ACROSS AN OCEAN OF STARS

BOOKS IN THIS SERIES

BAEN BOOKS by ROBERT E. HAMPSON

ACROSS AN OCEAN OF STARS

by

ROBERT E. HAMPSON

Set in the Black Tide Rising world
created by

JOHN RINGO

A Baen Books Original

Baen Publishing Enterprises
P.O. Box 1403
Riverdale, NY 10471
www.baen.com

ISBN: 978-1-6680-7254-7

Cover art by Kurt Miller

First printing, April 2025

Distributed by Simon & Schuster
1230 Avenue of the Americas
New York, NY 10020

Library of Congress Cataloging-in-Publication Data

Names: Hampson, Robert E., author.
Title: Across an ocean of stars / Robert E. Hampson.
Description: Riverdale, NY : Baen Publishing Enterprises, 2025. | Series:
  Black tide rising ; 14
Identifiers: LCCN 2024050620 (print) | LCCN 2024050621 (ebook) | ISBN
  9781668072547 (trade paperback) | ISBN 9781964856070 (ebook)
Subjects: LCGFT: Apocalyptic fiction. | Science fiction. | Novels.
Classification: LCC PS3608.A69589 A64 2025 (print) | LCC PS3608.A69589
  (ebook) | DDC 813/.6—dc23/eng/20250115
LC record available at https://lccn.loc.gov/2024050620
LC ebook record available at https://lccn.loc.gov/2024050621

Printed in the United States of America

10 9 8 7 6 5 4 3 2 1

DEDICATION

To Dad, forever my hero. I miss you.
To Mom, my first fan.
For Ruann, the love of my life.

ACKNOWLEDGMENTS

As with any story that takes place outside of one's own home and field of expertise, this tale benefits from the research and assistance of many people. First and foremost, I'd like to thank John Ringo for permission to play in his Black Tide Rising (BTR) universe. John, I still owe you for making me Suspect Number One if there ever is a real zombie apocalypse, so I've made you a brigand in exchange!

Many thanks as well to my friends and predecessor authors within BTR, Michael D. Massa, Charles E. Gannon, and Jason Cordova for conferring over continuity and the timeline of events surrounding the Fall. Thanks also to John Ringo and Gary Poole for invitations to contribute to the BTR anthologies. It was during a panel discussion by contributors to the first anthology that the seed of this novel was first planted.

The Hawaiian Islands hold a special place in my heart. No, I do not have family or historical connection to the islands but have always been fascinated by the geography, history, culture, and people. The multiyear course of developing, composing, and writing this novel saw the East Rift Zone eruption, the summit caldera explosion and minor eruptions, and the wildfires that devastated Maui. John Ringo wanted BTR to contain a message of hope, and I think this story invokes the spirit of the Hawaiian people to return to the Polynesian sense of self-sufficiency and exploration. To not just survive... but thrive.

For Hawaiian historical and cultural research, I am indebted to docents Karen and Ramona at the Bernice Pauahi Bishop Museum in Honolulu, HI. To readers, the best thing you can do for any museum is to visit and express interest. Docents and museum workers are a wealth of information and your first, best resource for research. I also thank the public information offices of Big Island Farms and Parker Ranch for information regarding their sustainability efforts. I am grateful to Big Island Runners, Kona-Kailua, HI, for information on Ironman and Xterra Games competitions and training in the islands. My thanks also to NASA for information on HI-SEAS (Hawai'i Space Exploration Analog and Simulation). My apologies for moving its fictional equivalent from Mauna Loa to Mauna Kea!

Where references regarding Hawaii culture and history are given, they are fictionalized, but the information for them and other details of Hawaii history and culture are sourced from *A Concise History of the Hawaiian Islands*, by Dr. Phil Barnes (Petroglyph Press, Hilo, Hawaii), *Kamehameha: The Warrior King of Hawai'i*, by Susan Morrison (University of Hawai'i Press, Honolulu, Hawaii), and *The Great Mahele: Hawaii's Land Division of 1848*, by Jon J. Chinen (University of Hawaii Press, Honolulu, Hawaii). These references were recommended by the museum docents and have been a great source of the details I wanted to enrich this story.

Not being a military veteran or dependent, I relied on good friends and advisors for information regarding military life, capabilities, culture, and the military facilities in Hawaii (including Joint Base Pearl Harbor-Hickam, Marine Corps Base Hawaii at Kaneohe Bay, Kawaihae Harbor, and Pohakuloa Training Area). I thank Michael Gants, James Copley, Jonathan LaForce, Jeremy Levitt, Philip Wohlrab, James L. Young, Kacey & EZ Ezell, Casey Moores, Douglas Miller, and David Fisher for their assistance in getting it right.

My heartfelt thanks to the best publisher in the business, Toni Weisskopf. Many Baen Books stars have influenced me—Larry, Dave, Jason, David, Sarah, Mike, Tom and John, thanks for your example, inspiration, and opportunities to hone my writing. To my friend and mentee, Brent Roeder, PhD, thanks for listening! To my biggest fan, Marjorie Hampson, you and Dad have been the best parents in the world. To my father, Len Hampson, I lift a toast. You lived a full life but are still gone too soon. You were my mentor, confidant, role model, and hero. To my wife, Ruann, and sons, Brian and Stephen, thanks for putting up with my storytelling, and the endless hours spent writing and editing!

Part One

EXPLORER

CHAPTER ONE
PROTOCOLS

This mission of exploration is of the utmost importance to the human race. Only by expanding into space can we ensure the survival of humanity.
—M.R. van Der Venn, tech entrepreneur and philanthropist

Ham Forsyth woke up in the dark. Waking suddenly in the middle of his sleep cycle left him confused as to his surroundings. He tried to concentrate, to figure out what had awoken him. Then he heard the screaming. It took a few more moments for him to process the sound and he was halfway to the door of his quarters before his brain registered the shrillness of the voices and the fact that it was actually two voices screaming at each other in Portuguese.

Oh God, they're at it again. He pulled back the folding door to his compartment and looked out into the Core of the habitat module. He saw closed doors with blue lights over most of them. Two doors did not—his own and one other. *Everyone has Privacy ANC set except for Angel and Wily, and they're the ones causing the disturbance! Christ, I wish they'd never come on this mission. I wish I had never come on this mission, and I'm the one that had to approve the crew!* He unfolded the door, fitted it back into its seals, and thumbed the pressure-sensitive patch next to the seal. A blue light came on over his door, and there was a faint sense of white noise as all sound deadened in the room.

Ham hated Privacy ANC. The acronym stood for "active noise cancellation," and it was an electronic system that exploited the physics of sound propagation and interference to mute sounds originating outside his quarters. It tended to give him a headache because the ANC worked by generating its own noise—tuned to interfere with outside sounds—and his inner ear interpreted the counter signal as pressure, almost as if he was underwater. Still, it cut off the noise from the rest of the hab—the "Hex" as it was called in the HI-SLOPE protocols—and suppressed any noise he made. He'd just have to deal with the discomfort.

Sitting in front of the small desk in his cramped room, using only the dim light of the ever-present Hex nighttime lighting, and the faint glow of a star field from the reinforced port behind his bunk, Ham opened the drawer containing his personal medication stock. Taking out two tiny pills, he dry-swallowed the pain reliever. Water was still short until Mugs finished the rebuild on the freshwater still, and the crew was encouraged to conserve water whenever possible. *Shit, it didn't stink bad enough with inadequate air circulation, but add in twenty-five people who can't shower and it was a surprise that more people weren't yelling at each other. Eighteen months in this hole in space; at least eighteen more to go.*

Now that he was awake and likely to have a headache until the meds kicked in, he might as well do some work. It's not as if HI-SLOPE ran on a strict day-night cycle. There would be a watch crew in the Command Module and probably someone in the Commons over in Hex One. *Oh-two-thirty, yeah, that was a problem.* He risked running into the CO if he went to either Command or Commons. "Prancer" fancied himself one of those self-made "Big Kahunas" who didn't require sleep to be at his best or most productive. He couldn't be more wrong, but no one dared tell him.

Ham could head over to the greenhouse in Hex Four. It was quiet, and usually smelled good. Even if the XO was up and about, she understood the need for quiet time. The problem was navigating Cores and Tubes this late at night; his eyes could adapt to the dark, but not well. Also, exiting his quarters would subject him to the sounds of Angel and Wily—Gabriel and Ylene Luca—the Fighting Brazilians. That is, unless they'd progressed beyond the argument to the inevitable make-up sex. Then again, that often meant *more* shrieking and shouting than the preceding fight.

"Angel." That was a laugh. Most of the crew came onboard with their own chosen call signs in violation of every custom, not to mention his own recommendations to Mission Control. Dr. Gabriel Luca styled himself as the Angel Gabriel. It fit his ego, just not his personality. "Devil" was more like it. Likewise, Commander Matthijs Rudolph van Der Venn had selected "Reindeer" as in "Rudy the Red-nosed," but the crew called him "Prancer" behind his back. Ham thought he knew what the crew called *him*, and at least it wasn't malicious. Or . . . he hoped it wasn't.

No, he was awake and stuck in his quarters, so he might as well do some work. He touched a raised pad on the desktop and a screen slowly lit—adaptive optics gradually increased the screen brightness so that his eyes could adjust. A backlight keyboard appeared, seemingly within the smooth desk surface. He could tap the virtual keys, gesture in sign language, or even tap Morse code and the motion sensors would interpret the gestures into computer input for him. The Virtual Environment decoders had been van Der Venn's great contribution to Society. They made his name a household word and earned him the money to finance this expedition.

Only the best VennSystems hardware for the Mission. If only he'd put as much thought into the crew. Ham grimaced with the irony of the thought. Crew selection was supposed to be the province of the mission psychologist.

If only.

A quick gesture with his left hand brought up his official mission log, and another activated voice entry. The screen now showed a slow pulsing red border that warned him that voice and video recording was active.

> Hamilton V. Forsyth the Third, MD, PhD
> HI-SLOPE Mission Psychologist.
> Deputy Chief Medical Officer's Record.

Ham made another gesture and a computerized female voice added: "*Sol Five-Five-Zero. Mission Year Two, Month Seven, Day Three. Zero-two-fifty-one Universal Time.*"

Once the computer completed the date and time stamp. Ham continued:

The Doctors Luca were engaging in behaviors again tonight that evidence a total lack of empathetic consideration for fellow crew. This makes the seventeenth episode I have logged since moving my quarters to Hex Two at the beginning of Mission Year Two. The fights and noise generally occur at night when most of the crew are in sealed compartments with privacy filtering. I seem to be the only member complaining, probably due to aversion to the ANC filters.

I have repeated my request to the CMO to screen them for evidence of heightened stress hormones, contusions, abrasions and the like, but he says that any such results could just as easily be attributed to energetic "mating rituals." Doc d'Almeida turned quite red while making the comment; he really does earn his handle of "Cro-Magnon" at times.

With the CMO unable—or unwilling—to support my contention that the behavior is damaging to the couple physically as well as mentally, I am unable to escalate my concerns to Captain van Der Venn. It is unfortunate; I was explicitly recruited onto this mission for my expertise in closed crew interactions. The couple's interaction with this crew is problematic and increasing stress, but van Der Venn won't hear it. The Lucas deny any problems, and Dr. Gabriel Luca counters any objection from his own expertise.

There's two problems with "Angel" leveraging his expertise. The first is, he doesn't have any. He was recruited out of an academic physiology department—trained in neurology, not human physiology. He also claims to have experience equal to my own psychology PhD (ignoring my MD), even though I know that he only studied enough psychology to run animal behavior experiments.

The second problem is that the Doctors Luca are close friends of the captain. When the mission plan was developed, van Der Venn overrode my choice of a husband-and-wife physiology and biomedical engineering team, and chose the Lucas, even though Wily's background is only peripherally relevant to actual mission expertise. Their personal relationship is messing with the crew, and I keep getting ignored whenever I point it out.

In other morale issues, several crew members confided in me their disappointment that the captain did not allow any Fourth of July observations last month and is disinclined to allow Thanksgiving next fall. The CO did not feel that we should celebrate National Holidays for just a quarter of the crew, and said that another quarter are from countries allied with the British nation we Americans rebelled against. It made a certain amount of sense given the fight that almost broke out between our British XO and her Irish husband after the fiasco last November Fifth. Still, the CO insisted on a celebration for Dutch Liberation Day just three months prior, and Sissy Bolinger's Songkran Thai New Year's festival right before that. There is an increasing disillusionment with van Der Venn playing favorites among the crew, and it's starting to show in work output. Until we reach our next mission objective, the crew is cooped up and festering. The lack of communications with Mission Control on Earth is especially trying. Even with a forty-five-minute communications lag, just being able to have some news from Earth would help.

Another gesture and the red border on the screen was replaced by green. The screen now showed a text translation and a prompt to approve the entry, save as draft, or discard. Ignoring the prompt, Ham spoke in a slightly different tone and pitch. "Hissy. Status of communications with Earth?"

The same synthesized female voice that had supplied the date, responded:

"*The AE-35 antenna pointing processor is still malfunctioning, Dr. Forsyth. Mr. Burbey projects repair and restoration of the AE-35 unit sometime today.*"

"Thank you, Hissy, and how long after the repair is complete can the crew begin personal communications with home?"

"*HI-SLOPE mission has been out of communication with Earth for seventy-four days. Accumulated mission data, system telemetry, and logs will require approximately thirty hours to transmit. Personal communication before completion of mission-critical transmission will require Command override.*"

Ham sighed. Even when communication was restored, they still would not be able to use the system for more than a day. Looking back at the screen, he swiped his fingers in midair, approving and dismissing the log entry. He then made the single-finger salute to bring up his personal diary. The entire screen turned a deep purple, and a small blue square lit up on the desktop. He pressed his thumb to the square and it turned the same color as the screen. Hissy's voice spoke: *"Privacy Mode One, Mission Protocols Deactivated."*

Sitting back in his chair, Ham relaxed slightly. For just a few minutes during Privacy One he could let go of the sham and ignore the Mission.

Ham Forsyth, personal notebook. I really don't know why I let van Der Venn talk me into this farce. Simulated mission or not, we've been stuck in this plastic jail for a year and a half. Make-work jobs and scripted conversations are bad enough, but these pretend equipment failures are just not realistic. Tree Rat is pissed. He's confident that he could have fixed the AE-35 in a day, but the Mission Plan called for an extended communications blackout. "To simulate real-world situations," according to Prancer. Fuck that. In a real mission we could have boosted for Mars or an asteroid base and gotten there in less than the two and a half months of this latest charade. Hell, Tree Rat says he could stand on the hull, aim with a telescope, and get an omni signal if nothing else.

My own personal Hell is that I designed the personnel list and interpersonal relationship protocols, yet nothing I could create has been as stressful as the preprogrammed disasters that the VennSystems jerks came up with. Prancer plays nice with his cronies and ignores everyone else. The Bolingers have dinner in his oversized cabin every night and talk book deals and movie rights. The Lucas play cards with the CO several nights a week, and they always try to invite Wyvern or Legs as a fourth. They usually have to settle for me or Cro, though, and it's pretty clear they don't consider us as peers. That's okay. We both detest bridge.

The rest of the crew acts like it doesn't matter, and in some ways it doesn't. The XO is professional and efficient even if her personal life runs hot and cold. She's the one who is really in charge with respect to the mission, and it's her debrief that NASA and the Mars and Beyond Consortium will use to decide how to construct long-duration missions. Everyone except Prancer and his cronies know that, but acting on it would be the next best thing to mutiny. As mission psych I find myself torn between counseling against it and leading the charge.

Ham paused, he started to gesture, and the screen displayed ERASE? CONFIRM OR CANCEL. He paused, not responding to the prompts, and turned to look at the simulated deep-space view through his "porthole." He considered his options for a moment, then gestured negation; the recording remained.

Abigail, I don't know if you still have access and have unlocked these personal notes or are waiting on me to make the first move and reach out to you directly. If something goes wrong, and you're reading these unedited, I just need you to know that things really aren't as bad as it sounds. I will have to move my quarters, though. I can't sleep with the ANC, and I can't sleep without it if Devil and Wily are screaming. Medusa says I can use the second half of the XO suite, and Cro said the same with respect to the CMO's suite. I hate to take the extra space from Medusa. She and Red need the ability to pull out the partition and have their own space if needed. Twenty square meters is just too small for two people—even a married couple, as shown by the Lucas. That leaves my best option to move back to Hex Three and put up with Cro's bad puns.

It's only eighteen more months. We're halfway there. I just need to think of the research papers! Well, that and the exposés. For now, it's a good thing these are private notes to be opened only after mission completion.

I will tell you this, though. I miss looking at the stars. I know I can look out at any time during our "day" and see them, but frankly, I miss just going out into a field, far from the city, and looking up at all of those stars. That's what I miss. Just you and me, Abi. You, me, and a literal ocean of stars.

I will make the first move, and I promise to send you a personal note the next time we're allowed to send them.

I apologize. I'm sorry. I shouldn't have yelled, and I should have listened.

There, I've said it, but I'm afraid it doesn't feel any better to think that you might not even see this. I really need to stop procrastinating and send you a personal message in the clear and not embedded in my log.

I didn't really mean what I said when we parted. I felt then . . . I still feel . . . that you have so much potential, and I was hurt that you chose a path other than the one that would keep you near me. There is nothing inherently wrong in your career choice. It was just the sense of impending loss speaking.

Then again, your words stung . . . because they're true. I *was* hiding. I *am* hiding from the world. I dreamed of space and thought that this was the way to realize that dream. It was selfish of me to drag you into this pale shadow of space exploration. Maybe with your choices you'll actually get there. What's sad is to think that you are *more* likely than I am to realize the dream. It's just that I chose this path and this mission, and pride wouldn't let me back down when Prancer screwed up all of my plans.

Pride goeth before a fall.

Please forgive me, Abi. Take care of yourself, I love you and I miss you.

Ham paused for a moment, hands poised, ready to erase the latest entry.

Why is it so easy to say that now that I may have lost you forever? Psychologist, heal thyself.

Notebook entry complete. Save; encrypt; lock entry against editing.

Ham stood up and the screen turned itself off. While he'd been at the console, the room lighting had gradually increased to something approximating twilight. Unless overridden, the compartment lighting would not return to full white light until the beginning of the simulated day. The low illumination was meant to ensure that he could go back to sleep at any time. Unfortunately, his head still hurt. He was also thirsty. Moving to the dispenser on the wall opposite the door, he placed a coffee mug under the spout and pressed the button for cold water. An amber light lit, the machine dispensed 25 ml of water, then the light turned red and the flow stopped. "Damned simulated emergencies."

Drink it fast? Or drink it slow? Ham opted for slow, taking small sips. He got two more headache pills and took them with the last of the water. *I should at least try to sleep.* As he lay back down on his bunk, the room lighting gradually faded out.

CHAPTER TWO

BREAKFAST CLUB

The irony of space travel is that THE BLACK is big, and ships are small. Orbital lift capacity and life support mandate small spaces and tight quarters. Only when we can duplicate a full planetary biosphere, and build it ourselves, can we afford elbow room in space.

—D.C. Gestner, construction engineer, HI-SLOPE

Ham grabbed a breakfast burrito with simulated egg and sausage and real hot sauce, filled his mug with coffee, and made his way back to Hex Three and Cro's small office in the sickbay. He and everyone else tended to get out of the Commons as quickly as possible, and this morning it was nearly empty despite being the designated breakfast shift. The Commons was meant to be a social environment. Mission psychologists, meaning Ham and the human factors consultant team hired by VennSystems, had stressed the need to have a social interaction area large enough for all mission personnel to gather as one group, or many small groups, for recreation, entertainment, and exercise. Thus, Hex One had been designed with a large, open-plan space on the second level, with tables, chairs, and comfortable seating sufficient for twenty-five persons. Kitchens, exercise room, and a small conference room would be on level one, connected by not only the Habitat Core access ladders, but a small, powered lift for transporting food and dining supplies. It had thin-panel screens with simulated views of Earth, bright cheery colors, and simulated grass on the floor.

Unfortunately, the Habitat Design Team hadn't figured on the ego of one Rudolph van Der Venn, tech billionaire and financial backer of the Hawaiian Island Simulated Long-Orbit Planetary Exploration, or HI-SLOPE for short. The Habitat consisted of six two-story hexagonal units and a three-story central unit. The concept was supposed to simulate a spacecraft with rotating habitation units around a central Command Module. Hexes Two and Five were devoted to personnel quarters, similar to Ham Forsyth's own. Every other Hex except for the Air Lock/Garage also contained two modular compartments that could be used as quarters. Those were intended for the CO, the XO, department heads, and watch crew.

The problem was that van Der Venn wasn't content with using both modules in Hex One for his expanded personal quarters. He'd indulged his ego by converting the entire first level into his own personal suite with large bedroom, office, private kitchen, private dining room with his own steward, and a private lift to the upper level. As a result, kitchen, dining, seating, exercise, and entertainment facilities for all remaining crew was relegated to half the intended space, all on the second level. The loss of the main kitchen also meant the loss of crew ability to cook their own meals. Condensing exercise and dining space unnecessarily limited exercise hours and sharing that space with entertainment options meant that the crew tended not to use the Commons to gather.

It also had one additional limitation. One hundred forty square meters looked like a lot of space on the floor plans but fitting all of the functions into that space meant either cramming in too much or leaving something out. Van Der Venn got rich by writing big checks, but then personally micromanaging each guilder. He chose to leave things out, and one of those was the hygiene compartment for the Commons floor. If anyone needed the bathroom, they had to go to the Core of the Hex, climb the ladder or spiral stair to Level Three, then traverse the "hamster tubes" across the top of the habitat to one of the other Hexes. Once that was done, it was much easier just to stay in that Hex and avoid the (now nonexistent) crowding in Commons. The greenhouse in Hex Four and "hangar bay" in Hex Six ended up as the most popular spots for small group socializing.

Commons was deserted this morning, as usual. The mandatory exercise rotation didn't start until midmorning, and the thin-panel "windows" and entertainment screens had been shut down along with the simulated communications blackout. Sickbay was small, but thankfully empty most of the time. The crew was disgustingly healthy...physically...and Cro was good company despite his puns. They used an empty diagnostic bed as a table and the doctor's precious vintage rolling physician stools for seating.

"Caveman." Ham nodded and addressed the CMO as he entered sickbay.

"Shrink," Anson replied, pouring his own coffee from an antique French-press coffee maker into a delicate china cup. The doctor justified the extravagance with a scientific report showing that the press-style was the best method for steeping coffee or tea in free fall, especially since it captured all of the grounds and leaves. He also argued that china and fine porcelain were lighter and stronger per gram than plastic, metal, or ceramic. How he had managed to continue to grind his own beans and tea leaves without violating the simulation's weightless and closed-circuit air systems protocols was a mystery, yet somehow Cro always had fresh coffee and tea.

With a hulking frame, dark complexion, heavy brows, and five o'clock shadow within minutes of shaving, Anson Robert d'Almeida looked every bit the Cro-Magnon that his medical colleagues had bestowed as his mission handle. The problem was that Dr. d'Almeida always wore a white or pale blue button-front shirt, necktie, and white medical coat. The image of a caveman in a coat and tie always caused a bit of cognitive dissonance for Ham.

"Dude. It's Hawaii. You don't have to wear a tie." It was an old argument. Ham had been trying to get Anson to wear a Hawaiian print shirt and lose the tie for months. The mission had preprogrammed "supply drops" every six months, with allowance for ten kilograms each of personal cargo in addition to fresh food and consumables for the "mission."

"No, Hamilton, we are in space. If I were to relax my standards, I am certain that someone would force me to wear spandex." He had a point. The HI-SLOPE Mission Planning Board had pushed for simulated space uniforms for all crew. VennSystems had a beautiful spandex-and-lycra uniform designed that looked like something right out of a 1960s TV show. Fortunately, the mission parameters specified that the crew needed to be able to have personal items available, and

Ham had been able to argue that regular clothing was an important "comfort item" essential to stress relief.

"Point," Ham replied. "Not to mention that you'd look like Duke." Anson just snorted and continued drinking his coffee. "So, Anson, buddy, about the spare compartment…"

D'Almeida looked up with a big grin on his face. "I knew you'd come begging. You've been there what, six weeks?" Ham nodded. "Right. Since the last supply ship."

The mission plan allowed personnel to move compartments either by a direct swap with another crew member, or via planned rearrangement coinciding with the six-month "supply ships." The most recent supply had come early, for some reason, but not been made available until it matched some astronomer's computation of transit time from Earth. HI-SLOPE had been planned to fit twenty-five crew members—if not comfortably, at least adequately. The residential Hexes each had ten wedge-shaped compartments for individual occupancy, and two for hygiene needs. The Command Module had two compartments on its lower level to accommodate pilots or emergency personnel. The remaining three crew were allocated "officer" accommodations consisting of double compartments with a removable center wall. The commanding officer, executive officer, and chief medical officer quarters were sited in Commons (Hex One), Greenhouse (Hex Four), and Medical/Laboratory (Hex Three), respectively. While the CO had arbitrarily expanded his compartment and the XO was married—using both compartments with her spouse—the CMO didn't use his second room. The compartment that would have housed the XO's husband was vacant in Hex Two, but it was directly above the Doctors Luca and wouldn't solve Ham's need to escape the disturbance.

Ham looked down. "Yes, you did predict it."

"Of course. You have classic acoustic hypersensitivity with a level-four psychosomatic tympanic response." Anson poured another cup of coffee and pointed at Ham. "You get tension headaches and can't sleep, then run around grumpy all of the time."

"Psychosomatic? Are you analyzing me, Doctor?" Ham raised an eyebrow, knowing it would annoy his heavy-browed friend.

"Hell no, I leave the head-shrinking to you, Dr. Fraud."

"That's Freud."

"You know what I mean." Anson took a moment to drink his coffee. "Psychosomatic means that the physiological reaction simply follows from the mental reaction to inner ear discomfort. It's a real problem, and not just in your head. You feel physical pain from the adaptive noise-cancelling feedback. I could fix it for you with a small stimulator on the tensor tympani."

"No thank you, Doc. I don't particularly like having my head cut open."

Anson snorted. "As opposed to you opening up everyone else's heads with psychoanalysis? You can have the compartment, but I warn you that I won't let you analyze me—" He cut off as a loud chime sounded.

"*Attention.*" Hissy's synthesized voice sounded over the intercom. "*The A-E-thirty-five antenna pointing processor has been repaired. Communication with Earth Mission Control has been reestablished and will commence with stored transmissions.*"

CHAPTER THREE

THE BLACKOUT

The importance of simulating a crisis cannot be downplayed. All it takes is a "Golden BB" micrometeorite puncture to end a mission or knock out a system for weeks or months. We train for the unexpected and rare.

—D.W. Burbey, PhD, simulation designer, Mars-and-Beyond Consortium

The CO had called a ship-wide conference. There was no space in HI-SLOPE large enough to hold all of the crew, at least no space not already occupied by growing plants or space buggies, so it would be held over the intercom system. Van Der Venn was in his "dining room"—what *should* have been a conference room for use by all crew but appropriated by the CO as part of his Command Suite. From the angle of the video pickup, Ham could see that the Bolingers and Lucas were present with him. *That figured; Prancer couldn't sneeze without the sycophantic Bolingers there to wipe his snot. It was a bit surprising that Devil and Wily were there, too.* Prancer was an extreme narcissist and a Europhile. Americans and Canadians were merely "acceptable," and the only non-Anglo crew were Sunan Bolinger and the Lucas. "Sissy" Bolinger was supercargo because the mission didn't really need an artist, but Prancer had wanted something from Aidan "Balls" Bolinger, and Balls wouldn't join the mission without his wife. *Rather surprising, because Ham was pretty sure Prancer and Sissy had been at it between the simulated zero-gee sheets. Behind or in front of Balls's back was the other question.* Ham knew that the journalist's psych profile indicated he'd swing both ways.

Ham wasn't sure what the relationship was with Angel and Wily. He knew they played bridge a lot, but they never seemed like quite the sexual play-toy types. Despite biweekly arguments, Angel and Wily were happily, monogamously married. Fighting was just their version of foreplay, sort of like Klingon sex. Angel was quite famous in Brazil— there may have been some connection there, perhaps a philanthropic project, but Ham was betting more on a profit motive. There was no particular need for Wily's linguistic skills on the mission, but she could fill in as a communications technician. Again, HI-SLOPE had recruited spousal teams where possible. Ham had thought it would add stability, but in fact, three of the four married couples on the mission were more disruptive than stabilizing.

Ham and Cro were in the med-bay. Medusa and Red—Executive Officer Morgen Kirby and husband Steven—were in the Greenhouse. Medusa was paying attention, but Red could be seen tending his plants in the background. Mission pilots K.C. "Wyvern" Seville and Sean "Littleshawn" Haley were on watch in the Command Module. Everyone else was in their personal quarters. *Oops, no, Bridget Litchfield was in the Commons running on the treadmill. Being cooped up had to be hard on "Legs."* The athletic life-systems engineer had told Ham on more than one occasion that she missed being able to run marathons. Personally, Ham couldn't see it. Getting out of exercise was one of the greatest reasons for going to space in his opinion.

"No, I *told* you, the communications system is working perfectly." That was D.W. "Tree Rat" Burbey, their communications engineer. If it communicated, Tree Rat could fix it.

"But we haven't *heard* anything from Mission Control!" There was almost a whine in van Der Venn's voice. It was one of his less endearing traits. First, he'd yell, then he'd whine, then he'd yell again. He'd already yelled at Zach "Lugnut" Ludwig, their teleoperations specialist, falsely accusing him of tying up all the communications bandwidth playing *Halo*.

"That's not true," continued Tree Rat. "We received all of the backlog telemetry. Forsyth and d'Almeida have both received their journal subscriptions and Mugs has his home-brewer's digests."

"Then why doesn't Mission Control respond to us? I have *business* to attend to. Aidan has to file his updates and Dr. Luca has to address the U.N. Bionics Council!" *AHA!* Ham thought. *That's the missing piece of the puzzle. Angel was working on biomimetic implants. As usual, Prancer wants something from him, too.*

"Look, this isn't getting us anywhere." Medusa broke in with an authoritative voice. She was efficient and competent—everything Prancer was not—and usually managed to defuse potential conflicts. Ham suspected she had psychology training, but all their XO would say on the subject was that she'd "read it in a book." "Engineer Burbey, please recheck the incoming circuits and run diagnostics on both outflow and inflow. Mr. Hlavacek, please assist."

"Got it." "Half-Check" was the systems engineer—he would have been in charge of the engines in a real space mission, but in HI-SLOPE he had a choice of working with a simulated engine room or applying his skills to the multiple mechanical and electronic systems that made the habitat work. "I'll get Lugnut to help me set up a ping-back. Maybe we can use one of his gaming servers."

Tree Rat made a face. He was in his quarters, and the camera angle revealed a poster behind him with a picture of an angry squirrel. Ham wasn't sure whether DeeDub's constant scowling or the poster contributed the nickname "Pissed-Off Tree Rat." But it was certainly the case that Tree Rat looked pissed at the current direction of the conversation. "Sure, while you're at it, why don't you have Redshirt One and Redshirt Two suit up and climb out on the hull to check the high-gain antenna!"

"Yeah, sure, we'll do that!" answered Matt "Redshirt One" Asnip, immediately. He was grinning and literally bouncing in his seat. He and his roommate, Redshirt Two, were the designated "Away Team," conducting everything from geological exploration to external habitat repairs.

Beside him in their joint quarters, Steve "Redshirt Two" Schaper elbowed him in the ribs. "Psst, Idiot. We don't *have* a high-gain antenna on the hull," he said in a loud whisper.

"Oh. Yeah, sorry. I forgot." Redshirt One's expression fell, then brightened again. "I know! We can take a Broomstick out and set up a parallax receiver!"

"Yeah. No. We're not in space, dude."

"Oh, cool, so we can just take a rover over to the Farside and set up there."

Asnip wasn't able to complete the thought before Schaper interrupted again. "Dude, you're embarrassing me. We're on Earth, dummy."

"Wait, I thought we were conducting the meeting in Mission Speak? Isn't this the Tuesday morning planning session?"

"NO!" shouted several voices in unison.

"Oh." Asnip looked chagrined and disappointed.

"You know, it might *not* be a bad idea to send the Wonder Twins out, though," mused Tree Rat. "Our communications run through Mid-level Support Services. We've got a buried high-capacity fiber link running down slope to Hale Pohaku. They relay everything from the VennSystems offices in Hilo along the same fiber that Keck uses to communicate with their telescopes at the Summit."

"Wouldn't it be easier to just go up to the Mauna Kea Observatories, then?" asked Angel. "After all, it's the highest point with the best chance of reception."

"Dude, that's three thousand feet straight up!" "...and cold!" the Redshirts said simultaneously.

"Yes and no," said Tree Rat with disgust. "And not really relevant. You should know this." He glanced around; it was obvious that he was checking images on multiple monitors. "All of you should know this, it was in the Mission Packet. Our communications are all by digital fiber. Even the observatories don't use radio, their images are too high bitrate. It's all fiber. Mission Protocol specifically excluded any radio in HI-SLOPE except our encrypted suit-comms so that there would be no stray signals violating Mission Protocol."

"Well, we're certainly off Mission Protocol now," someone said.

"Exactly. We are *off* Mission Protocol as of this very minute. Something is wrong with our communications. A *real* problem and not a simulated one. I say we break Protocol and send Redshirts One and Two down to Hale Pohaku to let them know we have a problem and get *someone* out there working on fixing their end of it." He paused a moment, then added, "Because for damn sure it isn't on *my* end!"

Prancer was looking mulish. The mission was his baby, his idea. He'd set up the mission to simulate deep space exploration of at least three years' duration, and he clearly didn't want to have to end it only halfway through. If outside service of the habitat was required, it would end all pretense of a self-sufficient mission. Medusa was looking more thoughtful; clearly, she was considering the idea. Most of the crew knew that ultimately the XO would make the call required for safety of the crew no matter what the CO had planned. The only problem was that if she bucked the CO on this issue, the mission was broken anyway.

Mutiny was such an ugly word.

CHAPTER FOUR

A VIKING

Every crew needs its red shirts.
—J.T. Kirk, famous ship captain

"Redshirt One to Death Star, Redshirt One to Death Star, we have cleared the asteroid field and are headed for Tatooine." The voice coming over the speakers in the Command Module was accompanied by video of a reddish, rocky terrain.

Wyvern touched a control on the console and responded: "Redshirt One, this is Wyvern. Please confine yourself to acceptable transmission protocols."

"Oh Darth, honey, are you going to blast me out of the sky like Alderaan?" was the reply.

"No, but I can cut off your radios. You know it's an encrypted channel and no one else can listen in. You'd be all alone just like Princess Leia—no friends, no family, no record collection." Wyvern's voice was all professional, as was her expression.

"Ouch, Wyvern, you sure know how to hurt a guy." Redshirt One continued in a slightly more serious tone, "Okay, we're over the lip of the cinder cone. The rover wasn't happy about that. Redshirt Two and I had to pick it up and lift it over the worst of the rubble at the top. I'm not sure the batteries can take another run on that slope. I almost think it would be faster to walk. It's only two miles. It won't be much faster in the rover." The little electric cart was designed for simulated asteroid exploring. With a top speed of ten kilometers an hour and limited

25

gearing to prevent excessive motion in low gravity, it had never been meant to traverse outside the cinder cone in which the HI-SLOPE habitat was located.

"Redshirt One, this is Cro. It might be three kilometers in distance, but it's over half a kilometer elevation change." D'Almeida was also sitting in the Command Module with Wyvern, the XO, and Tree Rat. It was shipboard night but none of the crew were asleep. Most were listening in on the consoles in their quarters. "I happen to know you've been neglecting your exercise. You might be used to thin air, but you're still going to get short winded on a fifteen to twenty percent grade."

"Roger that, Doc."

"The sun was bright and high our hearts when first we set a-Viking..." The voice paused for a moment and the camera swung up to take in the clear blue sky. "Well, the sun *is* bright, but it's kind of cold. Tell me again why the Hab is on a reversed day-night cycle?"

"C'mon, Matt. You know the answer to that. Cut the chatter." The new voice was Schaper's, Redshirt Two. The camera swung back down, then around to show the second man in his lightweight "spacesuit," walking carefully on the crumbled lava, about the same speed as the rover was moving. "It's so that we don't see all of this in the daylight." He gestured; a twisting road leading down to a small cluster of buildings could be seen in the distance beyond him.

The Mauna Kea Mid-Level Support Facility was just around a curve and upslope from the Ellison Onizuka Center for International Astronomy, at an elevation of 9,200 feet. It provided support services and housing at Hale Pohaku for astronomers working the high-altitude telescopes, and was connected by a steep, switchbacked road that climbed another four thousand feet up to the telescope observatories at the summit. It wasn't even ten kilometers, straight-line distance, but the road covered nearly twenty-five kilometers as it snaked back and forth along the side of the shield volcano. HI-SLOPE was sited inside a cinder cone almost exactly midway between Hale Pohaku and the summit—easily within sight of the road if not for the crater walls that stood taller than the habitat and obscured everything except for the sky. The added advantage of a reversed schedule of day vs. night ensured that any "daytime" activity within HI-SLOPE would see only the Hawaiian night sky, with its remarkable view of Northern and Southern Hemisphere stars.

"Redshirt Two, this is Cro. Watch your temps. I know it's cold out there, but your suit will overheat in a hurry with the exertion. Take it slow and easy. Drink plenty of water."

"Preaching to the choir, Cro. I've got this. Redshirt Two out."

The doctor turned to the XO. "I'm worried about them. Neither one of them has been doing enough exercise, and they haven't been 'outside' in over two months."

"I wouldn't worry about it, Doc," said Tree Rat. "Don't forget where we found them—hiking and camping in Haleakala."

Asnip, a Canadian farm boy born within sight of the Rockies, and Schaper, a German farm boy who'd left the farm to hike the Alps, had met when they'd both been on vacation in Hawaii. They'd signed up to hike and camp within the barren crater of Maui's extinct volcano and decided the experience—and the companionship—was exactly what they were looking for. They became inseparable friends, and opened their own hiking, camping, and wilderness guide service regularly escorting lowland tourists to the summit of Haleakala for sunrise "at the top of the world." They eventually branched out to providing extreme tours on all of the islands and had come to the attention of van Der Venn when they assisted the VennSystems planners with site selection for the HI-SLOPE facility.

"It doesn't mean I'm not going to worry about them, Tree Rat." D'Almeida turned to the side and set up a separate monitor to display the two men's medical readouts.

Two hours later, they were approaching the main building of Hale Pohaku. "Redshirt Two to Command. Y'know, I hope they've got a two-twenty-volt outlet for charging the rover. It is purely going to suck having to wait twice as long for it to charge off a one-ten."

"Roger that, Redshirt." Wyvern had been replaced by her copilot, Littleshawn. The physical contrast between the five-foot-two-inch pilot and the six-foot copilot wasn't evident over the comm, nor did it seem to make much difference in person. They both had a similar temperament, with great attention to detail, and both had affected the "Midwest drawl" of American pilots and astronauts, and they worked—and spoke—efficiently in all aspects. Only the pitch of their voices made it possible to tell which of them was "operating" the habitat and comm channels.

"I *told* you we needed an AT-AT!" Redshirt One didn't seem to be addressing anyone in particular as he took his turn walking alongside Rover One. "Huh. That's strange. What's a tour bus doing up here in the morning?"

"Littleshawn, would you please pan the camera over to the bus?" Cro had stayed in the Command Module for the team's entire descent, muttering about heart rates and blood oxygenation. Something had caught his attention and he pointed it out to the XO. The two conversed quietly for a moment, then she nodded to the copilot.

"Ah, Redshirt One, Medusa wants you to move the rover closer to the bus. We have an anomaly," Littleshawn drawled into the comm.

"Tell him to stay back," the XO added.

"Roger that. Redshirts, Medusa says to use the remote console to move the rover. You two hang back."

As the rover-mounted camera got closer to the tourist minibus, the XO called the image up on her own screen and enlarged it. "That's funny... Is that... a bone?"

The doctor looked over at the enlarged video. "Humerus, most likely."

Tree Rat snickered. Cro made a face and continued, "No pun intended. The humerus is the long arm bone. That one looks like it's from a human adult."

"Redshirt One, please confirm—" Littleshawn was interrupted as an outburst came across the comm.

"What the— Oh fuck no. Shit, fuck." There was more cursing as Redshirt Two came into the screen holding scraps of clothing in his gloved hand.

"Redshirt One, Redshirt Two. Please clarify." There was a pause in the cursing and the sound of a throat clearing.

"So much for hanging back," Medusa said in a stage whisper.

"Command, this is Redshirt One." Asnip finally responded. "We've got the remains of three bodies. Mostly bones and scraps of clothing. The clothing is not—repeat, *not*—cold-weather gear."

"Tourists, then?" Medusa turned to Cro and raised an eyebrow; the doctor just shrugged. "Away Team, this is the XO. We need you to enter the main building. Please take the camera with you."

"Roger that, Command." The video feed bounced and shook as the camera was removed from the rover. "Got it. Redshirt Two is opening the door." There was a muffled scream and the sound of retching. "Oh, merciful God . . ."

"Redshirt Two, get your helmet open. No, get your helmet *off*!" Cro stood and leaned over the copilot and shouted into the comm. On the medical screen several indicators began to flash red. "Redshirt One, *do not* let him throw up in his helmet!"

"Fuck no, Command, the room is full of bodies. They're torn and cut and bloody—all over the damn place. It reeks even through the suit filters. If I open Steve's helmet, he'll lose it for sure." The normally irreverent Asnip was uncharacteristically serious.

"Get him outside, then," ordered Cro, "and turn up his oxygen by two percent." The doctor paused, then added, "But make sure he doesn't hyperventilate."

CHAPTER FIVE
FIRST CONTACT

The worst part of space sickness is the risk of upchucking in your helmet. I'm surprised no one has invented an airsickness bag for astronauts.

—A.R. d'Almeida, Chief Medical Officer, HI-SLOPE

It was almost ten minutes before Schaper's voice came back over the comm. "I'm okay now, Doc."

The XO looked over at the doctor, who checked his monitors, then nodded. "Away Team, this is Medusa. What is your status?"

"Medusa, Redshirt One. We have three bodies outside, in advanced decomposition. There are more inside. I went back and did a count. There's eight more in the reception area of the main building. Various states of decomp; lots of damage. Frankly, it looks like a wild animal attack, but I've never heard of wild boar at nine thousand feet. Maybe a rabid goat would do it, but I don't know what else. We don't have that kind of predator on the Island—certainly not up this high."

"Redshirts, this is Eggnog. Can you get me some close-up video of the bites?" Pearce "Eggnog" Haley was the crew's nurse practitioner and medical tech, as well as wife to copilot Littleshawn. Like many of the crew, she had been only partly listening to the audio channels while going about her regular activities. She and Ham were in the medical lab; Forsyth was reading a journal article while Haley analyzed the crew medical data. They had both perked up at the recent outburst, and Haley had set one of the large sickbay monitors to echo the screens in the Command Module.

"You were an investigator." It wasn't a question. Ham knew her background. Hell, he knew *everyone's* background.

"Right. Get me a picture of the bite and I can tell you what made it." She'd worked her way through school as a private detective, studying during long surveillance operations and supplementing her coursework with forensics. "North Carolina had displaced predator species all the way into urban areas. We'd get a complaint that the neighbor's dog was tearing up trash and find out it was hogs or coyotes. Even had one of those guys that went crazy with 'bath salts' and tried to bite everyone."

"Roger that," replied Redshirt One over the comm. "I'll take the camera in."

"Negative. Get to the communications room! That's our highest priority." That was Prancer, surprising everyone since this was the first indication they'd had that he was even watching the mission.

"Redshirt One, just take some quick shots on the way in." Medusa, as usual, was trying to find the practical way around the CO's erratic orders.

"It's okay, Command. I've got this. Gimme the camera, Matt. You go." Redshirt Two's voice sounded tired and weak.

"Redshirt Two, this is Cro. Take your oh-two back down one percent but raise your suit pressure by ten kay-pee-ay. Cadaverine is probably diffusing through the seals, so ten kilopascals will push enough air out to counter it."

"Cadaver-what?"

"Cadaverine, putrescine, and a few other amines are what make that decomposition smell. Turn up your suit pressure, take a big, long drink of water, and swallow several times to pop your ears."

"Okay, people, let's get them moving," barked Littleshawn. "Redshirt One, you need to go through the reception area. There is a double door on the left, leading to the offices. Follow the corridor all the way to the end and up the stairs. Communications is the third door on the right. Report when you get there." He paused, then continued, "Redshirt Two, when you are ready, give us camera and commentary."

"Okay," Redshirt Two still sounded a bit shaky, but his voice firmed up as he talked and the video started to show scenes of the tourist receiving area. "Just inside the door, there's two people, one is stripped naked. He's all bloody around the mouth, but it looks like he's been shot. Next guy fully clothed." There was the sound of Schaper audibly gulping and trying to keep his stomach contents down. "His throat's been cut. Something jagged. Also, he's missing an arm. Stump was pretty bloody."

The gruesome scene was repeated as camera and crewman moved farther into the room. "Woman, older, evidence of plastic surgery. Naked, that's how I can tell, before you ask. Heavy coat next to her, so this was probably a group heading up to the summit, although why they'd be here and not at the visitor center around the curve is strange.

"Male, young, Islander, looks like. Fully clothed, there's a shotgun near him and his fingers are bent weird; might have been stripped out of his hands while he was holding it. I've seen pictures of that. Oh. Yeah. Here's a clear bite. Small, round, not very sharp."

There was a sharp intake of breath from Eggnog. Ham didn't even look. "Human," he said.

"Human," she agreed.

"Human bite, I've seen 'em before," continued Redshirt Two, his voice cold and distant. "This body is Keano Ikaia, by the way. Communications tech. I hunted with him a time or two. The rest of it's more of the same. More human bites. I think . . ." He paused. "I think, maybe I should have Matt's back. I'm taking the shotgun and going in."

The jostling camera showed Redshirt Two picking up the discarded firearm and moving through the doors into the office area. There was very little light except for the automatic headlamp on the space suit. There was hardly any indication that something had happened back here. Some papers were knocked off a desk and a few chairs and fixtures were askew.

At the top of the stairs, another headlight could be seen at the third door. Redshirt One was fighting to open the door. Together, the two managed to force the door open, pushing against a desk and knocking a computer and monitor to the floor. Inside the room was a mess.

Aside from the computer and monitor that just landed on the floor, there were cables dangling loose from the various computers and equipment racks in the room. Of the dozen or so computer monitors, all but three appeared to be damaged. One even seemed to have a ragged hole punched through the screen; it was roughly the size of a human fist. Keyboards were dangling from the workstation surfaces or lying on the ground. Several showed frayed wire where the cords had been ripped apart. One keyboard had been snapped in half, the keys themselves scattered on desk and floor.

"Command, this is Redshirt One. We're in the communications office. It's an absolute mess. Someone went to town on the equipment here."

"This is Redshirt Two. Some of it is still working, though—there are green LED lights in one of the equipment racks. To be fair, there are also many yellow and red lights, too, but there is power and something is running."

"Redshirts, Command. *What* is still working? How about the phone?"

"Command, Red One. No phone—no, wait, there is a phone, but it's smashed. Black plastic bits on the floor, and the buttons are mixed in with a broken keyboard. The handset is missing. No idea where."

"Command, Redshirt Two. There's a console over here labeled 'H.I.-S.L.O.P.E.' The system case has a green light on it. The screen is wrecked and the keyboard is missing. Let me see what I can piece together from the remains."

"Understood, Two. Check that first. One, look for radio—shortwave, ham, local walkies, anything like that."

"Roger, Command." Asnip looked over at Shaper, who had removed his gloves and was opening his helmet. "Are you sure that's a good idea, Steve?"

"Matt, I can't do this with gloves on. Screw the mission rules! Besides, we can talk without Big Brother listening in." He sniffed. "Damn, it stinks in here. Not like downstairs, though. More like an outhouse."

Redshirt One decided to emulate his partner, taking off gloves and removing his helmet. "Yeah, might as well take it off, you can't get in behind the racks with a big-ass bubble on your head."

"Yeah, got it." Redshirt Two, then started to swear. "*Damn it! One* intact keyboard and it's the wrong type. The only other keyboard is missing keys."

"What the fuck is the wrong type?"

"It's some damned character set that isn't English. Japanese, I think. Too many keys and the wrong kind of connector."

"Give me that one. I think I saw something about 'Subaru' and some Japanese characters over here. It's one of the units with yellow lights. Let me see if it works."

"Yeah, sure. I'll just have to use this broken keyboard and hope I don't need a 'J', 'K' or Backspace." Redshirt Two bent over the back of the intact monitor he had just moved onto the desk, then straightened. "Okay, monitor's up. Blue light, it has power, let's see if we have a signal. Ah. Good, it's coming up." He reached for his helmet. "Command, this is Two. I have the HI-SLOPE console up. Strange, though; it looks like it's already logged in. The screen header says, 'Emergency Notification System' with a blinking cursor."

Ham's voice broke in on the conversation. "Medusa, this is Hummer. That's an emergency override to our simulated communications failures. I insisted that the outside world had to have a way to get us messages even in the middle of a planned 'emergency' or real breakdown. It sounds like someone down there was trying to do that."

Back in the medical lab, Haley looked at Ham and mouthed the word "*Hummer?*" Her eyebrows arched to emphasize the question. Ham sighed. "Long story... but the short version is that in most circumstances, you don't choose your own call sign, your teammates do. Cro suggested 'Eggs' as in 'Ham-and-Eggs' or even 'Seuss' for Dr. Seuss's *Green Eggs and Ham* but you're 'Eggnog' and 'Seuss' is too difficult. The Redshirt boys started calling me 'Ham-V' using my initials, which then morphed to 'Humvee' and then 'Hummer.' Not my favorite, but my military friends told me that your call sign is your call sign until you screw up famously and earn a new one!"

Over the comm, the XO queried, "Hummer, you're sure of that? Any confirmation?"

"Yes, have them look in the lower right-hand corner. There should be a page or screen ID reading '13.1AO' for Authorization Override section thirteen, part one."

"Roger that, Hummer." Back on the comm line to the away team, the XO repeated: "Redshirt Two, confirm screen ident 'One-Three-Dot-One-Alpha-Oscar.' It should be in the lower right of the screen."

"Screen is not in the best of shape. Lower right is a bit blurred, Command. I make out One-Three-Dot... something... something... Oscar. Close enough?"

There was a change in background when the XO switched to the internal comm. "Hummer, close enough?"

"Close enough, Medusa. That's the override." He thought a moment and added, "Someone needed to tell us something. Something important."

"Agreed, Hummer. I'm beginning to wonder what it was." The background noise changed again as the link switched back to the away team. "Two, I'm going to need you to cancel out of that screen. It *could* explain why messages aren't going through if the system is locked in override mode."

"Roger, Medusa. Escaping out now." There was a scream from somewhere distant from the helmet comm systems. "What the . . . ? Damn. We screwed up."

Eggnog noticed that Ham blanched, then muttered to himself. "We fucked up. I fucked up. I didn't question why the door was barricaded from the inside . . ."

The voices over the comm began to panic.

"Where did he come from?"

"God, he *stinks*!"

"He's naked, too! Oh, I did *not* need to see that today!"

"Watch out! He's trying to bite!"

"Aaagh! Get him off! Get him off!"

There was the sound of a shotgun firing, then the comm went silent.

CHAPTER SIX

BREAKDOWN

Command is a hierarchy. HI-SLOPE is no different. Whether you call them CO, XO, and commanders, or CEO, vice presidents, and department chairs, the mission will only succeed if there is a clear chain of command.

—Col. Morgen Kirby, USAF (ret.),
Executive Vice President, Mars-and-Beyond Consortium

"Okay, people. We have protocols for this, but the CO hasn't made the call. It looks like it's up to me, since it's been three days. Before I make that call, give me some options." XO Kirby was holding the meeting in the air purification room underneath the greenhouse. It was a good-sized open space, but at present, there were only five persons present: department heads and one subject matter expert. For this meeting, they also needed one of the other features of the habitat—privacy. HI-SLOPE was monitored by sensors to monitor air quality but had no *overt* video or audio surveillance. Unfortunately, that didn't mean it didn't exist. The burbling of water through the algae tanks, the faint hiss of water pumps and moving air served to obscure sounds inside the room from being picked up outside.

"Send another expedition. No, wait..." Lugnut paused in the middle of his statement. "What do you mean we have protocols for this? We have a protocol for losing Mission Control?"

There was only the ambient sound of the room for a moment before Ham looked at the other three department heads, then answered. "The insurance companies demanded that we have a full set of emergency plans for everything from Mauna Loa blowing her top to a zombie apocalypse. Medusa, Tree Rat, Doc, and I wrote a literal book full of plans for every contingency."

"We have a contingency plan for a Zombie Freakin' Apocalypse?" interjected Lugnut. "Man, that is so cool."

Medusa smiled at the youngest crew member's enthusiasm. "Something like it, anyway. The point is, I wrote the sections on what to do if we lost communications with Mission Control, what to do if we lost crew members, and how to interact outside the Hab in an emergency. Rudy signed off on them, but he has *not* acted on any of those contingencies. I'll make the call, if necessary, but I want options, first."

"Alright, send me and Half-Check. We're engineers, we can figure this out." Tree Rat had been arguing ever since they lost communication that the Redshirts had been the wrong individuals to send.

"Too risky. We have plenty of robots. Send one of those." Ham had been countering with that suggestion for as long as Tree Rat had been talking about going himself. It was one of the reasons for the meeting.

"How about it, Lugnut? Can we send one of your teleoperated toys?"

The youngest member of the crew bristled. "They're not toys, XO." Lugnut was twenty-one and considered among the world's top ten experts in semiautonomous vehicles, even at his young age. He'd started building robots in middle school, and by high school he was winning competitions across the country. By college, he was winning them across the world, including two DARPA prizes for space exploration robots. The coveted Defense Advanced Research Projects Agency awards had brought him to the attention of Ham Forsyth when considering the HI-SLOPE crew. Van Der Venn had objected, but Ham had convinced him that anyone could teleoperate the robots, whereas Lugnut could adapt to the unknown and even design new ones.

"I don't have line of sight. If we had an antenna tower I could do it. Put a hexacopter on station for eyes and a crawler on the ground."

"Why not use the hexacopter to relay?" Tree Rat again. From the look in his eyes, use of a drone was finally beginning to appeal to him.

"I could, but then I'd lose contact any time I had to bring the drone in."

"What about an antenna, then?" Medusa asked.

"I suppose we can ask Scorpio if he can spare a truss. We've got spare parts for the hamster tubes in storage."

"I'd prefer to keep this close for now. I'd rather not bring the whole Hab in on this right now. You know how decisions by committee can be." Medusa grimaced. "How about just taking a look around?"

"Altitude's the real problem." Lugnut looked thoughtful for a moment. "Hmm, I guess it depends on what you want to look at, and whether or not you want to have a real-time signal."

"Preprogrammed course?" asked Tree Rat. "But what will you base the course on?

"Look, boss, if you want real time, I have to stay in line of sight. With my . . . 'toys' . . . as you call them, that means above the crater rim. That gives you a nice wide-angle view, but no close-ups, since it's a minimum of three, maybe four hundred feet up once you take into account distance and angle on our artificial horizon. All of the professional gear is designed to take a fix strictly on the Hab, or on a star plot, just like it would on Mission." He broke into a great big grin. "On the other hand, I do have a *real* toy at my disposal—my GPS-enabled quadcopter. It has a high-res zoom camera that records, too."

"Mr. Ludwig. I believe it is against Mission protocols to have any GPS or cellular-capable devices in HI-SLOPE." The XO cocked one eyebrow and gave him a stern look for a moment, then smiled. "On the other hand, it could be very useful, so go on."

Lugnut looked sheepish, every bit the shy kid just out of his teens. "Well, yeah, I know. But I *just* got it before we moved in. Anyway, I can program it with our GPS coordinates and that of the Onizuka Center. We still have problems with avoiding anything in the way, but I can program it to go . . . oh, call it one hundred fifty feet straight up, then directly horizontal to the Center, then down to a twenty-foot hover. Whatever we want it to do will have to be programmed ahead of time, though. It will be recording video, not transmitting in real time."

The fifth person in the room in the room had been silent so far, mostly looking at his hands the whole time. Now he looked up. "We need video of the people. Close-ups. I need to see what happened to them," Dr. d'Almeida said.

"Not a problem," said Lugnut. "I can program in a three-sixty pan, and fifty-foot spiral at twenty feet up. The video is the new ten-kay standard. Ten thousand pixels across. We can zoom it up on a computer and it will still look like the original."

"Okay." The doctor seemed satisfied with the answer.

"How are you planning to launch it?" asked the XO. "Rudy and Command get an alert on all air locks. We can bring Wyvern and Littleshawn in on this, but they will find out."

Lugnut opened his mouth, paused without saying anything, then closed it again.

Ham interjected "Yeah, about that…"

Tree Rat held up a hand. "No need. Rover Three's fully automated and programmed for a standard Hab external diagnostic later this afternoon. Can you set the quadcopter to ride the rover out, execute the program on command, then land once the rover is back in place?" Lugnut nodded. "Good. We don't need to bring Wyvern and Littleshawn in at this point, but we *will* need Bigfoot. He's scheduled to monitor the diagnostic."

Ham turned to Medusa. "You're the XO. You can act on the emergency protocols if the CO doesn't. Why are we keeping this a secret?"

"Because the CO has been throwing tantrums for the last two days. Right now, Sunan Bolinger is the only one who can stand to be near him. He threw Aidan out, yelling something about screwing up the book and movie rights. The Doctors Luca asked *Steve and me* to play bridge with them last night because Rudy won't let anyone else in his quarters! Legs said there was an airflow alert in his quarters that she monitored on the life-systems panel. Turned out to be a jammed air vent; something rather heavy had been thrown at it. Doc and I have been discussing whether he needs to be relieved under Section Twenty-five."

"And you didn't consult the mission psychologist?"

"No, Hummer, I didn't. This is a command decision, fully in accordance with emergency protocols, and doesn't require all of the department heads. Besides, I already knew what you would have recommended."

Cro grunted. "We all do. On the other hand, I imagine we all would say the same thing."

"Oh." Ham at least had the sense to look chagrined.

"For now, I want to keep this close, and strictly an off-the-record fact-finding effort. Once we know more, I'll do what I have to. But I'll have evidence and know exactly what we're walking into when I do it. HI-SLOPE may have a change in command, but we'll not go down in history as the first 'interplanetary' mutiny."

CHAPTER SEVEN
EYE IN THE SKY

The best part of my robots is that I can set them up to be fully autonomous. Combat is fast, my algorithms are faster. It's the next best thing to artificial intelligence.

—Z.J. Ludwig, seven-time Robot Battles champion

Unlike many of the crew call signs, "Bigfoot" Neil Frandsen had carried his nickname most of his life—in fact, no one ever called him anything *but* Bigfoot. At exactly six feet in height, he was not the tallest member of the crew, but his size-fourteen-triple-wide feet caused many uniform and space-suit problems for the genial Canadian geologist. He was also one of the oldest crew members. He almost hadn't made the crew, but Dr. d'Almeida swore he was one of the fittest. Bigfoot attributed it to a lifetime in the field—surveying, analyzing, and testing. Even before joining HI-SLOPE he'd consulted with the Mars-and-Beyond Consortium and had selected the simulation site before van Der Venn had muscled in and taken over the project. His exo-geology and asteroid mining simulations and protocols for the mission had been rolled into the simulation once Ham had selected Bigfoot for the mission. Well-liked by all, he was quick with a story, but also willing to listen—a rare combination.

"Okay, kid, your baby's back in the barn. Give it a few minutes for decontamination and wear a shipsuit when you go in the Garage. I don't suggest bringing it all the way in. You can set it up in my cubby in the glovebox."

Zach Ludwig bristled at being called a "kid" but Bigfoot reached out and tasseled the teleoperator's unruly hair. "Ah, don't take it hard, Lugnut. When I was your age, the seismic surveyors up on the tundra gave me a hard time until I showed them I knew the PZS triangle so well, I could set up and solve a three-station triangulation—vertical *and* horizontal—in my head faster than they could plug it into their fancy calculators. No one knows robots better than you, and we all respect you for it...kid." Bigfoot grinned and Lugnut grinned back.

"Thanks, Bigfoot. Actually, I might just leave the 'copter sitting on Rover Three. I don't need a physical connection to get the video, and there's still plenty of charge in case the boss wants another mission." Neither of the men commented on the fact that "the boss" in this case was the executive officer, and not the commanding officer.

An hour later, Lugnut was replaying the video on a large monitor in the medical lab.

"Hey, Cro! Get over here. You're the one that wanted the close-ups. What are you doing?" Ham called back to the tiny office partitioned off of the clinical space.

"Just reading my backlog. CDC reported some new influenza strain several months ago and I'm reading up on it." The doctor joined Ham, Tree Rat, Lugnut, and Medusa in front of the screen.

"Okay, not much at the actual visitor center. I had real-time coverage until the drone descended, so we only have the three-thousand-foot view as I widened the spiral and found the big tour van at the Commons building." Lugnut tapped his tablet. "Here, I'll freeze and zoom in, but there's not much to see. No one there. Maybe they got scared off? Anyway...resuming. Once I locked in on Hale Pohaku, I programmed the descent and return, then pointed the camera toward the buildings."

"There's the front door, pretty much what we saw on the rover cam," confirmed Tree Rat. "A few bones and scraps of clothing. How long ago did this happen? There were intact bodies inside, right? Predators?"

"I've never heard of predator species this high up," supplied the XO.

"Goats?" countered Tree Rat. "They'll eat anything."

"I'd be more likely to believe pigs or feral hogs, but here it's not so much the altitude as the barren lava."

"Actually," began the doctor, "decomposition is surprisingly fast at high altitude. The freeze-thaw cycle and temperature extremes accelerate the breakdown. We have higher UV, and the air swings from dry to humid depending on the trade winds. Any microorganisms and insects that can survive the extremes are very efficient." He paused and appeared to be mentally calculating. "Figure three to four times as fast. You can get down to bare bones in about . . . oh, six weeks."

"Can't really see inside the building; the doors are reflecting the sun. This new video standard is broad spectrum, though, so let me pause it and see if I can digitally polarize the image." Lugnut made several adjustments using the tablet from which he was controlling the playback. The image froze, then the lighting changed, and the video clearly showed bodies through the glass doors. "Ta-da! X-ray vision!"

"Ugh," said Ham. "These bodies are mostly intact. So, slower decomposition than outside, Cro?"

"Yes, very likely. Hmm." He pointed to one of the bodies on-screen. "Zoom that?"

"Got it." Lugnut touched a control and the image zoomed in on one of the bodies.

D'Almeida stood up and moved closer to the screen, inspected the image for a moment, then tapped the screen. "Not 'mostly intact,' Ham. That one's missing an arm." He pointed to another place. "This one's missing a foot."

"Traumatic amputation?" asked Medusa.

"Very traumatic. Those are bite wounds. Human, not animal."

"Ouch," she replied.

"Y'know what I *don't* see?" asked Tree Rat. "Rover One."

"Did we see tracks? I thought there should be tracks for the rover, the road surface isn't all that good," Ham mused, then looked over at Lugnut, who was just staring at the screen, slack jawed. "Lugnut, did we get an angle toward the road? Lugnut? Zach? *Zach!*"

"Oh, sorry. Yeah. Sorry, this is . . . That's just not right."

"It's okay, Zach. It's affecting all of us that way. Now, can we fast-forward to the point where we can see the road?"

"Um. Yeah, three more orbits and we should start catching the road." He restarted the playback and sped it up to the point where the camera now showed the road and entrance to the parking area. "This is the best angle. There's only two more orbits. This position won't come back up before the 'copter headed home."

"Zoom again?" asked Tree Rat. He pointed to one corner. "Right here?" Once the picture was enlarged, he smiled. "Yup, that's a double track. One coming in, one coming out."

"But we haven't seen it on the video so far," countered Ham.

"Yeah, but Lugnut programmed it to go directly, not follow the road. Besides, it was at high altitude. We should have a better angle on the return flight." Tree Rat turned back to Lugnut. "Was the camera locked forward?"

"No, actually, I had the 'copter take a slow return and rotated the camera the whole way to get a wide-angle pan. It's still pretty high, though."

"Good enough, we can use your 'magic zoom' if we need to." Tree Rat and the others sat back to watch the long video of the return flight. The quadcopter was crossing over the rim of the crater housing HI-SLOPE when Tree Rat spotted it. "There. The rover. There's someone on it."

Once again, Lugnut paused the playback and enlarged the image of the rover high on the slope of the crater wall. "Batteries must have run out. I knew the rovers weren't designed with enough storage capacity."

The image showed a nearly naked figure lying across the seat of Rover One. "Is he . . . tied up? Who is it?" asked Medusa.

The figure's wrists and ankles appeared to be secured with gray tape. A black cloth covered most of the head, obscuring the features.

"That's Asnip—Redshirt One. That's a knife scar there, on his chest, and the tattoos are right," said the doctor.

"How can you tell? They're both tattooed—identically they always said."

"They're a bit different." Naturally, the doctor would be familiar with everyone's scars and markings. "Matt had a knife design worked into his left sleeve because of the knife attack he survived before he met Steve."

"Not to mention he's not wearing Steve's fake Rolex," added Ham.

"Fake? I thought it was real!" said Medusa.

"No, not the one he wears," supplied Ham. "He's got a real one. Family heirloom and all that. He just doesn't *wear* the real one. Same thing as Matt. He's got some coin that's a family heirloom... 'Sitting Liberty,' I think he said. He carries a replica in his pocket on a chain."

"Why the hoodwink and restraints, then?" Medusa went back to her original question.

Lugnut turned to Ham and whispered: "'Hoodwink'?"

"It's what they called the hood they used on someone about to be executed, Zach," Ham whispered back.

"Oh. Ugh. Gross."

"Well, just speculating, but those *were* human bites we saw." The doctor was rubbing his chin, the permanent five o'clock shadow making a scratching noise as he thought. "And the last transmission said that someone was naked." He paused and rubbed some more. "That rings a bell. Something in the backlog of messages." Cro pushed back his stool and returned to his office.

"Is he alive? Lugnut, you said the camera was multispectral. Can you give us infrared?"

"Sure, Mr. Burbey! I can do that." The image on screen faded to blues and greens. There was a bright red rectangle in the back of the rover, but the body was only slightly yellower than the rest of the vehicle. "Oooh, the battery overheated. I need to check the scale." After a few moments of varying intensity on the screen, most of the image settled back to the original, with blue ground, dark green rover, and light green body. "That's the right scale. Not much warmer than the plastic seats on the rover."

"Not good. Not good at all." Ham was shaking his head. "We'll have to ask Cro to confirm it to be sure, but that's more than just hypothermia. That's a dead body."

"See that brighter trail, there?" Tree Rat was pointing to the screen again. "Leading up to the rim. Lugnut, do we have a camera view of the inside of the crater?"

"No, sir, the camera was pointed inward, just like in this shot. The inside of the rim will be just out of view."

"Why? I thought you were going to orbit until you could get Rover Three back into the right position?"

"I didn't *need* to. Mr. Bigfoot gave me a transponder and I was able to track directly into the rover bed and land it."

"We've got to send it back out, then. We need to look for Schaper!"

"Whoa, whoa, whoa, people!" Medusa held up her hands. "This is too big, now. I need to brief the CO, first. Zach, what do you need to send the drone out and give us real-time video the whole way?"

"I can do it on my tablet, but it would be better from Command—bigger screens and all that."

"Okay." Medusa slumped for a moment, then stood up. "Time to beard the lion. Meet me in Command in thirty minutes."

CHAPTER EIGHT

CHANGE OF COMMAND

Artificial Intelligence is no match for natural stupid.
—N.H. "Bigfoot" Frandsen, seismic surveyor

The screaming from Hex One could be heard throughout the Hab, carried through the open hamster tubes connecting each Hex. The tubes were officially kept open for air exchange unless HI-SLOPE was undergoing evacuation or hull-breach drills, at which time airtight doors isolated the Hexes and additional doors sealed the area of the "breach." Unfortunately, this was one time when the crew wished for the isolation, or some other way of *not* having to listen to van Der Venn bellowing at his executive officer. It was more than an hour before Medusa joined the others in the Command Module's control deck. Pilots Seville and Haley were at their stations, while Ludwig was at the engineer's position with Burbey and Hlavacek standing behind him. Most of the rest of the crew seemed to be either on the opposite side of the deck or peering down into the Core from the deck above. Notably absent were the Lucas, the Bolingers, and the doctor—the two couples most likely because their patron was in such a bad mood, the doctor presumably following up on his vague recollection connected to images of the bite victims.

The main screen showed video from the quadcopter, currently resting on the back of Rover Three as it exited the air-lock doors of Hex Six. Once clear of the doors, the propellers started to turn, then blur. They briefly rose out of view of the camera as the speed increased enough to provide lift. The drone was airborne.

"Back over to where we found Rover One, Lugnut." The XO's face was grim. The entire crew had heard the CO "fire" her, and her counter by asking him what he intended to do—throw her out an air lock?

"Yes, ma'am. With real-time control, I can keep it to twenty feet AGL the whole way."

"No need, son." That was Bigfoot, sharp-eyed as always. "He's right there. One hundred thirty meters out, twenty-two degrees less than true west . . . I call it"—he closed his eyes for just a moment, then opened them, nodding to himself—"about fourteen degrees upslope. You'll need another . . . thirty-two meters altitude at a course of two-four-eight degrees true."

"How does he *do* that?" Half-Check muttered. Next to him, Tree Rat just shook his head.

"Got it. Thank you, Mr. Bigfoot. One-thirty meters less two for camera angle. Adding thirty-two. I'll let the GPS do the rest."

"Shouldn't we be flying this thing?" Wyvern asked Littleshawn.

"Speak for yourself. I trained as an astronaut, not a drone pilot," he replied. "Let the kid do his thing."

"Give us infrared, Zach," Medusa commanded. "Let's see if he's still alive."

The screen turned to blues and greens, with a bright yellow outline of a human right where the former surveyor had said he would be. "He's alive, or at least pretty hot," someone said. A couple spots were a brighter orange, including the face and head, but also several other points along the body. The screen returned to normal colors as the image increased in size once the drone was close enough to hover over the body. The hotter spots on the body seemed to correspond to lacerations or abrasions, including one poorly bandaged area on the left shoulder.

"Note the watch," said Ham. "That's Redshirt Two. It's Steve Schaper."

"Doc? Are you seeing this?" Littleshawn asked over the comm. When there was no answer, he switched channels and called his wife. "Pearce? Honey? Are you monitoring this?"

"Yes, Sean, I'm here," came the instant reply. "Cro is occupied, but I am monitoring. He looks critical. That wound is too hot, and so is he. It's probably infected and for him to be that hot . . . I mean, look at the sweat on his face, it's not warm enough out there for him to be sweating. He could be getting septic. We need to get him into the med-bay right away!"

"I'll go," volunteered Tree Rat.

"Me too," said Bruce "Moose" Dennison. The Australian power-system engineer was not particularly tall but was regularly seen to bench-press twice his weight on the fitness station in the Commons. Together, the two big men would certainly be able to carry the slight form of Redshirt Two.

"Wait," said Medusa. "Bigfoot. Send Rover Three over there first. Let's see if we can rouse him and he can get onto it, first." She seemed to think better of it. "Oh, *can* we talk to him?"

"The rovers are tied into comm systems. He's not wearing his helmet. I don't see it or, frankly, most of his suit." Wyvern was checking her controls. "We don't have any external speakers on the Hab."

"Oh! You are *so* going to love this!" Lugnut pressed a control on his tablet, then reached out to the console and adjusted another control. The Command Deck was filled with a buzzing sound. "Lipstick mic on the 'copter. Now listen." The buzzing of the rotors increased in volume, then started to change pitch.

"*Bzzzzzzzz——Rrrrrrrredzzzzzzshirtzzzzzz—zzttwozzzzzzz! zzzzzzzzzSSSSteeeeeevezzzzzzzz!*"

The words were slurred and filled with buzzing, but clearly audible.

"Blade-pitch modulation! One of my own inventions!" Lugnut said proudly. The figure on screen stirred. His head turned, and the watchers could see cuts and lacerations all over his face, including what looked like a bite mark. "Oooh. He's been bitten. That's probably why he tied up Redshirt One and put a hood on him."

"He tied up Matt? I didn't think they ran that way!" said Littleshawn. The grin on his face faded when he saw Wyvern just shaking her head.

"Right. I'm going," said Tree Rat and headed for the Core. "Madam XO! Please authorize use of the emergency air lock!"

"Authorized, Mr. Burbey."

"*Stop! Do not open the air lock!*" A very red-faced and out-of-breath Anson d'Almeida jumped down the last rungs of the Core ladder onto the Command Deck. He looked as if he had run the entire way from Hex Three. Considering that the hamster tubes were meant to mimic connecting passages on a spacecraft, they were also rather cramped and rapid transit was difficult.

"Bloody Hell, Mate! He's frickin' bleedin' out up there." That was Moose; his Outback accent came to the fore when he was stressed.

"Hold, gentlemen," ordered Medusa. "Explain, Doctor. Quickly, and in words of few syllables. A man's life is at stake."

Cro panted a moment, breathed deep, then said, "We have to invoke Emergency Protocol 2020."

Lugnut whispered to Ham, "Which one is that?"

"It's the airborne pathogen isolation protocol."

"Huh?"

"Sort of like a zombie protocol."

"Oh cool, a real-life zombie apocalypse." Lugnut grinned. Ham just shook his head.

The doctor was still trying to catch his breath. "The CDC reports I saw...before the comms went out." He coughed and swallowed. Ham handed him a water bulb from the wall dispenser; the doctor nodded his thanks. "There was an update in the queue. H7D3 they're calling it. Never saw a dee-three variant before this." He paused and drank deeply. "Looks like the flu. People ignore it, but some *die* from it. Then it gets worse...*much* worse. Actually, it *got* worse."

"Worse than dying?" asked Wyvern.

"Yes." Cro was getting his breathing under control. "Yes, much worse. If you thought all the rumors about SARS and MERS and all the other viral diseases were bad, this is...well, it's worse than Ebola, dengue, and all the others combined. There's a second stage where twenty to thirty percent die outright. About half of the survivors go crazy. Like savages or something. They scream, run around naked, and try to *bite* people!"

"Oh. My. God!" exclaimed Ham. "The people at Hale Pohaku."

"Right. The infection gets in the blood. The infected attack healthy people. Once bitten, they're infected and become savages themselves. The last message in my download was from the CDC. It's worldwide and out of control. Too many governments had given up on controlling it and were evacuating their leaders."

"Fuck. It's the end of the world," said Tree Rat.

"As we know it, yes," confirmed the doctor.

After a long pause, Littleshawn whispered, "But I feel fine..."

Wyvern and the rest of the Command Deck personnel just gave him a dirty look.

Multiple voices started speaking at once. Conversation on the Command Deck seemed to be centered around two arguments. Cro was saying that Schaper was dangerously infected, and this new influenza threatened the whole habitat. Tree Rat and Moose argued that they could go out in suits and keep Redshirt Two isolated in the Garage air lock until he could be treated. The voices rose in pitch and volume until a loud alarm sounded.

"ALERT! HULL BREACH! THIS IS NOT A DRILL!"

CHAPTER NINE

BREACH

Even more important than the mission, we must be cautious with the composition of the crew. The cramped quarters of a spaceship are no place for ego.
—H.V. Forsyth, MD, PhD, Crew Selection Lead,
Mars-and-Beyond Consortium

Hissy's synthesized voice issued from all speakers and could be heard echoing from the tubes connecting the Hexes—as could an ominous sound of airtight bulkhead doors slamming closed. A scream came from the deck above as something—or, more importantly, *someone*—was caught by one of the closing doors. The alarm continued: "ALERT! HULL BREACH! LOSS OF STRUCTURAL INTEGRITY IN HEXAGON TWO. HULL BREACH IN HEXAGON TWO. EMERGENCY PROCEDURE TWO-ZERO-TWO-ZERO IN EFFECT. ATMOSPHERIC CONTAINMENT PROCEDURES INITIALIZED."

"Shit." The XO reached over Wyvern's shoulder and pressed her thumbprint on the control pad. The alarm silenced, but the room lighting had dimmed and red lights pulsed next to each console and over each doorway. "First. Who screamed? Is anyone injured?"

"Just my pride." The voice from the upper level belonged to "Malut" Fisher, their Aleutian astronomer. "The door caught my hair. Scorpio cut me loose. I've lost a chunk, but it will grow back."

"Good. Second. Mr. Hlavacek, please take your station and tell us about this breach."

Zach Ludwig stood up, allowing the engineer to work his console. "Ma'am. It's from Hex Two, the Quarters One Module. Lower Level, Gabriel Luca's quarters. It's . . . No. This doesn't make any sense, ma'am." He paused and looked back at the XO. "It's the maintenance panel. Used to install furnishings when the Hab was constructed. It's not damaged, it's unbolted!"

"Lugnut! Swing your camera around!" Once the camera was repositioned, Medusa continued: "Oh, those fools!"

On screen they could see two figures straightening up from exiting through the one-meter-wide hatch. Even at this distance, Angel and Balls could be identified as they began to carefully make their way across the crumbled lava rock toward their fellow crew member. It *had* to be painful since the only boots in the Hab were part of the "space suits" stored in Hex Six. The thin-soled shipboard shoes probably let them feel every sharp edge and corner of the lava. Bolinger stumbled and fell, catching himself on his hands, then knees, before carefully standing back up.

"Lugnut. Warn them off. Do that trick and talk to them."

"Ma'am, the battery is low, I haven't recharged it since the survey of Hale Pohaku. I can keep it on station and give us video, or I can use the modulator. I can't do both."

"Medusa. Ma'am. I can check and see if they are wearing their comms, or if someone answers in their quarters," Wyvern offered.

"Do it."

"Yes, ma'am!"

The initial queries went unanswered, but when Wyvern keyed the comm for Angel's quarters, Wily answered.

"Wily! This is Medusa. Tell Angel he needs to get back in here. It's too dangerous." On the screen they could see a figure inside the hatch, gesturing and speaking to the people outside.

Wily's voice came back on the line. "He says no, *Senhor Camisa Vermelha* is hurt. He can help." In the background they could hear shouted words from another person. Sissy was also present, and she, too, appeared to be shouting out to her husband.

"Ylene, please tell him that Dr. d'Almeida says it is too dangerous. There is an infection that kills. Steven is infected. It killed Matthew and all of the people down at Hale Pohaku!"

There was a pause and Wily shouted out to her husband again; after a few moments, her head disappeared from view again and she returned. "He says Doctor should have said 'probably.' Steven is only *probably* infected, and the disease at Center is only *probably* the one he read about. Gabriel says Steven *is* hurt and needs a doctor. Gabriel knows physiology; he is a *médico*. He also says d'Almeida is *covarde*— a coward."

Ham put a hand on Cro's shoulder as the doctor began to shake. "Easy, big guy. Not now. Later." The doctor held back but was visibly angered.

"Gabriel says do not speak to you. He will turn *comunicador* back on when he returns." The channel went silent.

"Okay, Devil, I understand, he has the ego. Why Balls? Frankly, he doesn't strike me as having any." While no one in the crew really got along with the Bolingers or the Lucas, Ham held the Bolingers in particular distaste. Prancer had overridden his recommendation for an exobiologist and mining specialist, and added Aidan and Sissy despite Ham's official report that the couple would not integrate well with the rest of the crew.

"Maybe he finally figured out where he left them?" suggested Tree Rat.

Lugnut had expressed concern over the quadcopter's batteries, so Bigfoot moved Rover Three around the Hab and toward the two men carefully making their way toward Schaper. The drone landed on the bed of the rover, positioned to allow the camera to remain pointed at the scene. The high-resolution video was zoomed in as Angel and Wily reached the injured man.

Angel bent over Redshirt Two and first checked over the neck and then the shoulder wounds. He touched a hand to the forehead and pulled it back quickly. He turned and looked directly at the rover and made a "come closer" motion.

Lugnut and Bigfoot looked at the XO.

"Go ahead, might as well. They're out there and they'll be in isolation for a minimum of seventy-two hours anyway. The 'hull breach' protocol will keep Hex Two sealed off for at least that long." She turned to d'Almeida. "Doc, how long does this H3-D-pio whatsit take to show symptoms?"

"H7D3, ma'am."

Ham noticed that now d'Almeida was doing it, too. There was a lot of "ma'aming" going on here. It made sense. Medusa had stood up to Prancer and had taken charge in the emergency. They were all treating her as if she *were* the captain, and the fact that they'd heard *nothing* from him seemed to make the change in command official.

The doctor continued, "The flu-like symptoms act like any other influenza, just with a high mortality. A week to ten days incubation, three or four of mild symptoms, then the fever, nausea, vomiting, dehydration hit. Around Day Five the survivors appear to get better, but by Day Seven, about half of them start going crazy."

"So, we quarantine them for two weeks?"

"No. The blood-borne pathogen is much more virulent. Direct infection, either a bite from an Infected or getting their blood on you, takes about twelve to twenty-four hours to show symptoms. People complain about intense itching, rip off all of their clothes, and start attacking."

"Blood. Like that?" Medusa gestured toward the screen. Angel was now bent over Redshirt Two and appeared to be providing chest compressions. He stopped for a moment and wiped at his eyes; his face and hands were covered with blood.

"Oh shit. *Merda. Scheisse. Skit. Kak...*" The normally urbane doctor tended to curse in multiple languages when upset. Several of the crew had very surprised expressions and Tree Rat's eyebrows kept getting higher. Cro continued: *"Hovno. Bok. Merde..."* and the list continued.

"Czech, too. I'm impressed. What was that last one?" Halfcheck asked Tree Rat.

"Urdu, I think. He's also starting to repeat himself."

As the doctor began to run down, Ham noticed that Balls did not seem to be assisting in the resuscitation. "Just exactly *what* is Balls doing?"

"Going through Red Two's pockets?" Lugnut said, tentatively. The view magnified as he controlled the zoom again. "This is probably all I can do until we get the drone recharged."

"Going through his pockets? What the hell?" Ham began, then stopped. "The watch! Steve's *watch* is missing! Balls just put something in his pocket... there's a chain. Oh, Christ on a crutch! That's Matt's coin. He's a thief! A. God. Damned. Thief! Dammit! When I get my hands on him...!"

Now it was d'Almeida's turn to calm down his friend. He placed one hand on Ham's shoulder and used the other to turn his chin so that they were face-to-face. "Hamilton. You will not need to. They will both be dead within the day. The CDC said that barely one percent of the people survive a direct blood-to-blood transfer."

"But we don't know that Steve is infected."

"No, but Matthew was. Did you see the chain? Zachariah, can you replay the video?"

On the screen, the video jumped back in time, and Ham could see Bolinger clearly put a coin on a chain into his pocket—it gleamed red in the sun. Red with blood. The same close-up also showed Ball's hands, and the bloody cuts he'd sustained during the earlier fall.

The crew watched, transfixed, as Angel and Balls eventually lifted the limp form of Steve and carried it over to the rover. Bigfoot maneuvered the vehicle back to the habitat and parked it outside the open maintenance hatch. Before he completely lost battery power, Lugnut once more switched the drone's camera to infrared mode, and they could all see that Steve Schaper's body had begun to cool.

True to his word, Gabriel Luca reactivated communications with Command once he was back inside. He seemed unusually subdued. He still didn't believe Cro's cautions about the virus, even when both Ham and Medusa confirmed that they had inspected the stored transmissions received after the end of the communications blackout and confirmed the reports from the CDC.

He may have believed it once the screaming started later that night.

Commander Kirby—Medusa, acting CO—ordered Engineer Hlavacek to permanently seal off Hex Two from the rest of the complex and turn off the comms before the seventy-two-hour Hull Breach protocol expired.

CHAPTER TEN

THE END OF THE WORLD

Planetary Protection? It's more important to protect the fragile life on and from Earth. Eggs, basket, one each. One major crisis and "Poof."
> —B.C. Litchfield, biologist and life-systems engineer,
> HI-SLOPE

Ham and Tree Rat were in the central Hex trying to search through the accumulated communication backlog for more information about H7D3. The main console for Comms was on the second floor of Hex Seven, but the Command Module had an additional level—Level Three, also known as the Core. The name partly derived from the floor-to-ceiling (and ceiling!) electronics panels, including auxiliary monitoring and emergency consoles for each system and subsystem. It also referred to the fact that it was the central hub for the access tubes to the other Hexes. Comm monitoring was a two-foot-wide panel with a physical keyboard, a small monitor, and auxiliary input-output jacks. There was even a hard-copy output printer directly adjacent to the sealed, red-lit hatch to Hex Two. Tree Rat had the lone chair, typing and muttering at the small monitor screen and occasionally throwing perturbed glances at Ham, who was hovering over his shoulder. Legs had just come off-shift from the Greenhouse and was sitting on the threshold of the hatch to Hex Four. She'd had to adjust the life-systems pressure balances with the loss of Hex Two.

Lugnut was half in and half out of the ladder hatch to Level Two, having just handed Tree Rat a bypass patch cable from the Primary

61

Comm console on the level below. "Yeah, I guess I should have realized something was up when Twitch went off the air a few weeks ago." He was idly fiddling with a small device, spinning it on the end of a finger, then moving it through a complicated orbit that complemented the gyroscopic effects from spinning. It had three lobes like most of the spinners Ham had seen before, but it was all black, with thin red arcs inscribed along each lobe. The arcs were open at the ends and crossed in the middle. It took Ham several more moments to realize that it looked just like the universal biohazard symbol.

"Twitch?" asked Legs. "What's that, a game show?"

"More like a gaming channel. News, walk-throughs, charity games, releases, DLCs, and reviews." Lugnut sighed. "Man, I've missed Bacon Doughnut, he had the best feed. At the time I thought it was because Mr. van Der Venn had discovered my stream and shut it off. Now we know they're off the grid for real."

"Wait, you mean you've had an open channel even during the programmed blackout? I didn't think that was possible!" Ham was surprised, and looked at Tree Rat, who was in charge of comm systems. "You knew?" he asked Burbey. Tree Rat just shrugged. "Go on, Zach."

"Sure. I mean, I had finally gotten a digital copy of *Halo 4* and needed access to the DLCs." At Ham's raised eyebrow, he explained, "Downloadable content. Most of the video games these days have more content and competition online than in the release packs. Anyway, those VennSystems guys may have installed our network, but they were sloppy. I've owned the network from Day One."

"So, this 'Twitch,' you say it had news? Anything about the virus?" Ham *really* wanted to press some more about how Lugnut had managed his illicit communications, since maintaining the illusion of a deep space mission had been part of Ham's own duties. However, it was all a moot point, and the opportunity to get uncensored news was too good to pass up.

"Well, Professor Bro-man and Dan's Gaming both ran segments on it. Bro-man and Bacon Donut were mostly just comparing it to *Doom*, while Dan was covering the speculation over who created it. One of the followers said some sci-fi writer in Tennessee did it, another said it was some professor in North Carolina. Initially everyone thought it was just another Four-chan joke."

"I could see my ex-husband's twin doing something like this," Legs interjected. "He was a notorious internet troll. Four-chan loved him and called him the 'Internet Lord of Hatred.' A nice enough guy, but on the internet, he was a real jerk."

"Anyway, they also had reports of teams in the big city 'harvesting' the zombies for vaccine. There was this funny government dude at a press conference complaining that they were violating the zombies' civil rights."

Ham sighed. "Yeah, I could see that. While others quoted that old saw 'the hardest part of a zombie apocalypse is pretending not to be excited.' I bet there were plenty of folks who wanted open season on Infected."

"Totally ignoring the fact that these people are victims of a disease," came Cro's voice over the comm. "I mean, with all the effort put into a vaccine, did anyone even start looking into a cure? What are we even going to do with millions and millions of zombies? Let them starve? Die of exposure?"

"Zombies are brain dead. No brains. That's why they're always going 'Brainzzz,'" Legs giggled.

"I'm serious! We don't know if there's gradations of the disease. There might be victims who don't lose all of their faculties. What happens if a true genius gets the virus? Do they become normal? Are there nonviolent Infected? Could they be trained to look after themselves?"

"Trained as a slave labor force, Cro?" Ham asked, quietly.

"No! I mean, that's my point. It's unethical. All of this is unethical."

"This is a fun conversation, but it's not solving our problem," Tree Rat interrupted. "Lugnut, get on the Comm board and toggle Charlie Alpha Five for me."

"Aye, aye, Cap'n Tree Rat!" Lugnut said as he disappeared from the hatch. "There, how's that?"

"I said *Five*, Lugnut," Tree Rat responded. "That was Charlie Alpha *Six*!"

"No, that *was* Charlie Alpha Five. You've locked me out of Charlie Alpha Six. I *can't* toggle it."

"Oh, right. Sorry," Tree Rat mumbled as he turned back to the keyboard. He continued muttering for a few more moments, then sat back and smiled. "Okay, that's got it. The comm logs are now in a searchable database. I can't get them into the common server, but we can at least work from the Command consoles below us instead of this tiny piece of crap." He waved dismissively at the communications subpanel.

"Yeah, who even puts together a state-of-the-art spaceship network based on a smart-home system?" Lugnut's voice came up from the lower deck. "Oh, yeah, this is 'Veedeevee' we're talking about here."

"I thought you said you 'owned the network from Day One'?" Ham asked.

"Puh-lease, that's not hard. I could build a better system out of my watch. In fact, I did exactly that for my master's thesis project at MIT."

Legs stood up and walked over to look over Tree Rat's shoulder, then moved to look down through the hatch at Lugnut. "How is that any better than this tiny screen and keyboard?"

"VR goggles, virtual keyboards ... all the space you want. In fact, my game console could have done all of this and projected a full-room hologram as a display."

Ham looked over at Tree Rat and raised an eyebrow. Tree Rat just shrugged in return.

"So, you could have done this already and saved us the trouble?"

"Well, not exactly. Mr. Burbey won't let me."

"Yeah," Tree Rat grunted, getting up from the small chair at the auxiliary console. "That's why I locked out Charlie Alpha Six. This kid will take over anything, but at least he listens."

"Why exactly are we doing it this way, then?" Ham picked up the patch cable to emphasize the point.

Tree Rat sighed. "Sure, let him run rampant through a five-billion-dollar space simulation. It's not like everything else hasn't gone to shit already." He disconnected the patch cable and started to coil it for storage.

"Already done," came the voice from below. "You *do* know that the only thing blocked by Charlie Alpha Six was Hissy's ability to see inside the toilets, right?"

"Hey!" Legs objected. "No spying!"

Tree Rat just put his hand up to cover his face. "Kid's got a point about the cheap systems, though."

"True, but I think it's a bit too late to take the VennSystems people to task for it." Ham turned and started down the ladder to the main deck. "Let's just see what we've got, and worry about Lugnut's misspent youth later."

Reaching the primary command deck, he stood in the middle of a blur of color and light. Stepping away from the ladder and moving toward the center of the room revealed projection beams from several points at the junction of wall and ceiling. Once outside the projection, he could see that it displayed a rotating holographic image of the Earth—at least it did until first Tree Rat and then Legs came down the ladder.

"Nice projection, but where did this come from?" Legs asked.

"It's my piloting display." Wyvern spoke from her position across the room without turning to look at the others.

"True, but I'm washing the display through my own system for speed and detail enhancement." As Lugnut spoke, red, green, orange, and black dots appeared on the projection of the Earth. There were four green dots, all clustered together about where Hawaii should appear on the map. A few red dots appeared in Washington State, California, Texas, New England, and others sparsely scattered across the globe, including one red dot in central China. There was a single orange dot in the middle of the U.S., with a large number of black dots filling the rest of the globe.

"So, what are the dots—people?" asked Ham.

"Nope! Servers." When no one reacted, Lugnut continued, "Black dots for where a server *should* be, but it's not answering. Red for an active address where the server answers a ping but is pretty much on autopilot. No real-time activity. Green is for active servers."

"That's ... it? Everything?"

"Pretty much, although to be honest, it's mostly public systems like universities, government services and commercial sites. Oh, and our VennSystems servers."

The Earth projection zoomed in on Hawaii until they were looking at a 3-D relief of Mauna Kea. There were two green dots near the top of the extinct volcano, and one at the very top.

"And this is us." Ham took a chair next to the pilot console, and could see that despite her prior apparent indifference, Wyvern was echoing the same view on her monitor.

"Yeah. HI-SLOPE and the Support Facilities at Onizuka and a

gateway server downslope from them. There's also something active at the telescope site at the summit."

Tree Rat cleared his throat. "This still doesn't tell us anything about people, just active computer servers. Probably the only reason we can see the summit is because someone at Hale Pohaku activated the override before things went to hell."

"Go back to the first display. The whole Earth." Wyvern finally turned and faced the rest of the room. She pointed at the hologram. "There. CONUS. That orange light. What is it?"

Lugnut zoomed the display, and faint lines appeared, outlining the individual U.S. states. "It's an active firewall. There's a server; it's active and it answers a ping, but I can't get into it. There's reactive routines that suggest someone is maintaining it, but it doesn't answer back."

"You've tried to get into it?"

"Of course. But I figured if they were still active, I didn't want to scare them off-line."

"Nebraska..." mused Ham. "Omaha?"

"It's Offutt Air Force Base." Wyvern clarified. "The Hole. It's where the Army, Air Force, and government hole-up when there's a crisis."

"Well. At least we have a government." Legs sounded rather more cheerful than any of them felt, looking at the vast expanse of black dots on the display.

"Trapped in a Hole at the bottom of a well." Tree Rat refused to be cheered. "Besides, it's the government, what good are they?"

"As good as we make it." Ham supplied. "We've got to help ourselves. So, let's get searching through the communications logs and see if we can work out a timetable and get a better idea what happened."

HI-SLOPE operated on a reversed schedule of day and night, such that daytime in the Hab was nighttime on Mauna Kea. Even though there were no direct viewing windows or ports, it meant that any regularly scheduled observations or EVA simulations would only see the night sky... and at eleven thousand feet of elevation, it was a clear and star-filled sky. An unending ocean of stars, just like a deep space simulation *should* see.

It also meant that daylight on the Hawaiian island was the middle of the night for the Hab. With Ham and Tree Rat involved in searching the backlog of communications, Medusa had suggested that Bigfoot and Lugnut send a probe back down to Hale Pohaku and Onizuka, but this time with continuous online video. The XO had proposed the mission for the very next "night" but was forced to reconsider when the geologist and teleoperation specialist reminded her that a continuous signal would require some way to maintain a line-of-sight connection with the 'copter. Since they would need to spend a large portion of their rest period awake, she decided to delay a day and ordered the pair off duty until the next evening.

In the meantime, Medusa put the problem of a relay antenna on Dean "Scorpio" Gestner, the construction specialist, as well as Half-Check and Moose, as representatives of Engineering and Power Systems, respectively. Scorpio reminded the XO that Burbey had already suggested mounting an antenna atop the Hab using the trusses intended to simulate deep space construction. Moose countered that an antenna tall enough to reach over the crater rim would be too tall for the lightweight/low-gravity trusses, and too heavy if they used the high-tensile-strength, high-gee construction beams. Half-Check suggested the compromise to put a small antenna on a rover and simply park it on the south rim of their cinder cone such that it could "see" most of the area down to Onizuka.

Rover One was still out in the crater with the bodies of Redshirts One and Two since Medusa had not approved a plan to retrieve either it or the bodies. Given that no one could decide how badly the rover was contaminated, she had deferred that decision until later. For that matter, the issue of decontaminating a crew member in a space suit had not been solved, so all procedures for prepping the relay antenna on Rover Two and the quadcopter on Rover Three took place in the Garage Hex with operators using one of the two glovebox units that had been set up to simulate vacuum conditions. Rover Two would use one of its two waldo-articulated arms to lay a physical cable from the comm interface on the exterior wall of Hex One to the rim of the cinder cone. Meanwhile, Rover Three was fitted with additional batteries and cabling to serve as a recharge platform for Lugnut's quadcopter and exploration drones. Three shifts later, the relay was ready, the quadcopter had been recharged, and Bigfoot and Lugnut were back in the Command Module with most of the crew on hand to witness the results.

"So, wait, what is everybody doing here?" Ham looked around at the crowded Command module. "I am certain that most of you have jobs that need to be performed right now."

"Not much I can't do from my console right here," answered Tree Rat.

"Ditto," said Scorpio and most of the other persons present.

"Okay, then, who *isn't* here?"

"Cro and Eggnog are in the clinic. Pearce says Doc's watching the feed with one eye while reading medical reports with the other."

"Yeah, that figures. He got through med school by virtue of his photographic memory. He takes it in and then analyzes it in his head later. Who else?"

"Mugs is chasing a hydraulic problem in the recycling module. He's up on top of a condenser, cursing."

"So, pretty much normal for him. Is it a real or simulated issue?"

"Frankly, ol' headshrinker, it's getting kind of hard to tell. Lugnut was asking me last night if I was sure this whole 'end of the world' routine wasn't another one of your simulated crises." Tree Rat gave Ham a particularly pointed look. "Is it?"

Ham held up his hands defensively. "It's not one of mine if it is. It's a bit too...real for my tastes."

"I think the point of our mission psychologist's question is *what* is everyone doing in Command?" Medusa asked as she climbed down the ladder from the core.

"Waiting for you, ma'am."

"Well, that's an answer, Mr. Ludwig. Not a good one, but it's an answer."

Ham noticed that no one was asking about van Der Venn, so he decided an indirect approach would be useful. "Has anyone heard from Crossbow?"

"Lalande? Not recently," said Medusa. "He reported in when Prancer locked himself into his quarters. Eggnog? What does his telemetry say?"

"Wait one...he's in Hex One. Seems to be sleeping," came the medic's voice over the comm. "Sorry I can't be more precise than that, we never got the upgrade that would have given us full remote medical telemetry."

"Damned cheap-ass Veedeevee software," muttered Tree Rat under his breath.

"Okay then, since everyone seems to be accounted for . . ."

"Uh, ma'am?"

"Yes, Eggnog?"

"I don't have readings for Prancer."

"Oh. Any . . . other problems with the system?"

"No, as you said, everyone—else—seems to be accounted for."

"I think I can answer that," interjected Ham. "Van Der Venn loved the idea of this space simulation but didn't think it should necessarily apply to him. I've noticed that he likes to turn off his monitoring. Just like he took over the whole level of Hex One and managed to lock us all out of it. That's not supposed to be possible, but obviously he built himself a back door into the system. He's probably sulking."

Medusa sighed. "Well, then. Let him sulk; he paid enough for the privilege. Lugnut? Is Wally ready to fly?"

"Yes, ma'am, although technically, Eva flew, Wall-E crawled, just like Bigfoot's rovers."

The XO sighed again. "You know what I meant, Lugnut."

"Yes, ma'am. Ready to go."

"Make it so, Mr. Lugnut."

CHAPTER ELEVEN

BREAKOUT

The myth of designed-in "back door access" in complex systems is just that...a myth. Have you ever tried to remember a password or access code you haven't used in a few weeks, let alone a few years? This is not to say there aren't forgotten logins and access pathways, just that they are seldom a result of baked-in design...which is why they present such a high risk.

—D.S. "Crossbow" Lalande, computer engineer,
Mars-and-Beyond Consortium Official Historian

Rover Three positioned itself in the middle of the crater, about one hundred twenty degrees away from where Rover One had stopped halfway down the crater wall. Rover Two was stationed high on the south rim, rather than the western rim over which Redshirts One and Two had traveled to reach the summit road. It would provide the most direct communication path to Hale Pohaku.

The quadcopter drone was airborne again, and this time live video was being monitored in Command. Instead of a screen, though, the video was now projected holographically using the same system that had previously shown the map of the Earth. Even though the drone camera only provided a two-dimensional image, Lugnut was running a custom program to convert the ultra-high-resolution video into an image that could be viewed from anywhere around the holoprojection.

Scorpio was the most familiar with the construction of the HI-SLOPE habitat, followed by Tree Rat due to his involvement in writing the simulations and emergency protocols. The two kept darting in and out of the holoprojection to point out features of the slope and road down to Hale Pohaku and the Onizuka Center.

"There, those are tire tracks," Scorpio said. "Rover One?"

"Nope, too wide," Tree Rat answered. "Besides, we should see tracks going both ways. We know they planned to stick to the road; those tracks are in scree." He was referring to the small loose stones that covered the slope of the extinct volcano.

"That's risky. Scree on a shield volcano isn't just pebbles, some of it is volcanic glass. Sharp stuff. It could puncture a tire or the dust could erode the wheel bearings. Lugnut, can you hover just a minute and zoom in?"

The image zoomed into the tracks.

"Okay, XO? Medusa? Permission to follow the tracks?"

"Approved. Lugnut, as Scorpio directs, do it."

"Great, okay, Zach, let's come back up-slope a tick and trace the tracks back up toward us."

"You have something in mind, don't you, Dean?"

"Aye. Yes, I do, DeeDub. Let's see where they lead before I say anything, though."

"What is that?" Ham pointed at a dark smudge against the side of the HI-SLOPE cinder cone. "A cave?"

"Tunnel," corrected Scorpio. "It's the construction access tunnel. It was supposed to be closed off, but not filled in to accommodate the sealed supply conveyor."

"Where does it connect?" Medusa's voice had a tightness telegraphing her anger. She clearly had a suspicion about the answer.

"Originally it connected underneath all of the Hexes, but once all of the interiors were completed, all but two entrances were filled in: Command Module and Hex Six, the Garage."

"There's a tunnel under us?" Lugnut asked. "Cool. Is it like the old steam tunnels under the MIT campus? We had such fun LARPing down there."

"Why am I not surprised you were into live-action role-playing?" Tree Rat muttered under his breath.

"No, there's nothing actually in the tunnel, it was just an access that didn't require going over the crater rim."

"But, what's the surprise? Isn't this how the six-month supplies come in?" Malut asked.

"Yes, but it's supposed to be a sealed conveyor into the stockroom off of the Garage."

"It's been months. How are there tire tracks leading from it? What vehicle? Who?"

There was the sound of a throat clearing from the access to Level Three above them. "It's Prancer. That's his 'personal buggy.' It's how he escaped any time he felt hemmed in." Dennis "Crossbow" Lalande very carefully made his way down from the Hub. There was a gash on his right temple, and dried blood in his hair and on his cheek.

"Crossbow? You're hurt. You need to see the doc."

"I will, XO. You need to know this, though. Van Der Venn hit me in the head and stuffed me in the kitchen, then closed and locked the door. Fortunately, I know the unlock code, since he likes to pretend I'm his 'dining steward' while I work on software designs for him. I've known about the hatch in the floor of his dining room for several months. He had a habit of locking himself in and not answering the comm. In reality, he was nowhere in the Hex. He had me create a false biosignal so that he would just show as being alone in quarters."

"So, the one person who most insisted we not break simulated mission protocol was playing hooky?" Ham mused. "Yeah, that fits. Damn. I should have seen it."

"Not just you," Medusa said with a grimace. "Okay, so, no contest, I'm really in charge. Lugnut, turn the drone around and follow those tracks downslope."

A few minutes later, the drone flew over a military-style utility vehicle with the HI-SLOPE logo on the side. It had what looked like a closed compartment for a driver, one or two passengers up front, and an open roof and seating in the back. A folded-up space suit was on one of the seats, indicating that those seats were likely meant for suited passengers.

The vehicle was stopped alongside the summit road, and the driver's door was open.

"Flat tire. Just what I was afraid of," Scorpio said. "Prancer bailed. He probably figured to grab a car from Hale Pohaku."

Once the drone was over the support services buildings, Medusa had Tree Rat call up a still image from the earlier run.

"A jeep is missing. He's long gone."

"Good riddance."

CHAPTER TWELVE

LETTERS HOME

Even soldiers get letters from home. NASA allows email and video calls between astronauts and their families. HI-SLOPE must give the opportunity for "communication with Earth" ... even if we have to add communications delays and filter anything that breaks the illusion. We owe it to the participants to provide all of the same conditions as a long-duration space flight. That includes letters to and from home.

—H.V. Forsyth,
meeting of the HI-SLOPE board of directors

My Dearest Abigail:

It figures that I would finally work up the courage to email you when I don't even know where or how you are, or even if you survived this "zombie apocalypse" we're just now discovering. I can only hope that your new job gave you some protection.

Cro—that's Dr. d'Almeida—says that the outbreak occurred just as we entered the last simulated communications failure. I can't believe that VennSystems or MABCon didn't see fit to warn us. At least it appears that someone at Onizuka tried to get a message through via the emergency override. It also appears that same person bit and infected Asnip, who in turn infected Schaper.

Two and a half months. I can't believe it. We sat here safe and ignorant for two and a half months while the end of the world happened; longer if we include the growing problem that was kept from us to preserve the illusion of this farce of a simulation.

So, here we are. Cro says the virus attacked too fast for traditional vaccine production. He has some ideas, and his reports from the CDC have some suggestions, but for now, we don't have immunity. We're trapped in our little bubble until someone comes for us, or we figure it out ourselves. He doesn't think the Infected—that's what he calls the zombielike humans—can survive in the thin air and cold temperatures up here, but that doesn't mean the *virus* won't survive.

He also goes off onto long rants on the ethics of everyone involved in studying the disease. He thinks that the idea of harvesting live Infected to make vaccine is repulsive, while at the same time wishing he had live samples of his own.

I worry for his sanity—but then I worry for all of our sanity. This situation is so much more than any of us signed up for.

On the other hand, we're safe ... for now.

Lugnut's going to package all of the crew emails and blast them out to all the servers he's identified that might represent survivors. He's trying to hack military servers and thinks the ISS base-station might still be active. I hope—we all hope—he's right, and the letters will get to our loved ones.

I pray that it's not too late. I am so sorry how we left things. I regret what I said, and hope you'll forgive me. "Have faith," you said. I just have to have faith that you're out there.

Be careful, Abi.

Survive.

The emails and messages could simply have been stored and sent on with Hissy—the HI-SLOPE computer's near-AI responded to voice commands and had access to habitat status. It was useful at storing and retrieving information, such as logs and reports, but it didn't *think*; therefore, it didn't really know the difference between a personal log and an email. Since the messages were to be sent via Lugnut's game server, everyone brought their messages on flash drives instead. Zach plugged each into his tablet and then compiled them all into a single package.

"I've studied the old ARPAnet and Usenet in my college classes. They didn't work anything like the modern net, which is why I'm recreating that technique for this message drop." Lugnut was tapping away at his tablet while Tree Rat configured the communications panel.

"Ah, you don't trust that ICANN is still operating?" Burbey asked as he rearranged several colored blocks inside the open electronics system.

"The Internet Corporation for Assigned Names and Numbers might still be running, but it's in California, and most of those servers are dark. Email programs rely on ICANN to tell them where to send email with direct computer-to-computer routing. ARPAnet and Usenet sent messages from computer-to-computer—keeping the ones addressed to its local users and forwarding on the rest. There's an old InterNIC server in Chantilly, Virginia, which appears to still be online, and an even older one in Menlo Park, California. A few years ago, some guys at Stanford and SRI tried to recreate a HOSTS.TXT master file of major international servers. It's huge, but it's likely the best hub for point-to-point relay."

"What about military servers?" Ham asked, knowing that the young computer and robotics specialist had been able to hack his way into and out of many secured computer systems.

"I can throw messages at socket twenty-five, but since I don't have an active socket pair with port eighty, there's no guarantee they will accept my HTTP. I can try pinging port one-forty-three or one-fifty-eight, but anything higher is likely to be firewall and honey-trapped. I'm planning on targeting every server with NNTP on port one-nineteen. It's the layer Usenet operated on and remains active on most networked servers."

"Is that English?" Wyvern asked.

"Sockets, or ports, are essentially subroutines built into a computer for communicating over the net. They are numbered in order of assignment, complexity, and age. So low numbers are older, but still included in almost all general purpose and network computers. The numbers run from zero to over sixty thousand, but anything over one thousand twenty-three is a custom or secured function. The lower the number, the older the function. Thus, twenty-five is the original email protocol, although it was replaced by two-twenty, five-eighty-seven, nine-ninety-three, and nine-ninety-five for secured mail. Zach is not sure there is enough network function running to fully realize those newer protocols, so he is going old school. Port eighty is the original HyperText Transport Protocol. HTTP is the backbone of the internet and is the language websites and applications are built on. It's also the first port blocked by a firewall; that's a combination of hardware and software which isolates and protects computers from bad stuff. One-forty-three and one-fifty-eight are older email standards, and more likely to be functional, but still have the risk of being nonfunctional due to network failures. One-nineteen is the old Usenet news relay. Usenet messages were sent from computer to computer, with each relay point adding their own news articles, and sending/receiving mail messages. They didn't require anything other than a list of computer addresses to connect." Tree Rat answered the question without ever looking away from his task.

"And 'honey-trapped'?"

"A honeypot, or honeytrap, is a computer server that looks vulnerable to intrusion but is really a security trap. If a black hat gets caught in a honeytrap, they open themselves up to hacking by the white hats who set it up," Lugnut said.

"It's a trap the good guys set up to catch bad guys," Tree Rat clarified.

"Oh," Wyvern replied, wisely not asking for more clarification.

"Okay, set to go. Mr. Burbey, are you ready?" Lugnut looked up through the Hub at the communications engineer.

"All set. Why don't you bring up that global map of servers, and we can track the bounces."

The slowly turning globe filled the holoprojection area on the Control deck. The four green lights in the middle of the Pacific glowed brightly, then a blue line extended northeastward to California. The line touched on a red light on the edge of San Francisco Bay, then that light turned blue. After several minutes, multiple lines fanned out along the western coast of the United States. A thicker line crossed the country and intersected with a red dot in Virginia. Once again, the dot turned blue and after a delay, multiple lines fanned out along the East Coast.

"Good. The first one hit the SRI server and was relayed. The old InterNIC server in Virginia also accepted the packets and relayed. Our messages have gone out and we just have to wait to see if anybody reads them."

"Messages in a bottle," Medusa said.

"Ma'am?"

"We've put our messages in a bottle and cast them out to sea."

After watching the blue lines spreading over the globe for more than an hour, the XO called an official meeting. HI-SLOPE originally held twenty-five simulated astronauts. The deaths of the Redshirts, Lucas, and Bolingers, and the absence of van Der Venn brought that number down to eighteen. The Hex Two breach would have subtracted another three, if Mugs, Crossbow, and Ham had been in their quarters. As it was, the greatest loss had been by Lee "Mugs" Smith, who'd lost a display case filled with his father's military ribbons and medals. Crossbow lost several classic history texts, and Ham lost a digital picture frame with family photos. Clothing, tools, and computers were all redundant and supplied from HI-SLOPE stores. They'd been limited to one hundred cubic centimeters of personal items, mimicking orbital cargo lift limitations. And it wasn't as if the items were lost forever, just out of reach until they learned more about the virus and could open up the sealed quarters.

"Alright, people, first order of business." Medusa had moved the meeting to the cafeteria. It was crowded, but there was seating for everyone. "Quarters. Mugs, Crossbow, and Hummer are locked out of Hex Two. The interdeck sealed as well as the main connecting passages to the other Hexes, so it may be possible to reopen the upper deck, but for now, we have to continue the seventy-two-hour Hull Breach protocol. On Dr. d'Almeida's recommendation we're going to keep everything sealed for two weeks.

"That means we need to redistribute the quarters. Hummer, you've moved to Hex Three, next to Doc, so that leaves Crossbow and Mugs. Suggestions?"

"Prancer's gone. There's a double in Hex One," Crossbow supplied.

"Just so long as we change the sheets and wipe everything down with ethanol. That dude was *nasty*!" Mugs added.

"Don't we have a water limitation?" Medusa asked.

"Not anymore!" Mugs grinned.

"Do I need to supply the codes to end the simulation?"

"You should probably do that," Ham said. "Although I suspect that our hydraulics engineer has his own overrides in place, not to mention alcohol."

Tree Rat and Scorpio coughed, but the word "Redshirts" was unmistakable. Mugs just smiled.

"Good. Make it so. Crossbow, configure Hex One back to separate quarters and you and Mugs can clean it up. Does this mean we can get the kitchen and exercise room back on Level One?"

"Wait," Eggnog interjected, "isn't there an open hatch in Prancer's quarters?"

"No. Hex One has a 'basement,'" Lalande told them. "The Core goes down all the way, but a hatch closes over it just like the interdecks. At the bottom is a whole 'nother level with storage, food prep, office, telecom booth, and even another bedroom. There's an air lock that leads out."

"How do you know this, Crossbow? And why doesn't it show up on habitat monitors?"

"Well, in the first place, the storage room is where he stocks his wines and scotch. He used me as his dining steward because I'm a pretty damn good cook. I'd use the lower-level kitchen because it's not tied into main air circulation. He'd also occasionally have 'guests' to entertain down there, so there's no monitors. He swore me to secrecy and threatened my family."

"He hated this place and really didn't want to be here but had to put on appearances." Ham looked at Medusa. "You've *always* been the authority here, Colonel."

"Huh. I guess I have. Okay then, that's out of the way. Next, we need to plan a trip to the summit."

CHAPTER THIRTEEN
BEGIN AGAIN

Every day is a new wave. To the surfer, the only thing that
matters is the next swell.

—E. "Duke" Oleson, surfer and power-systems engineer,
HI-SLOPE

"Okay, if we're going to the summit, we need a plan." Medusa
addressed the rest of the HI-SLOPE crew assembled in the newly
reconfigured commons area of Hex One. "First off, what is it that we
plan to accomplish when we're there?"

"The first thing we need to do is check out the functioning server
that Lugnut mapped for us," Tree Rat replied.

"Functioning server? I thought we just sent messages to servers
across the country. What's different about this one?"

"The servers that showed up as red on my map are only responding
automatically to messages and pings. They can perform all of the
functions they used to do—provide file access, run a game, relay
messages—but they don't really have any users interacting with them.
At least, there's no signals coming out of them that indicate user
activity." Lugnut called up his holographic map of the Earth and
pointed to the server nodes they'd used to relay the crew emails. "This
one here in the center of the country—the orange one—has an active
firewall. There are signals coming in and out of it, but they're
encrypted. There's still no way to know if this is someone alive sending
messages, or just responding to challenge-and-response with

automatic protocols. Until I can crack the firewall, we just don't know there's actually anyone there. There's a couple more of those, too, that I missed on first survey. There's one up on Kauai, which makes me think that they're military firewalls. That one is likely the Pacific missile test range.

"If that's the case, what about central Oahu? If you think those two are military, especially the one in Nebraska, there's at least one on Oahu that is a dug-in bunker—the Navy listening post." Erycke "Duke" Oleson claimed to be a Hawaii native, even though he'd only lived in the islands since childhood. On the other hand, as a surfer, he knew much more about the islands than anyone else in HI-SLOPE, having explored them looking for the best surfing locations.

"That should be here." Lugnut pointed to a red dot in the center of the most popular island. "There's only automated traffic, and not a lot of it, either. It doesn't mean there's nobody there, it just means they're not talking right now."

Medusa brought the group's attention back to the four green dots on the map. "Back to the summit. You said one of these is HI-SLOPE. What are the others? They are almost in a line, so they can't be just the telescopes."

"We won't know till we get there. This one is us." He pointed to the second dot in the line of four. "The one to the northwest is probably the summit; to the southeast is Onizuka. There's an Army base below that, likely accounting for the fourth. We know that Onizuka's incoming and outgoing signal activity is probably just relaying our signals. The Army base is just a mirror, but still active on our local network. The green dot says there's a computer at the summit and it appears to have some activity on it, but we won't know until we get up there. That's why I need to be part of the team that goes."

"I'm not so sure," Ham protested. "It's dangerous for everyone given what we've seen so far. I think this mission needs to be people who can fight and defend themselves. We have to be very careful."

"Well, then, send me back down to Onizuka. The last radio message from the Redshirts was that he shot whoever it was that attacked them. Either we have a dead body or a badly injured person— an Infected. In the latter case, we can certainly take on one person."

"We don't know that at all. Steve could have missed or there could have been more than one Infected. It's just as much of an unknown going back to Onizuka as it is going to the summit," Tree Rat said. "I'm going...with your permission, ma'am."

"So, that's Tree Rat. Who else?" Hands went up around the room—Ham, Lugnut, Scorpio, Cro. "Doc, no. I don't think so."

"If there's more of these Infected out there, I need tissue samples. Also, if somebody gets hurt at the summit, I may be the only chance that they're going to survive."

"Very well, but with that large a team, how is everybody getting there? Are you walking? Wearing the isolation suits? We need a plan."

"We can always go back down to Onizuka. Fix the tire on Prancer's little buggy and take it to the summit."

"Lugnut, we may have to go after it, but we know we've had at least one Infected down at Onizuka."

"Excuse me, XO, but it's even more of an unknown at the summit," Tree Rat interrupted. "We know about Onizuka, but not about the Mauna Kea summit telescopes. I'm happier going to an area where we know the risks."

"What are you saying?"

"That we need transportation for a large party, and that we need to be armed if possible."

"Armed with what?"

"We have limited ability to make some defensive items, but it's probably best to go back to where we know there's a higher probability of arms and armaments. Keano Ikaia was a hunter. He'll likely have stuff in his quarters. So, Lugnut is right. We need to go back down to Onizuka before we head to the summit."

Medusa thought on that for a moment, then nodded her head. "If that's the case, then I'm a little more comfortable sending the doc with you when you go down there. That means you people need to consider yourselves his bodyguards if you're going to do this."

"That would be acceptable," Scorpio told them.

"Good. That's the first part of a plan. Onizuka for the vehicle and weapons. Maybe another vehicle from Hale Pohaku for the trip to the summit. Doc, collect your samples, then get back here."

"Cadaver tissue is one thing, but I need live tissue if we can get it."

"We'll cross that asteroid when we come to it. Alright. Next step. What are the plans for the summit?"

☙☙☙

The deliberation regarding goals and team members for each of the objectives continued for another hour before Medusa called a halt. "Okay, everyone, we're still on reverse day-night cycle and the away team needs to go in daylight. Since you'll be departing after our simulated evening, everyone who's going—go get some rest." As people began to file out of the common room, she turned to Ham. "Hummer, you know the simulation protocols better than anyone here. Can we change our day-night cycle?"

"If we do that, it has to be gradual," Doc d'Almeida offered from where he was handing out sleep aids to the away team members. "It's a problem well known by shift workers for decades. Too abrupt a change in schedule causes irritableness, insomnia, headache. People make serious mistakes."

"What you're saying is that if we can change the schedule, we need to do it slowly." Medusa nodded and turned her attention back to Ham. "Do we have a protocol for this?"

"We do. It's built into the termination schedule, but we can activate it at any time. It takes about a month, as we shift our schedule by thirty minutes a day. That's twenty-four days for the twelve-hour shift. It just requires the commanding officer's override. So, it's up to you."

"Got it. Let's go ahead and get that started."

CHAPTER FOURTEEN

SCAVENGING

Look, you all know the fairy tale: an engineer always overestimates the time it takes for a repair, and then does that repair with baling wire and duct tape. It doesn't work like that. You have to have the right tools and enough supplies to fix or construct on-demand. Give me a 3-D printer, lathe, mill, and welding rig, and I'll make you whatever you want.

—B. "Moose" Dennison,
power-systems engineer, HI-SLOPE

The team headed to Onizuka included Tree Rat and Lugnut to check out the communications room. Scorpio would go in case of salvage, and the doctor was going in order to collect samples . . . if that was even possible. Bigfoot was going as security and a person who knew their way around volcanoes, tundra, and harsh environments. None of them had real weapons, although it was hoped that they would find some in the dorms and utility areas at the mid-level support facility. There was at least one weapon that they knew of—Keano Ikaia's shotgun was somewhere in Hale Pohaku. Tree Rat reasoned that there would be more in his quarters, and possibly at the security station. Instead, the group had several improvised weapons, courtesy of Moose, who'd used some scrap pipe to make clubs. He was also working on a couple of long knives, but those wouldn't be ready for this trip.

The other hope was that they would be able to find one or more working vehicles in addition to Prancer's currently disabled SUV. It appeared to have been customized to carry HI-SLOPE personnel in their space suits. The doctor had explained that staying in the isolation suits was best to protect them from the H7D3 virus. There was no known natural immunity and no readily available vaccine. Added to that, the isolation of the past eighteen months meant that everyone in HI-SLOPE was highly vulnerable to what some of them were now calling the "zombie virus."

One additional piece of information that had come out in their planning was that it wasn't only Hex One that had a hidden basement level. All of the Hexes had a lower level left over from construction; however, not all were accessible. Scorpio showed them how the bottom level of the core of each Hex had the potential to open into a hatch leading down underground to where the plumbing and electrical infrastructure for each Hex was located. Underneath Hex Six—the "garage" for the surface exploration rovers and mining robots—was another garage for utility vehicles. Hex Six also had the exterior access "air lock" that had been used by the Redshirts, and the floor of its inner chamber lowered down to an identical air lock underground that could be used for simulating landing missions. From there, they would access the tunnel through the wall of the cinder cone and join up with the road downslope.

Ham desperately wanted to be part of the away team returning to Onizuka. He'd sacrificed time, energy, and his own personal family commitments to HI-SLOPE. It had all been done with the best of intentions. Now he heard muttering from several crew members about leaving and trying to find their families. Cro had told him that half of the people who contracted the zombie flu died. With no immunity to the fever, they could expect many fatalities. The survivors risked becoming Infected. Still, people would cling to the slimmest hope.

Would HI-SLOPE even continue once they'd seen what waited at Onizuka and the summit?

Ham had no answers, but plenty of questions. He wanted to be out there seeking answers to those questions. For now, he was stuck inside watching the monitors as the group approached the buildings at Hale Pohaku.

Tree Rat and Scorpio planned to clear each building one at a time, starting with the Commons. The first order of business was to retrieve

Ikaia's shotgun. Next, they planned to enter the Commons building and take out the Infected that killed Asnip and Schaper. Once the building was clear, Bigfoot and Lugnut would stay behind while the latter tried to learn more about which communications channels were still open and active. The others would look into transportation and anything they could use for defending against the Infected. The final objective was Cro's samples, although his safety was the top priority.

Much to the surprise of the away team, the underground garage contained two small golf carts. They were designed to seat only two people, with a small cargo-carrying platform in the back. The seats were oversized and could accommodate a person in the HI-SLOPE simulated space suit. With five members on the away team, it was easy enough to slightly overload and fit three people on one cart, then two on the other. There was additional storage in the garage with automotive tools and spare wheels, batteries, and tires for the carts and Prancer's SUV, so Tree Rat decided to take that spare tire, several sets of batteries, and the tools with them in case they needed to get any scavenged vehicles mobile again. That way, even if they didn't find anything useful at Onizuka, they'd have sufficient transportation for the summit expedition.

With transportation assured, the away team set off for Hale Pohaku while Medusa and Ham monitored from the command deck. Lugnut kept up a continuous commentary, likely to cover his nerves. The youngest member of the team wasn't used to risk, and it showed in his nonstop talking about the environment and what every member of the team was doing. Tree Rat had tried to get him to be silent, but Medusa broke in over the comm and told them to continue the running commentary. It helped her keep tabs on everything that was happening with the team.

After a brief stop to check and make sure that Prancer's SUV would be functional once the tire was changed, the team proceeded on to Hale Pohaku. When they pulled up outside the Commons building, they noted one more body just outside the front door. It was not decayed as much as the others, but had what looked like a gunshot wound, and a lot of blood had pooled and dried on the ground beneath it.

"Do you think that's the one that attacked Matt and Steve?" Ham asked over the comm.

"It would seem likely. It's a fresher body, and it's been shot," Tree Rat replied.

"He's also only about five days dead," Cro reported, as his suit camera showed him bent over the body.

"Let's hope there are no more waiting inside?" Medusa told them.

"Only if our luck changes," Tree Rat growled. "Let's get inside and take a look around. I'll go first—to the left; Scorpio, you go right. Lugnut and Doc stay in the middle. Bigfoot, keep an eye on the rear for us."

Acknowledgments followed, and the team carefully entered the building. It was dark inside, and the suit cams didn't reveal much other than what could be seen in the moving light from handheld flashlights. The team swept the whole building before reporting back.

"All clear; nothing moving inside here. All rooms are empty except for the bodies in the changing room."

"What about the communications room?"

"I'll walk Lugnut in there and Bigfoot can stay with him while Scorpio, Doc, and I check the dormitories."

In the end there was little to find elsewhere in the complex, just a few more bodies that appeared wasted away—victims of the initial flu-like symptoms of H7D3. There were several small commuter cars in the parking area, but nothing that could operate on the high inclines or rough off-road conditions. However, farther down the road at the gift-shop part of the Onizuka Visitor Center, there was a high-clearance pickup truck and a commercial utility vehicle used to haul people to construction sites. The keys turned out to be behind the checkout counter. Strangely, there were no bodies in the store, so the whereabouts of the vehicle owners was unknown.

CHAPTER FIFTEEN

ASCENT

So, what does a pilot do when there's no actual vehicle to fly? We train. We run simulations. The HI-SLOPE Command Deck is one big simulations. The other thing we do is to be professional nitpickers. A pilot has to be meticulous; we have to find the faults that everyone misses. Give me a piece of machinery, and I can tell you how it works, how it fails, and what it will take to get it working again.

—K.C. "Wyvern" Seville, pilot, HI-SLOPE

Ultimately, the exploration of Onizuka yielded little information. Dr. d'Almeida had his samples from the dead Infected, and the flu victims. Lugnut confirmed that all communications channels were open, and that the additional active servers on the island showed evidence of independent activity, not just relaying HI-SLOPE activity. They now had three full-sized vehicles, plus the golf carts, and only five people to drive them back to the habitat. The decision was made to load one golf cart in the bed of the pickup and leave the other—along with one set of the spare batteries they'd brought from HI-SLOPE—at Hale Pohaku to support further exploration at a later time.

Tree Rat was disappointed at not finding much in the way of weaponry. Ikaia's shotgun had been recovered, but it was badly damaged. After shooting their attacker, either Asnip or Schaper had used it as a club. It was being brought to HI-SLOPE with the rest of the salvage, but Moose would have to work on it before it was usable.

Ikaia's quarters yielded a small-caliber pistol, probably only used for target practice, although they did find pistol, rifle, and shotgun ammunition in Keano's quarters. The security office likely had more firearms, but they were locked in a safe with no way to open it. Cro still wanted samples from a live Infected. He also wanted to transport the newest body back to his lab, but Medusa refused the request. As it was, the entire crew was going to need to undergo decontamination just from having been in the vicinity of the bodies.

Lugnut's investigation had yielded more interesting information once the away team had returned and undergone decontamination and quarantine. Once he was able to communicate directly with the Hale Pohaku servers, he was able to expand his list of suspected human activity. A possible active server was located in the town of Waimea. It was likely to be the one belonging to the headquarters and offices for the Keck Observatory telescope at the summit. That news alone filled the team with hope of finding survivors—if not at the summit, at least on the island, and with a chance to contact them.

Additional servers on the U.S. mainland were also upgraded to yellow with the suspicion that there was intelligent—even civilized—activity in the area, although the servers themselves were not actively maintained. Many were on military bases clustered in Texas, Florida, Indiana, Tennessee, North Carolina, and Northern Virginia. In the big cities, however, not only were the servers not actively maintained, but most of them had gone dark due to either damage, neglect, or power failure.

Medusa announced the results to the rest of the crew as a good news/bad news situation. The good news was that there were likely survivors out there. The bad news was that they were hunkered down and isolated. The crew argued over whether this meant they should stay isolated or go try to find another group and possibly improve their own chances of survival. Cro argued that due to their isolation, they had no resistance to the virus and would easily succumb to the influenza phase, which reports indicated was fatal in a high percentage of the cases. Tree Rat argued that the resources at HI-SLOPE were too limited. Remaining there was hiding in a hole until they ran out of food and water, or simply died of boredom.

No matter the justification, there was near universal agreement that a trip to the summit was necessary. They still required a means of contacting other survivors and needed to check for radios or other communications equipment. There was also the chance of survivors active at the telescopes, and perhaps they could help each other.

The conversation then turned to who should go to the summit. There was strong argument that it should not be the same individuals who had gone to Hale Pohaku. Rather, the duty and risk should be shared or even rotated to give others at least the chance of getting out of the habitat, even if only for a short time. Unsurprisingly, quite a few voices spoke in favor of rotating personnel for the upcoming mission, including a joint appeal by Malut and Wyvern.

The Aleutian astronomer argued that her prior employment as an astronomer in Alaska accustomed her to the same clear, cold conditions. More importantly, the facility where she worked also supported ocean navigation via analysis of the Earth's magnetosphere. Wyvern's justification was that her pilot and navigation training also included astronomy, and since she had trained for spacecraft, she would be the best person to assist the Aleutian astronomer. If anyone could repurpose astronomical instruments for long-range communications, those two were the logical choice. Lugnut and Tree Rat countered that so far there hadn't been a system that the two of them couldn't crack. Cro disputed their counter, saying that exposure to the conditions at Hale Pohaku argued against them going on back-to-back missions.

Ham inwardly debated whether to volunteer for the mission himself. After all, who better to understand what was happening with the fall of civilization than a psychologist? In the end, Medusa ended the argument by telling them she would take all of those arguments into consideration and would announce the summit team the next morning. With the vehicles that had been recovered it might even be possible to take a larger team if the risk warranted it. It also meant that more away missions were possible in the future.

Ultimately, Medusa decided that she would lead the summit mission herself, leaving Ham in charge in her absence. Moose, Malut, Wyvern, and Mugs would accompany her in Prancer's vehicle, which would comfortably hold five people in suits, and had a small, enclosed cargo area at the back. If they needed more carrying capacity, she'd call for Half-Check and Duke to join them with the pickup truck.

"Moose" Dennison, the power-systems engineer, would check any solar, battery, or diesel generators at the summit that were capable of supplying supplemental power to Onizuka and HI-SLOPE. HI-SLOPE's power came from a nuclear generator, just like an actual spacecraft. However, it was still possible for the habitat to pull more electricity than the generator could supply, and solar panels at the crest of their cinder cone usually handled the additional need. Now, the prospect of an extended time with no outside servicing meant ensuring that even their backups had backups. Moose had also been working on more weapons. Each team member now had a club and large knife, and Mugs and Moose carried machetes. The life-systems/fluidics engineer wouldn't have much to do in his specialty, but he'd had martial arts training with bladed weapons, and would work with Moose to check each building for Infected before allowing the rest of the team to enter.

The five members of the team bundled up in their isolation suits and loaded into Prancer's customized SUV. The open seating area in the back accommodated four persons in suits, while the cab was sized for only one suited (or two unsuited) people. In this case, that was Medusa, who'd claimed the privilege of driving. Weapons and supplies were dumped in the small cargo area at the rear, and the group headed out for the summit—only two miles in direct distance, but well over one thousand feet in elevation change. They were exiting the tunnel just as the eastern sky was beginning to brighten, although dawn would come quickly at this elevation. They each took a moment to look up at the star-filled sky. They had time; it would take the better part of an hour to navigate the rough road and narrow switchbacks toward their destination.

"*Enterprise* to shuttlecraft, come in, shuttlecraft," Littleshawn Haley's voice came over the comm.

"I thought we were going with 'Galileo'?" asked another voice.

"Can it." There was a tinge of irritation in Medusa's response, but Ham was certain that was just nerves. "We've barely left the garage. We need to wait on full sunup. We'll call you when we get to the summit."

"Enjoy the stars, then."

"Roger that."

The telescope installation at the summit of Mauna Kea was a complex of plain white cubes and silver domes. The thin, cold air at the over thirteen-thousand-foot elevation provided very little temperature or atmosphere interference with the telescopes. At Mauna Kea's summit was the world's premier visual astronomy station. It was normally busiest at nighttime, when the domes would open up and the telescopes would appear. Yet even in the day, the air was frigid, with the telescope housings kept at ambient temperature to prevent icing or fogging due to the heat differential. Light snow and frost were present on the ground, but as a whole, the moisture content of the air was low, another reason for locating telescopes there.

The most surprising feature at the summit was one that had Wyvern squealing over the comm. "A helicopter! They have a helicopter!"

"It had to have been an emergency. I didn't think helicopters flew this high," Ham replied over the comm.

"Oh, they can fly this high. They just don't like to, and hovering is nearly impossible above ten thousand feet. The issue is less about maintaining this altitude but whether or not they can take off again after they've landed. A helicopter departing from a high-elevation landing pad like this needs to fly at the warmest time of day and with the lightest possible load. It doesn't make sense for this to have been an evacuation flight; it seems more likely it was an emergency landing or a retrieval."

"Retrieving who? Or should I say, retrieving whom?" Medusa asked.

"Prancer?" Wyvern replied.

"Huh. Yeah, he would have wanted that backup. So, that means there's likely at least one live person, or a dead one, or a zombie. Prancer went downslope."

"In that case, it's time to start clearing the buildings. Mugs, you're with me." Moose opened the back hatch and pulled out clubs and machetes forged from steel bars and sharpened by a laser cutter. Medusa carried the small pistol recovered from Hale Pohaku, and everyone else had clubs and knives.

The first building was open, and appeared to be under construction—only a framework was present—and there was no place inside to house people or instruments, so Moose and Mugs bypassed it. Next was a large building with UK and Canadian flags on the side. After a few minutes, Moose came out and pronounced it clear, while Mugs moved on past the array of eight radio dishes to the helipad and a small support building. Moose told Wyvern to hold back from inspecting the helicopter until they had checked all the buildings.

Sitting in the open for nearly three months meant that Wyvern would need to do an extensive check, and probably perform repairs before it would fly.

The road curved around to one of the largest domes—actually a squared-off cylinder with a Japanese and U.S. flags on the side of the building. Several of the domes were built atop buildings where staff would work during the day, or when not actually looking through the telescopes. This dome actually had a sizeable building next to it, and a parking lot with two cars. The detached building would be a good place to start looking for resources. Mugs reported that he could feel a heating system turn on automatically after he'd opened several of the interior doors.

Another promising site was the next facility, a wide, low building with two domes on top, and two more cars outside its entrance. Malut identified it as the Keck Observatory, with a known auxiliary research building in Waimea, the farming and ranching community twenty miles northwest, and ten thousand feet down the mountain. Again, it was pronounced clear, and the pair proceeded around the complex of buildings and domes. However, once Malut announced that Keck was most likely to have the resources they were looking for, the rest of the clearance procedure was cursory, mostly just looking for survivors.

Medusa gave permission for Wyvern to check the helicopter, with Mugs assisting and standing guard, while Medusa and Malut did a more thorough inspection of the Keck facility. Moose continued to check around the power systems at each of the telescopes while also looking for radio and other supplies the habitat could use.

Ham sat in Command, monitoring the away team. If Medusa was going to leave him in charge, he needed to know what was going on with her mission. He noticed that there were several cars scattered across the complex. Mugs had brushed up against one outside the Subaru telescope, and Moose had checked a few more at Keck, pronouncing them "old, cold, and full of mold."

Ham doubted there was any mold. After all, the air at the summit was cold and dry year-round. He got the point, though. The cars had been sitting there since the zombie flu hit—if not earlier.

But if there were cars, what happened to the people? Were they evacuated?

Or still there?

CHAPTER SIXTEEN
AFTERMATH

I have loved the stars too much, to be afraid of the dark...
until now.   —S. "Malut" Fisher, astronomer, HI-SLOPE

After an hour of maintenance, Wyvern climbed into the pilot's position and flipped the switches to start up the helicopter. After several attempts, mostly resulting in the whining of various motors, the twin engines began to spin up with a loud roar. Wyvern engaged the rotor, and lifted the craft several feet off the ground, before settling it back down and cutting the engines. The sound brought Medusa and Malut out of the Keck building, as well as caught the attention of Moose, who'd been taking some electronic equipment back to the SUV.

"So, it works," Medusa said as she approached.

"Mostly," Wyvern replied. "It would be good to get it to a lower elevation and do a full PM cycle on it. The last entry in the flight log is ten weeks ago. Last pre-check was a week before that, and the last full cycle was four months ago. No preventative maintenance in four months is not horrible, but it needs to be taken care of."

"You can take off from here and fly it?"

"It's sluggish. Not really enough lift. I'd need to fly with no more than one other person."

"But it flew."

"Only in ground effect. The moment I get farther from the ground than the length of the rotor blades, I'll lose lift, and then it gets tricky."

"So, no flying us back to HI-SLOPE."

"Nope, not to mention we don't have a clear space to land."

Movement caught Medusa's eye, and she turned to see Moose waving from next to the truck. Mugs was already moving away from them in a different direction, and she turned to see several figures emerging from the building next to the Japanese telescope.

"Oh, shit."

"Medusa? Away Team? What's happening?" Ham called over the comm.

"We have Infected. They must have been hiding and come out when they heard the chopper."

"Helicopter or helo, not a chopper...uh, ma'am."

"Not the time, Wyvern, we have incoming."

An hour before, Mugs had declared the building to be clear. Now, multiple figures were coming out of it. The away team and those monitoring suit cams back at HI-SLOPE saw what appeared to be seven individuals, mostly male, with two females. That part was obvious because they weren't wearing any clothes. There was dried blood around their mouths and blood and dirt was caked on their bodies. They didn't lurch or shamble the way the TV shows and movies depicted zombies; they were moving quickly and the cold thin air didn't seem to be affecting them very much. Their faces looked angry, but with unfocused eyes. They screamed and they moaned and made other noises that were simply not human.

"Get out of there, get out of there, get out of there!" Ham yelled into the comm.

Another voice came on. "Smith, you told us that building was clear. What happened?" Tree Rat wasn't in Command, so he must have been monitoring the feed from his quarters.

Wyvern's body cam was moving, jerking back and forth. Mugs's cam remained steady and you could see from the slight posture adjustments that he was settling into a ready stance. He brought his machete up, and with a few movements of the blade in front of him, it was obvious that he was treating it as a martial arts sword and getting ready to fight. "There was nothing moving in there. No sound, no heat, no motion. The heat kicked on while I was in there, though—maybe they defrosted?"

"Don't let them past you," Medusa said as she started moving in from the side. She and Malut had been at the next telescope around the circle. She sighted her small pistol and fired once, twice. She hit each time, but it was obvious that the rounds had no effect.

"Reports say the Infected have extremely high adrenal activity and very low prefrontal and temporal activity. They're not going to feel pain," Cro added. He, too, was monitoring from elsewhere.

"Head shots. Go for head shots!" Malut was breathing heavily from exertion and anxiety. Her suit provided more oxygen then was naturally present at this thirteen-thousand-foot elevation, so breathing that hard risked hyperventilation.

"Calm down, everybody. Just don't let them reach the helicopter," Medusa instructed.

"Head shots!"

"Yeah, I know that book, but it also said they shot everything and everyone with twenty-two-caliber pistols and rifles. The only way a twenty two is effective for a head shot is if you do it from an inch away. The author was an idiot."

Ham knew the book; it been popular some years back. The son of a famous movie producer had written a book about a worldwide war against zombies. Opinion on the book and resulting movie had been equally divided—it was a good book, it was a bad book, it was an okay book but entirely unrealistic weapons handling. All of that was irrelevant now, because the Infected were almost on Mugs, and Medusa was about to close with them. Moose was still some distance away, but he, too, was brandishing his machete as if it were a sword. Malut was heading for the helicopter instead of the oncoming crowd of Infected, while Wyvern was rummaging inside the pilot compartment of the helicopter, clearly looking for the club she'd put down while performing maintenance.

"Kee-YAH!" Mugs screamed his martial arts yell as he laid into the Infected. His machete cut deep, and blood flew everywhere. Six of the seven Infected were on him. Before he could make much headway in reducing their numbers, the seventh turned in response to the gunshots and headed for Medusa.

Medusa shot at the oncoming Infected but missed and hit the mass of bodies surrounding Mugs. He was still moving, and each cut was accompanied by a spray of blood. She was lucky she hadn't hit him with a stray bullet, so she decided to wait until the Infected was closer. She shot again from only a few feet away. She couldn't miss, but the rounds had no effect. The bodycam showed the slide locked back on the pistol.

The pistol was out of ammunition.

Medusa's body cam showed a face filled with rage. Its teeth were bared—yellow, with dark stains between them.

Blood and bloody tissue.

A hand with fingernails long enough to be considered claws swiped at the body cam and the picture was lost just as the comm recorded Medusa's scream.

Moose's body cam showed that he was closing on a pile of bodies where Mugs had been fighting. The only movement appeared to be the Infected; the microfluidics engineer was nowhere to be seen.

Malut's body cam showed Moose hacking at the bodies in the pile, pulling them out of the way and uncovering Mugs. His suit was torn, and one sleeve—no, one *arm* was missing. One of the bodies on the far side of the pile avoided Moose's blade and jumped up to run toward the helicopter. The power-systems engineer turned zombie slayer gave one last chop, cleaving an Infected's head open, and rose to give chase, but he was too late.

The astronomer had moved toward the Infected to keep it from threatening the helicopter. It swiped at her, and its claws caught in the fabric of her isolation suit. It was designed to mimic a space suit. It was not as thick, but it was still strong enough to resist casual cuts. The force exerted by the Infected must have been remarkably strong for the material to separate at the arm seams the way it did. Moose caught up and swung his machete at the Infected's neck. It cut deep; the creature jerked once and dropped, spraying blood from the severed carotid artery...

...right onto Malut's exposed skin where the suit failed.

"They're all down, but we have..." Moose paused and made some strange sounds before continuing.

"We have casualties."

The beaten and battered away team returned to HI-SLOPE. They were met with stunned silence, even though Moose had managed to find both a ham radio, and components to attach telephone and fax capability to the fiber-optic link that supplied their email and "official" communications.

Wyvern was uninjured, thanks to actions in her defense by Mugs and Medusa. The same could not be said for Malut, who'd suffered bites and a bad laceration to her chest, both of which had torn her suit. Cro had her placed in a secondary pressure suit designed to simulate a rescue bubble. The device was intended for rescue from vacuum exposure and had fittings for an external air supply. It also had glovebox fitting to allow the surgeon to operate without exposing the person inside.

Mugs's and Medusa's bodies were carried over the rim of the HI-SLOPE cinder cone and laid out beside the bodies of Asnip and Schaper.

HI-SLOPE was now down nine people and missing both CO and XO.

Medusa's death was nothing short of a crisis for the continuing existence of HI-SLOPE. Tree Rat and Ham argued over who should assume the leadership of the group. Tree Rat felt that since he wrote many of the simulation parameters, he should lead the group. Ham argued that as doctor, Cro should lead. After all, he was the one who knew the most about the virus. The doctor deferred, claiming he had too much to do—treating Malut, taking samples, and studying the ones he already collected. Many of the remaining crew argued that since Medusa had left Ham in charge during the summit missions, he was in charge now.

That left a very vocal dissenting minority, with Tree Rat arguing that they should take the vehicles and helicopter and go off to find other survivors. Moose and Lugnut set up the ham radio, and Scorpio erected an antenna at the rim of the cinder cone. They were starting to pick up voices of survivors, although many of them were pleading for assistance.

Wyvern told the group that they had an obligation to use their skills to help survivors rebuild. Ham and Cro argued that they weren't even sure any of them could survive without a vaccine—Malut was already showing signs of the fever portion of H7D3, and they were keeping her in isolation, and watching carefully to see if she turned into an Infected.

The argument wouldn't be settled quickly...or quietly.

INTERLUDE

MESSAGE IN A BOTTLE

What do you do when you stumble? You pick yourself up and you run. You. Just. Keep. Running.
> —B.C. Litchford, life-systems engineer, HI-SLOPE

My Dearest Abigail:

It's been six months since the grand experiment we called HI-SLOPE ended.

Our innocence ended with the deaths of Redshirt One and Redshirt Two. Our illusions were shattered by Prancer's disappearance. Our confidence was broken by Medusa's death. The death of the dream happened when Tree Rat and the others left six months ago.

Oh, they stuck around for a month. Malut had told me she wanted to go, but Cro wasn't ready to release her, so she convinced Tree Rat to wait for her. She was very sick for almost a week, and still weak from injuries sustained from thrashing around while she was unconscious. After that, Cro wanted blood and tissue samples. Once she was up and moving around on her own, she told him he'd poked and prodded and punctured her with enough needles. She was done.

And leaving.

Tree Rat, Wyvern, Scorpio, and Malut left.

I'm really surprised "Red" Kirby decided to stay. After Medusa's death, I expected him to be in mourning and refuse to associate with us. Instead, he seemed to just dig deeper into his work in the greenhouse. He doesn't socialize much, but his work is good. He was never that talkative, so, I guess this is just his way of grieving.

Now we are down to twelve. We have enough space and enough supplies to survive for a few years. We hope to have a solution before it gets to the point that we run out, but the new radio is revealing that survivors are scattered. They're also not much better off than we are.

We don't actually know where our people went. There was a brief radio message that someone had spotted a helicopter over Maui. Apparently, there's boats pulling survivors from the Molokai Channel. We keep trying to contact the Keck office in Waimea and the HI-SLOPE offices in Hilo. Lugnut says there's no servers active in Hilo, Kona, or Honolulu. The servers associated with the Hawaiian Volcano Observatory are still automatically reporting every rumble and quake, but none of the big population centers are showing intelligent activity.

Crossbow has taken over monitoring the ham radio. He's making a log of call signs, but we don't know the identity or location of these voices . . . yet. Most of them appear to be boat captains, since the majority of signals are on marine bands, although there's a few on the amateur band—ham radio operators were everywhere before the Fall, and it seems that they are making an effort to spread information far and wide.

It makes me think back to your stories of that boat captain you worked for one summer during high school. What did they call him? Captain Bubba? I do wonder what happened to all of them when the Flu hit. Was it safer at sea?

So far, we're just listening. For the first month, Tree Rat didn't think we should broadcast. But he left.

Now? Maybe we're just afraid.

Bigfoot sat down with a map to plot out where he thinks survivors would be located on the mainland. Heavy tourist areas are out, as are big cities, but the ranchlands of the Great Plains, scrub deserts of the Southwest, northern tundra, and mountain ranges are the best bet.

Cro confirmed that the Infected at the summit were dormant because of the cold. That's a good thing. It means they won't be just wandering around up here at the high elevations. He also said that if we cremate the bodies outside, we won't risk infection if we have exposure to the air. We'd have to cremate all of Hex Two, though, to use it.

There is always the risk of attracting Infected to warm locations that make them more active. That's what happened at the summit. The automated heating system in the building Mugs checked warmed them up, then the sound of the helicopter attracted them.

Moose says that in the future we should stop skulking around and start with bright lights and loud noises. He says it's also something to keep in mind for working at lower elevations.

We'll eventually have to go down there.

But when?

The future. The future is unknown.

But the one thing we do know is that we have neighbors. The ranchers in the high country in the middle of the Big Island have survived, and can produce food. They are active on the radio, but again, we haven't reached out to them. Frankly, I'm afraid of their reaction.

I hope you're out there, Abi, surviving. Whether it's with the military or with the civilians. We've only gotten marine band signals from near the islands, so at least we know they are around. We have no way to get a military signal.

I tell myself that you would want me to have faith, but it's so hard. What kind of just God would do this to Humanity? Then I think again at what humans are like, and I can sort of see His point. The CDC reports said that humans did this, so it gets pretty hard to blame God.

And so, we survive.

I want to have faith, Abi. I want to think you got through this—that we will get through this.

I just hope you get this message in a bottle.

～∞～

"Professor!" Lugnut called from the Hex Core. He'd started calling Ham by that name after discovering an automated server with old videos. He'd taken a liking to *Gilligan's Island* and decided that the mission psychologist fit the part.

"In here, Lugnut." Ham was sitting in the greenhouse with my voice recorder.

"Professor! Bigfoot says you have to hear this. There's something on the radio."

"Okay. I'm guessing from your excitement that it's something new?"

"Yes, it's from off the coast of the Eastern U.S. They call themselves 'Devil Dog Radio.'"

Part Two

SEAFARER

CHAPTER ONE

CAPTAIN HAOLE

I love the sea. It is both foe and friend, scorned and lover. Some would say that one must be good to those whom they love. The sea doesn't care. It will aid you and hinder you equally. You must be firm and fight for your life, but that just makes the love grow deeper.

—B.L. "Bubba Haole" Gnad,
boat captain, Bubba Haole's Fishing Charter

Brian "Bubba" Gnad stood with his legs spread, shoulder width apart, knees slightly flexed as he manned the wheel of his thirty-seven-foot sailboat, *Storm Chaser*. He'd long learned to move *with* the swaying of the boat, and the short, wide fireplug was known for keeping his balance despite anything the ocean could throw at him. It was never more evident than when he stood free of any other support, sipping from the open mug of coffee in his hand.

But it was getting a bit choppy out and becoming a bit more difficult to keep the coffee in the cup, and not on the deck. He eyed the dark clouds gathering on the northeastern horizon.

"Storm coming in," said the man emerging from the hatch to the belowdecks cabin. "Tully" Roberts was a couple inches taller, and about half the mass of his captain.

Captain Bubba grunted at the irony, given his boat's name, but remained silent for a moment longer as he studied the clouds. "Dark, but not roiling along the front. Heavy wind and rain, but nothing like the tornadic systems I used to chase in Oklahoma."

107

"I don't know how you could do that. I figure if I was in one of those storms, I'd find I wasn't in Kansas anymore."

Bubba snorted and eyed the slim man with shaggy white hair. "Well, duh. You look like a dandelion, Tully. You'd be carried off by the wind in an instant. Still, all the equipment's pretty much the same as the storm chasing equipment I had back then—although the *Bubba Truck* Marks One and Two were outfitted better than this boat."

"But not your Viking, I bet. Besides, you had shelter."

"Why do you think I christened the Viking *Bubba Truck Mark Three*?" Bubba turned to his business partner with a twinkle in his eye. Looking back at the storm front, he continued, "From the looks of this, we should be able to make Lehua before it gets here."

"Maybe, but not Kamalino Bay. We'd have the bulk of the island between us and the winds, shouldn't we try?"

"Let's get to Lehua first, then see if it's worth it."

Lehua was a sunken volcanic caldera, due west of Barking Sands Beach on Kauai, and just off the northern tip of Ni'ihau. In contrast, Kamalino Bay was most of the way down the leeward side of Ni'ihau and was inset into the southwestern part of the island. Mount Pani'au, and the "pu'u" and "mauna"—hills and mountains—of the island center blocked the worst winds from most storms, but proximity to land didn't seem safe these days. The caldera formed a nearly circular bay, open to the north, shielded by the walls of the extinct volcano, and was utterly bereft of humans.

Bubba could use Lehua for a storm shelter, but the surrounding land wasn't suitable for people to live, hence why it was safer than the bay. Ni'ihau had been sparsely populated before the Haole Flu, and now there was hardly anyone on shore. But that didn't mean there was no one.

Ni'ihau was a restricted island. General tourism was discouraged. Residents had to be approved by the family owning the island. It wasn't completely insular—there was regular trade and travel, mostly with Kauai, which was only twenty-five miles to the east. The islanders had wanted a simple life. They'd hoped that they could avoid H7D3 and had banned travel even before official news of the deadly infection was released.

They accepted their own people home, though. Maria Thomlinson was a student at UCLA, and even though she'd left home against the wishes of her parents, she'd been encouraged to return for her safety and their peace of mind. She "borrowed" a small boat from the docks at Hanapepe, on Kauai, and headed for Ni'ihau in the middle of the night. The Coast Guard had tried to stop all small-boat traffic around the islands, but the girl had grown up navigating the channel by day and night, and she knew how to keep away from the red-and-white cutters.

Maria returned home and brought H7D3 with her. Within two weeks, there was no intelligent life on the island.

The storm hit just before *Storm Chaser* reached the sheltered cove of Lehua. Bubba and Tully reduced sail as much as possible, but with winds out of the northeast, the north-facing cove offered only a little protection. They spent some of their precious fuel motoring around the leeward side so that they could drop anchor in the shadow of the seven-hundred-foot volcanic crater walls. The Coast Guard lighthouse on the peak of the island was barely visible as the heavy rains set in, although mercifully that rain was mostly coming straight down, and not blowing horizontal to the sea.

"Better get on the radio and tell Mamabear we're not going to be back until after the storm blows itself out," Bubba told Tully.

"Aye-aye, Captain," Tully responded. "She'll be worried. Anything else you want to pass along?" Tully reached for the marine radio to call back to their base at Kamalino.

"She should probably tell the shore party to stick to the shelters on the beach and not try to go any farther onto the island. I know she has parties out looking for supplies. Given the noise of the rain, the thunder, and the lightning it's probably going to stir up any Infected, so it would be a good idea if they stay close enough that they can get out onto the water."

"Even with the lightning."

"...Especially with the lightning."

The population of Ni'ihau had never been high and yet for some reason the scavenging crews still kept running into Infected. While the first stage of H7D3 had a high fatality rate, the second stage robbed any survivors of human intelligence. Victims complained of intense itching, then ripped off all their clothes and began attacking those around them. Even six months after what most people would have considered the fall of civilization—and four months after Bubba and others started trying to clear the Infected off Ni'ihau—they still kept encountering them. It was almost as if there were many more people on the island than officially recorded.

Most people called it the "Zombie Flu," although news reports from the mainland called it the "Pacific Flu." Out in the middle of the Pacific Ocean, it earned the name "Haole Flu" since it was brought to the islands by nonresidents. When it first came to Kauai, tour boat and fishing boat captains set out from the harbors at Nawiliwili and Hanapepe Bay. Towns and cities were quickly overrun, but staying out on the water was safe as long as no one in your crew was infected. All too many succumbed to the disease, though, and six months later, they still barely had enough trained crew to operate all of their boats, even with pulling survivors from the ocean. If you lived in a town or any settlement of more than a handful of people, the best chance of survival was to hunker down, isolate, quarantine yourself, and hope that you had enough water and food to last until it was safe to come out. The problem was that the Infected would eat anything, drink any water, no matter how foul, and they seemed to survive more so in the lush tropical conditions of the lowlands of the Hawaiian Islands. For most of the survivors, there was never a safe time to evacuate. It took teams of them with weapons to clear a small area and make it safe, and both personnel and weapons were scarce.

Bubba had hoped that, with its low population, Ni'ihau could be cleared and made a safe haven. He quickly discovered that they didn't have the weapons needed to fully eradicate the Infected, and the isolation limited the supplies they could scavenge. There were plenty of hunters in the Hawaiian Islands, but hunting was by special permit only on Ni'ihau and discouraged on Kauai; rifles and shotguns were rare, and there were very few handguns except in the hands of police and military security officers. The residents who worked the boats might have a small firearm hidden that they wouldn't admit possessing. Unfortunately, even when weapons were present, there simply wasn't enough ammunition to go around. Knives, machetes, makeshift swords, boat hooks, and spears were the most common weapons. There were plenty on the islands but recovering them was also part of the problem. One had to be armed to go up against the Infected...in order to search out weapons to fight the Infected.

Supplies were short, but that didn't deter Bubba and his people from trying. They pulled survivors out of the ocean, and off the beaches of Kauai, and worked diligently to clear and scavenge in small areas off the leeward cost of Ni'ihau and north shore of Kauai. A small community had built itself up at Kamalino Bay, but with the lack of resources and continued difficulty with Infected, the general consensus was that they would soon need to find another refuge.

"Okay, Mamabear reports that they've all hunkered down there. They've double-anchored the boats, pulled a few ashore and tied them off, and retreated to the old Thomlinson manor. They aren't expecting too much storm trouble, but they're keeping watch anyway. She also says that Kapua Kekoa's team was scavenging around the coffee plantation and found a couple more survivors. They want to talk with you about trying to do a harvest and maybe transplanting some of the crop, but that's for later. Kimo Mikala reports that he's perfected his bow and arrows and will be making more and training the shore teams. He took down a goat and speared a boar, so there will be a feast when we get down there."

"Very good. Okay, Tully, get that hatch and let's call it a night." Bubba was sitting at the table in the galley, two glasses in front of him. Each had about an inch of amber liquid. "It's the last of the Tullamore Dew, but a stormy night like this need something to light a fire in the belly."

Tully sat down opposite Bubba, lifted the glass, and toasted his captain with the Irish whiskey. "May seas be ever calm..."

"...and the wind be ever in your sails."

CHAPTER TWO
SETTLEMENT

Ni'ihau is the "secret island" of the Hawaiian people. It's a place for native craft and the traditional Polynesian way of life.

—Urban legend

No, no, it's not.   —E. Comeau, Kauai survivor

The storm lasted all night into the wee hours of the morning. Daylight came late, with heavy overcast and occasional light periods of rain and gusty winds. The remnants of the storm could still be dangerous to an unprotected boat on the open ocean, but the rest of the trip down to Kamalino Bay would be in the lee of the larger island. Even though its highest point was twelve hundred feet, just twice the elevation of Lehua, the island was two to five miles across its east-west axis, which was sufficient to blunt the force of wind and rain. Even with that partial protection, it still took two hours for Bubba and Tully to join the rest of their settlement.

Sixteen boats were in the bay, most at anchor in the water, with two smaller catamarans pulled up onto the beach, and a much larger boat tied up to a narrow pier that extended just far enough out from the beach to keep a boat like the one-hundred-eight-foot Burger sportfishing yacht, with *Simple Gifts* painted across the transom, from running aground. Two boats out of the total collection belonged to Bubba. He'd run a combined sailing, fishing/scuba operation out of Nawiliwili, the port associated with Lehui, the largest city on Kauai.

Bubba had sailed his Viking 62 sportfishing yacht, the *Bubba Truck*, while Tully had conned the Tayana 37 *Storm Chaser*. The rest were the remnants of forty-eight personal and tourist boats that left the western Kauai port of Port Allen, attached to the town and bay of Hanapepe. They'd lost many, but also managed to recover several boats, including *Simple Gifts* and a personal cruising catamaran—a Leopard 42— named *Hole in the Water*. The *Gifts* wasn't ready to sail, yet, since it was still being cleaned of the ... debris ... left by the owner and crew who'd fallen victim to the Haole Flu just after leaving port.

Many boats had been lost when their crews went zombie, resulting in collisions and groundings. More were lost when a crew simply chose to sail off. Crew were often lost to accidents and Infected attacks while salvaging or inspecting boats found adrift. Very few of the people rescued had practical sailing and boat operation experience, leaving the survivors short on trained crew. That led to harsh decisions whether to salvage boats at all. Preference was given to sailboats, even though they required more crew and more training, since fuel supplies were limited. They would collect food, fuel, and other supplies, but unless the boat was worth keeping, it was usually scuttled or left in a protected anchorage, if possible, to salvage later.

The *Simple Gifts* was an exception, and it was one they'd paid dearly for. Bubba had found it adrift off Hanalei, Kauai. The islands attracted the rich and famous; there were stories that many tried to fort-up in their hundred-million-dollar estates for several weeks before calling on friends or employees to come take them off the land. Bubba and a three-person salvage crew boarded the yacht to find five dead people, one live Infected locked in the head, and two *very* hungry Dobermans. Two of Bubba's crew were lost that day, one to the Infected and one to a dog attack, but the yacht itself was worth saving. On the other hand, they'd been cleaning it of blood, feces, and rotted meat for the past two months.

The fourth boat they'd salvaged was pulled up to the shore on a boat ramp next to the pier—opposite the Burger—with its bow ramp dropped into the sand. The LCM-8 landing craft had been built by the U.S. government for the Vietnam War, and was essentially a barge with a flat deck, slightly raised sides, and a ramp at the front. It was one of two found tied up in a small inlet just outside of Pakalala Village. The first landing craft was empty and had been stripped of all interior components, including engine parts and instruments. The second craft, named the *Landin'C*, had been found loaded with fifteen drums of gasoline and diesel fuel, a large liquified propane tank, a forty-six-foot-long cargo-shipping container, and surrounded by eight dead bodies.

Landing craft like the LCM-8 models were quite commonly used by private shipping companies in the Caribbean and around the Pacific islands to carry heavy loads and even vehicles between islands. Their shallow bows allowed them to be pulled right up to the sand—just drop the ramp and drive cargo onto the beach. In this case, the *Landin'C* was registered to the Thomlinson family, owners of a large number of private properties around Hawaii, including the island of Ni'ihau. The shipping container held household goods, likely destined for that island. The contents had been inventoried, and included seating and bedding, which the refugees used around camp, as well as clothing, sundries, and nonperishable food. The most valuable find, however, was the fuel, which could be used in all their boats, as well as any other vehicles they might find.

The eight bodies found around the LCM-8 were not Infected but appeared to have been two different groups who'd fought over possession of the prize and had killed each other. It also looked like a ninth person had survived the fight and attempted to crawl away, but was found over one hundred yards away, bled out from multiple gunshot wounds. He'd only had a pistol—empty—and Bubba figured he was the last survivor. On the other hand, there was evidence that someone had tried to shoot the locks on the shipping container and the pilothouse of the boat and managed to puncture one fuel drum. That drum was only one-third full, but all of it was good fortune for the refugees, especially since one of their number was experienced at picking locks. The salvage was one of the main reasons they were all still alive and sheltered on the island coast.

The settlement was not a permanent one. It mostly consisted of tents and lean-to shelters. There was one residential building near shore—a manor house owned by the Thomlinson family, hence the pier and landing ramp for the LCM-8. Most of the refugees were hesitant to use the house, since all those inside had succumbed to the Haole Flu. Superstition—plus the fear that perhaps they hadn't found all of the Infected—caused most people to avoid staying in the building at night and only use the kitchens during the day.

Bubba and Tully came into the bay to see people repairing damage from the previous night's storm. At least one tent had overturned and blown several yards down the beach; a couple of lean-tos had collapsed, and one of the fishing boats was listing in the water. A porch pillar had snapped, and they could see saplings being held against the splintered wood by two people, while a third lashed them in place with vines.

Erna "Mamabear" Comeau stood in front of the tables and chairs assembled on the lawn outside the old Thomlinson house. There was really no place inside large enough to hold the entire gathering. With more than seventy people currently in the settlement, meals and meetings were held on the lawn. After all, outdoor dining was common in the Hawaiian Isles; weather was typically mild, and even the daily rain showers were little more than a sprinkle. Mealtimes and assemblies did require a diverse collection of tables and chairs, ranging from the manor's fancy dining room set to a chrome dinette, to a table and benches carved and shaped from driftwood.

The settlement didn't have an official leader, but everyone listened to Mamabear. "Okay, I know most of you have been expecting this sooner or later. Food supplies aren't critical, but we can see certain items starting to run low. There's only so much we can hunt on this island, and it simply does not have good space to grow crops."

Ni'ihau was the oldest of the eight major islands of the Hawaiian Archipelago. It was known as the "Forbidden Isle," and was the most overgrown, which was itself part of the problem. Despite its fertile soil, the island was almost completely covered by dense tree growth. Clearing it to grow crops would require tools and labor that were not available. The neighboring island of Kauai was so much better suited for agriculture, but the combination of higher population and more towns and villages meant more victims of the Haole Flu, and greater numbers of Infected hiding and hibernating in dark places.

Mamabear spoke for a few minutes about the state of supplies, particularly food, then turned the meeting over to Captain Bubba with the admonishment that they all keep the discussion civil.

Bubba stood slowly and walked slowly to the front. It was obvious his knee was bothering him since he was leaning heavily on his cane.

The cane, a straight wooden dowel with a glass oval on top, when combined with Bubba's trademark white camp shirt and wide-brimmed hat, made him look like a character from that dinosaur park movie that had been filmed on Oahu.

"I don't think I need to reiterate all of the problems here. Resources are tight and if this group grows much larger, food will begin to be a problem."

"So, we just step up the scavenging. What's the problem?"

The interruption came from Jackson Toivo. He'd been a fishing boat captain with one of the larger tour agencies on Kauai and had run a fleet of five fishing boats out of Port Allen. For the past couple of months, he'd been taking small parties over to the leeward coast of Kauai for "scouting" expeditions that many people simply assumed were actually scavenging expeditions.

"The problem, Jackson, is that you've been consuming more resources than what you've been scavenging," Bubba said.

"I only use my fair share. After all, I scavenge most of the fuel and canned goods."

"And somehow manage to use it all."

Toivo had been insistent on using their fuel motoring back and forth between Ni'ihau to Kauai. He'd claimed it was more efficient than sailing upwind, but almost everyone else knew that Toivo was simply not as experienced with sail given that so many from his crews had succumbed to the Haole Flu.

"Except for the LCM and everything we've scavenged from derelict boats. That amounts to about ten times what you've scavenged so far," someone muttered.

"So far! If you'd let me guide larger parties, or even commit to going yourselves, we'd be able to gather more from the Island!" Jackson shouted back. "The Island" was almost universally understood to refer to Kauai. Most folks didn't refer to Ni'ihau at all.

"It's too big a risk, and we don't have enough people," Bubba countered.

"Well, rescue some more! You're the one that keeps pulling more people out of the water. Put them to work! So far, they've just been more mouths to feed. Well, make them work if they want to be fed."

"And essentially treat them as slaves, right? Otherwise leave them to die?"

"Well, if they're not going to work for us, I don't want them here using up our supplies—*my supplies*—and that of my people."

"I noticed it's all men in your crew, Jackson," said another voice. "If it's the end of the world, and we have to repopulate, just exactly how are you going to do that?"

"Take what I need," replied Jackson.

"And the rest of us?"

"Well, I suppose you can just let your little socialist paradise go the way of all the previous ones." Jackson stood up and leaned in toward Bubba, stabbing a finger into his chest.

"Move it, Toivo."

"Make me, commie."

Tully pushed in between the two men, but shouts and accusations ramped up among the rest of the people present. Mamabear tried to keep it civil, but it was clear that most people had taken sides. Toivo had been vocal in pushing for more clearance operations on Kauai. He wanted to push past Port Allen into Hanapepe and Eleele, and then east toward the Poipu resort area. From there he claimed that he could push all the way to Lihue, the county seat of Kauai County and the largest city on the island.

The other faction wanted to avoid the risk and potential loss of life associated with the clearance operations. Most of the group's food was coming either from fishing or salvaged goods, but the more conservative faction argued that they needed to be planting crops and hunting for meat. The more they depended on goods salvaged from Kauai, the more likely that any food would be ruined by weather or Infected. Several times Toivo had reported finding a storage warehouse that should've been full of food, but they'd found only ripped packages and smashed cans indicating that it had been raided by looters or used as a shelter by Infected. Often, they encountered the Infected sheltering or trapped inside.

At least, that was what he reported. There were suspicions some of the salvage was being hoarded.

What Toivo was proposing was to gather all able-bodied persons and make a push to flush out and kill all the Infected throughout Kauai. Bubba, Mamabear, and many others didn't think there were enough people to effectively clear the Island to a point they'd be safe planting crops. At the same time, he wanted to reduce ration consumption by the "Four L's"—elderly, ill, lame, or lazy—that five to ten percent of the survivors who could not or would not contribute to the community.

"Look, we know that the last census said there were less than one hundred people on Ni'ihau. Yet somehow, we seem to have killed a couple hundred Infected despite a fifty percent fatality rate for the Haole Flu! Hawaii had a homeless problem, and it's been that way for the past thirty years. Even with Kauai's official census at seventy thousand people, we *know* there were people living here who were not officially recorded. Ni'ihau proves that. Who's to say we don't have tens of thousands of Infected on the Island? I just think it's going to be so much harder than what Jackson's telling everybody," Bubba told the assembly.

"They won't last forever, it's an island. Nobody else is getting here to replace them. Once we get them rounded up and wiped out, we won't have this problem."

"And look how well that's worked here on Ni'ihau," a voice called out from the crowd. "There was an attack by the *'ino'ino*—ugly savages—during last night's storm."

CHAPTER THREE

DECISION TIME

The ancient Hawaiians drilled holes with fire-sharpened sticks. They made weapons out of flakes of obsidian from lava rock and fishhooks from bone. So why in the heck didn't they clear any farmland in the middle of their own private island?
—Jackson Toivo, boat captain and owner, Cap'n Jack's Tours

Maybe it was because they destroyed their fields in 1941 to keep from giving the Japanese makeshift runways ... Or maybe it was simply because they knew they could buy stuff online, stick it in a boat, and have it carried twenty-five miles to their houses. —Brian "Bubba" Gnad

The conversation continued to devolve, with shouts and accusations. All pretense of civility was soon dropped, and a few others started squaring up, preliminary to an actual fight. Bubba looked over at Tully, who was sitting in a folding camp chair next to Bubba's. Tully nodded, stood up, put his fingers in the mouth, and let out a shrill whistle. "Enough!" he bellowed.

Mamabear stood back up. "This meeting is not about whether we stay or go. There's enough people on each side of that question that we aren't going to reach agreement. The question here, is that *if* we go ... *where* do we go?"

"We need somewhere we can grow food," came one response.

"Somewhere we can get supplies and weapons to fight those savages," was another.

"Someplace we can be safe."

"Yeah, with no zombies."

"I just don't understand why we can't stay here? We cleared it as much as possible; there's houses we can use if we just clean them out."

"We don't have the resources we need for growing crops. We need clear fields and open land to grow crops, and we need to be growing enough to supplement our food," Bubba told them.

"So, chop down the trees and clear the ground!"

"We have one saw, one axe, and we're still struggling to find a good way to sharpen them both ever since Jimbo dropped one of my whetstones over the side of his boat when he was sharpening his gaff." Each fishing boat had a hooked pole with a sharpened barb for landing large game fish. They'd been used enough over the past six months to require sharpening, lest the barb fail to puncture the tough skin of the game fish. Each of the fishing boats was *supposed* to have a sharpening stone, but when Bubba had asked for them, to pool resources, Toivo had announced that all the fishermen working for him had somehow managed to lose theirs. Bubba had the only fishing boats not under Jackson's wing, and the loss of the whetstone he'd loaned out left him with the only one available to the settlement.

"I don't understand why this is a problem," Jackson sneered at Bubba. "The native Hawaiians made do with obsidian axes and dug holes with a fire-hardened, sharpened stick. This island was supposed to be for those who wanted to practice the old ways. Where are their tools?"

"On a barge somewhere with another weekly shipment of twenty-first-century goods. Look, we have some battery and electric stuff, but too many things need to be charged with our limited number of solar panels. We don't have that many gas-powered tools; we have a decent amount of gasoline for small tools, but no two-cycle oil. Without that, a gas-powered tool won't last past the first usage. So, we can't run our gas-powered tools, and without electricity we're not running—or recharging—electric tools. Ni'ihau was only primitive in press releases to the outside world. It's a private residence and resort; they depended on their modern luxuries as much as anyone. We've gotten pretty much everything we can get from this place," Bubba told the group. "We need to go somewhere where we can actually grow crops without having to landscape the whole island."

"You're all idiots," Jackson growled. "We can grow crops on Kauai."

"But what are we going to do, build a wall to keep the Infected out? We all know how well that concept worked on the mainland to seal the southern border."

"Give me the people to go out and clear the savages. We'll do what needs to be done if we all work together. And before you ask again, yes, we build walls, fences, and barricades to hold what we own."

"And keep the lion's share of salvage?"

"Well, the people who do the work need to be rewarded for their efforts," another one of Toivo's people muttered.

"We're not starting this argument again. Back off, you two," Mamabear admonished them. "Let's get back to the question of *where*. We have a vote for clearing Kauai. Bubba?"

"I agree Kauai is closest. It has resources we need, certainly has fertile soil that will grow plentiful crops, but there's no way to completely isolate those areas, wall or not. We need to go farther."

"Oahu? Where all the city folk and tourists turned Infected? You expect us to go there?"

"Possibly. It's not my first choice, but it's possible we could land on the north shore or maybe check out the leeward side. We have to stay away from Pearl; there was a report early on of an explosion somewhere in the Harbor. After that, almost everybody pulled out of the Molokai Channel was sick and dying with blisters and burns."

"A nuke carrier went up?"

"No, that wouldn't happen," said Mickey Ganz, one of the retired sailors who'd moved to Kauai after getting out of the Navy. "Shipboard nuclear power plants can't blow up, despite what you saw on movies and TV. There are too many safeguards, and frankly there's not enough fuel. However, there was an SSBN undergoing a resin exchange."

Before Mickey could continue, Mamabear held up a hand. "Resin exchange?"

"Yeah, they can be pretty nasty. Nuclear reactors are cooled by water circulation and have to be watched to make sure heat versus pressure is kept steady. If a reactor gets too hot, the pressure will rise, and it's possible to crack the casing. It wouldn't be a bomb, just a lot of steam. However, the cooling water gets 'dirty,' so to speak. It gets circulated through resin, which is like a great big water filter, and over its service lifetime it can pick up a lot of toxins. The resin needs to be changed out periodically, and it's a dry-dock job. It's touchy, toxic, and needs to be handled with utmost care. So, if there was an overpressure, spilled resin, or steam explosion—*that* could crack a reactor casing—and it would be like a dirty bomb went off."

"So, Pearl Harbor and Honolulu are right out," said Toivo. "I always said they could never handle true disaster. Too much reliance on modern supply chain, too many touristy areas. I'll bet Waikiki's overrun with savages."

"Well then, what about going west? Johnston Atoll, French Frigate Shoals, even Midway! There's enough small islands that won't be populated or overgrown, and we can go looking for the *Yukon*." The new speaker was Phil Charles, a former coastguardsman who had been rescued after H7D3 ran rampant through the Kauai Coast Guard station. When rescued, Charles related about how his Coast Guard station had been alerted to a collision between two naval ships in the ocean north of Kauai. The Henry J. Kaiser-class replenishment oiler USNS *Yukon* had suffered a collision with another ship north of Oahu. His cutter had been called out for rescue operations and pulled sailors out of the water at the site of the collision while the supply ship attempted to sail for Midway Island.

"Look, the *Yukon* was supposed to provide 'gas, grub, and gear' to last year's Pacific FleetEx," Phil continued. "They sailed from San Diego, but before they even got to Hawaii, PacFleet called off the exercise, ordered the ships to home ports, and told the submarines to scatter. *Yukon* and its cruiser escort, the USS *Port Royal*, headed for *Royal's* home port of Pearl Harbor. They were warned off as they approached the islands and took station fifty kilometers east of Pearl to await orders.

"Things were getting bad in Honolulu, Coasties were pulling lots of untrained boaters out of the channel and losing half of our personnel to Infected. The marines at Kaneohe Bay started evacuation flights, even sending a C-130—of all things—to Pohakuloa Training Area! Why, they thought a C-130 could land on a one-klick airstrip, at two klicks' elevation, is beyond me. I heard it didn't end well, but I digress."

"You do that a lot, Phil. So, finish telling us about your white whale . . ." The heckler snickered at his own joke.

"Yeah, right, so anyway, the *Yukon* and *Port Royal* moved in closer and started taking the refugees off helos from Kaneohe. They could spread out on the big deck of the *Yukon*. The *Port Royal*? Not so much. A bunch of refugees went zombie on both ships, but it was really bad on the cruiser; the bridge crew was attacked and they went off course. While trying to correct, they rammed right into the stern of the *Yukon*, damaging the steering gear and twisting a shaft. You know how those Ticos had all of the superstructure cracks in the eighties because of the aluminum? Well, the other problem with aluminum is that it burns. My cutter arrived as the *Royal* was fully engulfed in flame. There was nothing we could do but pull bodies out of the water. Pulled some Infected, too, which was why we never made it back, either, but the *Yukon* slowly sailed off, supposedly heading for Midway. The last radio contact was that they'd stopped at French Frigate Shoals for repairs, still alive, and with their own Infected under control."

"Uh-huh, we've heard about your Flying Dutchman before, Phil. A miracle ship filled with so much food and fuel we'll never go hungry or run out of gas. It's a myth and a waste of time and resources."

"I swear it, man, I saw the ship, and we had all of the radio messages with her crew. The *Yukon* was fully stocked, and there's no way a ship stocked for a thirty-ship, fifteen-thousand-person FleetEx would be depleted by a couple hundred crew and refugees. We need to at least send some boats up to French Frigate Shoals. It's got gasoline, kerosene, diesel, bunker, fuel oil, and even JP-4 for aircraft. Besides the food, there's machine shops, tools, weapons, firearms, ammunition, everything we need. I don't disagree that we should be heading to Molokai, but we need to go and see if the *Yukon* is still there. Those survivors need a home, too! We can help and we need those supplies."

The group conversation devolved into jeers mixed with shouts of agreement. Bubba thought about the problem. Midway was over one thousand miles west-northwest across open ocean. French Frigate Shoals was four hundred miles, with no major landfall in between. It would be a fifteen-day, one-way trip in the wrong direction just to the Shoals. The Hawaiian Archipelago was *long*, it stretched from the undersea volcano of Loihi to Midway Island. Fifteen hundred miles in total. There were hundreds of small islands, reefs, and shoals, and with the exception of the eight major islands of the State of Hawaii, most were less than one square mile. If the *Yukon* had made it all the way to Midway, it was well beyond the range of all but two of their boats, and they simply didn't have the fuel to go that far.

"I understand, Philip, and you're right; we need all of that. But if it's still out there, I really don't think it's going anywhere and we just don't have what we need to reach it yet. Let's get ourselves set up and then see if we can figure out a way to go find the *Yukon*. That's one of the reasons I think we need to go to Maui Country. Molokai, Lanai, and Maui are better situated for farming and fishing in the shallows between them. Molokai also has plenty of wild game; Maui does too. After we're settled, we can see about a longer exploration."

"Hey, we got chickens over on the Island," called the heckler from before. "That's wild game."

"Yeah, thunder chickens," said another voice in the crowd, eliciting a laugh.

"Molokai and Lanai are just as overgrown as Ni'ihau," said Toivo. "You will have the same difficulty setting up farms there. Maui had twice the population of Kauai, so you'll have even worse problems with savages."

"That's true, but the Kalaupapa peninsula on Molokai is almost sea level, it's mostly flat, very low population, and it's isolated from the rest of the island. The locals farmed and fished. That's where we should go."

The group erupted into angry shouting, and Mamabear had Tully whistle for attention again. "*Quiet!* We're not going to resolve this now. Now pipe down and get everything cleaned up. Sleep on it, and we'll talk more tomorrow night after dinner."

CHAPTER FOUR

THE LEPER COLONY

I said Hansen's disease, not Hampson's disease.
—T. Roberts

Mamabear had ended the meeting, but it didn't really break up, other than into smaller groups that seemed to be rehashing the earlier arguments. Fortunately, no fights broke out—this time. Mamabear, Tully, and Bubba went from group to group, attempting to calm the situation and reassure them all that matters would continue to be discussed before a decision was made. Toivo also made the rounds, but rather than calming, the people he talked to seemed more riled up after he left.

Eventually, everyone returned to their boats, tents, or shelters. Tomorrow would bring more work, just surviving, and the conversation after supper would be . . . acrimonious.

The next day dawned with the mild weather typical of the island paradise. Light rain overnight had left a few puddles, and the air was thick with humidity. Toivo's teams left before dawn to attempt salvage on Kauai's southern coast. Bubba and Tully took *Storm Chaser* and *Bubba Truck* out into the deep water west of the island for fishing, and the shore-side teams continued cleaning *Simple Gifts* and gathering supplies for that day's main meal.

That evening, once Mamabear finished her part of the meeting, Jackson opened with the main topic from last night.

"Why in the hell would you want to go to the leper colony?"

Once again, there were shouts and interruptions.

"It's over two hundred miles away. We don't have the fuel for that."

"There's lepers there; are you trying to kill us all?"

"They are no better than savages themselves. I've heard there's no discipline. They're rough, crude people and you'd put us in their midst?"

"How are we going have the supplies needed to even get there?"

"Are you crazy?"

Tully whistled the group back to order. "Enough."

"Leprosy was cured in the 1950s. There have been no active cases on Kalaupapa in sixty years," Bubba began. "The descendants and people who were healed continued to live there because they've been isolated and ostracized for all of their lives. If you know the history of Hawaii, you should know Father Damien's legacy. Kalaupapa colony has been peaceful and orderly for more than one hundred years. More than that, they have farms and gardens. There's switchbacks up to the main part of the island, which is rich with wild boar, deer, goats, and more. We can hunt on Molokai proper, and there's likely to be arms and ammunition at the hunting camps.

"The peninsula is surrounded by cliffs and rocky shores, but they have a port deep enough for a yearly barge and they always stockpiled a year's worth of supplies at a time. The biggest risk is whether any survivors would accept us, so we have to have something to offer them—like fishing and trade." Bubba leaned on his cane as he finished, allowing the people to think through his logic.

The murmurs continued for a while. There were still a few negative comments, but none were shouted out, or as loud as before. Most of those came from a small group around Jackson Toivo. After a while, a man stood up and approached Bubba, motioning for Mamabear and Tully to join them. He was tall, thin, dark-haired, broad-shouldered, and had sun-darkened skin. He was the perfect image of Duke Kahanamoku, the Olympic swimmer from Hawaii who gained fame as a professional surfer. Akoni Keoki, called "Kōkee" by his crew, had participated in the evacuation of Port Allen, bringing eleven refugees and his crew of six over on one of the large catamarans normally used for sunset dinner cruises and snorkeling expeditions along Kauai's Na Pali Coast. Lately, he'd been operating with a crew of two, scouting and exploring around Kauai, and looking for survivors. Bubba knew he'd been ranging farther than just the west coast of Kauai and sailing farther and farther out. He hadn't realized just how far until Kōkee spoke to him.

"They would welcome you."

"What?" Mamabear exclaimed. "How do you know this?"

"I've been there. It's a long trip on a sailboat—two hundred miles and change if you stay clear of the other islands. A small sailboat like *Hole in the Water* would take three days' sailing only during daylight hours. Your *Bubba Truck* will probably make it in a day if you burn the fuel. We took almost a week out and three days back with the wind. There's only a handful of people in the old colony: the Catholic priest and six survivors out of the old families plus a few refugees. They're trying to farm but there's just not enough people to work the land. They have one fishing boat with a broken engine and the half-empty yearly barge which ran aground nearby. One of the younger men built an outrigger canoe and has been fishing for them. It supplements their food, but the group is failing. They got the better part of a year's supplies from the barge, but the colony won't last much more than three months unless they get more people."

"Bubba, you knew?" Mamabear looked at him with suspicion.

"No, I suspected. I didn't know for certain, but this changes things. We need to let them know."

"But how are we going to get there? Do we have enough fuel?"

"We have fuel for the Burger, Viking, and *Landin'C*. The catamarans have the range and can sail it. We'll need to stick to their speed, so we could tow anything too slow."

"We won't have much left."

"It's true. We have a decision to make. We could all pile into the *Gifts*, but from the sounds of it we need to take boats we can fish and trade from. We could tie off several boats and tow them, but it's not ideal."

"Going to need the fuel drums that we found on the barge," Tully said.

"Not to mention refilling what we've used so far."

"How do we do that?" Mamabear asked.

"Hanapepe," Bubba sighed. "I don't like it, but Jackson will get his wish. We need to secure a beachhead to have a safe space to operate from in Hanapepe Bay and Port Allen. We should be able to restock from the tanks at the marina, and maybe scavenge more in town. Then we should give people the choice whether to stay with Jackson or go with us."

"I suppose that will make Jackson happier. He gets his island beachhead and a start at clearing the region. He can lead his people... and you can lead the rest, Bubba."

"Oh, hell no. I don't want to lead."

"Too bad, Bubba, you're the man with the plan," Tully told him.

Bubba sighed. "Okay, Kōkee, tell the folks what you told us, and I'll fill in the rest."

Tully got the group's attention again, then Kōkee got up to speak while Bubba watched Jackson. Toivo's eyes narrowed as he started to hear support for the Molokai plan, but then they widened as he realized that his plan to engage in more clearance operations on Kauai would be part of the agreement. Several of those around him turned to whisper quietly. A brief smile lit his face, but quickly fled to be replaced with a neutral expression.

He's probably thinking about the fact that not everyone will want to stay on Kauai, and trying to decide whether that's good or bad, Bubba thought. *Well, I suppose that's true for both sides. We just have to hope that we have enough people to make a difference when we get there.*

With a tentative plan, Mamabear called the assembly to end; it was time to eat. The cooks brought out fish and vegetables from their rapidly dwindling stock of canned goods. There was rice to ensure that everybody got the calories they needed. The meal was more extravagant than rationing would strictly allow, but the prospect of being able to scavenge and collect supplies from one of the Kauai towns buoyed their spirits and everyone seemed convinced that there would be more supplies once they had their toehold on Kauai.

Much to his surprise, Toivo came up to speak with Mamabear. "Hmph. I guess it's for the best. I'll need every able body for two to three weeks. We'll push to clear as much as we can in Eleele and Hanapepe. After that, we'll divvy up the supplies and get you out of here in hopes the folks at Kalaupapa can hold out for another month. Some of my men have been working on mapping resources along the shoreline up to Barking Sands."

Jackson hadn't included Bubba in the conversation, and it annoyed him. Not to mention the fact that the man was essentially demanding that everyone in the settlement go to work under his orders.

Bubba snorted, drawing Jackson's attention.

"It's okay, I'm not heartless. I'll even let you keep *Landin'C*. My people took a second look at the other LCM and think we can get it running. I'll go along with this plan—for now—but you don't get to take everything."

"Gee thanks, I wouldn't want you to throw too much support to my plan."

Jackson snorted in return. Bubba knew this wasn't the end of it. The discussions over who went, who stayed, and what supplies would go with either party wouldn't be pleasant.

One of the first things they would need to do would be to get the *Simple Gifts* ready to sail. It would be able to carry the most people (not to mention comfortable sleeping arrangements) but would consume a lot of their fuel—second only to the LCM. They wouldn't need to travel at high speed, though, since they'd be keeping pace with the sailboats.

Bubba and Kōkee sat down with charts and maps to figure out their best course and choice of boats for the journey. The route to Molokai would take them around Oahu with its big cities and military bases. That was where the real danger was likely to be lurking. They'd heard voices over the marine radios and knew there were a few boats in the waters off the northern and western coasts, but nothing about the eastern and southern coasts near the military bases at Kaneohe Bay or Pearl Harbor.

Bubba knew better than to expect anything positive out of Honolulu and the tourist areas stretching from Waikiki to the North Shore along the windward side of Oahu. Radio reports and news—while those were still broadcast—painted a bleak picture of massive death toll from the Haole Flu, followed by the Infected attacking in every population center. Whatever happened in Pearl Harbor had left people sick and dying downwind. There were supplies to be had at the military bases, not to mention fuel at Red Bank and armaments in the storage depots of the leeward shore. There was also the possibility of survivors in the central portion of the island, but the risks were high, and the benefits so uncertain, that they knew it was not the time to chance it.

The Molokai Channel was only twenty-five miles wide, but likely to be the most congested if there were survivors on boats. Several days of sailing, boats filled with survivors and zombies—or worse, pirates. Then contact with the Kalaupapa colony survivors, convincing them to combine efforts, and building a new home.

Easy sailing...

CHAPTER FIVE

CLEARANCE OPERATION

The Hawaiian love of the food product Spam dates back to the time of the Ali'i, or elites among the Polynesian leaders. Meat was rare in the common diet, and pork was reserved for the elites. When Spam was introduced, courtesy of American soldiers, even low-income islanders could afford to add pork to their diet. Spam became popular and ingrained in Hawaiian culture.   —V. Landrum, schoolteacher, Kauai

Compared with life pre-H7D3, it wasn't as easy as simply picking a destination and setting sail. The first step was salvaging enough food, supplies, and fuel from Kauai to ensure that both the group that left and the group that stayed had a decent stock. Teams of four were organized, with each consisting of one person with a machete, two with spears, and one with a maul or sledgehammer. Firearms were still scarce, and the few owned by the survivors were kept in reserve in case a clearance team encountered trouble. The spears were bamboo, sharpened and fire-hardened—the ban against civilian bamboo-cutting having ended with the fall of civilization. Machetes and large knives were fairly common around Kauai for cutting brush, cleaning fish, and more, so there were plenty of those for each team conducting salvage to be armed with one or more bladed weapons.

The plan was to secure a beachhead at Hanapepe Bay. There was a tall fence outside the marina and port facility. It was damaged in several places, but the first teams would push through to a hardware store to obtain additional fencing and materials to extend that barricade. The marina fence was six feet tall, and was not entirely enough to stop Infected, but it could be reinforced and made taller. As long as the fencing lasted, they would extend that barrier to enclose as much cleared territory as they could manage. After that, it would be necessary to use local materials such as wrecked cars, metal siding, and even scavenged building materials to create a secure perimeter extending out from the harbor.

Jackson's team set sail for Hanapepe first, taking three days to secure a beachhead. They suffered one casualty, a twisted ankle, but that was nothing compared to the evidence of deadly battle found at the site. Broken glass, shattered doors, ripped-up fences, and quite a few human bones indicated a deadly battle had occurred sometime in the past, likely when the Infected first overran the town. Some buildings had already been scavenged, but most had not. The best result was a store with cartons of dry and canned goods in an untouched stockroom. The worst case was another where packaged food had been torn open and soiled by the Infected.

The shoreline around Hanapepe Bay was bisected by one of the many small rivers that drained the rainy highlands of the Garden Isle. The Hanapepe River was navigable for about a mile and divided the area into two prime targets: east was Port Allen and the town of Eleele, west was the lightly built Hanapepe. While the east held desirable resources, the west offered a securable space to set up camp—a large park and recreation facility right next to the bay.

Once Port Allen and a nearby hardware store were secured, some of the fencing was used to reinforce and repair existing fences surrounding the tennis courts and baseball stadium. More fencing was scavenged from around the baselines of two more baseball fields to create a total fenced area of sixteen acres. Even better, a twelve-acre National Guard station and armory was immediately adjacent to the secured area, along with a Salvation Army soup kitchen, restaurant, temple, and thrift store.

With immediate residential needs satisfied, attention turned to clearing Eleele, then eventually the small towns of Waimea to the north and Kalaheo to the east. A particularly attractive target was the eight square miles of coffee plants and processing facilities between Eleele and Kalaheo. Even farther was the Pacific Missile Range Facility, north of Barking Sands Beach. The entire facility was fenced, which either meant that Infected were excluded, or concentrated within that region. For now, it was out of reach, but Toivo had already stated his desire to shift to that location if it could be secured.

Bubba wasn't sure which was a more attractive concept: the possibility of tools and weapons, or unlimited coffee. Perhaps both— if they could manage to crack into the Guard armory before his flotilla sailed, they could afford to station guards while harvesting coffee and cocoa beans. There was even talk of transplanting some of the bushes into pots and loading them into the LCM to take them with them to Kalaupapa. For the time being, Bubba's goals aligned with Toivo's, and their respective followers united in a common goal:

Salvage, and clearing the area of Infected.

"This one's clear," Charlie said, coming out of the house. Several wrecked cars were already being moved up to incorporate this neighborhood of Eleele into the secured perimeter extending out from Port Allen.

"Infected?"

"None. No Savages here."

"*Signs* of Infected, dumbass?"

"Also, none."

Jon Ko sighed. Charlie wasn't his brightest team member, mostly a follower. That much was evident by his use of the derogatory term "Savages" adopted by Toivo's people. Still, he wasn't afraid to enter houses. "Okay, mark it with a green circle and let's keep moving."

"Hey, Charlie, you *did* remember to make a bunch of noise and flash your light around, right?" Daniel Kapua was not about to let Charlie Young forget about the house they'd cleared two days ago. "I'd rather not go into a building and find out that an Infected was sleeping in a dark basement and you overlooked him."

"Hey, it worked out okay. I got him with my spear."

"Yeah, but he still grabbed me. If I hadn't been wearing my rain gear, he would've bitten me."

"Whine, whine. Would you like some cheese with that?" Edmund Peevy asked Daniel.

"Shit, man. You know how long it's been since I had cheese?"

"Well, maybe we can find you some. The Hanapepe side is starting to move into the commercial district."

"Are you kidding? Eight months without refrigeration? It'll be bad. We'll have to make do with cheese in a spray can."

"Ugh, that's as bad as eating Noni fruit. Tastes like vomit."

"But it's good for you. Healthy, unlike spray-can cheese!"

"You guys shut up," Ko growled. "I think I heard something."

The sound came again, an arrhythmic tapping. It wasn't Morse code or anything, but it caught their attention.

Tap . . . tap . . . tap tap . . . tap.

"Charlie, are you sure you checked everything?"

"Yeah. I mean, like it's not like these houses have basements or anything."

"Ah, right. I keep having to remind myself that you guys really are idiots," Ko told them. "You didn't look for a crawlspace, did you?"

"What do you mean a 'crawlspace'?"

"The house is elevated; you have to take steps *up* to the door. It's a precaution against storm tides and tsunami. You looked for access hatches and trapdoors, right?"

"Sorry, boss."

Ko sighed again. "Right. Okay, by the numbers. Charlie, you're going first and taking the machete. Daniel's got his spear and going second. I'm handing Edmund my sledgehammer, and he'll follow. I'm last, since I've got a handgun. Actually, Edmund, give your spear to Daniel; he'll carry both. Look for any small door or hatch that could lead underneath."

The clearance team reentered the house, checking the first and second floor again. They didn't expect to find anything different but they needed to reassure themselves that no Infected could come up behind them while they were checking for access underneath the main floor.

They found the access in the kitchen next to the pantry. Charlie said he'd thought it was just the door covering the water heater.

"That would be fine if it wasn't for the fact that the water heater is over there." Ko pointed to the four-foot-tall cylinder next to the sink on the opposite side of the kitchen.

The tapping came again from somewhere beneath their feet.

"Alright, Charlie, you're opening it. Daniel, Edmund, stand on

either side. Be ready, but don't overreact—so far, Infected don't tap—"
Even as he spoke, the tapping changed and went from no rhythm to a
familiar one. "And they certainly don't tap 'Shave and a Haircut.'"

Charlie opened the door and the four of them looked into a dark
space. The three men stood ready while Jon called into the space.

"Hello?"

After moment, a female voice called back. "So, you *are* intelligent.
Do you want to come in, or should I come out?"

This took them all by surprise. Most the time when they found
survivors, they were huddled scared in darkness. Many were even
mute with fear, but this voice sounded confident, as if she were
expecting them.

"'Intelligent' is a matter for discussion, but it would probably be
best if you came out." Ko turned to his team. "Weapons down, but
ready."

A few moments later, a small, slight woman with gray hair came
into view. She had to duck to fit through the short door. Charlie and
the others backed up to give her room, but their stance said that they
were still on guard. As she straightened up, it was obvious that she had
nothing in her hands, and she clearly wasn't an Infected.

For one thing, she was dressed.

Her clothes were worn, dirty, and frayed around the seams. On the
other hand, she didn't look pale, emaciated, or sickly like so many
refugees. She came fully into the kitchen and stood slowly. It looked
painful, as if she spent a lot of time hunched over. After stretching for
moment, she smiled at them. "I'm Vanessa, Vanessa Landrum."

Charlie, Daniel, and Edmund just looked dumbfounded.

The leader spoke instead. "I'm Jon Ko."

"With a C or a K?" she asked sweetly.

"With a K," he said. "K-O, Ko. The boy with the machete is Charlie.
The one with the spears on your right is Daniel; on your left is
Edmund. So . . . you were tapping. Why? For that matter, why were you
hiding if you were tapping to get attention?"

"I heard movement. I didn't know if it was those creatures or if you
were actually humans—intelligent, that is. I don't consider the
creatures to be human anymore."

"So, you tapped?"

"I thought I heard voices, but I wasn't sure. Humans would've found the door and called out. The creatures? Not so much. I tried to avoid a rhythm; the creatures respond to bright lights, loud sounds, but they *really* respond to rhythm."

"You seem to know a lot for someone who is hiding out in a basement."

"Oh, that's just my secure spot. I live on the upper floor and spend a lot of time on the roof watching, but I had been inventorying supplies when I heard sounds outside. I hid until I could tell who was out there. I take it you boys are from the group down at the marina?"

"Yes, ma'am, we secured a beachhead for salvage. Some of us are going to move off to start a new colony. The rest are going to stay here and secure the area."

"Oh, that sounds good. You'll be needing some help, then."

"Well, most people want to help, but we've found some who can't . . . or won't. What are you offering?"

"Oh, odds and ends. I go out at night and explore a bit. I can help your teams figure out where they need to go. I was a schoolteacher before that. The schools around here are mostly vocational so I know a little bit of woodworking, metalworking, cooking, home economics. I even taught science for a while."

"Well, then, I suppose we should help you get out of here and have you report to the big boss."

"The one who's staying? Or the one who's going?"

"Hmm. Perceptive. Yes, I can picture you as a schoolteacher. Both, I think."

"Well, then, let's be about it! Jon, boys, I have some canned goods down there. You might want to gather those up, and I have a few other items that I think might be very welcome." She pulled out a flashlight and shined the bright light back into the crawlspace. Charlie was clearly taken aback. Isolated refugees usually didn't have uncommon supplies like batteries.

Vanessa laughed as she saw the reaction. "I have a few things put aside. I scavenged from time to time, and my Walter left me his revolver."

"Ma'am, I think we definitely need to get you to see Jackson *and* Bubba soon as we possibly can."

"Oh, no doubt about that, but I think you're going to want to get my canning and preserves before we do that."

"Preserves as in jams and jellies?" asked Daniel.

"Oh, yes. I did mention that I taught Home Ec, right?" Vanessa laughed. She led the group down into the crawlspace. After a couple of turns to place them once again firmly underneath the house, it opened up into a depression in the earth. The central area had been dug out and closed off with plywood sheeting. They'd noticed plywood covering the windows from the inside, which was one of the reasons for checking it carefully. Now there was a clue that this very capable person in front of them had found a way to secure her space, not to mention supply and defend herself since the fall of civilization.

Jackson and Bubba would be very eager to meet her. She was likely to find herself courted by both factions. He just hoped it wouldn't devolve into a fight.

Inside the enclosure they found rough shelving along three walls. On the shelves were metal cans from a supermarket, as well as glass containers with metal tops filled with all manner of preserved fruit, vegetables, and other products.

Each team was equipped with a small, collapsible wagon. Theirs was out front, and Jon sent Edmund out to get it. They quickly loaded it full with the items from Vanessa's stronghold, but there was so much, the wagon couldn't hold any more. Each of the men loaded up their backpacks with cans and jars and bottles, and would still need to make at least a second, if not third, trip to retrieve it all.

It would be welcome, indeed. It wasn't too difficult to find food, but all too often, Infected had found it and either eaten it or contaminated it. There was still food to be found in some of the stores and restaurants, not to mention individual houses and dwellings. That didn't mean there was variety, though. Having the supplies and the *knowledge* to can and preserve food would be very welcome indeed.

CHAPTER SIX

SUSPICION

Fifty percent of U.S. coffee plants are within a four-mile plot of
land on Kauai...and we greatly appreciate that fact!
—B.K. Esteves, Merchant Mariner (ret.)

Vanessa wasn't the only survivor they found. However, she was the one
in the best shape, and able to join in the clearance efforts. Fortunately,
she'd had plenty of stored food supplies that had *not* been added to the
common storehouse until after the prior supplies were ruined. Her
diet had become somewhat deficient in meat, and she was greatly
appreciative of the salted fish Bubba provided when she sat down to
meet with him and Jackson. The latter had already expressed his
opinion that she should join his clearance crews to point out areas with
a heavy concentration of Infected or areas that had already been
damaged or already picked clean. For his part, Bubba listened to the
former teacher talk of scavenging, canning, and past experiences
hunting and butchering her own meat. Her skill set would be essential
on Molokai, and he hoped she would choose to join their group.

It surprised Bubba that Jackson was beginning to show grudging
support for his plan to migrate to Molokai. They'd spent considerable
time discussing supplies and what Bubba's people should take with
them...which is how the talk turned to the nearby coffee plantation.

"You need to take coffee. Coffee makes for excellent trade goods.
There have to be people out there desperate for their morning coffee
fix. How long has it been since you had a nice cup of joe, Bubba?"
Jackson asked him.

"We had a pretty good run of salvaging from boats, but we had to ration it, and then ran out a month ago, so I can see your point."

"Are you going to try to secure the whole plantation, Mr. Toivo?" Vanessa asked. "That's a lot of territory, over three thousand acres. Are you just going to go in and scavenge, or are you planning on people living there and reactivating the big harvesting machines? You know they run on an alcohol-gas mix and not diesel, right?"

"Wait, you know about coffee harvesting? Oh, wait, what am I saying? Of course, you do. Is there anything you *don't* know, ma'am?" Jackson asked, sarcastically.

"Well, I don't know how to sail a boat...yet. But my Walter was a mechanic, and he worked on a lot of the equipment over there. The machines reach much taller than a human can, so the crops over there are taller than can be harvested by hand. The harvesters were custom-designed, and ran on an ethanol mixture, which is a bit unusual for farm equipment, but the coffee cherries don't like diesel fumes. They had island electric and a solar array for the processing equipment and roasters, and a distillation setup for the ethanol."

"I suppose we should start pumping out the underground tanks from some of these gas stations," Bubba said. "We can probably gather enough ethanol in various forms to mix with the gas as long as we don't touch Tully's Tullamore Dew."

"We need to make the best of it this year, then; prepare enough fuel to run the machines for a single harvest. So, a raid, and not a full-on occupation. Afterward, we can work on extending our cleared perimeter to the plantation and as far past it as we can."

"That's over four million plants in three thousand acres, gentlemen."

Bubba whistled and sat back. He pulled out a handkerchief, took off his hat, and wiped at his receding hairline. "I suppose that'll do for a start, Jackson. After that, you'll probably have to start harvesting by hand."

"And processing, too. So, *how many* people are you leaving me, Bubba?"

Bubba didn't answer.

"You'll have to hull it, clean it, roast it, and then store ground or whole beans. All of that was automated, but they have facilities for doing that by hand, over at the visitor center. It's low capacity, but it's probably just as well," Vanessa told them.

"Speaking of the visitor center. What do you suppose they have already processed and packaged?" Jackson asked her.

"It will be almost all in whole bean form, especially the fifty-pound bulk they sell to roasters. There should be hand grinders in the gift shop for the city folk who wanted to pretend to be coffee connoisseurs. You could probably load up and take a lot of that stock with you and replenish from the first harvest."

"I'd like to try to have that harvest before Bubba and the rest leave."

"To be honest, now that we know we're getting decent salvage and low encounter rate, plenty of people are having second thoughts about going to Kalaupapa. We're up over seventy-five people. It's probably a fifty-fifty split right now, but not everybody can work."

"Not everybody *will* work, for that matter."

"The rate we're finding people, I don't think we'll have a problem with finding enough people to stay, and to be honest I'm not sure even forty will go. At this point I'd be happy if it was twenty and enough just to man the boats."

"Yes, I know. I feel the same. Give me three clearance teams and about twenty people total to start putting things back together."

People came and went as Vanessa continued to fill in Jackson and Bubba about resources in the area. They'd been talking with minor interruptions since lunch, and it was now later afternoon. Several of the clearance crews, including Jon Ko's, had returned to assist in supper preparation.

"Why didn't you eat chicken?" Bubba had asked Vanessa. "Lord knows, there's chickens everywhere in Kauai running wild."

"Have you ever tried to catch a wild chicken? They run around and make noise. Noise attracts the Savages, as young Charlie called them. I'm told you prefer the term 'Infected.'"

Toivo snorted, and Bubba just grimaced.

"My Walter just called them Creatures, but I think your name is more accurate. Anyway, say you catch a chicken, you have to prepare it. I didn't have hot water for cleaning it and I'd have to build a fire to cook it. Trust me, you do *not* want to eat raw wild chicken. The diarrhea would be worse than starving."

"So, cook it on a wood fire," Ko said.

"Where? In my kitchen? With a risk of setting the whole place on fire? On a rooftop here, the Creatures would smell it and attack."

"Oh, yeah. I get it. You ran out of canned meat, too, I guess."

"Oh, dearie. I haven't had meat for protein since the Spam ran out."

"Ooh, Spam," said Ko. "I miss Spam."

"Spam Musubi," Bubba added. "Spamburgers."

"Sweetie, there is nothing better than a thick slice of fried Spam with mustard on a toasted bun, but I was eating it straight out of the can," Vanessa told them. "I still miss it, though. Mr. Toivo's people should see if they stockpiled any Spam up at the Navy Exchange. It's just off of Barking Sands Beach."

"I'll be sure to put it on my list," Jackson said, drily.

Despite the focus on clearance operations, an undercurrent of unrest started to simmer as teams worked through their way through the towns of Hanapepe and Eleele and found survivors. It had become clear that people were separating themselves into three groups. The first group backed Bubba's plan to go to Molokai. A slightly smaller group backed Toivo's plan to remain on Kauai. The smallest group consisted of the "infirm."

Within any grouping of humans there were five to ten percent who couldn't do the heavy work necessary for group survival. A small percentage simply *wouldn't* work, the rest were too sick, too young, or too old to do heavy labor. Toivo had proposed a Work-to-Eat policy and, as much as it offended Bubba, he had to agree that everyone they fed needed to support the community. So, the "infirm" filled in with jobs that were easy, such as inventorying the results of the clearance and salvaging operations.

Toivo's group took the lead on securing Port Allen and the immediate surroundings of the marina. Bubba's group had secured the bayside park area. The infirm mostly stayed within the fenced-in confines of the park, while Jackson's and Bubba's teams moved out past their perimeters into Hanapepe and Eleele, respectively. The Hanapepe River separating the two groups was crossed by only two vehicle bridges, and a pedestrian, swinging bridge, which served to minimize conflicts... except at mealtimes.

The conflict between the two groups simmered at a low level while they focused on their separate objectives. East of the river, just past

Port Allen, was the power station for the island, with an extensive solar power field, as well as fuel tanks, machine shops, and a small commercial district. West of the river were the park, armory, several restaurants, and thrift shops, a bakery, and the larger of the two residential districts. Eventually, the two groups would have to share the salvage, in order to accomplish their goals, but that was currently a bone of contention.

Bubba's supporters were mostly from the fishing and tour industry around Kauai. They supported the Molokai relocation since they saw the need to have a secure base where their families could live on land and have the chance to grow crops. There also seemed to be a larger proportion of Hawaiians who had lived in the islands for several generations.

Toivo's group consisted of a few of the Port Allen boat operators and a disproportionate number of rescues. This was surprising to many, given that Toivo thought that too many resources had been spent on sea-rescue operations. On the other hand, most of those rescued had been pulled from boats that they didn't know how to operate. They wanted to stay on land and not return to the sea.

Both groups performed clearance and salvage in their respective areas and were *supposed* to deliver everything to the community stockpiles. Those were located at the park, for consumables, and at the port for fuel, boat, and fishing supplies. There were arguments for a common depot for salvage, but neither group could agree on where that should be located, or who should be in charge. As a result, there was an undercurrent of suspicion that not all salvage was reported, or equally shared.

CHAPTER SEVEN

THE KU INCIDENT

Hawaii for Hawaiians! Rise up, kane and wahine! Drive off the haole and reject the white man's religion. Return to the Gods of Polynesia and they will bless our land.

—Laurentino Edgar Vale Serra, aka "Kuwahailo"

Not all of the infirm were totally useless. One such was Larry Vale. He claimed that his family was from Hawaii, and he certainly looked like any Hawaiian surf bum of indeterminate age. As with many of the survivors, he only had the clothes on his back, and wore brown board shorts and a blue aloha shirt with pink flowers. He clearly looked like he'd spent too much time in the outdoors, with sun-bleached white hair, and his exposed skin was weathered and blotchy. Vale's face was thin and yellowed, the skin pulled so tight it almost looked like a skull, supposedly due to a strange endocrine disorder. He claimed prior experience in warehouse management, and Mamabear had assigned him to keep the inventory of supplies.

He told Bubba and Mamabear about his concerns one morning about a month after they started clearance of the island.

"I'm seeing fewer stocks reported by Toivo's teams. Quantities were high right after they secured the harbor, but once they moved out past the Eleele Shopping Center, the numbers dropped off," Vale told them.

"There was a big grocery store there. What about salvage from there?" Bubba asked, looking at a map of the area.

"Mr. Toivo said it had been ransacked already."

"Past that area is mostly residential. It's slow going and low yield until you get to the river," Mamabear said.

"That might be," said Bubba, "but there's not much in the way of stores on this side of the river. What's the proportion of supplies turned in by the Hanapepe group?"

"Two, maybe three to one. Hanapepe to Eleele, that is."

"Hmm. Okay, we need to keep an eye on this."

"Yes, Mr. Bubba, sir. Oh, I should also mention that I overheard two of the Eleele workers bragging about an arsenal of weapons all hidden in the back of a closet in a town house. At least three rifles, a shotgun, two pistols, and a thousand rounds of ammunition each. I haven't seen any of that turned in for inventory."

"They kept it at the port?" Mamabear asked.

"Maybe, but it also doesn't make sense. Hawaii law is death on private guns. You hear of stockpiles like that on Hawaii Island, and maybe on places with wild boar and deer, but not on Kauai."

"The two also mentioned lots of alcohol, drugs, and a whole bunch of that expensive Haole survival food."

"So, the owner was probably rich or politically connected. You'd expect to hear about that on the north shore, what with the billionaire mansions, but not on the south shore. I wonder," Bubba mused. "Do you think Toivo knows? Or are they keeping it from him, too? If there's drugs, I wouldn't be surprised if they didn't tell him."

"They said he told them not to turn it in."

"Oh."

"I just thought you should know."

Most of the community gathered for a common meal since all food was supposedly accounted for in the common stocks. With virtually everyone working on clearance, there was no difference in calorie requirements, so everyone got the same meal. Tonight, it was reduced to a small amount of watery fish stew, a tiny serving of canned vegetables, and some crackers.

The grumbling started almost immediately, mostly from the clearance crews who felt that much more should have been available. Bubba had seen that day's catch from his fishermen and agreed. While it hadn't been as large as some days, there had been more fish caught than represented by the stew. One of the Hanapepe teams had encountered a bakery the previous day, so there should have been sufficient flour to make flatbread, and not resort to stale crackers.

Meal planning was also one of Larry's duties, and as mealtime went on, there were increasing calls for him to account for what had happened to the food. By the end of the meal, it was obvious that tempers had begun to rise. As was her custom, Mamabear stepped up to address plans, progress, and the organization of the next day's work teams.

It was when she announced the latter that the fecal matter truly impacted that rotary impeller.

"Where's the food?" someone yelled from the back.

"Calm down. We are working on an inventory. We have the food gathered in a central location, and the inventory is balanced with projected need, so we may have to tighten our belts at times."

"No. No, it's not. I know we pulled in more than this." The voice came from one of the team leaders for Eleele.

"Yeah? Well, maybe you didn't turn it all over!" said another voice.

"I know we brought in enough fish to each have some, instead of this pitiful stew!" one of Bubba's fishermen added.

"We found a good supply of salt, though. We needed to salt some of the current catch to preserve it for later." Bubba also tried to calm the situation.

"Sure, but we had a good catch! Why didn't you put more in the pot? It would have been better than this . . . sauce."

Vale finally spoke up. "There simply was not enough to go around. Resources are limited and we have to make sure that everybody gets fed."

While it was an answer, it wasn't a satisfying one. While Toivo wasn't sitting anywhere near him, Bubba could still hear the man mutter, "Not everyone deserves to be fed."

It was true that there were those who gave everything they could, while others did the bare minimum. Still, there was no reason to deny food to anyone. This sentiment led down a dangerous road of throwing people aside who couldn't keep up, no matter if it was due to age, illness, or attitude. After all, why should they waste resources pulling survivors out of the ocean or out of their boarded-up homes? Bubba looked over and saw Vanessa Landrum—people had started calling her "Gran" recently—sitting with Jon Ko and knew what his answer would be.

"Some of the clearance teams have been keeping what they found! They've been keeping stuff for themselves!" a voice called out.

"Who said that?" Jackson shouted. "Come say it to my face."

No one responded to Jackson, but one of his team shouted back, "Yeah? Well, so what if we keep a particularly nice piece of jewelry, a bit of worthless cash, or the occasional can of Spam? That's not hoarding, that's just being practical!"

"So, you admit it! Damned hoarders!" said a man a few feet away.

And there it was.

Jackson Toivo stalked over to Bubba, his whole posture showing barely controlled rage. "You will stop this! You will stop this, now!" yelled Toivo, getting up into Bubba's face. "My people are doing most of the work. Now you're accusing us of stealing it?"

"People are beginning to wonder just what's been found versus what's been turned over. For example, like what happened to that cache of weapons your people found?" Bubba wasn't reacting particularly well to Toivo's hot breath in his face and pushed him back with the foot of his cane against the other man's breastbone.

"Weapons? You mean like the armory your people cleared? There's no weapons on this damned island! The guardsmen took them all with them!"

Mamabear tried to separate the two men and failed. Fortunately, Tully came over and forced himself between the two. It didn't stop Toivo's rant, however.

"You're too soft! You and your people want to run away instead of doing what it takes to take back this island."

"I'm not threatening you, but if you're having so much trouble finding salvage, then how are you going to stay here?"

Toivo shoved Tully out of the way, then advanced on Bubba. Bubba spun his cane to bring the large oval head to bear, ready to strike Toivo with it.

Toivo took a swing at Bubba, who took the hit on his upper arm. He went numb down to his fingers from the blow. He swung the cane...

...and never connected. Kōkee deflected the cane, then reached out to grab both men by the neck. Neither man had the strength to fight the Hawaiian fisherman, and they knew it.

"Stop it! You need to see this!" He adjusted his grip physically, turning their heads to look in the same direction.

Vale was standing at the back of the crowd with an expression of satisfaction. As he saw the three looking at him, he turned away, and began moving toward the kitchen facility.

"You two have been set against each other. Vale's behind this. Something isn't right here."

Bubba backed up a step, but Toivo moved to close the distance before Kōkee's words finally sunk in. He put his foot back down and turned to the Hawaiian.

"You have proof?"

"No, but I think we should go check the inventory ourselves." When the men looked back toward Vale, the man had disappeared.

"Yes."

"Agreed."

The salvage was supposed to be kept in the thrift store next to the soup kitchen, just past the athletic fields. Only sufficient food supplies for the current meal were kept in the kitchen, with the remainder kept in a locked storage shed between those two buildings.

As they advanced on the buildings, Kōkee called their attention to someone disappearing behind the storage building. When they got there, the man was nowhere in sight, the door was locked, and there was a horrible smell coming from the shed.

Toivo was the first to identify it as rotting fish. "I think I know what happened to today's catch."

None of them had the keys, those had been entrusted to Vale and Mamabear. Kōkee backed up and kicked the door. The metal door dented slightly and sprung loose from the frame. Inside, the storage building was an absolute mess. Several days' worth of rotting fish was dumped on top of the packaged food, which was piled haphazardly in the middle of the floor. Cans were crushed, cardboard was torn, and plastic packaging was ripped open. On the walls, in feces and blood, was written The wrath of Ku.

"Oh shit."

"Literally. I'm sorry, Bubba," Kōkee said.

"This is . . . this is . . . savage," Toivo said. "It's worse than the Savages. They're mindless. This is malicious. I'm going to hunt him down and kill him."

Bubba just nodded. He couldn't find the words to express himself.

He never considered himself a bloodthirsty man, but Toivo was right. It was bad enough they had to fight the Infected, but to have one of the people they had rescued do this? It was worse than mindless.

It was evil.

He didn't know who Ku was, but Bubba knew that neither he nor Toivo could let this go.

Bubba held out his hand. The other man looked at it for several moments, then shrugged and accepted the handshake.

"Alright," Jackson growled. "Let's get back to work."

CHAPTER EIGHT
WE ARE VOYAGERS

You mainlanders have it easy. Want to go somewhere? Get in your car and drive. On an island, you drive thirty miles, then you need a boat. On the mainland, you can cover five states in a day. In Hawaii? The nearest U.S. state is twenty-five hundred miles away. —D. Wells, boat survivor

After the Ku Incident, the perimeter was pushed out day by day. After each team cleared a building, others were ready to erect fencing and place physical barriers to increase the secured area outward from the marina. The bay itself became filled with ships and other floating resources to support the growing community. A multi-bedroom houseboat was now anchored just far enough offshore to be protected from Infected, and served as a combination headquarters and hospital. The vessel had been found stuck on a sandbar at the mouth of the Po'owaiomahaihai Ditch up near the coastal town of Waimea Town. It had solar panels and compact wind generators providing just enough electricity to provide power for medical instruments, making it a valuable resource for treating survivors and maintaining health of the clearance teams.

They all knew that there weren't enough supplies—yet—to extend the perimeter more than a mile out from the harbor. There were simply too many houses once they got more than three quarters of a mile from the waterfront. They still continued clearance operations but would soon have to stop extending the perimeter. Jackson called it "clearance level Delta." As he explained it, Alpha was absolutely secure and Omega was entirely at the mercy of the Infected. Delta at least meant that infected numbers were reduced and the chances of a surprise attack were low.

They had hoped for more hardware and grocery stores, but past their current perimeter the area was largely residential with no useful retail. On the plus side, southeast of their beachhead was a solar power array for the port, and Mickey Ganz was working with several others—including some new rescues—to isolate the town power grid and bring the port systems online.

Next to the solar array was the start of the coffee plantation, and with guards to protect the workers, they'd started manually harvesting coffee. It was slow, and low yield, because they could only put a dozen people in the field at a time and an equal number on overwatch to protect them from Infected attacks. Many of the people declaring for the Molokai migration joined the harvesting, rationalizing that they would need high quality trade goods.

The National Guard armory was a bit of a disappointment. Apparently, the guardsmen had grabbed all the issue weapons for themselves when civilization fell. However, an unexpected find was a small gunsmith shop, which at least yielded a few more handguns, a couple shotguns, and a high-powered rifle that apparently had just been repaired, but never picked up by their owners. The gunsmith also kept a supply of ammunition for testing the repaired firearms. Given the limitations on ammo sales in the state, he'd apparently been quite stealthy in his acquisition of common calibers. While not *plentiful*, it was still enough to ease worries that people filling the overwatch and security positions would run out.

There was also enough to ensure Bubba would be able to equip his own people with weapons for their voyage. It was time for that to happen and a firm departure date agreed upon.

Six boats would be leaving Hanapepe for Kalaupapa. They were chosen primarily on the basis of fuel, passenger capacity, and ability to sail. The only motor vessels were the Viking 62 *Bubba Truck Mark 3* captained by Tully, the Burger 108 *Simple Gifts* captained by Bubba, and the LCM-8 *Landin'C* captained by a retired merchant mariner named Bernardo Kaimana Esteves, or "Nardo" as he identified himself when he was rescued from his own capsized boat months ago. Two catamarans—

the forty-two-foot private yacht *Hole in the Water*, and a sixty-five-foot Gold Coast tourist cat, *Sunset Gold*—would join them. Bubba's Tayana 37 *Storm Chaser* with Keith Duke at the helm completed their flotilla.

Thirty-six people would set sail with Bubba, while forty-two remained with Jackson Toivo. At least Mamabear and "Gran"— Vanessa Landrum—were accompanying them and were riding on the *Gifts* with Bubba. In fact, Gran had taken over all of the logistics and coordination for the float, surpassing even Mamabear in her organizational skills. The two also handled meal preparation for all the boats, distributing as needed each morning and evening. Bubba was a bit intimidated, but at least he wasn't inclined to start up his own harem. Jon Ko was working as crew on the *Gifts*, as he and Gran had made it clear that they were a couple.

The *Landin'C* was repacked with supplies in the shipping container, two ATVs and a RHIB—a Rigid Hull Inflatable Boat—on the deck, and a dozen fuel barrels. The cargo container was carrying trade goods that Bubba hoped would entice any survivors on Kalaupapa, or any other settlements they might contact. Each of the vessels had been filled with fuel, with *Landin'C* and *Simple Gifts* carrying additional fuel.

Feelings were mixed as to whether the flotilla *wanted* to find more survivors, particularly on the seas. They were always conscious of pirates. Kōkee and Bubba both confirmed finding boats during their expeditions where the occupants had come to a violent end inconsistent with attack by Infected. Nevertheless, they would rescue anyone who needed rescuing, and it would be beneficial to find survivors on land.

That didn't mean Bubba ignored the fact that the flotilla, especially the landing craft with its obvious stocks of goods, was a very tempting target.

With many tears, hugs, and handshakes the group gradually separated into "Bubba's Flotilla" as it was being called, and the "Hanapepe Camp," which would be staying behind. Bubba and Jackson met one last time in the "radio shack" constructed in one of the motor pool buildings at the National Guard armory. A lot of animosity had been put aside after Ku's machinations.

"Keep in touch, haole," Jackson said grumpily.

Bubba grinned. The competitiveness wasn't gone, just suppressed for now. He shook his rival's hand. "Marine band as far as we can, and we'll set up that ham radio antenna when we get there."

One of the most important finds during clearance had been radio equipment. The National Guard armory had military, marine, and amateur band radios, but lacked an antenna mast. Piping and wiring from various hardware and electronic stores had solved that problem, particularly under the supervision of Mickey Ganz, who'd been a machinist's mate on submarines, and hence was nicknamed "Boomer," and Nardo Esteves, who'd been a radioman when he'd first sailed as a merchant marine sailor out of Manila. Given that both of those men would be accompanying the flotilla, they'd stocked the equipment to do the same at Molokai.

In fact, the reason why they were meeting in the communications room was because Jackson had just received word of communication with a group holed up in the old Sandia Labs building at the Pacific Missile Test Range fifteen miles to the northeast, at the westernmost extent of the island.

Bubba laughed and congratulated Jackson on growing his colony. "You're going to gain almost as many people as you're losing, and we haven't even cleared the harbor!" He was going to miss the verbal sparring with the pushy tour captain.

Jackson laughed, briefly, but his face quickly returned to his usual dour expression. "I spoke to Kōkee, too, and I know you have to do what you have to do. The truth is, we need to do *everything* we can if we're going to survive. Keep in mind, though, we're always at your back."

"Is that supposed to make me feel better?" Bubba asked, a smile quirking the corner of his mouth.

"Hmph. Maybe. But if there's problems, if you run into trouble—call us. Especially if you get into a big fight. We'll come show everybody who's boss."

"Me," they both said together.

The two men shook hands, then turned when the young radio operator called out. "Sirs, we have another contact. You two should hear this."

He turned some dials, flipped a switch, and a young female voice came over the radio. "This is Devil Dog Radio coming to you from the Mayport Naval Station in Florida."

"More survivors." Once again, Bubba and Jackson had spoken at the same time. They looked at each other with blank expressions.

"Change your mind?" Jackson asked him.

"Nah, too far away to make a difference to me."

"Okay, Bubba. Well, now we know there's survivors on the mainland. When we meet them, we'll show them what Islanders can do! Go on, get out of my sight."

Bubba tipped his hat, grabbed his cane, and headed for the boat ramp across the street from the baseball stadium.

The voyage to Kalaupapa would be just short of two hundred miles. It was ten miles from Hanapepe Bay to the southernmost point of Kauai, off Poipu Beach. From there, it was seventy-four miles across the Ka'ie'ie Waho Channel separating Kauai and Oahu. Circumnavigating Oahu would add another sixty-five miles. From the Makapu'u Point Lighthouse at the southeastern tip of Oahu, it was forty miles across the Ka'iwi or Molokai Channel to Kalaupapa.

A motor yacht like the *Simple Gifts* or *Bubba Truck* could easily cover the distance in eight hours, but the sailing vessels would be facing a quartering wind. The tourist cat, *Sunset Gold*, with its large sail area meant they could almost keep up with a motor yacht when sailing downwind. Unfortunately, the trade winds blew from east-by-northeast to west-by-southwest, and overall, the flotilla needed to sail east-by-southeast, with the wind thirty degrees off the port bow. Moreover, the flotilla needed to keep pace with their smaller boats, *Hole in the Water*, *Storm Chaser*, and *Landin'C*. While modern boats had autosteering and could sail at night, the lack of civilian maritime "traffic control," proximity of land, and the possibility of encountering derelict ships limited their options to only sailing during daylight hours.

The plan was to sail across the channel to Oahu the first day, and anchor for the night off Kaena Point. They would then take one to two days to slowly sail along the Oahu coast, scouting for resources and survivors, before crossing to Molokai. There was risk, however. Mickey Ganz worried that the suspected resin exchange explosion at Pearl Harbor could have damaged other vessels that would still be leaking toxic materials. Philip Charles's report of the evacuation of Kaneohe gave little hope for survivors or resources without major clearance operations.

Bubba and his captains would have to balance curiosity and inquiry against caution and safety.

CHAPTER NINE

OFF KAENA POINT

We've almost never had an accident.
—Submarine tour operator

The flotilla was approaching Kaena Point on the second day of sailing. They'd gotten a late start the first day, and sailed slowly toward Poipu Beach then beyond, to get a good look—through binoculars—at Lihue, the county seat of Kauai County. They passed Bubba's home port of Nawiliwili but saw only wreckage from boats which had been inexpertly piloted, or on which crew members had turned before the boats could clear the bay. He and Tully had not returned since the day they'd escaped with *Storm Chaser* and *Bubba Truck*, and from what they could see, that had been the right decision.

There was discussion about whether it was worth checking out the navigable portions of Huleia Stream, and the head of Nawiliwili Bay, or even to check out the Wailua River, up north, under the supposition that refugees might have been able to escape the city and flee upriver. In the end, Bubba just radioed the information back to Jackson, who promised to send one of his boats experienced in shoreside scavenging to check it out after they recovered the survivors from Barking Sands.

The extra time and distance ate up the rest of the day, so the flotilla sailed away from Lihue and anchored off Kawelikoa Point, with the ridge of land forming the point between the boats and the wind. The ships had to anchor away from the rocky shore and allow distance between boats, but they were still able to cluster enough that

Mamabear, Gran, and their team of cooks could prepare a meal for the whole group using the galley on the *Simple Gifts*. It was not a completely protected anchorage, and they needed to distribute food via the inflatable motorboats, but it was safe enough for the time being, and they'd be able to make the crossing to Oahu by the next day.

The next morning, the flotilla spread out and raised sail where they could. The motor yachts, *Bubba Truck* and *Simple Gifts*, were in the center of the formation, taking lead and trailing positions, respectively to better match speed with the sailing vessels. *Hole in the Water* was the smallest and slowest of the catamarans, so it shared the lead, slightly ahead and to port of *Bubba Truck* to set the speed for the flotilla. Trailing behind both boats was the large tourist cat *Sunset Gold* on the starboard side of the flotilla. Trailing on the port was *Storm Chaser*. *Landin'C*, with its valuable cargo rode in the center of the formation. Since *Simple Gifts* was the largest boat, with the combination of powerful engines, sophisticated electronics, and plentiful storage, its position in the rear of the flotilla allowed them to both guard and coordinate the flotilla as a whole.

At any given time, inflatables from the *Gifts*, *Truck*, and *Gold* might be in the water, transferring personnel, meals, or supplies between the boats. The six boats required almost thirty crew to man the sails, bridge, and engines. Each had at least one trained sailor, but the others had mainly been trained after they were rescued from the ocean of Kauai. The "passengers"—that is, people not originally trained in maritime operations—had all been trained to handle basic functions before they left. They were distributed according to age and ability, but no one was present who didn't have a job contributing to the operation, both afloat and once they reached their destination. The ages also ranged from a boy of eight who had been the only survivor on a family sailboat, to Bubba and Mamabear, at age sixty-five and sixty-eight, respectively. There were also four teens who had worked tourist boats, and were currently tasked as lookouts.

One of those teens, Yori Hamasaki, was currently standing beside Bubba on the flybridge of the *Gifts*, keeping an eye on the flotilla and the open ocean around them. "Land, about ten miles ahead, sir."

Bubba took the binoculars from Yori and looked for himself. This was likely Kaena Point, the northwesternmost point of Oahu. He handed the binoculars back and keyed the intercom. "Kiwi. Radio the other captains, we're going to reduce sail and slow our approach."

David Keith "Kiwi" Wells had been a lawyer visiting Kauai for a convention when H7D3 caused the airports to be closed. Finding it impossible to return to his native New Zealand, he'd made it to Nawiliwili where he'd been unsuccessful in buying a boat for himself. He'd even approached Bubba in an attempt to buy *Storm Chaser*, but Bubba refused to sell. When Kiwi explained that he'd owned both sailing and motor yachts, and even raced in an America's Cup qualifier, Bubba decided to give him a trial, and if he was as skilled as he said, he'd take him with him as he left Lihue for a safer port. Even though no such "safe port" had been found, Kiwi had remained and was now the "captain" of the *Simple Gifts*, with Bubba coordinating the flotilla.

"Radar confirms Kaena Point ten degrees off the port bow, eight miles ahead," Kiwi responded. "Do you want me to call a halt? Or just slow to half?"

Bubba thought on it a moment. The course would bring them off the leeward side of Kaena Point, famous for being the site of the radar installation that had actually detected, but misidentified, the Japanese planes that attacked Pearl Harbor on December 7, 1941. "Any surface contacts?"

"A lot of clutter, but nothing moving."

"Okay, clutter's expected, but could be hazardous. Let's have everyone drop sail and come to a stop about five miles off the Point. The MVs can explore a bit before we decide on a course."

"Aye aye, Commodore. Depth finder says we'll likely have to close to within a mile to anchor off the western coastline, although we likely have two miles along the North Shore."

"Got it. We'll use engines for station keeping until we check things out, then we can find an anchorage for the night."

"Acknowledged."

A moment later, Bubba heard the report echoed over the radio, then the responses of five captains as they confirmed the order. They'd no sooner finished the roll call when *Hole in the Water* reported a sighting in the water ahead. He wasn't too surprised—after all, Kiwi had reported scattered debris. That supposition was challenged a moment later.

"What the hell is that?" came Tully's voice over the radio. "A capsized boat?" He heard Tully talking to Boomer, who'd gone over to *Bubba Truck* to check out a possible engine problem.

It took a few more moments before Mickey's voice came back over the radio. "Commodore, that's a submarine. It's got a long, white rounded hull, with what looks like a conning tower on one end. It's little more than a cover to keep water from entering the passenger hatch and has a pretty characteristic shape."

"A submarine? Navy?"

"Nope, civilian. It's one of those Lemuria subs that operate off the tourist resorts of Waikiki, Lahaina, Kona..."

"What's it doing out here?"

"Drifting, most likely. They have limited range, being battery operated. They can dive and maneuver in circles, but they have to be towed out to their operating area, and passengers come out on ferries."

"Huh. Okay, since the flotilla is slowing, Boomer, you can take a RHIB over to take a look."

"No can do on the RHIB, Bubba, it's almost back to you with young Dalia. She's been assisting me and I sent her back for some more tools."

"Send the *Truck*'s dinghy, then."

"Faster for us to go," came Tully's voice again. "Plus, we'll have a better viewing angle."

And they'll *have a worse shooting angle, too,* Bubba thought, filling in what Tully was deliberately *not* saying over an open radio.

"Understood. Increase speed and break formation to go take a look. *Hole in the Water*, wait for *Truck* to cross your bow, then angle to starboard and take the lead. All boats, reduce sail and speed, but don't come to a stop. I've got a bad feeling about this, and I want everyone to maintain the ability to maneuver." Bubba had been tempted to sign off with something like "*Simple Gifts*, out," but he, personally, wasn't commanding his own boat, it was more of a flagship. "Commodore out," while appropriate, just wasn't his style. "Bubba out" was his style, but seemed somehow inappropriate, like he was avoiding responsibility for the flotilla. His growing unease told him that the responsibility would soon become relevant.

With the *Bubba Truck* headed to their port side, Bubba wanted to make sure they didn't ignore their starboard. He told Yori to keep an eye out on that side, since they were best situated to detect a vessel coming up from the stern or starboard. The thirteen-year-old looked back at him with worry, but Bubba clapped him on the shoulder. "You've got younger eyes than I do. I'm headed down to the enclosed bridge to keep an eye on the radar."

The boy gulped but nodded his head. Once Bubba started down to the lower deck, Yori shifted to be able to cover a wider arc and raised the binocs to start scanning the sea.

He's a good kid. It's my job to make sure he has a future, so let's just hope my gut is wrong, Bubba thought as he descended the ladder.

As he entered the darkened pilothouse, his vision took a few moments to adapt from the full sun of the flybridge. Bubba took off his sunglasses and placed them in the pocket of his white linen camp shirt. His regular glasses hung from a gold chain around his neck, and the transition helped speed up the adaptation to the darkened bridge. Heavy tint and polarized glass on the windows made it easier to read instruments, particularly the surface and weather radar sets, and reduced the moving reflections off the surface of the water. He moved over beside Kiwi and looked at the radar.

"Anything out of the ordinary?"

"Lots of small returns," Kiwi told him, but pointed to two particular spots. "Larger returns well to port and to starboard, but they aren't moving."

"Not moving as in drifting? Or not moving as in dead in the water and holding position?"

"Uh. Ouch. I didn't think of that." Kiwi reached for the console displaying the radar image and pulled open a drawer with a keyboard. A few keystrokes brought up a menu onscreen, and he chose a function to replay the past few minutes of radar imaging. He frowned and rapped his knuckles against his bald head. "They aren't drifting."

"Yeah. They're waiting. Hand me the mic."

"Private or public?" Kiwi asked.

"Hmm, public will spook whoever it is, but it might make them act prematurely. Not everyone has the encrypted side band, though, so a private hail won't reach all boats. Let's keep it public for now."

Kiwi nodded, handed Bubba the microphone for the marine band, and checked the broadcast channel.

"All boats, be aware we have surface contacts to port and starboard. Too large for buoys, too far out for dive platforms, but they're fixed in position."

Bubba released the talk button and waited. He heard a number of responses, from simple clicks to brief bursts of static. There were five of them, meaning each of the other captains had acknowledged, without giving away more information.

"That's got them spooked, look." Kiwi pointed to the radar. Both of the targets had started moving. The one to southwest was clearly a boat, but the one to the northeast seemed too small, or at least too low to the water. As they watched, the latter target began to speed up.

"It's fast. Too big for a RHIB or even a Jet Ski, but still really small."

The radio crackled again, but this time a voice accompanied the noise. "*Simple Gifts*, this is *Bubba Truck*. It's definitely a tourist submarine. Boomer says it's the *Lemuria XIV* out of Waikiki. There's a guy on deck and he's waving."

"Approach with caution, *Truck*."

"Roger that, *Gifts*. He's . . . wait . . . he touched his ear and is now reaching for something . . . Oh shit, veer off! Veer off, Boomer, he's shooting at us."

Bubba could see *Bubba Truck* turning to port, which was going to bring him right into the path of the fast mover.

It was an ambush, alright.

CHAPTER TEN

PIRATES!

> Every normal man must be tempted, at times, to spit on his
> hands, hoist the black flag, and begin slitting throats.
> —H.L. Mencken

"Ah! Now he's shooting at *us*!" Philip "Flip" Charles called from *Hole in the Water*.

"Flip, turn ninety degrees to starboard, make your course two-two-five degrees and raise sail. You'll be running downwind and can get some speed up. Break for open water and get clear," Bubba told him.

"And if there's more of them out here?"

"We know there's more, but you're the smallest, and at the moment, you've got the chance to be fastest. If you can stay clear, you can circle around behind."

"Coasties don't run, Bubba."

"You're not running, *Hole*, you're repositioning. Implement Bird Protocol."

A laugh came over the radio. "Understood, Bubba."

While it was true that the forty-two-foot Leopard catamaran was small, it was also fast. Turning downwind with full sail would allow it to quickly accelerate, then turn northward and sail across the wind to quickly come up behind the flotilla. As long as they didn't turn into the wind and lose headway, their speed would be an advantage. They also had an ace up their sleeve.

"Bird Protocol" referred to David "Birdy" Birdsall, who had earned

165

top marks in shooting during his Army days. Several highly successful business decisions had left him with the time and money to collect firearms, continue training, and hunt. He'd come to Hawaii to hunt wild boar, and had participated in numerous organized hunts on Molokai, the Big Island, and had even been invited to hunt on Ni'ihau. He'd been waiting on Kauai for the permit to come through when the Haole Flu hit.

To skirt state regulations on "assault weapons," Birdsall had only brought his "curio and relic" rifles: an M1903A4 Springfield and M1D Garand. Both models had been official U.S. Army designs, seeing use in both World Wars, Korea, and Vietnam. They were both also more than fifty years old, qualifying them as collector's pieces under Title 18 of the United States Code, chapter 54. That didn't stop them from being powerful and effective, both using the ubiquitous .30-06 cartridge, and both also capable of being used as sniper rifles with the appropriate optics.

Birdy was their sniper, and it was Flip's job to get the *Hole* and Birdy into position to fight back against pirates.

Bubba had designated the surface target to the northeast—directly to port relative to the flotilla's position—as Bogey One. It was moving fast, much faster than such a small boat should be able to do in the open sea. "*Bubba Truck*, do you have eyes on Bogey One, yet?"

"Just getting that now, Commodore," Boomer's voice came back. "Thirty-ish feet, low gunwales, central pilothouse with a cloth cover all the way across the beam. I'm seeing two barrels sticking out of a cupola up front, and an obvious pintle-mounted weapon in the stern. Damn. That looks like..."

There was the sound of two muffled voices speaking in the background. Micky and Tully were likely discussing the identity of the craft.

Boomer came back on the radio. "Bubba, it looks like a PBR—patrol boat, riverine—a brown-water navy boat from Vietnam."

"PBR? That's got to be unstable as hell on open water."

"I know, right? It's bouncing around like a sonuvabitch, but it's pretty damned fast. Those things had jets, back before jets were popular."

"Oh? Ah, yes, because shallow rivers could have stuff that would foul the propellers. You know, I heard of a collector who bought several and had the engines upgraded with modern impellers. He used them for racing, but I never heard of one operating in anything rougher than the Intracoastal Waterway."

"Right, plus the only navigable rivers in Hawaii are on Kauai. Our problem now is those twin fifties in the bow. No idea if they are operable or have the ammo, but . . ." There was the sound of breaking glass. "Okay, can confirm, at least one of the fifties in the bow is operable *and* has ammo."

"Break off and let Bird Protocol take care of it."

"Breaking off now."

On the radar, Bubba could see *Bubba Truck* turn starboard, to allow the souped-up river boat to pass it to port. With the speed of the two, relative to each other, the encounter would be extremely short and at the closest approach, *Truck* would be too easy to hit with the machine guns on the PBR. *Truck's* turn started to reverse back to port, and it looked like they planned to come back around and chase the PBR.

Yori yelled down from the flybridge, "Smoke coming from *Bubba Truck*. Something got hit."

"*Bubba Truck*, report status," Bubba called on the radio. The radar now showed that boat's turning radius opening up and slowing down. The radar return for the PBR had also turned slightly. Whereas it had been heading for *Hole in the Water's* former position within the flotilla, it was now headed for *Simple Gifts*.

"We got shot up, and it's bad," Tully radioed. There was a grunt, and a hint of strain in his voice before he continued. "I've got some glass in my face, and a slug in my upper arm. Boomer got grazed, by the same ricochet—probably why I'm still standing, but that's not the big problem. The port side took a long burst, and we've lost that engine. We're listing and dragging on that side. We got pulled to port before I got the starboard engine throttled back. I'm going to continue this turn and follow that bastard. I'll ram him if I have to."

"I hear you, Tully. I take it Boomer went down to check the engine?"

"Yes, he suspects an oil line got hit, and he's going to try to patch it if he can and get us some power back. We're no good to you running on one leg."

"Understood, Truck. Let me know your status once Mickey reports back."

"One more important piece of info, the front twin-fifty is firing slow, likely only one barrel. No one's at the rear fifty, but it's got a big mother of a tube slung underneath. It's the size of an M-88."

"Oh heavenly...they've slung a mortar? I thought that was a Coastie myth?"

"Boomer says it's real, he met the guys that did it, and of course bubbleheads have to try *everything* so he says his boat got one to work, too."

"Are they using it?"

"Not yet."

"Small favors. Stay with us, Tully. I've got to pay attention to the starboard side, now. Bogey Two's closing in."

"Looks like a tug, sir," Yori shouted down a minute later.

"Well, that would explain how they got the submarine out here," Bubba muttered to himself.

"It's not as fast as the PBR," Kiwi told him, motioning to the radar. "Bigger, though."

"I should think so. Even if it's a brown-water tug, it would have a deeper draft and wider beam to support powerful engines. Its low speed could be a ruse. What's its course?"

Kiwi pulled out the keyboard and tapped in a few commands. The billionaire who'd owned *Simple Gifts* had clearly insisted on the best electronics, and likely owned the company, since he'd noted the logo on the instrument panel was also engraved on glasses and plates in the galley, as well as embroidered on linens and personal items.

Lines extended forward from each return on the screen, clearly extrapolated from the past several minutes of radar scanning. The flotilla had only short lines extending forward. The exceptions were *Bubba Truck*, which had a wide cone, likely because of the recent course changes, and *Hole in the Water*, which was picking up speed as it rapidly moved to the southwest. The tourist sub was static, and the two bogeys had long lines extending in front of them.

Simple Gifts was at the center of the plot, with *Landin'C* slightly ahead and to port. The line extending from Bogey Two was aimed right between the two craft.

"As I thought. They're zeroed in on the LCM. Probably wondering what cargo we're protecting and treating us like a convoy. They probably figure we're the real threat, and the others are just a screen. Either they had some passive spotters out, or they've been trailing us."

"Or they had a more powerful radar."

"Not likely, Kiwi. I used to work with this stuff when I was a landlubber. I don't think they'd have better range unless they had a taller mast, and from the size of that tug, they don't."

"Ah. Yes. I see. I take it you plan to intercept."

"Well, they're going to have to work harder to get our landing craft. Increase speed to fifteen knots and turn to starboard as soon as we're clear of the 'C. Tell Nardo to reverse until we're past, then swing to port behind us."

"...and *Storm Chaser*?"

"There's not much they can do, there's no armaments at all on board. If they run too fast to port, they risk the PBR; running starboard risks being in the path of the tug. Duke's greatest advantage is maneuverability, so tell him to open the distance. If we end up with people in the water, he's the best bet for recovery." Bubba watched as Kiwi made a couple of annotations on the radar glass with a wax pencil. "I'm heading back up to relieve Yori. Women and children go to the salon. I'll handle lookout and radio from the flybridge."

As Bubba headed back to the ladder, Kiwi started relaying the commands to the rest of the flotilla. Relieving the teen lookout, Bubba focused his attention on Bogey Two. As reported, it was an oceangoing tug, typically used to position vessels in harbors. He could read the name on the side of the wheelhouse—*Nonee*—and recognized it from an article regarding sale of the tug by a well-known pineapple company. He didn't recall the specifics, but it would be consistent with use by the submarine tour company.

The tug had a tall pilothouse up front, and low afterdeck with winches and pulleys dangling from spars jutting over the side and stern. There were several ten-foot cylinders on the aft deck, and something was being towed along one side from a boom. He could see a small wake where the cable met the water, and again about eight to ten feet behind. There were men standing on the fore- and afterdecks holding guns, and with the change in the *Gifts*' course, they were rapidly closing.

He didn't have long to think about what they could be towing, since a panicked voice came of the radio. "Bogey One is firing something in the air!" He recognized the voice as being Leilani "Lily" Apikalia, herself a tour boat captain, who was currently assisting Duke on the *Storm Chaser*, now the ship with the best view of the onrushing PBR.

"Lily, are they firing at you?" Bubba asked.

"No, they're firing back at the *Bubba Truck*. Something going up in the air, then landing with a big splash and explosion. Duke's in the bow trying to get a good look and trying to see if he can rig a harpoon or something. That little boat is all over the place, though. Not shooting or driving straight."

"That's the mortar, then. A river boat's just not stable on sea, and doubly so with the speed they're going." He paused a moment, so that the other captains would know he was switching focus. "Tully. How's it looking?"

"Not good," came Tully's voice. "Boomer's down below working on getting hydraulic pressure back in the port engine. He just got it patched and we had a near miss off the bow and it blew out again. They're close to having our range, but as Lily said, it's a crapshoot whether the deck's going to pitch under them and throw them off target. If they get us it won't be pretty."

"Get your noncombatants off. Put them in the dinghy and *Storm Chaser* can swing out and pick them up." Bubba paused again. "Lily? Duke?"

"Understood, Bubba," replied Lily. "*Storm Chaser* is turning north for pickup."

"Good, now I have to get back to—"

"FISH IN THE WATER!"

"What?" Bubba was confused. *Fish?* The voice was Nardo on *Landin'C*. He wouldn't be talking about... "Oh, crap. *Torpedo!* Brace for impact!"

A trail of white extended from the side of the tug toward *Simple Gifts*. The yacht was directly in line with the oncoming "fish."

"Evasive—"

"Not fast enough, Bubba," Kiwi interrupted. "The only thing to do is pray."

Bubba wondered if the Old Gods would hear a prayer from a lapsed Catholic/Wiccan. Perhaps Asatru, then; the Vikings would understand this situation. He didn't have long to contemplate his fate as a loud *clang* sounded and a sharp vibration rang through the boat.

"What was that?"

"A dud," came a new voice on the radio. James "Genghis" Young was a retired military historian, assisting Nardo on the LCM. "Probably a Mark Forty-six they jury rigged. Odd that they towed it, though, that's dangerous. A Mark Forty-six is designed to be launched off a deck or dropped from the air."

"Where would they get torpedoes? Pearl?"

"Unlikely. If something went boom, there would have been damage to the resupply stores. There's a bunch of old munitions bunkers uphill from Waianae, though."

"Oh, lovely. So, they've likely got more."

"Yes, but they'll have to rig them, first. Look lively, though, you're about to have company."

"Joy."

CHAPTER ELEVEN

DAMAGE CONTROL

"Observe, orient, decide, act" beats "Jury rig, fail, react, repeat"
every time.   —P. Charles, former Coastie

The next few minutes were chaotic, and Bubba realized that this was
what was referred to as "the fog of battle." Multiple voices came over
the radio, telling of the encounters between the PBR and *Bubba Truck*.
Tully radioed back that three of his crew were headed west in the
dinghy to meet up with the *Storm Chaser*. Meanwhile, *Storm Chaser*
reported that it could see the dinghy and was slowing to intercept. *Hole
in the Water* reported its position only by radio clicks—three fast
clicks, then one, two or three slow clicks for "clear," "circling," and
"closing," respectively. Meanwhile, the PBR continued to fire its mortar,
now swinging it, firing off rounds almost continuously toward *Truck*.

The starboard engagement certainly wasn't quiet, either. Shooters
on the deck of the *Nonee* shot out windows on the *Sunset Gold* in
passing and were now shooting at *Simple Gifts*. The tug wasn't coming
in a straight line, changing heading each time *Gifts* changed. The yacht
was trying to keep itself between *Nonee* and *Landin'C*, while the tug
was trying to counter Kiwi's movements to get around them to
threaten the LCM.

Despite all the maneuvering, the tug and yacht were about to pass
each other. At least they wouldn't get a clear shot at the landing craft,
since Nardo was doing his best to keep *Landin'C* behind *Gifts*, and
Genghis was working on their own surprise. The gunmen on the tug

deck were now shooting at the big yacht, and Bubba could hear breaking glass and *ping*s as rifle rounds hit his boat.

"Get everyone down below. You need to be belowdecks," Bubba shouted through the hatch to the enclosed bridge. He heard Kiwi relay the order down to the salon, and Mamabear's acknowledgment. Jon Ko shouted back up to ask if he was needed, but Bubba really didn't want any more targets where they could be hit directly or by ricochet.

The two boats passed, and the flurry of shots died down. Bubba could see two men on the tug's aft deck lifting a tubular object up over the gunwale with a winch. Another man was pulling something out of a long green case on the deck. He tried to see what the item was but could only catch glimpses as people moved back and forth across his line of sight.

"Genghis, it looks like they're rigging another torpedo. I also see someone pulling out a thinner tube, about four feet, maybe a bit more. It's also about four to five inches in diameter."

"Hmm, torp first. Are they setting up on the deck, or pulling out the torpedo?"

"They've pulled it out and have it attached to a boom."

"Do they have a hatch cover open behind the head? Attaching wires?"

"Yes, that's exactly what they're doing. It's dangling from the boom while someone is fiddling with the side, about five inches behind the head. By the way, it's eight feet long, dark green with red at the head, and with four short fins at the back."

"First guess was correct, then, that sure sounds like a Mark Forty-six. Also, they're rigging for sea launch, just like the other one. That's foolish, and we shouldn't interrupt the enemy while they're in the process of making a fatal mistake. It's amazing they got the first one to launch. Doing it during battle is asking for a malf."

"So, we have time?"

"Yeah. Tell me about the other weapon. Is it also dark green? Pistol grip and scope at the midpoint?"

"That's right. Looks like . . . a bazooka?"

"Not quite, but close. It's a recoilless rifle most likely. Given the vintage of the torps, I'd say M67, they're both Vietnam era, and that's consistent with the Waianae bunkers. Our pirates stumbled into vintage MilSurp. There's a reason those bunkers are off-limits, though. EODs won't go in there, and there's only so many bomb disposal robots to go around. That whole complex is a powder keg, and if these idiots haven't already lost half their number, it's only a matter of time."

"Should I worry?"

"Yes, the M67 launches a six-pound, three-and-a-half-inch round designed for taking out tanks. They don't want what's on our ships, they want to threaten us into giving them the landing craft."

"Well, we can't have that, Genghis. Get your surprise ready, and we'll set them up for you."

"Ready in three more minutes, Bubba."

Genghis planned a very rude surprise for the pirates. He was up on top of the container in *Landin'C* with a few items from David Birdsall's curio and relic collection. Along with his "antique" M1 Garand, Birdy had brought an M7 grenade adapter with him.

Birdy told him it'd been an accident, and frankly, was surprised that no one had noticed it when the gun case was inspected on arrival. The rifle, adapter, original scope, and all of the vintage WWII and Korean War paraphernalia had been on display at a competition for Garand collectors the month before traveling to Hawaii. All of the components were still in the secured case, and it never occurred to the collector that the parts were still there. It didn't occur to the inspectors, either. If there had been someone familiar with collectible firearms, they might have recognized the threaded cylinder with three springlike prongs... but Genghis had yet to meet a TSA inspector who was truly knowledgeable about guns. If it wasn't on the specific list of banned items, they tended to ignore it.

Now, with Birdy's Garand, the M7 adapter, some grenades from the NG Armory, and special blank rifle rounds Birdy made in the gunsmith's shop back on Kauai, Genghis was ready to fight back against the pirates. Nardo and Kiwi had been playing a game of keep-away, but now his perch on top of the shipping container on the deck of the LCM-8 was his own private payback nest.

Just so long as the grenade doesn't go off when ejected from the rifle, he thought. He then keyed his portable marine handset twice, paused, then twice again.

꩜

"*Landin'C* is ready," Kiwi called up from below.

"I heard," Bubba replied. "You can open the gap a bit and let Bogey Two see them. Bogey One is now inside the formation as well."

"*Bubba Truck* has also picked up speed. It's likely that Boomer got their port engine fixed."

"Affirmative. However, with only Tully and Boomer aboard, they might not have a chance to radio."

"Didn't Tully say he was going to try to ram them?"

"He said it, but Bogey One has a considerable lead." Bubba debated whether to stay in position to lay eyes on the formation or descend to the enclosed bridge where he could watch it all play out on the radar. Viewing the radar won out, and he descended the ladder onto the bridge. There wasn't much he could do up top, and he could only look in one direction at a time whereas the radar would show him the whole layout at once.

Once in the darkened interior, he looked at the radar. Bogey Two was just about to clear the stern of *Simple Gifts*, which would give them a direct view of the landing craft. It would also give Genghis a direct view of the pirates. Bogey One was still ahead of *Bubba Truck*, headed directly for *Landin'C*. *Storm Chaser* was now well to the north and had stopped as it picked up the dinghy from *Truck*. *Sunset Gold* had turned downwind, to south, to open up the area around *Simple Gifts* and *Landin'C*. The screen was zoomed in to focus on the action near *Gifts*, so the final boat was right on the edge of the formation. *Hole in the Water* was reentering the fray from the southwest and was likewise about to come into view by the tug.

The only problem with being inside was that Bubba couldn't see the surface action. With the bogeys approaching so close to his boats, he really needed to see what was happening on the decks of the pirate's boats.

"You just got here," complained Kiwi as Bubba went back to the ladder. He flashed the captain a grin of apology, and quickly headed back topside, where he picked up the binoculars and looked out at the tug.

The man with the M67 was now up and starting to take aim to the stern in an attempt to shoot at *Simple Gifts*. Despite the lack of return fire, they still saw the large yacht as the biggest threat—or prize.

Bubba gave a feral grin at the lesson the pirates were about to learn. He could see Genghis lying prone atop the shipping container on

Landin'C, and there was brief flash of reflection from Birdy sprawled out on the tarp that stretched between pontoons on the bow of *Hole*. His range to Bogey One was actually shorter,

There was the sound like a sharp *crack*, followed by three more, and the PBR started to jerk. The sudden movement enabled the mortar to make a lucky shot, and an explosion bloomed on the foredeck of *Bubba Truck*.

At nearly the same moment, Genghis launched his first grenade, and the puff of black smoke beside the tug's wheelhouse must have spooked the pirate captain into a sudden movement, because two things happened at once: the swinging torpedo hit the gunwale and swung free, and the M67 gunner staggered as he was lining up a shot on *Gifts*. The lurch caused him to pull the trigger prematurely, and the armor-penetrating projectile missed its target, splashing into the sea off the starboard aft side of the yacht.

The miss wasn't the worst consequence, however. There was a chortling over the radio as Genghis keyed his handset. "That happened in 'Nam, a lot, they said. The idiot didn't check his backblast area." In order to reduce recoil, the rear of the M67 was open, allowing the exhaust, or backblast, of the rocket-propelled projectile to exit out the back. The gunner had been standing directly behind the wheelhouse, facing portside aft. Even without the sudden stumble, his backblast would have taken out two of three of the men working on the torpedo. As it was, they got lucky, and the rocket exhaust hit the wheelhouse, instead, causing all the windows to break, and a fire to start in the interior.

The torp handlers weren't completely spared, however, since the impact caused the wires to spark, igniting its propylene glycol dinitrate fuel. The torpedo swung around by a single point of its harness, spraying exhaust on all three of the pirates. The torp then swung out, breaking its tether, and dropping into the ocean.

"*Fish in the water!*" Bubba yelled into the radio. "Bogey Two fish is *live* and in the water!"

"What's the target?" Tully radioed back. The torp had been pointed ahead, and on the tug's starboard side, which meant he was the likely target. On the other hand, the sportfisher had been hit by a second lucky—or unlucky, depending on point of view—mortar round, and was slowing down, with smoke bellowing from the portside vents.

"Heading is"—Bubba checked the flybridge compass—"five degrees true."

"That's right for us." Tully sighed. "I can't maneuver worth a damn. Boomer's injured, and port engine is completely out."

Bubba looked for options. "Um, Tully, sit tight," he said in an odd tone. The torpedo wake was five degrees off due north. Tully, Boomer, and *Bubba Truck* were due north, not on the direct path of the torpedo, and it passed the stricken boat.

Headed directly for Bogey One.

This Mark 46, it seemed, was not a dud. Moreover, there appeared to be a considerable stock of flammables on the small boat. The explosion, and secondary explosions, almost spread to *Bubba Truck*, but that boat was rapidly falling behind the fast mover.

One bogey down.

Bubba's attention turned to Bogey Two. The fires on deck had spread, and flames started to appear near the tubes that might still contain torpedoes. Genghis launched a couple more grenades, one of which landed on deck, but then his gun apparently jammed. Birdy took four more shots, picking off the one remaining man standing on deck, then put three more through the windows of the pilothouse.

Bubba keyed the mic again. "*Hole in the Water*, *Landin'C*, get clear."

Flip turned to the north and headed for *Bubba Truck* to see if they could render aid. Nardo turned south and ran the throttles up on the landing craft's powerful engines. They had pulled up even with *Simple Gifts* when a large explosion lit the deck of the tugboat.

Bubba felt a sting on his cheek and put his hand up to touch it. His fingertips came away wet, and he pulled his hand back to look at them. Blood. Whether a piece of the tug or shrapnel from exploding ordnance, he'd have his own memento of the day.

Both of the pirate vessels were now flaming wrecks. A few survivors jumped off the PBR, but there were no survivors from the tug. That just left the shooter on the sub, but frankly, with no support ship to move it or relieve anyone aboard, he wasn't going anywhere, and was no longer a threat. He was a problem that could wait for later.

Bubba looked down at *Landin'C* and noticed that Genghis was no longer sprawled across the top of the shipping container. On the other hand, the rifle and a couple of grenades in a bandolier were still there.

"Nardo? Where's Genghis?"

"Mr. Young? He atop big box."

"Ah, no, he's not there. I haven't seen him since you made that sharp turn to get clear of the explosion on Bogey Two."

"He not? Oh, oh!" The merchant mariner started to swear in Portuguese.

Bubba sighed and made the announcement. "Man overboard. Send the 'Zod to the LCM's previous position and please pull Professor Young out of the water."

CHAPTER TWELVE

RECOVERY

I'd have succeeded, too, if it wasn't for those meddling British.
—Edward Teach, aka "Blackbeard"

The flotilla had won the day, but at a cost. Two people had been grazed by gunfire, and several more had suffered cuts when the pirates' guns had broken glass on the various boats. The *Bubba Truck* was a total loss. In addition to the machine-gun fire that had caused the original damage to the port engine, the mortar rounds had destroyed the foredeck, which meant that most of the cabins had been trashed. One final round in the fishing cockpit had cost them the port engine for good. It had also cost them Mickey Ganz.

Tully had been pulled out of the water by *Storm Chaser*, having taken a round in his thigh, and a through-and-through in his upper arm. Gran and Flip had worked on him to remove the bullet from his leg and ensure there was no blood vessel damage in the arm. He'd live, but would walk with a limp, and there was a question whether nerve damage would cost him the use of the arm—that is, if infection didn't take him first. Of course, Tully claimed that he'd fight off infection by sterilizing it with alcohol—Tullamore Dew, to be precise. He wouldn't be captaining a boat for a while.

Of James Young, there was no sign.

"I thought he was supposed to be some rock star swimmer at the Point?" Flip had asked when they finally called off the search.

"No, he said he swim like rock," Nardo responded.

The flotilla, now five vessels, sailed south to anchor off Keawaula Beach, leaving the wreckage of three boats behind. There was also one drifting tourist sub, its lone passenger having abandoned it to attempt to swim to shore.

The flotilla spent the rest of the day licking their wounds and trying to figure out what they would do next. Bubba sat with the group he'd come to call his advisors: Mamabear, Gran, Jon Ko. Kiwi was taking the place of Tully—who was sleeping—representing the boat captains. The group was missing, and mourning, Boomer, and Bubba had not yet figured out who could replace the endlessly inventive former submariner.

Of almost as great a concern was the loss of a boat. They still had plenty of capacity to carry their now thirty-four people, but they'd lost some of the diversity in type and function. They'd been told that Kalaupapa had no functioning motor vessels, nor had Kōkee mentioned any sailing vessels. *Simple Gifts* was too big for fishing close to shore, even if it was technically a sportfishing yacht. *Storm Chaser* was a good utility workboat, and the catamarans were merely adequate as fishing platforms. Fishing for big-game fish that would feed a whole colony required a motor vessel the size of *Bubba Truck*. The five vessels also represented a significant portion of the working long-ranged vessels from Kamalino and Kauai, although Jackson had hopes of clearing, repairing, and reactivating several of the boats still at Port Allen. They'd accepted the fact that they might lose or break a boat, leaving them short unless they salvaged one and made it seaworthy again. Unfortunately, they'd counted on having Boomer to do the repairs; his absence felt like a great hole in their hearts and in their capabilities.

"We have to push on. The survivors on Kalaupapa won't last on their own. We are as critical to their survival as much as they are critical to ours," Mamabear told Bubba.

Bubba didn't answer right away. He was sunk in the depression of what-might-have-beens and what he could've done better. Jon Ko reached out and placed a hand on his shoulder. Bubba hadn't really known the man before. Ko had been on Jackson Toivo's clearance teams, but after rescuing Gran he supported the prospect of moving to a place where they could farm and grow their own food. His deepening relationship with Gran cemented that feeling, and he proved to be a fast learner and hard worker when it came to the boats.

Ko had been a storeowner on Kauai, with no unique skills except for knowing and understanding people. In this moment, he knew what Bubba needed. "None of it is on you. Look, you cannot second-guess this. I was managing the store late one night when some kids came in and decided to rob me. I had a teenaged clerk who refused to cooperate, so they shot and killed him. I grabbed a two-by-four and ran after them. As they ran away from me, I could hear the other kids yelling at the one who'd pulled the trigger. We didn't get robbed that night, except for a twenty-year-old boy robbed of his future. I blamed myself, but after a considerable amount of time and grief counseling came to understand that it was not my fault. It was the fault of the kid who pulled the trigger. It was the fault of four boys who decided to rob a convenience store. They were eventually caught and sentenced, one for murder and three for manslaughter. After the trial I had to decide how to forgive myself even if I could never forgive them.

"It's a hard lesson, Bubba, but this is on the pirates, not on you," Ko concluded.

"So, what do you want to do, Bubba?" Kiwi asked. "Push on or go back?"

Bubba thought for a while. "We stay the night. Everyone needs to set their anchors and we can run lines between boats if we need to. Have everyone come over to *Simple Gifts* for a meal. Mamabear and Gran, it doesn't have to be fancy, but we should have a meal together. Then, in the morning, we push on."

It was a solemn evening meal. The galley on *Simple Gifts* had an oven large enough to bake bread, and they'd scavenged flour and yeast in Eleele before sailing. Gran had also set aside a carton of Spam they'd found in the storeroom of a grocery store in Hanapepe. While the front of the store had been well picked over, the storeroom had not. They'd found a treasure trove of canned and packaged good: canned meat, vegetables, fruit, crackers, grains, and other goods. Thus, the meal of remembrance consisted of fried Spam sandwiches, a treat for the native Hawaiians and curiosity to the haoles who had joined the group.

It was also something of a joke pertaining to Professor Young, who'd claimed never to have tasted Spam; whereas Boomer had mentioned he'd had it all too often in the Navy and never wanted to see it again. When Tully told that story, accompanied by a ration of whiskey, it was enough to lighten the mood to the point where the group could tell jokes and stories and celebrate the lives of the two lost friends. After the meal and wake, everyone returned to their respective boats.

Bubba went up to the flybridge and sat watching the sun set and light up the nearby shoreline. By day they'd seen the usual sights associated with the fall of civilization: burned-out buildings, crashed cars, and trash everywhere. In the gathering twilight, he could see a few flickering lights of cooking fires on the slopes and ridges of the Waianae mountain range. At least one of those lights appeared to be up on top of Kaena Point near the old radar tracking station, and a couple more were down the coast toward the towns of Makaha and Waianae.

Campfires or cooking fires were a risk these days. The alternative was cold, raw meals, but at night, the lights could attract Infected. Even now, the smell of cooking food risked doing the same. However, those lights would be a matter for another day. Surely, there would be other crews willing to take the risks of exploring, clearing, and making contact on land. Right now, it was not his job. In the morning, Bubba and his flotilla would resume sailing toward Molokai. He continued to watch and to think until he couldn't keep his eyes open. He finally retired for a few hours of troubled sleep before rising with the dawn to greet the new day and new decisions.

The boat captains gathered again for breakfast, while everyone else ate from rations in their respective boats. The purpose of the meeting was to determine the course they'd take around Oahu, and whether it was worth taking extra time to study the effects of H7D3 on Hawaii's most populous island.

The leeward side of Oahu had been lightly populated but would expose them to being downwind of whatever had happened in Pearl Harbor. It was the most direct course to Kalaupapa, and they'd have an opportunity to get a look at the small towns and communities where refugees and survivors were more likely. They'd also see for themselves regarding the status of Pearl Harbor, Honolulu, and the resort areas such as Waikiki.

The alternative was to sail back to the north and around Kaena Point, then follow the North Shore around to the windward side of the island. That transit would continue to take them around slightly more populated areas than the leeward shore until they reached Kaneohe Bay and whatever was left of the Marine Corps Air Station. In addition to the somewhat denser population, that shoreline had been home to many large private homes, estates, and mansions of the rich and famous. Two particular features made it more likely that the windward side of Oahu could have organized survivors: the Island Cultural Center, and the Ka'a'awa Ranch. The former was a combined church and university-run park that hosted students from all over the Pacific, showcasing the native cultures (and historical hunting, fishing, farming, and building practices). The latter hosted sustainable aqua- and agriculture and ranching, while also providing tours of its picturesque movie sets and filming locations. Both sites had the advantage of skills useful in the absence of electricity and technology, as well as the means to implement them. It would be a great shame if one or both of the groups hadn't managed to survive; they'd be an incredible resource to help others rebuild some semblance of community and civilization.

"It's risky going downwind of Pearl, but I think we really need to get a look." Mamabear had fallen back into her role of matriarch. Where Bubba was the acknowledged leader of the flotilla, Mamabear led their hearts, particularly after the previous day's disaster. Bubba simply did not feel up to the task of leading this particular meeting.

"Sure, but there's the chance of survivors at Laie and Ka'a'awa," said Marietta "Steph" Stephanidis, who would be taking over as captain of the *Hole in the Water* for this leg of the journey while Flip Charles joined Bubba on *Simple Gifts* to provide information from his Coast Guard background.

"We do have a way of checking, though," Gran told them. "After I learned that you wanted to sail past Pearl, as well as what you think happened there, Jon and I took a scavenging team over to the local high school. We grabbed a bunch of chemicals that might be useful for medicines and other purposes. You know, like iodine pills, just in case. Anyway, we've got a Geiger counter from the physics classroom. It's old, but just needed a change of batteries. Most schools stopped teaching that kind of science, but their Geiger counters and test sources are usually just stashed away in a classroom closet. So, we can check for radiation if folks are worried about that."

Gran Landrum's experience as a teacher had already paid dividends. She was one of the best cooks and was now teaching younger members of the flotilla on how to make better-tasting meals from their supplies. She had assisted with treating Tully and had promised that she would soon be up to speed on engine repair. The woman was unstoppable, and if she said that something was okay, the rest believed her.

"If it's the old standard with a great big disc on one end that looks like a microphone, I second Gran's comment. We used them in the Guard. We never knew when an interdiction might reveal someone trying to smuggle bomb components."

"Yes, but only if we go that way," Bubba said with a sigh. "It sure would be nice to see if there's any organized survivors on the East Coast."

"Split up and go half each way?"

"After what happened yesterday? No, I don't think that's a good idea."

"Well, then, why not go leeward, then around to the Marine place?" asked Nardo.

"I'm not sure I like the idea of sailing into the wind while we're off of Pearl and Honolulu," protested Kōkee. "It might be better if we took the windward course around the North Shore, then run with the wind down the east side where we can set sail and move downwind quickly if we need to. Then as we round Makapu'u and Koko Head we turn west. We keep our distance, but also have the wind to our advantage while we check out Honolulu and Pearl. In an emergency, we just turn south and open up the distance."

"Makes sense," said Steph. "That way if we *do* have to sail into the wind, we're in open water. I like it."

"Me, too," Bubba said. "We can satisfy our curiosity and stay as safe as possible."

"So, we take a day to explore, then on to Molokai." Mamabear looked at the faces of the captains and advisors, then nodded her head.

"Then Molokai, before it's too late for *their* survivors," Kōkee added quietly.

CHAPTER THIRTEEN

DESECRATION

A date which will live in infamy.
—F.D. Roosevelt, President of the United States,
address to Congress, December 8, 1941

With the decision made, the captains went back to their boats and
prepared to set sail. Once they rounded Kaena Point, they'd be sailing
almost directly into the wind. For that portion of the journey, they
moved to about two miles offshore. The water was deep enough for
stability and safe maneuvering, yet close enough to watch the land
through binoculars. If the teenage lookouts on the larger boats
reported anything interesting on shore, a smaller boat could move
closer to shore to check it out. They passed through the same area as
the pirate encounter of the previous day, but there was no sign of the
submarine or any wreckage. Given prevailing wind and sea currents,
those items might not reach land until the Philippines or Indonesia,
more than five thousand miles away.

The area around Kaena Point was a forest preserve, with not much
to see at the shoreline. The lookouts reported occasional flashes from
up on the ridge near where the satellite and radar installations had
been located. There was nothing on the radio, however, and those
occasional flashes were completely random rather than a rhythmic
form of signaling.

The flotilla sailed past the North Shore tourist and surfing town of
Haleiwa, and turned northeast, directly into the wind. Or it least, it

should have been. Bubba noticed that the wind heading seemed to be shifting, so he had the sailboats move out into deeper water to tack upwind, while *Simple Gifts* cruised just offshore under power. Bubba had put the sailing portion of the flotilla—plus *Landin'C*—under Kōkee's leadership for this portion of the float. So far, they'd only used about ten percent of their total fuel, but a slow survey of the land would certainly use that up, so it was better to keep the vessels under sail as much as they could. Bubba and Yori watched the shore, and Bubba kept up a running commentary for the other boats.

As they motored past the landmarks of Shark's Cove, Sunset Beach, and Banzai Pipeline, Bubba half expected to see one or more die-hard surfers out on the strong North Shore waves. After all, a *true* surfer would not let something as trivial as the end of the world keep them from chasing the perfect point break. It saddened him to see beaches devoid of humans and littered only with the debris of their passing.

After passing Turtle Beach, they saw the short, irregular peninsula of Kahuku Point, and prepared to turn southward along the Windward Coast. The towns and cities on this side of the island were more populous, so the sailing vessels would remain well offshore for safety. At least until Kaneohe Bay.

Passing Laie, Yori called Bubba up to the flybridge and handed him the binoculars, pointing out the double row of palm trees leading inland to the Mormon temple. The building still gleamed white in the sun, and the beach and streets leading up to it seemed remarkably clean and well kept.

Someone was alive and still looking after church property, which gave hope of finding survivors at the island culture outposts. Unfortunately, while they saw occasional reflections and a hint of movement on the hills overlooking the beach, there were no overt signs of intelligent life. On the other hand, as the rest of the flotilla joined up, and the collection of boats turned into Kaneohe Bay, they could see fishponds that also seemed relatively well cared for.

Dalia, who was acting as lookout on *Sunset Gold*, reported seeing something in the water moving at a speed greater than what would be accounted for by simple wave action. As she described it over the radio, Gran broke in to say that it was likely an outrigger canoe. If true, it seemed that some survivors had gone back to the old ways and built a vessel they could use for fishing and trade. It would be worth sending someone back to the area to see about establishing contact. That was for another day, though, and they needed to keep moving.

The area around Kaneohe and the Marine base was a disappointment. The town was burned and badly damaged. The same was true of the military base, with the addition of evidence of several explosions. Apparently, the last marines did not surrender calmly. For the first time, the lookouts reported spotting a group of naked figures chasing something or someone between buildings.

Yori reported 'ino'ino out and hunting. Infected numbers were high enough that they feared nothing and no one.

Bubba's people had yet to encounter large packs of Infected, even in the towns of Eleele and Hanapepe and the areas of West Kawai. In those locations, and even from the occasional scavenging attempts all the way east to Lihue, Infected had been spotted in only ones, twos, and threes. They'd all heard reports on radio and TV, right before the end, about larger packs chasing and taking down uninfected individuals. They knew intellectually that such things happened, but it was a shock to see it with their own eyes. Faced with such savagery, it was hard to imagine trying to build any sort of community near the population centers.

They exited Kaneohe Bay and continued to the southeast until spotting the Makapu'u Point Lighthouse. Turning southwest, they were in a quartering wind, and could see building clouds to the south. They decided to pick up speed after rounding Koko Head, both because of what appeared to be an oncoming storm, and the desire to not look too closely at the remains of Oahu's tourist areas. The famous Waikiki shoreline had changed, with two of the iconic hotel towers now just charred stumps of jagged metal. Fires still burned in many places, as evidenced by numerous columns of black smoke. More roving gangs of Infected were visible, and the many ports and marinas were virtually empty as everyone who could get in a boat and leave had attempted to do so. A few good-looking and powerful boats had been left behind.

The captains discussed whether it was worth a later trip to try to salvage any of them, but Steph reminded them that many would have been abandoned due to unseen damage or maintenance issues. After all, it had happened to her. The former dentist had owned a fifty-foot *Isara*, which was still in Nawiliwili contributing to the wreckage blocking the bay. The catamaran's engine had failed as she was exiting the marina. It was then struck by the boat attempting to exit behind her. Before long, the pileup rivaled any multicar highway pileup, with nearly the same disastrous results. She'd had to abandon ship and make her way to Port Allen in an inflatable dinghy.

It might be possible to recover some of these ships at a much later date, but the risk of finding a broken boat—or worse, one filled with Infected—simply wasn't worth the risk right now. Maybe not even for the near future. But those were all decisions for another time.

Finally, the flotilla passed Honolulu's airport and paused at the mouth of Oahu's most historic site, Pearl Harbor. Flip came up to the flybridge with Bubba and Yori. They'd been monitoring the air with the Geiger counter and had yet to detect anything out of the ordinary.

"Let's see what we've got here. Yori, can I borrow your binoculars?" Flip asked. "We should be able to navigate at least as far in as the harbor proper, as long as the channels aren't blocked."

Part of that morning's discussion was whether they should enter the harbor to check and see what facilities might be undamaged, or even still secured. While the land was flat, the view was not unobstructed, given the trees and buildings. In order to see into the harbor, they would have to enter it. If the air was safe, that was.

"Okay, Ford Island Channel seems to be clear," Flip told them. "I can't see Southeast Loch from here. That's where the sub pens and drydocks are located."

"So, you think we should go in?"

"Geiger's clear; Gran used a test kit to check for other contaminants. It's normally for drinking water, but the air's humid enough to set a cloth in the wind, then wring it out into a test tube. We're not going onshore, right?"

"Nope. As long as we can maneuver, I have no desire to reenact the *Nevada* incident and run aground in the channel."

"Got it. That memorial's right over that way. Two miles in, and on the starboard."

Bubba laughed. "Thanks for the warning." He then called down to the helm and suggested that Kiwi might want to come up to the flybridge to navigate into the harbor.

Sure enough, two miles in, they could see a clear channel to the west of Ford Island, and wreckage to the east where a massive explosion had occurred.

"We've got trace. Background's jumped from twenty-six to one-oh-two counts per minute," Flip called from the fishing deck. Jon Ko was next to him, dipping a water sampling tube into the harbor water.

Gran looked up as Bubba leaned over to look down from the flybridge. She was holding a rack of test tubes with liquids in various colors. "Water's dirty, but not dangerous."

"Is one hundred two dangerous?" Bubba called down to her.

"Zeros over Pearl Harbor, yes, definitely," she replied with a wry grin.

Bubba didn't react to the dark humor. "No, one-oh-two counts per minute."

"Ah, yes, the Geiger." She looked over at Flip, who nodded back. "Not dangerous—for now. It does suggest that something bad happened here. As long as we don't go over one-fifty, we're fine."

"Cracked or corroded reactor casing most likely, but it's a low-level leak," Flip clarified. "It should be okay."

"East is impassible," they could hear Kiwi say. Bubba turned to look to the main channel where the fateful attack had occurred on December 7, 1941.

From somewhere, a voice called out, "Hey, do you think we should render honors like the Navy folks do?"

Another voice answered him. "No, you idiot, that is only when passing the *Arizona*. We're not going that way; didn't you hear the captain?"

"Ah, okay. Well, at least we should be able to see—" The voice cut off, followed by a yell. "Oh shit! Oh fuck. Damn it, damn them all. *You damned dirty apes; you blew it up!*"

Bubba's attention was drawn to the horrific sight of an aircraft carrier run aground on Ford Island. They'd seen the carrier as they entered the harbor, but it was only once they were fully in the channel that they could see all of it. The deck was tilted, and it was clear fires had broken out throughout the superstructure. A jet fighter was dangling by its tail hook off the starboard edge of the flight deck. One of the elevators for bringing aircraft onto deck from the hanger dipped down almost to touch the water, and more aircraft had tumbled off the side.

The wreck was tragic, but that wasn't the worst of it. It certainly wasn't what had caused the outburst. The carrier hadn't actually run *aground* on Ford Island. The carrier had smashed into the bow of the USS *Missouri,* one of two iconic ships to be found in Pearl Harbor. That alone would have been tragic, but they could all see that the bow of the carrier had come to a halt on top of a low white rectangle marking a watery grave.

The USS *Arizona* had succumbed once again, this time to friendly fire, as the memorial was crushed and buried under the keel of a U.S. warship.

CHAPTER FOURTEEN

GATHERING STORM

Hawaii sits in a unique location with respect to tropical storms and hurricanes. Cyclonic storms require warm water, steering winds, and low pressures. While the waters around Hawaii are indeed warm, they're not quite warm enough. The trade winds blowing from the northeast to the southwest are actually too strong, and pressures are not low enough. It's like Goldilocks and the Three Bears. Hawaii is *not* "just right" for hurricanes.

On the other hand, every ten to fifteen years a cyclone will impinge upon the islands. When it does, the results can be devastating.

—Akoni "Kōkee" Keoki, crewman, Kauai Boat Tours

Since *Simple Gifts* was already in the main channel of the harbor, they continued through the clear Ford Island Channel to the spacious East Loch to turn back and head out to sea. While passing the mouth of the Middle Loch, home to several ships of the U.S. Inactive Reserve Fleet, they noticed that the amphibious assault ship that should have been in the middle of the bay was missing. The USS *Tarawa*, LHA-1, looked like a small aircraft carrier, although it mainly supported vertical-takeoff aircraft like helicopters, Harriers, and tiltrotors. Underneath the flat upper deck was a large open well deck to support landing craft and hovercraft. The fact that the ship was missing implied that someone had had the time and crew to get it moving after having been mothballed for several years. They all wondered where it might have gone, and if it meant that the U.S. Navy still had an active presence in the Pacific.

Bubba and his crew relayed all of the findings to the rest of the flotilla, which had remained offshore. "Well, I guess this answers questions about how well Pearl Harbor survived. Things were bad. So bad, I just can't imagine." They'd rejoined the rest of the boats and sailed past Barbers Point, at the southwestern corner of Oahu, to anchor for the night in the lee of the Waianae Ridge.

There'd been no further increases in Geiger counter readings; in fact, the reading had dropped below fifty counts per minute once they cleared the mouth of Pearl Harbor. On the other hand, downwind of Pearl just plain smelled bad. They had seen several places where fires continued to burn on the eastern side near the dry docks. Fuel supplies, lubricants, and even aluminum and magnesium structures could burn with no hope of being extinguished as long as something remained to fuel the flames. Fortunately, Barbers Point was not directly downwind of Pearl, and they'd sailed just far enough north that the island's western mountain ridge blocked the prevailing wind.

Everyone gathered once again that evening for a common meal and to discuss the day's findings. "There's still so much that could be gained from exploration of Pearl: the fuel depot at Red Hill, Tripler Hospital, the armories of Fort Shafter and Wheeler," Steven "Kela" Taylor was saying. He'd been a mechanic at Wheeler Army Airfield prior to retiring and moving to Kauai, and now helping keep the *Simple Gifts* running.

"Yes, but Red Hill's two or three miles inland, and uphill," Flip countered. "We'd have to either go in through the wreckage of the east harbor or clear our way through Honolulu. Besides, the pipeline is gravity fed. For all we know, the underground tanks could be empty from feeding the fires all this time."

"We've also seen too many roving bands of the 'ino'ino. We had it easy on Kauai compared to this," Jon Ko said. "If we ever do send scavenging teams onto Oahu, I'm sure I don't want to be among them. They need way more firepower and protection than what we have."

"Once again, we have a decision to make: go ahead or go back." Bubba had the senior people gathered to one side.

"I don't think there's any change from this morning. We have to go on to Molokai. There are people on Kalaupapa who need us. What's more, they have resources and land we need," Gran told them. "We also risk something bad happening to them the more we delay, right, Kōkee?"

"I don't think it's been too long. They had supplies. As long as they didn't get overrun, we'll be in time."

"I agree." said Flip. Kiwi, Duke, and Steph nodded agreement.

"Very well," Bubba told them. "Sleep well. In the morning, we sail for Molokai."

The first few days of the voyage had been pleasant tropical weather. Skies were clear in the morning, with only a few clouds in the distance. Increasing cloud cover and occasional light rain was normal in the afternoon.

Today was different. It dawned with dark storm clouds and swirling winds. The lack of ground stations to interpret satellite images meant that there was no weather forecasting, no warning of oncoming storms or prediction of storm path. Sailors had to revert to the old techniques of mariners from one hundred and more years ago.

"The barometer's falling, and it's falling fast," Kiwi told Bubba. "We have to make the choice to either find a more protected anchorage or push on to Molokai and get there before the worst of this breaks."

"How big do you think this is?"

"I'm not the one with the most experience in these waters. For that, you should probably ask Kōkee."

When Bubba called over to *Sunset Gold* to get the native captain's opinion on the weather, he was not happy with the news.

"The winds are currently out of the east again. That's not good. The falling pressure, wind speed, and direction indicate a tropical cyclone," Kōkee told them. "Yesterday we had southeasterly winds. Preceding a storm, that would suggest a track east of the islands, but this one *could* be coming on us from the south. It doesn't matter where the track is, we're going to get caught by it."

"A hurricane, oh joy."

"Or tropical storm, but right now, it makes no difference. While we wouldn't be sailing into the wind, if we try for Molokai right now, we're sailing into the storm. It will get much worse before it gets better, and I'd rather be on completely open ocean than in the Channel when it hits. Or a protected anchorage."

While the waters south of Hawaii were warm enough for tropical cyclone formation, the north side of the islands was much cooler. On top of that, the trade winds were mostly dry and from the northeast, pushing developing storms away from the islands. The exception was in El Niño years, when exceptionally warm water extended much farther to the north. Just before the Fall, Bubba had heard reports of a developing El Niño, and it occurred to him that conditions ripe for hurricane formation were perfectly in keeping with his luck since the Haole Flu hit the islands.

"Maybe we'll be lucky and it will miss us," Mamabear said to Kōkee.

"Only if our luck changes," muttered Duke.

"We'll know by the direction of the wind. When a storm passes windward of the islands, the winds go east, northeast, north, then northwest. If a storm passes leeward, the winds come east, southeast, south, southwest. It's out of the east now and could go either way. Frankly, if the winds shift south, we need to be protected as much as possible. We do *not* want to get caught out on the east side of a cyclone. The leeward side of the islands will *not* be protected. We could be driven ashore with our anchors broken. If that happens, being capsized is the least of our worries. The wind and waves could pick up even a medium-sized boat and dash it against the rocks. We need a protected harbor."

"Where are we going to find shelter, then, if the leeward shore is no guarantee of safety? Try to make it to Molokai?" Mamabear asked.

"No, Kalaupapa offers some protection from east or southerly winds, but its harbor is not enclosed. Also, as Kōkee mentioned, we'd likely be sailing into the storm," Bubba told them. "On the other hand, Barbers Point Harbor is nearby."

The captains had gathered on *Simple Gifts*, as they had taken to doing every morning. Currently they were on the enclosed bridge, and Bubba stepped over to the large table where he'd insisted they have physical maps. Kiwi and Flip had raided all of the offices in Port Allen to assemble a set of maps covering all of the Hawaiian Islands. He and others had gotten used to GPS positioning, but after the Fall, the potential loss of the GPS system had been on everyone's minds. It still worked, but Flip had noticed that positioning errors had begun to creep into the system in the form of deviations between where the GPS recorded their position and what they could actually tell from landmarks and channel markers. It was a worrisome difference, and they all hoped that someone somewhere was keeping an eye on the global positioning satellite system and had a plan for making sure that it continued to operate.

"Right here." Bubba tapped the map. "Barbers Point is a big empty harbor, but shallow enough for multiple anchors, and we can tie up to the pier on the south side, or even make use of Ko Olina Marina next door. We might even be able to pull the smaller craft out of the water; there's ramps on both sides."

"We don't know what shape the marina is in," Flip told them. "I'm not sure pulling out of the water is a good idea, and *Gifts* wouldn't be able to, anyway. A marina slip wouldn't fit her, but we'd have a choice of open-but-protected water or alongside a pier. It's certainly much better sheltered and protected from all sides."

"So, we get inside and prepare ourselves for a storm," Mamabear said.

"Right, and maybe even see if some people can shelter onshore instead of on the boats."

Barbers Point Harbor was a large squared-off body of water. It was primarily designed to serve industrial purposes, including tankers delivering fuel for Oahu. Once inside the protective breakwater, they could see long concrete piers on two sides, an unloading area parallel to the piers, and the petroleum tanks at the far end. It didn't have the tall derricks and cranes typical of a port serving container-based freight, but it did have the infrastructure necessary for unloading petroleum and other liquid goods.

Opposite the long pier was a jetty separating it from the Ko Olina Marina. The harbor itself was empty, with not even a tug or harbor pilot's boat evident in the area. The shoreside facilities appeared empty, and they could see large stretches of open land, enclosed by a tall fence that appeared intact all the way around the facility. The two large gates they could see likewise appeared to be in good shape.

The same was not true of the marina. It was shaped like a right triangle, with boat slips extending out from the short side, and the long side running parallel to the jetty separating it from the commercial harbor. Many slips were empty, but the accessway closest to the right-angled corner was a jumble of damaged boats and piers. Apparently, people had been in too much of a hurry to leave, and a pileup had occurred in the most congested part of the marina. They could also see makeshift barriers at the shore ends of several piers. It seemed likely that escaping boat owners had been mobbed by either Infected or people desperate to escape to the water.

There was no one in sight at present, but that didn't mean they weren't there. There wasn't a fence, but the pier was set apart from the land, and only connected at the rear corner of the marina. On the land side, a large shipping container had been placed to block access, and the pier itself was missing for about fifty yards where it would have connected back to the rest of the marina, including the jumbled wreckage. There were a sufficient number of open slips—they were all empty, just not all accessible—on that end of the marina for the entire flotilla. Jon Ko volunteered to lead a clearance team into the harbor to find out if the petroleum storage tanks were accessible and usable for replenishing their fuel stocks. Birdy also volunteered his services and guns to lead a team up the intact piers to the marina administration buildings to look for resources and signs of survivors as well as to ensure that the various blocks and barricades were sufficient to secure the access from the shore.

Bubba put a hold on those plans for the time being. They were reasonably confident about two-legged security, but they needed to ensure security of a different type. The discovery of the marina's wonders couldn't eclipse the reason they were there in the first place. A storm was coming, and they needed to prepare.

CHAPTER FIFTEEN
EYE OF THE STORM

I know what you're thinking.
—T.S. Magnum

"Okay, everyone," Bubba radioed all the boats. "Find a slip near the end and send teams to reinforce those barriers. Then get to securing those boats. We'll get *Gifts* tied up alongside the long pier, but let's not plan on using the piers to get between boats unless they are directly adjacent."

There were a few motor vessels, mostly twenty- to thirty-foot fishing vessels. Those could be useful if they were clean and operable, but those concerns were for later. Of greater interest were three highly unusual boats—well, at least one was clearly a *ship*—that were located in the farthest slip from shore, and alongside the jetty. None of the three was small enough to fit in a conventional slip, which might also have something to do with why they were still here.

Tied up to the end of a pier was a trimaran; the two outrigger hulls were sleek and low to the water. The central hull was also streamlined, but wider than required for a purely racing craft. It was still narrower than an open-ocean cruising tri, in which the pilothouse and cabin often extended out over the outriggers. It was clearly a custom build, and none of the mariners with Bubba could identify it.

The same was not true for the other two craft. Moored alongside the jetty pier was a long motor yacht with two decks above water to the rail, then a pilothouse and covered flybridge above that. There was also a covered area behind the flybridge attached to the radio/radar mast. The rear deck came down two levels, and had what appeared to be a *garage*, likely for the dinghy and sport watercraft. Flip identified it as a Monte Fino and suggested that it might be a fine addition to their flotilla, as long as they could scrounge fuel for it. Kiwi suggested that the latter could be as simple as checking the fueling port next door.

The most outstanding vessel was the two-masted ketch moored behind the Monte Fino. It was an amazingly modern-looking vessel, all gleaming white superstructure, two decks above the rail, with crisp black windows wrapping all around the salon and pilothouse. The main mast extended from just in front of the salon. The mizzenmast, also serving as the radar mast, extended through the roof of the salon just behind the flybridge. It looked to have a luxurious interior based on the rich wooden railing, bright brass, and pristine teak of the deck. This boat was quite fine and would be worth the salvage if the interior was recoverable, as long as the mechanisms for raising and setting sails had not been ruined from vandalism or lack of maintenance.

"Now, *that* could be useful," said Duke as he motored *Storm Chaser* past the ketch, sails furled.

"Indeed, sail and motor in a hundred-twenty, hundred-thirty-foot length? We could easily sail between islands on a regular basis," replied Steph. "I think I'm in love."

"Mine," said Flip.

His comment was met with laughter over the radio.

Winds had shifted again and were now coming from the north.

"That's good, right? It means the storm is passing to our east?" Kōkee volunteered to stay aboard *Sunset Gold* and Flip was back on *Hole in the Water*. Everyone else had come over to *Simple Gifts* to wait out the storm.

"Not necessarily. The winds have been too variable," Kōkee told them.

Heavy rain had been coming down for the past several hours. The wind was whipping the rain to the point that it was blowing almost horizontally. Bubba and Kiwi had taken turns keeping watch from the flybridge at first, but as the wind increased, it became much too dangerous to stay exposed, particularly that far above the deck. Everyone except for Kōkee and Flip was now gathered in the main salon and the enclosed bridge. Mamabear was leading part of the group in songs, Gran was teaching some of the less experienced how to tie knots, many of the older folks were playing cards, and the teens had a game of *Munchkin* in progress.

Kiwi was currently watching the instruments at the helm. The captains had decided to sit in the seats behind the bridge station so that any concerns or conversation were less obvious to the people below. He tapped the indicator that showed wind speed and direction from the instruments on the electronics mast. "Winds are up to forty knots and coming from the east. We're also seeing a storm surge."

"Oh, fuck!" Bubba exclaimed. "We're going to lose some boats. We tied up expecting wind, not storm surge."

"The change in direction also means the storm isn't passing to our east. It's coming right at us," Kōkee told them over a radio filled with static interference from the electrical activity of the storm.

"Is it too late to loosen the hawsers and ride the surge?" Steph asked.

"It's too dangerous out there, and it's only going to get worse," Bubba told them. "The storm surge means we'll get water inside, but most boats have positive buoyancy. They shouldn't sink."

"Shouldn't," said Nardo. "Glad I pulled LCM up boat ramp. It *will* sink if gets swamped. Also get cargo wet."

"*Storm Chaser*'s in trouble, Bubba," Duke said.

"I know, but not much we can do about it. We need to ride out the storm, then we'll see what we have."

The group became quieter, as everyone waited anxiously for the storm to pass. By late afternoon, Gran and her assistants had made sandwiches and coffee for everyone. It was as dark as night, but only four in the afternoon. Time seemed to crawl by as the wind speed and noise of the storm got louder.

Bubba and Kiwi had loosened the hawsers to their boats as the storm surge increased. From what they could see of the marina, all the piers were submerged. *Storm Chaser* and *Hole in the Water* were sitting awfully low in the water, and Flip had decided it was better to stay in *Gifts* with everyone else. He and Kōkee had loosened the hawsers on their boats, even though it risked them being tossed around once the storm surge passed. Unfortunately, no one could convince the native sailor to leave his boat and shelter with the rest of them.

The winds shifted to come from the south as the speed increased to seventy knots. "This is a Category One, at least," Kōkee told them over the radio in a moment of clear reception. "It's likely passing just to our west, and we might even get inside the eye."

Almost as soon as he said it, the winds seemed to slack off, and what they could see of the sky got brighter. Flip raced out the hatch to the rear of the bridge and up the ladder to the flybridge. He quickly looked around, and even before Bubba could follow him up, was sliding back down the ladder with one foot on the outside of each rail, descending as fast as he could.

"We're in the eye. From the looks of it, we have fifteen, maybe twenty minutes. Storm surge is receding."

"Okay, got it." Bubba turned back to the assembled captains. "Back to your boats. Assess damage, tighten the hawsers, and secure anything that came loose. Make it ten minutes and get back here."

A fast but orderly exodus of boat crews left *Gifts* to run to the other boats over piers that were just barely above water. Reports quickly came back that they had managed to have only minor damage... except for *Storm Chaser*, which had waist-high water in the interior. Nardo reported that he was headed to *Landin'C*. He would ride out the rest of the storm onboard and try to get the landing craft off the boat ramp as soon as the surge receded, so that it didn't get stuck.

Nardo did inform everyone that their cargo appeared in good condition. Bubba gave a sigh of relief. He had been worried that all the supplies they'd intended for the relief of Kalaupapa would be lost in the storm, and they would be more of a burden than salvation to the few survivors.

The crews returned in ten minutes, less a few who decided that they could, in fact, remain with their boats; most notably, Kōkee's entire crew of *Sunset Gold* elected to stay. Duke, Kimo, and 'Pua salvaged what they could from *Storm Chaser* and stored the soaked goods in the fish lockers in the cockpit of *Gifts*. They could deal with drying them out after the storm passed.

It was another ten minutes before the clouds, wind, and rain closed back in, this time from the southwest as the southeast quadrant of the storm closed in on them.

The last rays of sunlight had been fading as the storm clouds swept in and the winds built back up. It seemed as if they were of higher intensity and Kiwi confirmed that, indeed, the winds were reaching about eighty knots. It was still "only" a Category 1 hurricane, so they were getting off easy, although it certainly didn't feel that way. Bubba and his people sat huddled, waiting through the long night. No one wanted to sleep, although a few of the younger ones were taken to the staterooms belowdecks by their parent or guardian. They were the only ones who seemed to get any sleep at all.

When time for sunrise came, it was still dark. Winds were down to about twenty-five knots, and rain came in spurts. An hour later, they'd started to worry that the storm had changed its track and come back over them. However, soon the darkness turned to gray, and gradually to a lighter shade. The wind slacked off even more and only a light rain was falling. Bubba stepped out onto the deck and could see clearing skies and sunshine in the southeast.

The sight that greeted him was anything but sunny. *Hole in the Water* was flipped on its side. *Sunset Gold* was listing, but that appeared to be because one of its pontoons was up on the pier and not in the water. The pier itself had taken more damage, not just around *Sunset Gold*. It no longer circled the entire marina and disappeared for about twenty feet before where *Storm Chaser* had been moored. That boat was sitting low, with the railing and gunwales barely above the waterline.

Bubba looked over to the other side of the marina where the boat-launching ramp was located. He couldn't see *Landin'C* but noticed a faint line of exhaust over in Barbers Point Harbor, and soon saw the landing craft motoring over to the petroleum depot. Nardo had apparently pulled the LCM-8 out into the water as soon as the storm had slackened enough to be safe.

Only *Simple Gifts* and *Landin'C* appeared to have weathered the storm without damage. *Gold* was surely fixable, though, and they'd just have to make sure that the mast and keel for *Hole* were not severely damaged. The *Storm Chaser* might well be a total loss. The interior would have to be pumped out and stripped of all cloth and porous materials—to let them dry out, at the very least. The engines would likely need extensive work before it could be salvaged. They might simply not have the time to do so.

Bubba was looking around the marina, wondering if any of the other vessels might be salvageable, when he heard a voice calling. He looked to the stern and noticed someone up on the flybridge of the motor yacht docked behind them. A woman of about forty was waving in his direction, a child of maybe eight was standing next to her, and she was holding a child of around one year in her arms.

"Hey, over here."

The more he stared at the other boat, the more he realized there were many signs of occupancy.

"Hello. Have you been here all along?" Bubba called back.

"Yes, we saw you and your people come in right before the storm but weren't sure we should reveal ourselves."

"That's probably smart. What changed?"

"Well, we can see that you might need some help. Also, maybe you can help us. My husband is pretty handy; he knows mechanical stuff, carpentry, you name it. We don't really know how to operate a boat and could use some help there. If you have an extra person who can show us how to do this, we can learn fast. I mean, even if you can't help us with that, we can try to help in exchange for food and... um... hygiene items?"

Bubba made sure not to let a smile show on his face, or even to laugh. "I think we can help out. Our supplies are over in the harbor at the moment, though. As for food, we'll see what we can do. How many of you are there?"

"We have nine: my husband, me, our three sons, and my older daughter, plus three kids from the local Scout troop. My daughter was their scoutmaster... or assistant... or scoutmistress. Whatever."

"Wow, nine people, and your family is intact?"

"Yes, we know it's rare. We loaded up supplies and tried to get to one of the quarantine shelters when Scott got a call from Heidi. She was stuck with a bunch of Scouts whose parents never made it. There were more, but..."

"Say no more. We have a few kids like that," he told her. "Hey, I'm Bubba."

"Oh, where are my manners? I'm April. April Barkin." She set her hand on the head of the boy, who promptly squirmed out from under. "This is Theodore Calvin. He's seven. Thomas Sullivan is nine. He's helping his father down below; they're trying to get the stove working again. The little cutie is Ricky. Scott wouldn't let me name him Orville."

At that moment, a man came on deck, followed by a slightly older boy. The man was tall, with curly black hair, and thick mustache. He was also wearing a faded and worn red shirt in the aloha style.

Bubba's jaw dropped.

"I know, right? Doesn't Scott look *just* like Burt Reynolds?"

"Uh, yeah. You're right. He does," Bubba agreed, although he had to admit that the older actor was *not* who came to mind under the circumstances. "Um, so do you have *any* food? We're stocked reasonably well, but we'll need some at our destination."

"We do, but frankly, we've gotten so tired of Spam. When we got here, well, the owner must have *loved* the stuff. But without a working stove, it's . . . well . . . it's yucky."

This time, Bubba *did* laugh. "Yes, I know. You should talk to Gran about that. I'll introduce you to her and Mamabear, and they can work with you about a food exchange."

CHAPTER SIXTEEN

KALAUPAPA

You ask why people come to Hawaii and they answer: Sun, Surf, Weather. No one ever says people. Why did I come [back] to Hawaii? People needed me.

—B. Koa, priest, Church of Saint Damien, Kalaupapa, Molokai

Once the newcomers had been introduced around, Gran went over to the Monte Fino to see if she could do anything about fixing the stove. She suspected that it was as simple as rewiring the igniter and bleeding the propane lines, since the tanks appeared full, but the Barkins said that it had not worked as long as they'd been aboard.

They'd also said that the yacht belonged to the owner of a luxury car dealership, for which April had worked as manager. She'd been in the company offices the day the owner had come in, talking about getting off the islands and heading out to sea to wait out the Haole Flu. It had been too late for him personally, though, as he'd turned and attacked the office staff an hour after his arrival. April had been the one to put him down, courtesy of a metal bat she'd kept in her office ever since being on the receiving end of harassment by the person who'd previously held her job. She knew of the yacht because of parties he'd held for managers, buyers, and prospective corporate customers. He kept the keys in his office since he'd had a tendency to take visitors there after work.

The Scouts turned out to be a surprise, two girls and a boy. They all were well trained in many aspects of outdoor craft, include small boat sailing. Their troop had been a co-ed unit, aged fifteen and up, who joined primarily for outdoor adventures. In the Islands, that naturally included basic maritime skills. They immediately jumped in to assist with getting *Hole in the Water* upright, and *Sunset Gold* back on the water.

With a full exchange of food, supplies, and labor underway, Bubba turned his attention to his own flotilla. Nardo reported back that the petroleum depot did indeed have full tanks, and that the valves and pipes could be adapted to refuel their boats and any that could be salvaged from the marina. With the loss of *Bubba Truck* and *Storm Chaser*, and potential loss of *Hole in the Water*, they really needed to see if there were other boats that could be salvaged.

It soon became apparent that there was no shortage of useable boats; there were at least four readily salvageable boats in the marina. That included the Monte Fino, whose name plate identified her as the *Sails Proposition*, and the trimaran, *With the Wind*. These two were absolutely untouched. The best of the others had only a few bodies, and none of the mess associated with the Infected, such as the ketch, which was appropriately named *Eye of the Storm*, and a thirty-eight-foot Bertram powered fishing boat named *Doc's Side*.

That left Bubba and his captains with a choice of getting the "new" boats ready to sail or trying to repair their own. *Simple Gifts* had come through the storm with only cosmetic damage. *Sunset Gold* would need to be at least partially pulled out of the water to elevate the starboard pontoon to replace the propeller and repair the rudder. As suspected, *Hole in the Water* had a bent mast and damage to both pontoons. It was repairable, but not if it seriously delayed them. The same was doubly true for *Storm Chaser*; it could be pumped out, but the interior was a complete loss.

Again, it was all about time.

After three days of work on repairing and salvaging, refueling and restocking, Bubba called the leaders, now including the Barkins, to meet in the salon on *Simple Gifts* after the evening meal.

"I'm worried about how long this is taking, and how the folks are doing on Kalaupapa."

"They've lasted almost ten months on their own, Bubba," said Tully, now out of the makeshift sickbay, and hobbling around with the aid of a crutch.

"Kōkee, you said they were barely hanging on," Mamabear said to the captain who'd brought them news of the survivors at the former leper colony.

"That was mostly based on running low on certain supplies, and lack of people to fish *and* tend fields *and* repair things. I saw six people other than the priest, but he said a few were out trying to access the top side of the island."

"Those cliffs are over three thousand feet!"

"Yes, but there's an old trail from Kalaupapa taking people up a bit less than two thousand feet to the top. Tourists used to ride donkeys down from topside."

"Seems like a good way to have an accident," Bubba said.

"Yes, it's why they need some working boats to go around instead of over," replied Kōkee.

"Right. So, time is of the essence. We need to balance repair with recovery and relieving the colony."

"There's another way," said Jon Ko. "What if we send Nardo over with the LCM, plus a small boat with Kōkee, since they've met him?"

"And Bubba," said Tully.

"What? Me? No, my place is here."

"Your place is to *lead*, brother. We need you to make official contact and start getting things ready for us. There's nothing here we can't handle."

"Okay, then, Nardo, Kōkee, and I will go in *Landin'C*, but that leaves you without a boat captain. Without two, for that matter."

"No, *Landin'C* needs an escort."

"Kōkee can do that with *Sunset Gold*."

"No, my haole friend. It will be another week before *Gold* is ready," Kōkee reminded him. "If we do this, we should do it now, and not wait."

"Sounds like you should 'go with the wind,'" Flip told them.

"The trimaran? That will be quite the ride. A bit fast for an escort, but not a bad idea."

"It's settled, Bubba, whether you like it or not. I may not be able to operate a boat yet, but I can certainly captain. I can teach the teens to sail the ketch now that we have a few more to round out the crew. You go, and we'll be along later."

෬෧෬

After all the delays and adventures, it was a surprise that the trip to Kalaupapa took only five hours. Kōkee introduced Bubba to Bartholomeus Koa, the Catholic priest who'd been keeping the colonists active and organized to that point. "Ever since Father Damien, there's been a Catholic priest on the peninsula, even once leprosy was cured and the residents no longer needed to be quarantined."

"I'm happy to meet you, Father ... Koa?"

"Father Bart ... and they call you Captain Haole? It seems somewhat rude."

"Bubba Haole, actually, but just call me Bubba."

"Ah, good. Well, we did have a few newcomers since young Brother Aconi was here months ago." Father Bart motioned to the homemade outrigger canoe pulled up on the boat ramp. Another was offshore at the wreckage of the cargo barge that had run aground and spilled cargo on the rocky shore a half mile away.

"I see that. From the other side of the island?"

"Yes. They tend the fishponds on the opposite shore. The top of the island is still quite dangerous." He nodded toward a burly Hawaiian approaching from the beached canoe. "Brother Bear was trying to make his way down from the heights when one of my people reached the top."

"Br'er Bear?" Bubba said with a smile.

"William Bear, but people call me Wizardbear." The man held out his hand. "Kahuna Wizardbear, actually. I hear you have boats."

"Yes, there are more coming, but it will take a few more days to ready them all to get over here. In fact, if there's anyone that wants to help, we've got a couple of motor yachts, a fishing boat, and a two-masted sailing ship." Bubba eyed the man. "Kahuna, eh? A priest? What religion?"

"Brother Bear is a heathen, I am sorry to say." Father Bart hung his head and turned it from side to side, but it was clear there was no animosity in his words.

"Papist fool," Wizardbear replied, likewise devoid of rancor. "I'm Hawaiian. My religion worships the original Polynesian gods, such as Kane, Maui, Pele."

"Ku?"

"No. Ku is ... not good."

"We know. We encountered one of his followers."

Both of the clerics made signs. "Blessing be on you, brother."

"May Kane favor you, if you have met Ku."

"You two knew each other before . . . well, before?"

"Oh yes, Brother Bear and I have known each other for years. We went to Kukui High on Oahu many years ago."

"Uh-huh, the Nuts. You two do go way back." Bubba pointed out at the wrecked ferry. "So, was that before or after a delivery?"

"After, fortunately. The annual shipment is in the warehouse beside the dock, but some items are running low. Once I found the Father, here, I urged my people to come over and join forces. We have twenty-two people now, and fish. Your people and supplies will make that even better. Then we'll see what time and tide have left us."

"Right. So, if you have that many, and young people, too—anyone want to go back with Kōkee and help bring the rest of the fleet?"

Wizardbear grinned. "Oh, I can guarantee it. It will give the young ones something to do! You two go and do church stuff."

"Actually, I'm lapsed."

"As if that matters on this island." Father Bart laughed and clapped Bubba on the back. "Come and meet the rest of my flock."

Two weeks later, Bubba, Father Bart, and Wizardbear once again stood at the dock and watched as two large motor yachts moored offshore, while a fishing boat nudged the ketch up to a newly built pier. Catamarans and outrigger canoes mixed in the small harbor, as the final boat—*Storm Chaser*—sailed into view.

"Congratulations, Commodore Bubba. Your fleet has come in." The kahuna slapped the former charter captain on the back.

"And now we start the next chapter of our lives," said the priest.

"Of rebuilding civilization," Bubba corrected them. "On land and sea. We're going to take back these islands."

INTERLUDE

WEB OF HOPE

Tutu Kane (Grandpa) said that Browning, Colt, and Smith & Wesson will clear my path. Tutu Wahine (Grandma) taught me that Faith, Hope, and Love will clear the soul.

—Y. Hamasaki, teen survivor, Kauai

Dear Abi:

You told me to have faith, and I have to admit some of the news we've heard lately has given me faith that there are enough survivors out there, to eventually rebuild something. It seems too much to hope for rebuilding civilization, but it would be nice to be more than simply surviving.

The term "survivor" does have a ring of determination, though. It carries a sense that a person will do anything and everything required to not just survive but to thrive in difficult times. I do wonder if that term applies to us here in HI-SLOPE, though. All too often we seem to just be enduring. The last three months have been difficult. With reduced personnel, it becomes harder to ensure that all of the normal processes that make our habitat work are maintained and running in proper order. Lugnut does his best with the communications array, but Tree Rat was the expert. He fiddles and monitors, but I often find him just staring blankly at the racks of electronics. It seems the young gamer really did break the simulation on a regular basis to play games

213

online with his friends. Without that outlet, it's clear he's lost the excitement of being part of this grand adventure. He told me it's not so much the loss of the game servers but the sense of community, both online and in HI-SLOPE.

D'Almeida is working hard with his tissue samples from Malut. He was able to isolate the virus, but he says that the problem is that it expresses as both an RNA and DNA virus at different stages of the infection. He's not entirely sure that he can develop a vaccine without one or the other contaminating the product. I asked him if it was possible to create a vaccine using both components. He assured me that it was, and it would be faster than his current process. However, it would require collecting live samples and then inactivating the virus with radiation. The samples he's banked already won't work. Someone would need to get up close and personal with an Infected and risk getting infected themselves.

That caused him to go into a rant again about ethics. I just tuned him out. Most of us do. One thing that did come through was that even after making his vaccine, there would still be a question of testing efficacy coupled to unknown adverse effects of the inactivated virus.

That's another ethical dilemma we're going to have to wrestle with.

The one bright spot is that Scorpio's radio mast allows us to be in touch with others. We've been listening to the ranching community on this island, and a group on Kauai. They say that they're waiting to hear from a mission to establish trade and food production on Molokai. We haven't returned the contact yet, we're not sure we should risk exposure, but it would be good to look into trade between the islands.

We've also heard of other groups of survivors around the world, like this fascinating "Wolf Squadron" operating in the Caribbean. Apparently, they are now retaking land and working their way up the East Coast of the U.S. mainland. One of the biggest questions, though, is what remains of these no longer "united" states. Radio signals from a group in Texas suggests that they are organizing themselves around small population centers. They are even talking about electing a governor, senator, and working to restore some semblance of order. There's others starting to pop up in random places: North Carolina, Indiana, Utah, and Nebraska.

We haven't returned contact with many of the other groups, like that raving radio preacher in North Carolina. We heard that one of his neighbors has been securing local towns and moving back into the cities of the central Carolinas. They said he was an engineer, not religious, and was even pretty reasonable for a while after the Fall. Something happened to send him over the edge, though.

Most amusing to us is the so-called King of Florcubatamp. I'm sure he's just a nutter, too, but at least he's a witty one. None of us knows whether to take him seriously or not.

Closer to home, the ranch on the Kohala plateau is building a community, and they want to start expanding back down to the coast. It's sort of like the nineteenth-century "Mahele" where the rulers sat in the highest points of the Islands and controlled a wedge of land leading down to the water. If the ranch succeeds, they'll secure large portions of coast north of Kona and north of Hilo. That includes some quite productive land. If they can hold on to it, maybe we can come out of our self-imposed exile at some point. It would be nice to know that people near us and around us were thriving.

I have to hold to this hope. Every day they all look to me for leadership and inspiration and at times I just don't feel it, Abi. At times I just want to close my eyes and go back to those times we shared on the beach or on a mountain late at night looking up at an ocean of stars above us. Those stars were my inspiration for this mission—the reason I wanted to go out into space. That dream now seems impossible. We've been knocked so far back. The thing is, all of the technology is still here, we just need the knowledge and the will to use it.

"Hey, Lugnut, is it time for Wolf Squadron's broadcast yet?"
"Sure thing, Professor, they're up in ten minutes. I've been listening

in to marine band chatter out of Kauai. There's a Captain Bubba Haole recruiting a flotilla to head to some of the other islands. Hawaii might have its own version of Wolf Squadron."

"Wait, Captain ... Bubba?"

"Yes, that's what they call him."

"Hmm, that's too odd to be coincidence."

"What?"

"Oh. Nothing, just a stray memory."

"Ah, okay. You should also know that Waimea has been broadcasting, and they've asked for us by name."

"Just us?"

"Well, not just us. They've called for several of the telescope groups like Keck, also Hale Pohaku, Pohakuloa, HI-SLOPE, HI-SEAS, the volcano observatory."

"Oh, a wide broadcast, then. Another answer to discuss. Very well, I'll join everyone in the mess for the Wolf Squadron news in a few minutes."

I remember what you told me, Abi. I just have to have faith. That faith includes seeing you again. I have faith and believe that you survived and even thrived.

Please be out there. Please be happy. This web of hope is the only thing that keeps me going.

Part Three

IRON MAN

CHAPTER ONE

ESCAPE

Triathlon is the ultimate challenge . . . it's not just the run, the bike or the swim . . . it's you versus your body.

—L. Eller, owner, Run, Inc.

Lee Eller dreamed of shoes. He was in a store and surrounded by shoes for running, shoes for walking, shoes for cycling. His years of training had taught him the importance of appropriate shoes—walking vs. running, fast vs. slow, long distance vs. short, cycling and even water shoes. He felt frustrated, always reaching for a pair of new shoes and ending up holding an old worn-out pair with frayed canvas and missing soles.

In the dream he was heavy—too heavy—even more than when his weight had ballooned after college before he started running. He looked at his feet. The shoes were narrow, old, and worn, one lace was frayed, the canvas torn and the rubber peeling off. That wasn't right. He'd walked a lot when he was heavy and he needed shoes with a wide base, firm sides, and stiff insole—he never wore canvas and rubber once he got serious about running. These shoes looked too old, too worn out; he should have changed out the shoes well before they got to this condition.

His friend Chris was there, yelling at him—or at least Chris's mouth was open and he was saying something, but Lee couldn't hear it. Chris was a fellow runner and also a former heavyweight. He was wearing the 4XL-sized shirt that Chris had worn for a picture when they had lost a combined total of nearly three hundred pounds. Now Lee and Chris were both wearing the shirt at the same time, like a strange three-legged race. Chris was still yelling at him and trying to pull Lee out of the store.

Outside there were people, milling around aimlessly, blank stares, open mouths. No clothes, though. This was Hawaii, and people in bathing suits were not uncommon...wait...Hawaii? He'd been in North Carolina with Chris! But Chris was no longer there, just Lee and the crowd of strangers. A girl was beckoning him closer, mouth open forming words, but still no sound. She was on a bicycle, was holding another one for him. But no, he was naked! That would *hurt*! But oh, okay, he was in a swimsuit like Olympic swimmers wore, vinyl cap on his head and his race number marked on his chest with a permanent marker. He needed to change, because there were zombies crawling out of the surf, stumbling on the loose sand. He got on the bike and pedaled, but he seemed to be getting nowhere and the zombies moved closer.

He had to move, but every step felt like he was bogged down in thick mud and pulling against elastic bands.

He awoke with a start in the predawn grayness.

It was okay. He was safe. Well, as safe as he could be in a zombie apocalypse.

Lee Eller had been a runner...and a swimmer...and a cyclist.

It was quite the change for him, from sedentary college student on an ROTC scholarship, to a brief Army service constantly at risk of failing his fitness test, then a desk jockey with a big weight problem, to athlete and successful business owner. He'd started walking for his health, then running, cycling, and swimming. At first, he'd limited himself to single-sport races, such as marathons or long-distance cycling. A friend had challenged him to compete in a triathlon—a swim of at least a mile, plus a fifty-mile bike ride, then a half-marathon run—and he was hooked.

He'd come to the big island of Hawaii last spring, after competing in triathlons for several years. The Ironman World Competition held in the town of Kailua-Kona—commonly just called Kona—every October was considered the pinnacle of the sport, doubling the distance of common triathlons. Last year was his first Ironman, and rumors of an even more extreme competition convinced him to continue training for the upcoming "ExtremeIron" with a four-mile swim, one-hundred-fifty-mile ride, and fifty-mile ultramarathon.

There wasn't much money in the competition, except for someone like him, who'd been in the circuit for more than ten years. On the other hand, he'd developed a few profitable computer programs, built a company, and hired people for the day-to-day operation. The programs were popular for athletes and people wanting to track their exercise, and he made a comfortable amount of money. It was good income, and he'd sold off several software titles at a profit. That nest egg plus a steady income from writing software gave him the free time to train and compete, so he'd come back to the Big Island of Hawaii last spring and stayed. Lee had set his sights on the super-triathlon and knew that he would need to practice not only running on not level roads near sea level, but also cycling on the hills that climbed nearly three thousand feet in elevation to the ranching town of Waimea. There was also an additional one-thousand-foot incline on the cycling course as it rose over the extinct Kohala volcano, then descended to the coastal town of Hawi, followed by a speed run back to Kailua-Kona.

As long as Lee had a laptop and access to the internet, he could work—and train—anywhere, and so he did. He'd even met someone compatible in Hawaii. Malia "Allie" Noelani was a fellow triathlete who shared his love of extreme sports. He worked on his remote job while Allie worked at a T-shirt shop to support herself while finishing her nursing degree. The two of them managed to fit early morning and late evening training around their respective work schedules and a growing personal relationship.

That all changed one day as Lee and Allie were sitting at a café alongside Kailua Bay and saw naked people climbing out of the water and attacking the tourists on Ali'i Drive. They'd been riding that morning and left their bikes out behind the café. Backpacks loaded with training supplies, a change of clothes, socks, shoes, water, protein bars, wallets and cell phones sat at their feet.

That would have to suffice.

Without a word, they got up, tossed a few dollars on the table to cover their lunch bill, and rushed to their bikes.

"Where?" Lee asked.

"Not along the coast," Allie told him as pulled her bike out of the rack behind the restaurant. "We need to head upland, either to the Saddle or Waimea."

"The saddle is seven thousand feet up. Are you thinking of heading to Hilo?"

"No, the coast will be bad, think tsunami," Allie told him. "Also, I think we want to be away from other people."

"Where?"

"Kamuela—you know it as Waimea—is the waypoint on the ExtremeIron cycling course. It's a small town and people are all spread out because of the ranch lands."

"Away from the crowds..."

"...and the beaches, the ports, and the airport. I think we have enough time to grab the tsunami pack from my store, it's away from the beach, so we should be okay if we hurry. If you can manage a big pack, we can combine race packs into one and I'll carry them." Allie gave him a serious look, and Lee thanked his stars that he'd found such a sensible companion.

"Yeah, I—" Lee took a deep breath. "Whatever it takes. Let's hurry."

It took five long minutes to get to the store, and ten even longer minutes for Allie to come back carrying a large backpacker's frame and pack. It threatened Lee's balance on the bike, but there was nothing he could do but try his best. After that was a grueling forty-mile, nearly three-thousand-foot climb, but it was exactly what they'd been training on. With bikes, and only the possessions on their backs, they fled the growing zombie apocalypse in the town of Kailua-Kona. They rode high up toward the mountains, away from the sea. When they could not pedal, they dismounted and walked. They walked—and ran—for their lives.

CHAPTER TWO

RUNNER

Visitors never see the true strength of Hawaii and Hawaiians. We are descended from the resourceful Polynesians who colonized their way across the Pacific Ocean in sailboats and canoes. The islands are loaded with resources—fruit, vegetables, cattle, chickens. We are a people of great ingenuity and a tradition of perseverance.

—M. Maleko, co-owner, Paniolo Ranch Industries

Moving around the tent, Lee was careful not to disturb Allie. She'd taken sick a week or two after they had reached the uplands town of Waimea. She'd had a very high fever, and the local officials had quarantined her for two weeks in fear that she, too, would succumb to H7D3. After the fever broke, she'd been weak but lucid, requiring several more weeks in the refugee medical facility before she could join Lee in the tent city that was growing at the state Forestry and Wildlife station just a half mile outside Waimea. Once she had been able to join him, they'd been assigned a private tent so long as they both performed some service to the community. Lee worked hard every day in his courier job. While Allie was still regaining her strength and limited to light jobs, she began assisting in the clinic where the medical staff could keep an eye on her. She was now past the monthslong recovery and still worked at the clinic, assisting the staff and helping with administrative duties.

At twenty-six hundred feet in elevation, Waimea had a pleasant climate, cool at night, warm during the day, and frequented by light rains. It was ideal for farming and ranching, and famed for its "paniolos," the Hawaiian term for cowboys. In fact, the famous Paniolo Ranch, one of the ten largest ranches in the Americas, stretched southward along the central plateau from just outside Waimea. As an odd technological contrast, the town was also the site of headquarters for two of the observatories with telescope facilities on the summit of Mauna Kea. It had just under ten thousand residents before refugees started pouring in from the coastline. The first month was hectic, with refugees setting up tents and squatting in abandoned houses in the town itself. As residents succumbed to the disease, many people died, and many more had turned into the mindless Infected roaming the streets and hiding wherever food and water could be found—no matter how fresh or palatable. Town and ranch officials had moved refugees to Lalamilo Farm Road as attacks by Infected within the town had increased. Fortifications had been erected around the farms and greenhouses because it was compact, enclosed by vegetation and fences, and contained their food supply. The Paniolo "ranch house" headquarters was not so lucky since it was only separated from the town by a narrow stream. Ranch workers had barricaded the house and service building, and then then left it, seemingly abandoned. It had only recently been cleaned out and reoccupied. The town and ranch administrators fell back to the airport another half mile past Lalamilo Farm and set up their own temporary housing and medical facilities just outside the town. Some of the homes and businesses within Waimea were still occupied, notably the post office, hospital, and a nearby shopping center. Heavily armed groups made occasional forays into town, taking in food and bringing out supplies and medicines. Communication with the hospital was by radio, but for everything else, there was Lee.

Lee stepped out of the tent into the cool dawn air. This early in the day, the sky was clear and crisp. Later, the trade winds would bring clouds that would bump up against the surrounding volcanic peaks and drop a light rain, feeding the farms and nourishing the ranch's grazing lands. Lee walked, then broke into a slow run for the half-mile trip to "headquarters" at the airstrip. He grabbed a quick breakfast at the mess tent: rice and Spam with a bit of fried egg. What was once an unusual specialty breakfast called "Spam musubi" was now a staple because it was easy to prepare. Stocks—for now—were plentiful but were always subject to depletion when a new group of refugees were located. He headed out to the airport. It was only a quarter mile, no distance at all to a runner like himself. Approaching the small field, he passed the wreckage of a commuter plane where it sat at the end of the airstrip. He heard the sound of metal on metal as he came into view of the hangar facilities and saw Michael Horgan working a piece of red-hot metal on an anvil. The local blacksmith was making tools to replace the machine powered farming implements necessary to provide for the community.

The airport building served as the local "government" office until a decision was made about moving back into the ranch house or town offices. Lee quickly took the steps and entered the building. It was hot inside. In the post-H7D3 world, you learned to sweat and love it. As an athlete, he was well-acquainted with sweat.

"Lee! Good to see you. Last day of census. You're headed to the scout camp upslope of the town of Honoka'a, and you should be able to look down toward the town from there. Get a head count and an estimate of how much clearance we'll have to do to get to the Honoka'a-Waipio Road." Julian Thompson was the ranch foreman for Paniolo. He'd been injured protecting refugees as they evacuated from the grounds of the Hawaii Preparatory Academy in Waimea, so he'd been assigned a desk job coordinating the refugees and volunteers. Among survivors, there were those who absolutely excelled at their jobs—Jules among them. Most the remainder willing to work simply did the best they could. Lee counted himself among that number, and would have been surprised to learn that the Paniolo old-timers considered him to be in that top tier, instead.

"I thought Mud Lane was open? The folks at Rocking Chair Ranch said it was clear."

"They say it is, but it also runs through Hamakua Forest, so there's no clear sight lines. If we can go through Honoka'a, or at least as far as Plumeria Street, we can avoid dense cover and lessen the risk of ambush. That means getting close to Honoka'a, so we need some eyes on it before we try."

"Got it. Census at the camp, get close enough to put eyes on the town, then back here by sunset." Lee threw Jules a mock salute.

Jules just laughed. "Run on, Runner."

∞∞∞

"So, what's the *official* tally?" Lee handed over the last of his report from visiting every tent, every farm, ranch, outlying house, and camp in the area controlled by the ranch. He knew his own survey had accounted for over two hundred survivors, and according to Jules, reports from ham radio operators around the world suggested that the local region had had a very high survival rate for H7D3. Thompson attributed it to the climate and isolation, but Lee secretly suspected that the real reason was the attitude and capabilities of these rugged, independent ranchers and farmers.

Lee had trained to be an Ironman, but these were real men—and women—of iron.

"You accounted for two hundred and forty-seven. That includes the ranch, farm, and outlying areas. There's two still in the hospital, sixteen here at the airport, and the other runners came up with seventy-five. Three hundred and forty total. We need to start looking at the other side of Kohala Mountain, but that we'll have to wait." Jules paused, then grunted. "We had a courier up from Waikoloa." He turned and whistled toward the back of the room. A tall, well-weathered man approached. *An islander from his looks, but not Pacific. Caribbean?* "Lee, this is José Clavell, he's a former Army nurse, evacc'ed across the Saddle from Hilo. He's been practically running our clinic."

Lee reached out and shook the older man's hand. "We've met. You helped my friend, Allie Noelani. Lee Eller."

Clavell returned the firm handshake. "Ah, yes. Nice girl. Friend? Not girlfriend?"

Lee released the man's hand and looked down, surprised at the reaction he felt at the words. "It doesn't seem fair," he mumbled, then looked back up. "Somewhere in between."

"Good. She's smart and one of the lucky ones, and now she helps us. Call me José or 'El Coquí' if you like."

"El Coquí? Not sure I've heard that one, Doc." Jules prompted the former combat medic.

Clavell merely nodded. "Puerto Rican tree frog; named for their mating call—ko-KWEE, ko-KWEE!" He shrugged. "People call, I jump. Thus, I am the tree frog of nursing."

All three men chuckled. Jules continued. "Anyway, as I was saying, we've had a message from Waikoloa."

Lee held up his hand to interrupt. "Village or resort? I didn't think we'd had any contact with the coast?"

"Waikoloa Village. About ten miles down Route 190, then another eight miles downslope to the town. The message said that there was a group forted up at the golf course, and they've had several bad cases of . . . something. Not the Haole Flu, something else. They requested a doctor, but it needs to be an armed mission, and they need to travel fast. Doc's former Army, he knows guns. You've proved to be pretty capable yourself, so I want to send the two of you."

Prior to Kona, Lee had only fired a weapon in ROTC and Army qualification tests. Since Kona, he'd learned to fire shotgun and handgun, tutored by Horgan and supervised by the ranch's armorer and gunsmith, Jered van Tuyl. His bicycling pack now accommodated a cut-down semiautomatic shotgun and he wore an old .45 pistol in a belt holster everywhere he went. "Sure, but are we on foot or bike? No offense, José, but unless you've biked these hills, we won't be moving fast. One-Ninety isn't too bad, maybe a couple hundred feet of elevation change, and it's rolling, but we're twenty-six-hundred feet up. The coastal highway averages two-hundred-feet elevation, so halfway down the mountain means at least twelve hundred feet in elevation change. Eight miles? That's what, a minimum three percent grade? Fun going down but a stone bitch coming back up if you have to do it for eight miles."

Clavell laughed. "For this, my young friend, we will let someone else do all the work."

When Lee looked puzzled, Jules explained. "The ranch has consented to the use of a few horses. This is important. If we can establish a safe point at Waikoloa, we might be able to work toward the coast."

"But . . . I'm not a horse person. I'm mean, they've taught me to ride, but that doesn't mean I'm proficient!"

"Shouldn't be a problem, you'll have two other people with you. Cody Makano *is* a 'horse person,' and James Stephens is our 'horse whisperer.' Cody has family in Waikoloa and will serve as recognition and insurance that you don't get shot on approach, and Stephens is a veterinarian. He's also a radio mechanic and will help the survivors set up a radio for regular communication. We'll also send some packs of supplies."

"But if you have someone who's a local, why do you need me?" Lee was still confused.

"Because you're my insurance policy. You're going along to ensure that the party doesn't get shot getting from here to there. Everyone along the One-Ninety knows you, you've been everywhere. Frankly, you're the best runner and courier I have. I know that if the shit hits the fan, you can get word out by foot, by bike, or any means necessary. Van Tuyl says that your shooting and reaction time are very good, bordering on excellent. I'm sending you because I can count on you; because the best reward for a job well-done is a harder job." Thompson paused. "Oh, and one more thing, Lee..." He paused even longer, and his face lit up with a great big grin. "They've got a shoe store."

"Oh, crap. You had to say that." Lee turned red with embarrassment. "Okay. May God have mercy on my soul, but I'm in."

CHAPTER THREE

KITTING-UP

Rodeo! I mean, let's face it, the ranch has horses and people who know how to ride. Kohala is the American Old West condensed onto an island. It's too small for a cattle drive, so a rodeo is the next best thing.

—J. Stephens, veterinarian and rodeo rider

Lee got the courier assignments because it was felt that no matter the situation, he could get out of it—on foot or on bicycle. More recently, that had come to include riding a horse. There wasn't much call for swimming in the highlands, but if he had to swim his way to freedom, he would be able to outpace his pursuers. Anyone, or anything, that tried to deter him from his mission would be left in his dust. It was the gift, but also the price, of his athletic training.

For most of the courier missions he went on foot. If it was a distance longer than ten miles, he'd take his bike. Going on horseback was a rarity. The Paniolo Ranchers carefully guarded their horses and were reluctant to let anyone else handle them, let alone ride them. At the same time, they all knew that Lee was the best choice for getting a message through. So, they trained him on horsemanship as well as firearms. Lee had been introduced to the horses, taught their care and feeding, trained in riding, and taught a few tricks to help get himself out of trouble.

James "Darkhorse" Stephens had been a horse trainer before he came to Hawaii. He'd spent some time on the rodeo circuit on the mainland. Before that, he'd apprenticed with the famed Lipizzaner Stallions in Vienna, Austria, joining them first as a veterinarian, then becoming enthralled with horsemanship as he watched them train. There was no one better at racing, show jumping, or teaching those skills. He'd come to Hawaii for the weather, and settled on the Big Island since it was where they had horses and rodeos. At the ranch he met Iokua "Cody" Makano, who likewise was interested in rodeo, and the two of them helped organize and promote a high school rodeo in the town of Waimea. The two had planned some exhibitions on the other islands last spring, but the Haole Flu derailed those plans. On the other hand, it left the paniolos with the best people to teach their best courier what he'd need to know in order to do his job.

Lee met Stephens, Makano, and Clavell at the stables the next day before dawn. Darkhorse had taught Lee to inspect and adjust all of the tack and gear before setting out anywhere, let alone downslope. The ranch also had a rule that anyone using a horse on a given day *also* had to contribute to the care of *all* horses, including grooming, feeding, and mucking out the stalls.

The four men joined other ranchers in the general care and cleanup of the facilities before they started their assignments. Horses were led to specific corrals for feeding, gear was oiled and inspected, stalls were shoveled out, with all of the manure going into wheelbarrows destined to the steam plant for sterilization. After that, it would be earmarked either for fertilizer, or dried for fuel. It was hot, sweaty work, but once Lee stepped outside the stable, he cooled off rapidly in the firm breezes that blew over the uplands of the Big Island.

Hard work meant hearty appetites. As with farmers and ranchers the world over, morning chores came first and breakfast second. Food was tightly managed, although there were allowances based on the type of work a person contributed to the community. Breakfast was a firm cake of cornmeal, a single hard-boiled egg, mango slices, and two strips of wild boar bacon with a glass of diluted mango juice. It didn't feel as if food was rationed, but it was a tithe of the amounts he'd consumed when training for ExtremeIron. The Paniolo Ranch community had over three hundred mouths to feed, and only half of them worked jobs that directly provided food.

On the other hand, they had fifteen thousand cows, five hundred sheep, and the wild goats and boars. On the farming side, there were fields of corn, plots of strawberries, mango groves, and scattered plots of lettuce, tomatoes, sweet potatoes, and other vegetables. Even before the Fall, Waimea and the ranch area had been known for food production. That didn't even count the Waipio, Waimanu, Honokane, and Polulu Valleys downslope on the windward side that grew rice, taro, bananas, avocados, papaya, pineapple and sugarcane. Food was available but had to be farmed—and in the case of the valleys, it had to be traded for. Small farms were scattered through the tablelands in the center of the island, and along both the windward and leeward slopes. There was more produce than people left to tend it.

They'd gradually come to understand that while Waimea and the Paniolo Ranch had the highest concentration of survivors, there were many groups of ten to twenty survivors scattered throughout the island. Many of those had only standard consumer radio receivers— no broadcast capabilities. There were few two-way radios or walkie-talkies because there just wasn't a need for them on an island with cellular phone service. Connecting isolated groups *without* radio contact was the main job of couriers like Lee.

They had thought that survivors had mainly clustered around the central plateau until a hunting expedition had discovered that several of the lush rain forest valleys and fertile bottomlands to the northeast were also populated. In fact, one valley had no H7D3 victims despite regular visitors from Hilo and Waimea. True, several residents of Waipio and Waimanu Valleys had gotten quite sick with flu-like symptoms, but none had turned into Infected, and very few died of the initial symptoms.

Several of the older residents said that the valleys were often visited by the spirits of the Ali'i—the old Hawaiian rulers. After all, Waipio was where King Kamehameha won the battle that first united the islands, and Waimanu was likely where he was hidden shortly after his birth. The valleys were extremely fertile and some said—blessed by the old gods. It was no wonder the locals considered the valleys mystic and strange. The possibility of immunity to the Haole Flu was not out of the question, after all. Allie recovered, and Lee never got it, despite being exposed to all of the same infectious conditions.

Of course, there were others who said that the immunity could also be the work of the menehune. Legend said that the mysterious "little people" lived in the islands well before humans, and kept to themselves, only evident by their wondrous constructions. A few humans and children were supposed to be able to see them, and they befriended a few, granting health, fortune, and good crops. Whatever the reason, these outlying settlements and villages added a couple hundred more survivors to the Kohala region and provided much needed trade in foodstuffs to Waimea.

Thus, the stables were divided into two buildings. The larger one could house up to fifty horses, although before the Fall they'd had fewer than fifteen working paniolos. Now that they couldn't use powered vehicles or machinery, the ranch had trained and expanded to forty paniolos. Horseback was the best means to get around the 130,000 acres of ranch to tend the over tens of thousands of cows, sheep, and goats. A smaller building held ten stalls and served the couriers and guard escorts.

It was there that Lee's usual mount, a sixteen-hand, sorrel gelding named Oumuamua—Hawaiian for "scout" or "messenger." Lee shared access to 'Mua, but Darkhorse had told him that the gelding would be available any time he needed him. "Our best messenger deserves his Oumuamua."

Lee had groomed 'Mua the night before. He took his duties seriously and did the grooming whether he rode 'Mua that day or not. This morning, he needed to work out just a few tangles in tail and mane, muck out the stall, and oil the tack. With that cared for, and one of the buckles on the saddle replaced, Lee saddled up 'Mua and joined the others headed to Waikoloa.

There were two stops to make before they went. The first was at the ranch manager's home to pick up messages that would be given to the mayor of Waikoloa, and others to be passed on as survivors were encountered and other towns were contacted. The second stop was with the armorer. Lee usually carried a shotgun in a scabbard attached to his saddle. Jered van Tuyl, the ranch's burly, six-foot-three-inch armorer, had taken it upon himself to drill Lee in pistol and rifle skills as well as shotgun. While Lee was nowhere near as accurate as the paniolos and hunters, he'd be carrying all three weapons on this trip since they were headed into an unknown population center.

The shotgun was a Mossberg 500, shooting twelve-gauge buckshot. His rifle for this trip would be a Winchester 700 chambered in .308, paired with an old police-model SIG Sauer P210 pistol in 9mm. The weapon and caliber were the most common in use by hunters and clearance teams and could be most easily reloaded. While none of them would necessarily bring down a charging wild boar with a single shot, they were all was certainly effective on predators of the two-legged variety. To date, the paniolos hadn't encountered any organized highwaymen or bandits. There were reports of isolated thieves, and more than a few who sought to take advantage of the decline of civilization and police forces, but nothing more than two or three people at most ganging together. There was no doubt, however, that desperate survivors would grasp for any food, shelter, or other provisions, even if they had to take from those who had, rather than provide for themselves.

Outside the armory, Lee and his companions went to the warehouse for the packs and saddlebags they'd carry with them. For the trip down, they were taking some fertilizer and salted meat to Waikoloa. The goods were loaded in packs and tied behind each saddle. The slope would be mild at first, but steeper once they got closer to the village. They had originally planned to take a cart but couldn't spare the mules or horses. It would also have meant additional men to pull the cart, plus guards, not to mention someone to restrain the cart from running downhill on the descent. For this trip, they would take what the four could carry, and save bigger loads for later.

It was midmorning when the team was completely assembled. Once everyone confirmed readiness, the party set out to descend the slopes of the Kohala uplands.

CHAPTER FOUR
DOWNSLOPE

Many people arrive on Hawaii Island via Kona. Driving out of the city you see fifty- to one-hundred-fifty-year-old lava flows. The casual visitor to the beachside resorts will probably think that all of the island is lava rock, but once you get above two-thousand-feet elevation, you get trees, grass, and real soil. The same change occurs if you get more than twenty miles north, or even just a few miles south of the airport. That's just the leeward side. Hawaii is an island of contrasts.

—N. Maile, co-owner and household manager,
Paniolo Ranch Homestead

The distance was only sixteen miles, but the last six would result in an almost two-thousand-foot drop in elevation. Cody and Darkhorse would range ahead of Lee and José and keep an eye out for trouble.

The group had traveled ten miles down Route 190, to where it met the Waikoloa Road. They'd passed the branch to the Saddle Road, Route 200, about five miles back, which was generally the landmark Lee used to differentiate ascent and descent around the ranch and outlying houses. Saddle Road climbed another four thousand feet to the pass between Mauna Loa and Mauna Kea. That was the direction Lee normally took in the course of his courier duties.

It was always a surprise to realize that, despite the gently rolling terrain, they hadn't actually descended since Waimea. Cody pointed out that Route 190 had elevation markers as you got closer to the city of Kona, but not here, since the elevation didn't really change. Lee and Allie certainly hadn't noted them during their escape from the bay, but now that it was mentioned, Lee realized that aside from Saddle Road and Route 19 on the other end of Waimea, he hadn't really been down this particular stretch since that day.

The steep road was no easier on the descent than it would be for the same route returning uphill. At least the road was clear. Mr. Maleko—the ranch manager, part owner, and the closest thing to a government leader for Waimea—had sent teams out over the past six months to clear broken-down vehicles and any other debris from the roads that surrounded Paniolo Ranch and Waimea. Even Waikoloa and the smaller settlements seemed to have done the same, although they were beginning to see more dead vehicles as they approached the small town.

What Lee *did* remember of his escape flight from Kailua Kona was riding among lava flows and fields dominated by lava rock. Up on the plateau of the central highlands, the rock had long been broken into rich fields of fertile soil. Once he realized that Route 190 didn't really descend until much closer to Kona, he understood why the land around them was mostly grasslands, with a few stands of trees right next to the trees. Once they started to descend into Waikoloa, they began to see many more outcroppings of lava rock and course, rocky soil, but still none of the vast fields of lava from the nineteenth-century eruptions of Mauna Loa and the much smaller Hualalai, both of which loomed over the Kona coast.

"Zed at two o'clock," Cody announced as they started to see scattered buildings and the green-now-brown grass of a golf course.

"Got it," Darkhorse replied.

The Infected didn't seem to notice them, yet, but Lee was certain that once the smell of horse and human was detected, the Infected would orient on them and accelerate from a shamble to an outright run. The amazing thing wasn't the fact that the creature was naked—no, that wasn't amazing, they all were—but that it was standing barefoot on lava rock that was cutting its feet, leaving ragged, bloody strips of flesh behind.

Lee pulled the Mossberg out of its saddle scabbard. He brought it up to a low-ready position, but didn't shoulder or aim. Darkhorse and Cody were closer and would take the shot. Lee and José needed to be on the lookout for *other* threats, now.

The Infected's head came up, and it appeared to sniff the air. The wind was coming from behind them, over the center of the island, and the Infected was off to the side, but it appeared to smell them anyway, as it turned, sighted the men and horses, made a bloodcurdling shriek, and started toward them.

CRACK!

The Infected barely started moving before its head exploded. Darkhorse lowered his rifle once the creature collapsed, but then began to scan for more threats.

"Between the scream and the gunshot, that will bring them out," said Cody.

Sure enough, several more shapes appeared, moving out from behind a row of palm trees lining the right side of the road.

"That's your shoe store, back there, kiddo. Best we take care of these guys now," José said to Lee over his shoulder as he turned to take aim on the approaching pack.

"'For Shoes!' doesn't seem like much of a rallying cry," Darkhorse responded.

"How about 'For Survival!'?" countered Lee.

"That'll do nicely." Darkhorse and Cody each took aim and dropped an Infected.

José took several shots, but dropped his rifle and drew a sword as the Infected started to get closer.

"Saber?" Lee asked. Van Tuyl had been trying to teach him weapons, but the curved blade with the elaborate basket hilt was new to him.

"Navy cutlass. It's a chief petty officer's sword for repelling boarders at sea. Also good for driving off Infected, savages, and bandits," Clavell replied as he slashed the throat of an approaching Infected.

Lee brought his shotgun up. As the creature got closer, the weapon was much more appropriate. At this range, bullets tended to go right through them, which really did little to stop one of the mindless creatures. They didn't feel pain, and unless a bullet took them in the head, it did little more than delay them a step or two.

Twelve-gauge slugs, on the other hand, would make an Infected pause, at the very least. They were also good for mangling and removing limbs, organs, and heads at close quarters. The hazard was getting splashed by blood, though, so Lee tried to engage from at least twenty feet away.

Cody and Darkhorse had trained the horses well; they remained steady and under control even as the firearms went off above them. They'd remain so until the Infected got within reach, so it was important to maintain that distance. José relied on keeping his horse moving to dart in, strike with his sword, then keep moving. Darkhorse and Cody maneuvered to the edges to keep firing into the crowd, while Lee simply backed his horse up to maintain the appropriate distance.

It wasn't much of a fight. The three shooters spaced their shots so that each could reload as needed. Lee's extended magazine gave him five rounds plus one in the chamber. The stock-mounted shell carrier gave him his first reload, and he barely needed to reload from his saddlebags. José switched to cutting throats of the Infected that had been downed without headshots. They'd keep moving as long as blood was being pumped, and even a bit longer, so it was the only way to be sure.

In less than ten minutes, this fight was over. The four men spread out in a line and entered the parking lot of the small shopping plaza behind the trees. While their destination was a bit farther down the road, it was never wise to leave an enemy behind you.

Another twenty minutes confirmed that there were no other active Infected in this area. Darkhorse shot one more Infected with torn-up feet who appeared to simply be late to the party.

Lee did note that the shoe store in this center appeared to be one affiliated with a chain of sports outfitters, and his hopes were raised regarding finding footwear appropriate to long-distance walking and running. In addition, the windows and door were intact, and from what he could see of the darkened interior, it hadn't been trashed.

But all of that would have to wait.

There were injured people to treat, supplies to deliver and then gather up to send back to Waimea. There was also information to be gained about other events happening downslope. Shoes could wait. People? They came first.

They didn't see any more Infected around the area of the shopping center, but there was evidence of Infected "nests" nearby in the form of shallow, cleared depressions, ringed by mounds of trash. The groomed lawns of the golf course would have made comfortable sleeping areas in the shade of the palm trees and tall bushes lining the fairways. With the increasing rockiness of the surrounding fields, the landscaped area—even if now overgrown—would be perfect for unprotected humans to simply lie down and sleep without the need for overhead shelter.

If there was one thing the survivors had learned, it was that while Infected had no communications skills, no signs of higher intelligence, and certainly did not react to pain, they apparently still sought comfort, shelter, and food like even the most primitive of humans. Hawaii had had a large homeless population due to the nearly universal pleasant weather, and this same weather made it all too easy for the mindless Infected to survive . . . and even thrive.

One reason why Maleko, Jules, and the others were so reluctant to advance on the coastal cities was that they'd simply trade one "homeless" problem for another. As long as there was food and water— no matter how unpalatable—the Infected could survive.

Until iron men came to clean them out.

CHAPTER FIVE

THIS FALLEN WORLD

Some people think Hawaii's most popular sport is surfing. No, it's golfing. I mean, where else do you find golf courses in black sand, rain forest, and even in the middle of an airport?
—J. Clavell, Army nurse (ret.)

Jules had told him there was a medical emergency, but also critical information to be had in Waikoloa. It had been the reason Lee was sent, and not just José. They'd also been told that the local "government" had been set up at the clubhouse for the golf course. So, the four set out across the old fairway to a cluster of building with solar panels on their roofs. As they got closer, they saw a pair of tennis courts with tall fences around the outside. One was filled with tents and lean-tos. The other had several long tables, a couple of pavilion-style tents, and firepits.

"Using the fences as Infected defenses," José said quietly. When Lee looked his way, the man nodded his head in the direction of the tennis courts.

"Oh, emergency housing and dining. Makes sense," Lee replied.

"I wonder what they did with the pool?" Darkhorse asked. "Infected seem to sniff out water, and they will drink the most horrid-smelling and -looking stuff."

The question was answered as they approached the first of the buildings. A low fence surrounded what was clearly a drained pool, but there was an obvious gap in the fence, and there were internal barricades that appeared to lead farther inward.

"Probably a pit trap," José grunted. "Draw Infected in with the smell of fresh water. Well, fresh-ish, I guess. Then have the pool lined with stakes, and maybe grease the sides as well."

"Perceptive," said a weathered older man approaching them on foot. "You're too young for Vietnam." This was directed to José.

"Nope, Somalia, Sudan, Zimbabwe. They all had variations on the theme."

The man gave a respectful nod, then turned to address the rest of them. "I'm Scotty Thompson, Security. I did serve in 'Nam, right at the end. The only thing I refused to do was coat the stakes in shit. Zeds don't care if they get an infection. We trap 'em and shoot 'em. Arrows, lately, because we're running low on bullets. Follow me."

He led them around the buildings, then to a housing complex across the street. The buildings ringed a central courtyard, and there was only one open side, facing the street. Barricades closed off that side, and they could see that fencing had been added to the outer perimeter of the buildings, securing the whole complex. He rapped twice, then twice again on the wooden panel blocking the driveway, and the wall began to slide back, exposing the parking area.

"Your horses will be safe in here." He nodded to the teenaged boy operating the gate, who closed the barrier behind them after they rode through.

After the four dismounted, pulled their weapon scabbards from their horses, and handed the reins off to another teen, Thompson led them out through a small door in the barricade, then back across the street to the golf club buildings.

"Ahoy the house!" one of the guards called.

After a minute, the door began to rise, first slowly, then all at once as a man straightened up behind it and released the handle to allow momentum to open it the rest of the way. Behind him was another wooden barricade with small holes cut through at eye height, and just below.

"Two-stage barrier and gunports. It's nice to work with professionals, Mr. Thompson." Cody eyed the man curiously. "Any relation?"

"Julian is my nephew," Scotty told them. "Let's get you inside. Which of you is the doc?" He looked at Lee.

"Not me, I'm just the runner."

"I'm a nurse practitioner," José told him. "Closest thing to a doc right now. But don't let Lee sell himself short, he's more than just our runner. He speaks to and for Maleko."

Thompson raised an eyebrow at that, then led them to a side door of the main clubhouse. Lee wondered briefly at the fact that no one mentioned that he and his companions were heavily armed. Then again, it was a zombie apocalypse.

Inside, Lee was surprised to see lighting and moving air from ceiling fans.

Thompson noticed his expression. "Solar panel farms just downhill. Not full power, but it lets us keep the lights on. Also powers our radio."

"Radio?" Darkhorse had a puzzled expression. Lee knew that the man had experience with electrical and electronic systems and was supposed to help the folks at Waikoloa set one up if they didn't have one already. "So, you do have one. You're too low on the slope to reach the plateau from here, though."

"You're right. We can't talk to your people directly. We call Kauai, and they relay for us."

"Oh, okay."

"Right. In here for the patients." He'd taken them up a short flight of stairs into the bar area of the clubhouse. Several areas had been cleared out and converted to housing and other needs. The golf shop was filled with cots and bedrolls, while the bar seemed to have retained a few tables, but the restaurant now had all the tables pulled together into one, surrounded by chairs.

"This, and the tennis courts. Is it all of you?" Lee asked.

"No, just the folks who came to us from elsewhere. Many people choose to live in their homes. It's a risk because we haven't cleared all the houses of those creatures, but folks who live here like to be left alone. When we get enough people, we'll try to clear some of the unused houses and move them in. This is just the central meeting place and Mr. Peachtree's office. By the way, Doc, the patients are in there." Thompson pointed to the converted golf shop.

"Not a doc, sir, just a nurse," José corrected him.

"You saw combat."

José nodded but didn't say anything.

"Let me take the rest of you to Mr. Peachtree. He's the boss."

Darkhorse elected to head back to see to the horses, leaving Lee and Cody to go meet "the boss." Lee had the mental image of a rotund man, red in the face, wearing a white suit and fanning himself with a wide-brimmed hat. The name brought back memories of Atlanta and made Lee think of a wealthy plantation owner.

Much to Lee's surprise, Mr. Peachtree was anything but the image of a Southern gentleman. He was lean, with darkened, sun-weathered skin. He looked like a man who worked outside most of his life, but in shorts and an open, flowered shirt, Lee saw muscular legs and arms, and a relatively flat stomach. He was in his forties, maybe fifties, and looked vaguely familiar to him.

The office had once belonged to the golf course manager—as evidenced by the small nameplate outside the door that said exactly that. Inside, it had been stripped of all memorabilia, except for a single medallion draped over a picture of a woman of Peachtree's age. This one Lee did recognize, and with that realization, it all clicked. Cecilia Peachtree had won the women's division of the XTERRA World Championship on the neighboring island of Maui the year before he'd come to Hawaii. The off-road triathlon was not as long as either Ironman or ExtremeIron, but the fact that the swim was in surf, the bike course was in the West Maui Mountains, and the run was along trails in those same mountains made it a class all its own. Lee had planned to attend the games as an observer while training for ExtremeIron and had made contact with the local organizers for information.

His contact had been Reuben Peachtree. The man standing in front of him.

Lee held out his hand.

"Mr. Peachtree. It is good to see you again." Before he said the next thing on his mind, his brain registered that in addition to the medallion, a black ribbon crossed one corner of the portrait. "I'm sorry for your loss."

Peachtree's return handshake was firm, and his deep voice calm. "Thank you, Mr. Eller. It is good to see you as well. What's past is past, and we all have to live on in this fallen world." There was the trace of a wistful expression, but that faded as he turned to shake hands with Cody.

Peachtree motioned for the two to sit and joined them in a cluster of chairs around a small table. "I'd heard you made it out, but it's a surprise to see you with the Paniolos. I hope Maleko knows what he's got in you."

"He . . . they . . . treat me well, sir."

"Call me Ben. May I call you Lee? One athlete to another?"

"He's a true *iron* man, sir," Cody said. "We'd be lost without him. He keeps us in contact."

"You too . . . Cody, is it? Forget the 'sir,' you can call me Ben as well." The table had a clear pitcher of water and several glasses. Ben poured them each a glass and then leaned back in his chair. "Hmm. He's got you working as a runner. Literally, am I right?"

"Yes. My training partner, Allie, and I got out with all of our gear and our bikes. We were training the day Kona fell."

"You two are lucky, then. So is Maleko. I handled a lot of paperwork for ExtremeIron, so I saw your qualifiers. You have amazing endurance."

"He's contacted more outlying settlements and covered more distance than any of our other messengers," Cody told him. "That's why Jules sent him down here with us. We heard there was some important news in addition to the injuries."

"Right. To business, then. You might want to head right back up to the ranch when we're done. This needs to get to Maleko's ears and I didn't want to put it out over the radio. We don't know who's listening."

Lee's eyebrows went up at that. "Pirates? Or . . . wait . . . it's 'brigands' on land, right?"

"Worse. We have a problem. This is bigger than just our village or even just our side of the island." Peachtree took a sip of his water, continuing to hold the glass in his hand. "We had a visitor come amidst a bunch of those Fallen—the Infected, that is. They didn't touch him, and they seemed remarkably restrained at first. Didn't attack us while he stood among them, either."

His voice cracked, and he finished off the rest of the water in his glass, then refilled it before resuming. "Sorry, not a pleasant memory. So, about this stranger, he wasn't naked, like the Fallen, but he sure looked like them: thin white hair, sunken features, sun-damaged skin. He wore a tattered old aloha shirt and a loincloth. Symbols painted on his skin in mud and blood. He told us he spoke for the 'True King' and that we should know that Kuwahailo had returned."

The name didn't really mean that much to Lee, but he could see the shock on Cody's face. "Lauro Serra the psychopath? Called himself Ku? I thought he was in prison."

"He was, over on Oahu—Halawa Correctional. I guess the guards let folks out when things went south."

"I've heard of him. Of his case, that is," Lee said. "Killed a bunch of people and ate them?"

"Yes, he said it was a return to the old Polynesian gods. Said that he was the incarnation of Kuka'ilimoku and demanded human sacrifice. I heard he told a fellow inmate that Ku the sorcerer would send a great plague. I guess he considered H7D3 a validation."

"And this guy was Ku-whatever? Or just a messenger?"

"He told us he was a messenger, but that all who refused to worship Ku would be sacrificed. He told us to tell everyone that he'd be back. 'Go tell it on the mountain,' he said, then raised his hands and disappeared in a puff of smoke. The Fallen attacked us the moment he was gone."

"Serra, or Ku, or whatever name he uses, was fond of illusions and magic tricks. He escaped from custody a few times and loved the 'puff of smoke' trick," Cody told them.

Lee looked at him and raised his eyebrows.

"I had a cousin on Honolulu PD. Cops told a lot of stories about the hunt. Took most of the HPD and Five-O, and lots of Fibbies and Marshals. They'd have him cornered, and '*poof*' he'd be gone."

"How'd they catch him, then?"

"Smell. Five-O—the state police—had some cadaver dogs brought over on loan from the mainland, the ones they use to find bodies in disaster sites. It seems that eating human meat causes abnormal pain sensation and the victim ends up with sores from biting or scratching themselves. Those get infected and begin to smell."

"He was also mad as a hatter, and while he'd been pretty smart to begin with, he ended up a devilishly clever madman," Peachtree said. "Like, figuring-out-how-to-control-zombies level of insane. Anyway, our doc was coming back from a house call about the time this all happened. He was caught on the fringe of the crowd of Infected and was bitten. That's when we sent word to you folks. Maleko needs to know. We *all* need to know, and to do something. Our world has fallen so far, but there was still hope. This? This could cause us to fall so much farther."

CHAPTER SIX

SUPPLY RUN

At three thousand feet elevation, atmospheric air pressure is ninety percent of that at sea level. By the time you climb above six thousand feet, it's down to eighty percent. Above nine thousand feet, the air pressure has dropped to seventy percent. That's not just a percentage drop in oxygen, it also increases the difficulty of landing aircraft and taking off from those elevations. When temperatures increase, it gets worse.

—Captain M. Fowler, pilot, MCBH flight Penguin 4-2

"The scariest part of this was that the nutter seemed to have those Zeds under control." Scotty Thompson was leading Lee and Cody back across the street to the location where they'd left the horses. "I'm not sure how he did it, but they didn't attack him, and they didn't move on us until he disappeared."

"It's all tricks, Scotty. It has to be. I don't believe in reincarnated kings or gods or whatever. He's a madman who works for a madman." Cody snorted in disgust.

"A madman who thinks he's the reincarnation of the Polynesian God of war."

"Actually, from the reading that Jules... ah, your nephew, Mr. Thompson... had me doing, Kuka'ilimoku was the god of war, but didn't Ben tell us that the messenger called him Kuwahailo?" Lee asked.

"What of it?"

"Well, that incarnation of Ku was a god of sorcery."

"Ah. Yes, we shouldn't be surprised at the tricks, then."

The teen at the gate let them back in to the barricaded hotel courtyard. The horses had been taken to a back corner, directly opposite the entrance, where one building set directly adjacent to the parking lot formed a small green space with the larger villas that formed the outer perimeter of the complex. Darkhorse was brushing José's mare, while a teenaged girl did the same for 'Mua. Each horse had a feed bag attached over their muzzle.

"Hope they haven't had too much, Darkhorse," Cody told him.

"Just enough to make sure they are fresh," Darkhorse answered. "I take it that means someone's headed back this evening?"

"Yes. The manager had news that needs to get back as soon as possible. Lee's headed back, and one of us with him."

"Well, did you at least get your shoes, Lee?"

"Not this trip. No time to waste. They aren't going anywhere, though. I imagine I'll be back."

"Tell me what size, and I'll see if I can get them for you. I assume, Cody, that you are going back with him?"

"Yes, I am."

"Right. Good. Kiana's enthusiastic but doesn't have much experience with caring for the horses." Darkhorse looked over at the girl, and she blushed, but nodded in agreement. "And El Coquí is staying?"

"He'll go back with you the day after tomorrow once he is satisfied with his patients."

"Okay. I'll probably do some perimeter scouting tomorrow." He looked up at the sky and noted the position of the sun. "Sunset's in, oh, three hours. You'll have to take the upslope at a walk, so that's roughly an hour, hour and a half. You can trot or even canter up on Route 190 if you keep it slow until you get there. So, another hour. Twilight's not as short at elevation as it is at sea level, so you should have enough light."

Scotty grunted. "You paniolos have it all figured out, don't you? Why not wait until morning?"

"The Ku or whoever he was said he'd be back. There's no telling when, and since he specifically mentioned 'on the mountain,' there's no telling where. We need to get this message back right away."

"And, of course, the ranch is the center of power here on Kohala," Scotty said. "Okay, so you need to leave now. What if you run into Zeds?"

"Then I will fight them, and our runner will dismount and run." Cody turned to Lee. "What's your best time for ten miles?"

"An hour and fifteen, maybe twenty. Likely better than that if I'm being chased."

"This isn't Marathon to Athens, kid. You need to survive to pass on the messages," Scotty admonished him.

"I'm rested, hydrated, and not overfed," Lee assured him. "If I have to, I can outrun the horses."

"Okay. Well, gentlemen, good luck." Scotty shook their hands and stood back as Darkhorse and Kiana saddled 'Mua and Cody's stallion, Blaze. Lee and Cody performed an abbreviated check of their gear and were out the gate inside ten minutes.

The return trip did not require Lee to emulate Pheidippides, and they arrived before the light started to fade. The horses were tired, but not exhausted, and Lee was excused from their care to go see Jules as quickly as possible to set up a meeting with the head of their community.

Lee and Cody approached the old ranch headquarters building. The central building was still intact, but several of the outbuildings had burned in the early days after the Fall. It had been overrun in those days, since a residential neighborhood was less than a quarter mile away over a small stream. Makaio Maleko had been ranch manager—and eventually, owner—before the Fall, and his wife of eighteen years, Nalani Maile, the ranch's household manager. Nalani was trapped inside the manor house with ten people under her care, and Makaio led the surviving ranchers to reclaim the headquarters building after dealing with the immediate threats out of Waimea.

Parker Ranch HQ was iconic to the community. The last of the Parker family heirs had passed more than twenty years prior, leaving a trust in charge of the ranch in general, and the ranch house in particular. Nalani was the last executive of the trust, and she'd been the one responsible for hiring Makaio as ranch manager twenty years ago, before the two had bought the ranch and renamed it. The involvement of both of them in creating jobs and strengthening the community cemented their status as leaders of the ranch community and surrounding town even before the Fall.

Nalani met the two men at the door and invited them into Maleko's office. The ranch had a limited amount of electrical power, from solar and wind generation, but Lee noted that they used oil lamps and candles for lighting in the office. Nalani stayed and took a seat on a sofa that appeared to be recently recovered in cowhide.

"The Infected did such damage. We had to have so many furnishings replaced, but it would have been a shame to abandon the homestead. It has been here for two hundred years," she told them, motioning for the two to take a seat as her husband came over to join them.

There was a tea service, with what looked like small sandwiches, sitting on the coffee table in the middle of the seating area. Nalani poured tea for all of them as Maleko motioned for Cody and Lee to tell their news.

Cody told most of the story, although Maleko seemed interested in Lee's observations of Peachtree, the elder Thompson, and others at Waikoloa. "What do you think of this, Lee? You've been everywhere on the plateau, but not down to the coast, since you came here. Still, you've seen the mobs and the breakdown firsthand. What type of threat are we facing?"

"Sir, Infected aren't smart, but they're relentless. It's like any race. A driven person will ignore pain and weakness and push on, but the psychological battle will cause them to eventually stop. Infected don't have psychology. They don't stop, and unless you kill them outright, they just keep coming. A single man with a gun can kill dozens, maybe even a hundred, one-on-one. They won't survive a dozen that attack all at the same time. The only fortunate thing with the Infected is that they can't *get* to you all at once. The possibility of intelligence directing them? It's a bigger threat than I've ever seen."

Maleko sighed. "Yes, I agree. We are going to need more. More people, more weapons, more ways to fight."

They sat in silence for a few moments, and Lee could hear a clock ticking somewhere in the house. A distant chime began to sound, and Lee realized that somewhere on the floor was an old gravity-driven grandfather clock, and it was still in operation.

When the clock finished chiming, Maleko looked to his wife, who cocked her head to one side. The two obviously communicated something without words.

"Go home, you two. Lee, go see your wife. You're going to be busy for a while, and far be it from me to keep a man away from his girl." Nalani smiled a small smile, making it clear that this is what she'd been signaling to her husband. "I'm sending you to Pohakuloa tomorrow. It's time to rally the troops."

"Not my wife, sir, ma'am. Just my training partner."

Nalani cocked an eyebrow at him. "No? Or just not yet?"

Lee was left wondering what she meant; what she knew that he didn't. He let the issue drop and did as she said and went back to the tent he shared with Allie. They had a lot to discuss.

After telling Allie about his trip to Waikoloa and instructions to head up the mountain to the army camp at Pohakuloa, Lee prompted her to tell of her own day at the clinic. He found comfort in knowing that her work was routine, and as safe as it could be. He lay on his bedroll, unable to sleep, thinking about what Ms. Maille said, and how he felt about it.

"Something's bothering you," Allie murmured.

It was telling to Lee that she knew he was thinking deep thoughts. After all, he wasn't fidgeting or making it obvious that he was still awake.

Somehow, she just knew. She cared for him and knew when something was on his mind.

He cared for her, too, and knew it was time to broach a subject they'd been discussing well before the escape from Kona—and put aside in the struggle to just survive since then.

"You always know, don't you?" Lee replied, softly.

"Of course. I know you, Lee Eller."

"That you do, Malia Noelani."

"So, what is it? I know you're not the type to be afraid of an upcoming mission. Cautious? Wary? But not afraid."

Lee took a deep breath. "Us."

"Us?"

"Yes. Us. As in you and me. What we mean to each other, what our future holds."

"Oh. My sweetest Lee, we set that aside because it was too much to think about the future when we didn't know what the next minute would hold—let alone the next however-many years."

"We set it aside to concentrate on surviving. We've done that."

"So far."

"Yes, so far. So, what next?"

Allie sat partway up, supported herself on her elbow, and turned to look at him.

"What brought this on?"

"Oh, just something Nalani—Maleko's wife—said to me. She called you my wife."

"Hon, we agreed to wait."

"We did. But...is...is this enough? Have we waited long enough? Or too long?" Lee rose to mirror her position, looking across at her in the dim moonlight that filtered through the tent roof.

"Too long? You want out?"

"No. I want...I don't know exactly what I want, but I want you in it. Not out."

"You know I love you, Lee. We were so close before..."

"And then we had to ride for our lives."

"You took me by the hand—well, not literally—and we left Kona *together*. Then you sat by my bedside even when people told you it was too risky, that if I turned, I'd bite you and infect you."

"It wasn't worth going on without you."

Allie reached her free hand over to place it against Lee's cheek. "And here we are. I don't know what the future holds, but I want you in it, too. As for the rest? I don't know either. I do know that you have to go up the mountain tomorrow. Close your eyes, get some sleep, and know that I love you."

Lee leaned over and kissed her, then lay back and fell quickly asleep.

This was the longest distance, not to mention the highest elevation, Lee had traveled from Waimea for any of his missions on behalf of Paniolo Ranch. The town was just over 2,600 feet in elevation, while the Pohakuloa Training Area was at 6,400 feet, and twenty-three miles away from the ranch. Altitude would rob his body of a lot of its cardiovascular fitness, so walking, running, or biking was out of the question. He could ride a horse, but even that would be hard on the animal and wouldn't allow Lee to return with any trade goods from the Army facility.

Instead, Lee had been issued a wagon and two draft mules. 'Mua would be tied to the back and follow along to provide for an emergency exit if needed. He would also be accompanied by Richard Gunderson to act as guard for the wagon and to assist Lee if they got in a fight.

The two men left the ranch stables well after sunup. They'd be traveling in the shadow of Mauna Kea for much of the journey, and it was necessary to have full light as they turned upslope. On the other hand, the journey would take most of the day, at least six hours, given the increase in elevation, so they needed to move out as soon as the sun cleared the three-thousand-foot elevation ridge east of the town and ranch.

The two-person team also meant that Lee was once again acting directly on behalf of Mr. Maleko. In the previous mission, he'd been perfectly happy to let Cody take the lead, as one of the co-owners and senior paniolos at the ranch. This mission, however, was all on Lee.

As with the Waikoloa Village mission, the first five miles of Route 190 were mostly level. However, five miles out of Waimea, the Saddle Road, Route 200, began its ten-mile climb, gaining three thousand feet in elevation. At the 5,500-foot level, the Saddle Road was joined by a new highway being built out of Kailua-Kona to provide a shortcut between the Kona and Hilo areas. The new highway was still mostly just cleared and graded land with a gravel base; it was certainly not suitable for any sort of transportation designed for roads and trails, but perhaps that could change depending on the outcome of this mission.

The final seven miles was a much more gradual climb; the last one thousand feet of elevation gain to Bradshaw Army Airfield and the Pohakuloa Training Area. The sun was low on the horizon as they crested the highest point in the pass between Mauna Loa and Mauna Kea. The burned-out remains of structures at the airfield caused Lee to wonder whether the army base would be similar, but they saw intact buildings and a few lights behind an eight-foot-tall fence stretching along the road in both directions.

As the light continued to wane, Gunderson started to sort through the contents of the wagon for camping supplies in case it was necessary for them to camp out on their own. Lee dismounted the wagon and approached the tall gate and guardhouse. Sitting about twenty feet behind the gate was a tower, of obviously new—if crude—construction. He knew he was being watched and he could see the muzzle of a rifle sticking out from a viewing slit on the tower.

"Hello?" Lee was surprised that he hadn't been challenged already.

There was no answer to his hail. He thought he saw a shadow move within the guardhouse, but there was no response from there or the tower.

"Hello? I'm Lee Eller of Paniolo Ranch and the town of Waimea."

"Well, I guess you're not an Infected. You can talk. I'm Sergeant Robert Copley." The voice came from inside the guardhouse.

"Ah, well, no to the Infected part. I've been sent to ask for your help, or for supplies to help us fight the Infected and recover the coastal areas." It was disconcerting to just talk to a shadow in the steadily darkening evening. He'd much rather speak face-to-face.

"Sorry, not interested. Not authorized." The voice sounded tired, as if this argument had occurred many times before, although Lee wondered what that implied about other groups of survivors...

Or would that be thieves and brigands? If so, Lee couldn't blame him, even though he was feeling frustrated how the conversation was going. "Look, the people of Paniolo Ranch, Waimea, and even Waikoloa Village are facing a new threat. We need equipment, and as a military unit, you're obligated to help us."

"I'm sorry, but I'm not authorized to answer to civilians. Yes, the military swears an oath to the country and the Constitution, but my chain of command comes from the Army Chief of Staff. He's not here, and my command has not authorized release of equipment."

"Well, then at the very least, can we get fuel? I mean you've got fuel, right? For the aircraft and tanks and stuff?"

Copley laughed. "This isn't the first time so-called 'civilian authorities' have tried to commandeer my supplies or personnel. Did you see the burned-out wreckage at the airfield? We had a C-130 make a high-risk landing with a full load of marines. Someone went zombie on their approach and the plane augered in. Shrapnel took out the valves for the underground fuel tanks, and the fire consumed everything."

"Wait, what're these tanks on the rise right behind us?" Lee pointed back over his shoulder at a cluster of large tanks across the road from the gate.

"Drinking water."

"Dammit, is there no way you can help? There's a nutcase claiming to be the reincarnation of an old Polynesian god who wants to 'purify the wicked.'" Lee let a little bit of frustration come through, and it seemed to have an effect.

Lee heard Copley sigh. "Him again. Okay." A man dressed in worn army fatigues stepped out of the guard box and held out a piece of wood with a key tied to it. "Here, this key will open a construction office at the state park about a mile down the road. You can sleep there for the night, then come back in the morning. We'll talk to the captain—or maybe the lieutenant—and see what can be done."

The sergeant directed them about a mile past the gate to a site where the state had been building a new park facility for people crossing the improved road between Kona and Hilo. He assured Lee that the site and the construction office had been cleaned out and that no Infected should be expected this far up the side of the mountain.

"We had some tourists and the telescope staff at the Elison Onizuka Center, some of our personnel, and a few who managed to make it up this far. For the most part, the ferals don't come here," Copley told him.

"Huh, ferals. I haven't heard that term. We mostly call them Infected, and sometimes zombies," Lee responded.

"Or 'Zeds,' but that tends to be the Canadians and Brits. Whatever you call them, they're feral beasts."

"I guess everyone has their own name for them. Just so long as we don't ever discount how dangerous they are. I've seen them first-hand and was lucky to get out alive."

"Sounds like a story to share over a beer . . . if we ever have beer again. It doesn't do well at altitude. Anyway, I'll see you in the morning and we can resume this conversation. We'll need to come to terms on security so you can come inside to talk, but that needs to wait until full daylight."

"Understood. We'll see you then."

CHAPTER SEVEN

CONTACT

Hawaiian volcanoes are great training grounds. You've got
open space, high elevation, alien landscapes, and the clearest
skies you've ever seen. Just watch out for the geese.

—R.J. Copley, First Sergeant (U.S. Army),
Pohakuloa Training Area

The construction office was little more than a small travel trailer. It
was still on its wheels but had been braced at the corners to prevent
tipping. Copley had given them a key that they would return in the
morning. 'Mua and the mules were set loose from the wagon, given
food and water, and hobbled so that they couldn't travel far—not that
there was anywhere for them to go at this elevation; the ground was
rocky brown soil, and their hooves would be uncomfortable traveling
far on it.

Inside the office were a desk, several chairs, two cots with wool
army blankets, a water tap and basin, olive green towels, and a
chemical toilet. Much to their surprise, the office appeared to have
electricity, although not much. Flipping the light switch lit a single
incandescent bulb with a low-wattage yellowish glow. As Gunderson
readied himself for bed, Lee sat down at the desk and looked over the
papers that had been left by previous occupants: scraps with notes
about people looking for family, a set of military orders, and, under
the accumulated mess, the plans for the state park. When finished, it
would have picnic shelters, restrooms, and even a playground for

children. There was also a map of the surrounding area. Lee had seen its like on display at rest areas and state welcome centers. This one showed Kailua-Kona, Hilo, and what would be the new highway connecting to the Saddle Road. There was a star near their location, indicating the park, symbols for Pohakuloa, the airfield, and the Ellison Onizuka Center. The latter was located about six miles downslope along the Saddle Road toward Hilo, then another six miles upslope along a narrow road filled with switchbacks that climbed three thousand feet in elevation toward the telescopes at the summit of the dormant volcano, Mauna Kea.

He was surprised to note two additional sites marked on the map. Almost directly opposite the Onizuka Center, but on the slopes of the active volcano, Mauna Loa, was a symbol that looked remarkably like a miniature spaceship and was labeled "HI-SEAS." On the same road as the Onizuka Center, but halfway between there and the summit, the same symbol appeared, labeled HI-SLOPE. The symbols and names triggered a memory from Lee's first trip to the Hawaiian Islands. The slopes of the tall, rugged mountains hosted two simulated habitats for space exploration. He wondered idly whether anyone had been left at the sites when H7D3 came. He could ask Copley if they managed to get on friendly terms.

That led him to think about the situation. If Pohakuloa truly had no resources, then they were likely worse off than Waimea. There was likely no way to grow crops up here, and only a few wild goats. Still, the base seemed to have people—the sergeant had mentioned a captain and lieutenant, yet he acted as if he had authority. He was only a sergeant, though. What did that mean? Could he and Gunderson have stumbled onto a group of renegade soldiers? Was his mission actually putting Waimea at risk?

The questions and rough conditions did little to settle him for the night, and morning came with Lee feeling as if he hadn't slept at all.

Sunrise came early on the high volcanic slopes—even if only by a couple of minutes. Pohakuloa was at the highest point in the east-west pass between Mauna Loa and Mauna Kea. At twenty degrees north latitude, they were close enough to the equator that the sun came up almost due east for most of the year. More than that, the elevation only accounted for a two-minute difference in sunrise. Mauna Kea, being slightly east of due north, only shadowed the rising sun slightly during the summer months. Waimea was a couple hundred feet below the highest elevation on that part of the island, and the slopes of the dormant volcano began just south of due east, relative to the town. Those same summer months were the only time Mauna Kea did *not* delay sunrise on the plateau.

Lee and Gunderson were surprised to find that not only did the water tap still work, but the office had a small electric kettle. With the rising sun, they could heat water for coffee.

With the precious wake-up juice consumed, Lee heated a little bit more water so that both men could wash up. They then refolded the blankets and put everything back the way they'd found it. Gunderson relocked the office as they exited, and they went to retrieve their wagon. The horse and mules had wandered a few yards away but stayed near the water Gunderson had put out for them the night before. Lee topped it off from another water tap outside the office and let them drink a bit more before getting his gelding saddled and the mules hitched to the wagon.

Lee felt somewhat guilty that they hadn't set a watch the night before, but the climb and thinner air had fatigued them both. The sergeant *had* assured them that Infected were extremely rare at this elevation, and Lee was certain that between the animals and his own restlessness, he'd have been alerted if any danger had approached. Still, if they stayed any longer, it would be better to do so inside the fences of the military facility.

Copley had also pointed out a road directly opposite the park site that would take them to a side gate to the training area. It led them behind the rows of half-cylinder-shaped Quonset huts that seemed to comprise most of the buildings on the base. They came to another gate, beside a flagpole on the back side of the fenced-in area. Two soldiers were preparing to raise the flag, and Lee had Gunderson stop the wagon. Lee dismounted 'Mua to stand at attention as the colors were raised to the accompaniment of reveille.

Some military routines never changed, and there was great comfort in that fact. It was a good sign.

Copley, who seemed in a better mood this morning, met Lee and Gunderson at the gate after the flag ceremony. He was accompanied by another soldier, and they insisted on inspecting the wagon and their firearms. The long guns needed to be left in the wagon and were secured with plastic zip-ties through the magazine well and breech. They'd both be allowed to keep their handguns, but they were secured in the holster with a ribbon. The guard demonstrated that the ribbon could be broken, but it would delay someone long enough that they couldn't surprise one of the soldiers. Lee was also allowed to keep the knife he wore sheathed at his side. The guard had expressed approval of the Ka-Bar knife similar to what Lee had occasionally used during ROTC many years ago. That too, was peace-bonded, but again, if he really needed it, he could draw and use the blade after breaking the bond. The whole purpose was to provide a visible "safe" status, while still acknowledging that they were living in a zombie apocalypse and might need to act quickly in self-defense of themselves and others.

As with most places Lee visited, there was no real facility to handle the animals. The ranch had really been the only place he'd seen that used them for more than just a hobby. Inside the fence, though, there were several spots that would suffice to keep them corralled and fed. To the left was an enclosed motor pool and covered gymnasium, to the right was a dirt-and-scrub-grass area surrounding the flagpole. Another block up the street from the gate was another dirt-and-scrub area next to unused tennis courts. Gunderson settled on this last location since it was well inside the fenced perimeter. He could also use the area to unload the fresh fruits and vegetables they'd brought as trade goods. A young man in worn BDUs bearing a private's insignia assisted Gunderson with unhitching the horses and explained that he was assigned to watch over them, allowing the two men from Waimea to accompany Copley to the facility headquarters.

As they walked, Copley started to tell them a bit about the training area. It was originally designed for artillery training during World War II. After that, it was taken over by the Hawaii Territorial Guard. The HTG was the equivalent of the National Guard before Hawaii became a state in 1959. The U.S. Army took over in the mid-1950s and built the distinctive Quonset hut barracks buildings that the three walked past on the way to the HQ building. He also explained that the fenced-in area they were walking through was referred to as a "cantonment," a term borrowed from the British colonization of India, describing temporary troop quarters, as well as civilian support. Furthermore, he referred to PTA as the "garrison" rather than calling it a base, a camp, or by its initials.

Considering what Lee had just learned about the role of Pohakuloa for military training, the term seemed appropriate. However, what the casual conversation did not include was any reference to military supplies. He figured that would likely have to wait until they spoke with whomever was in command.

It was right after he'd had that thought, that the three men approached a square, green-roofed building at the center of the cantonment. A woman in crisp uniform stepped out the door as they approached, and Copley saluted. The woman returned the salute, and Lee noted a first lieutenant's insignia on her uniform.

The officer paused long enough to greet Copley.

"Ma'am, these are the emissaries from Waimea. I'm taking them to meet Captain Silver. It seems they've met our old friend, Ku."

"Oh. Very well, First Sergeant. He will likely unload all of that on me. I'll be back in the office in thirty minutes after I pick up the coffee ration. You can bring them by at that time. Carry on."

"Yes, ma'am."

Copley turned back to enter the building as the lieutenant left them, sharply, and Lee looked more closely at the man's uniform for his rank insignia. He hadn't been able to see it the night before, and he'd only introduced himself as "Sergeant."

The NCO noticed his attention and sighed. "Yeah, I know. If you know insignia, mine says 'Staff Sergeant,' and she called me 'First Sergeant.'"

"Three up, one down. Yeah, I wondered. I had an ROTC scholarship. Did my four years and got out as a lieutenant."

"Ah, not uncommon. Well, that C-130 crash I mentioned last night? It had Lieutenant Colonel Timmons and Command Sergeant Major Jessup; the base commander and senior NCO. It also had most of a company of Marines. We were expecting a battalion for training as it was, but they'd been delayed and the brass had to go to Pearl for a briefing. We lost twenty-two people in the crash, and the Haole Flu took so many more, including the major and first sergeant. I was the senior NCO, and Captain Silver and Lieutenant Cortez are the only officers left. I received a battlefield promotion, jumping two ranks, but we don't have a PX and I wasn't about to take insignia off a fallen brother."

Neither Lee nor Gunderson said anything in response. It simply drove home how everyone simply had to make do with what they had.

They entered the building and approached a desk in front of several closed office doors. The woman at the desk had a specialist—E-4— insignia, and Copley announced Lee and Gunderson for a meeting with Captain Silver. He was told that the captain was not yet in the building, so they were led to a side office with the plaque FIRST SERGEANT beside the door.

Copley led them inside. "Water? It's all we have to offer."

Lee looked at Gunderson and nodded. The wagon driver and guard spoke for the first time. "Could I interest you in some mango juice, then?"

Copley's eyes lit up as Gunderson took a steel bottle from the backpack he'd taken from the wagon. While it was not refrigerated, it had been stored outside the night before, and was still relatively cool. Plastic cups were produced, and juice was poured, with a double serving for the NCO.

"Don't worry, we brought more, and can set up trade."

The gift broke the ice, and the three settled into a more casual conversation as they waited for the garrison commander.

Lee learned that First Sergeant Robert—"call me Bob"—Copley had a brother in the New York National Guard. The last he'd heard from him was just before the fall of the big cities of the East Coast. Bob had come to Hawaii as part of the training detachment permanently stationed at the garrison, and frankly, hadn't expected to ever reach the E-8 rank. He'd been happy as an E-6 and had planned to retire as a sergeant first class in a few more years.

They also learned more about the ill-fated "Penguin-four-two" flight that had badly damaged their infrastructure. It was supposed to be the last flight out of Kaneohe Bay, with the senior officer and NCO of the garrison, seventy-five marines, and all the food and medicine they could pack onto the plane. A 3,700-foot airstrip at nearly 7,000 feet elevation and an overloaded C-130 were pushing the edge of safety, but Indo-Pacific Command had lifted peacetime restrictions to meet the needs for emergency operations in the wake of H7D3. Army and Marine battalions were nothing new to the garrison, since they trained mountain troops and infantry alike for Afghanistan, but since the battalion never arrived for training, it was decided to make the garrison the Army and Marine redoubt to preserve a military presence in the islands.

Unfortunately, the radio communication from the C-130 had garbled references to someone called "Ku," then the copilot had "gone zombie" as the flight turned on final approach, and Major Michael Fowler had to simultaneously fight for his life, and for the safety of the airplane. The plane scraped the ground with the right wingtip on landing, spun, and sent fragments of the starboard engines and propellers flying into the airstrip tower, storage, and support facilities. Another fragment sheared off the refueling valves linked to the underground fuel storage tanks, and sparks started the fuel burning.

The Marines had sent two corpsmen, a Navy doctor, and a Navy dentist, but the doc was killed in the crash along with the senior leadership and pilot. A Marine E-7 and one of the corpsmen were severely injured, but eventually pulled through—the NCO minus a leg, and the corpsman minus an arm. Pohakuloa didn't have its own doctors, only a combat medic among their fifty-odd survivors, so the surviving medical staff were welcome, although overworked at first dealing with crash and fire injuries as well as the Haole Flu. Still, with the survivors from the crash added to their numbers, the garrison had more than enough room, food, water, and even medicine, given that it was designed for more than twenty-five times that number.

What they didn't have were engineers to build power generation, recover the remaining fuel in the underground tanks, and allow the soldiers to move out from their mountain redoubt and rejoin the survivors at lower elevation.

CHAPTER EIGHT

COMMAND

I ___, do solemnly swear that I will support and defend the Constitution of the United States against all enemies, foreign and domestic...   —Oath of Commissioned Officers

Copley being the first sergeant went a long way to explaining why he seemed to be in charge. As far as the enlisted were concerned, he *was* in charge. The surviving E-7 hadn't been in sufficient health to take over the NCO leadership position, and Copley's promotion had been confirmed by the Chief of Staff of the Army.

"What?" Lee asked him. "How? Last night you said something about the Chief of Staff not being here."

"By radio," Copley replied. "We have radio contact with USSCUCC."

"Huh? I've been out a long time. I'm not up on all the acronyms."

"The U.S. Strategic Command Underground Command Center. Where General Brice and Under Secretary Galloway are located. The general is the senior surviving military officer, and Mr. Galloway is the highest ranking congressionally appointed official."

"So, effectively the Chairman of the Joint Chiefs and the Acting President?"

"Pretty much."

"Wait, is this USC place the Hole?"

"Got it in one."

Lee had heard from Jules that there were occasional radio signals from the bunker at Offutt Air Force Base outside Omaha, Nebraska. The Hole, as it was called, was famed through fiction as an old Strategic Air Command bunker sealed against nuclear, biological, and chemical attacks. It was known to exist, though, since it had been used as a safe command center for the president on 9/11/01. Up to this point, the U.S. leadership was not something that Lee or most of the folks at Waimea or Paniolo Ranch gave much thought, but now that Copley mentioned it, Lee was certain it would be important to Mr. Maleko and the others downslope.

After a few more minutes of conversation—and drinking mango juice—the lieutenant had returned to the office. With her arrival, Lee and Gunderson were ushered in to meet the garrison commander, Captain Silver. The senior officer was young, not even thirty by appearance, which likely made him younger than Lee. He was friendly enough, and seemed competent, just . . . overwhelmed by a job meant for an officer at least two ranks higher.

Lieutenant Cortez, whom they were formally introduced to next, was also young, about five years younger than Silver. She gave less of an "out-of-her-element" impression, but that might have been because she was well suited for administrative duties. She was friendly, and suggested many possibilities for trade, but none of it seemed to involve personnel or military weapons. Much as Copley had mentioned before, both officers stressed that they had no orders with respect to rendering aid to civilians other than one-on-one cases of refugees fleeing attack, arriving at the gates of the garrison. On the other hand, both mentioned having heard reports from other survivors of someone calling himself Ku and demanding worship or tribute. There were enough mentions to consider Ku a threat, although Silver and Cortez were uncertain about how serious he was.

Through both conversations, it became even more evident that Copley, even as a first sergeant, was technically the one keeping it all together in the garrison. Cortez had mentioned that in Officer Basic Training, she'd been admonished by her trainers to always listen to her NCOs. She acknowledged Copley's fifteen years of experience and turned the negotiations over to him to "exercise his best judgment."

Lee was frustrated. The garrison, far from being a secure bastion of military strength, was just a bunch of survivors hanging on but not knowing what to do. They seemed to be awaiting orders that hadn't come.

It gave him an idea, though. "You still have radio communication with the Hole, right?" Lee asked. "Can you contact them and at least *ask* if you're allowed to help us? I know that Jules mentioned reference to your general by this 'Wolf Squadron' we hear about in the Caribbean. Don't you think we should ask and find out what you're allowed to do?"

"Well, shit," Copley said. "No one here thought of that. Wait here, I'll go back and check with the captain." Lee remained in Copley's office while he went over to the offices across the hall. Gunderson had gone back to check on the animals and unpack more of the "trade goods."

He only waited for ten minutes before Copley returned and motioned for Lee to follow.

"It's thirteen-thirty. That's eighteen-thirty in the Hole—six-thirty in the evening, in case you forgot."

Lee laughed. "I used to race triathlons. We used twenty-four-hour time to simplify race-time calculations. So, five-hour time difference and they might have signed off for the evening?"

"Actually, it could be only four hours. Who knows if anyone even bothers with daylight savings time anymore? There should always be someone on the receiver, but it's uncertain if the general will be available."

"They're in the bunker. What else are they going to be doing?"

"Yeah, I know. That's what I told the captain."

Lea noted that, much like the construction office, the base had power, but not much. He could hear the sound of generators and had seen sheets of solar panels on top of several buildings. Very few electrical appliances were in use, aside from a laptop in the lieutenant's office and a tabletop fan in the captain's. The outer room with the specialist was the only one without windows, so it had incandescent lighting strung from the ceiling, and disconnected wires dangling from the fluorescent tubes. Periodically the lights would dim, and the generator sound changed pitch. The building where Copley had taken them for a cold lunch of prepackaged food smelled of cooking fires, and he could see oil lamps and candles on the tables.

It came as quite a shock when they arrived at another building that was not a Quonset hut and stepped inside to bright lights and air-conditioning. An array of computers and electronics racks covered two walls, and desks covered the other walls and the center of the floor. Each station was labeled with a name: JOINT BASE PEARL HARBOR/HICKAM, MARINE CORP BASE HAWAII/KANEOHE BAY, and PENTAGON. The computer screens and electronics at each of those stations were powered down, but several more were still powered up, including ones labeled PACIFIC MISSILE RANGE FACILITY, and OFFUTT. He also noticed a desk labeled HI-SLOPE where the screen was turned off, but the electronics rack was still active. It piqued his curiosity, but he needed to save that for later.

Much to his surprise, the answer to that question came almost immediately when he asked about the room itself. "Curious. You seem pretty sparing with electricity everywhere else, but this equipment is all fully powered, brightly lit, and cooled. You're saving it all for here?"

"Not really. This room has its own power source from high up on Mauna Kea. A rich billionaire built a space simulation habitat and buried an experimental generator up there—the kind designed for space stations and colonies. It's some form of nuclear generator, and they ran the power down here for communications equipment so that we would act as a relay station for them. There's also a relay at the Onizuka Center and up at the telescopes as well."

"Is there anybody still up there?"

"Unknown. We tried calling them, but their communications were FUBAR and we're not sure anything ever got through."

"Surely the power means someone is there."

"Maybe. But my understanding was that it was designed to be maintenance free. For us, it's one room of free power. Walking in here is like the Haole Flu never happened."

"So, no one has checked."

"Not that I know of. Someone might have, but not logged it. After all, we're supposed to be the only ones up this high." Copley sighed, as if he wanted to say more, but his expression hardened and he turned back to Lee. "Maybe later. For now, let's talk to General Brice and Mr. Galloway so we can see what they say about helping your civilians fight Ku."

∽◦∾

The conversation with the surviving leadership of the U.S, government took a rather surprising turn. Copley made the call and they patched in Captain Silver from his office to exchange authorization codes. The surprise came after First Sergeant Copley described the status of the garrison, and relayed what Lee and Gunderson explained about Waimea, the Paniolo Ranch, and the situation with Ku and the zombies. Then General Brice asked to talk to Lee.

Never, in his life before H7D3, would Lee have thought he'd be talking to the general commanding all U.S. forces, or the President of the U.S., but here he was talking to their equivalents. The conversation had revolved around leadership of the various communities he'd contacted, and how that might evolve into a cohesive government for the island. Mr. Galloway asked about population size and mentioned that he had the ability to confirm territorial governors. Those positions would have a set time limit, and would have to be backed by free elections, but if the people of Hawaii were to organize their government, it would be possible to deploy assets to assist. Lee was unable to answer all the questions, but they gave him food for thought and several topics to discuss with Jules on his return. It seemed that things were very likely to change in a drastic manner over the next few weeks.

He just hadn't realized that it would start now.

General Brice emphasized that military aid had to be prioritized to authorized government agents and representatives. She then asked Lee about whether he had prior military service.

Lee answered in the affirmative and described his ROTC scholarship and four-year obligation to the Army. He'd started to have trouble with his weight and failed a fitness test, so he'd just gotten out instead of continuing in the Reserves.

There was a faint, whispered conversation with someone who might have been Mr. Galloway, then she came back to ask about his life after the service. Lee described his bachelor's and master's degrees in computer science and electronics, respectively. He'd built a company that made devices and applications to track an athlete's fitness and training progress once he'd gotten involved in marathons and triathlons.

At the end of his story, General Brice was mostly silent, although he could hear conversation off-mic again. Lee was a bit disconcerted by the silence, and looked over at Copley, who was sitting at a device on the opposite side of the desk that he'd told Lee was a secure communications printer.

Captain Silver then entered the room, much to Lee's surprise. Silver smiled, as did Copley, standing up with a printout in his hands.

Back on the radio, General Brice finally spoke. "Mr. Eller? Are you willing to swear to defend and rebuild the United States of America?"

"What?" Lee was confused. Suddenly it all became clear. "Uh, yes, ma'am, or sir. I'm not sure of the proper address."

"'Ma'am' or 'General' will suffice, Lee. You can have a minute to think about this."

"No, ma'am, I don't need the time, and yes, ma'am, I'm willing. I put on the uniform once before, I'll do it again."

"Very good. Captain Silver, would you please administer the oath to Lieutenant Eller?"

Once again, Lee's thoughts whirled and jumbled. He was aware of raising his hand and swearing to defend the Constitution of the United States of America, but he couldn't let loose of the one thought that seemed to stick in his head:

Lieutenant?

"Lee, with your prior service, education, and track record running a company, I'm recalling you to service. You'll be more valuable to Waimea that way, and they can't ignore you. Troops will obey you, and you can give orders and access military equipment. I advise you to listen to your superior officers, and especially Bob Copley. Senior NCOs have kept young officers alive for many hundreds of years. You're officially commissioned in the Army Reserve and called to active duty as liaison to the Waimea colony. Make decisions wisely and help us rebuild the United States."

Lee swallowed the lump in his throat. He wanted to wipe his eyes but figured it wouldn't be a good idea in front of the captain and first sergeant. "Yes, ma'am. Thank you. I will do my best."

"We know you will," Galloway said over the radio link. "Now, time for us to get to supper, and for you to figure out your duties."

"Thank you, sir!"

The radio clicked off, and Captain Silver grinned and left the room. Lee collapsed in a chair and First Sergeant Copley held out a tissue. "Yeah, I know, there must be onion-cutting ninjas in here."

Lee just nodded, not trusting himself to speak.

CHAPTER NINE
FORGOTTEN WIZARDS

Hello, we've been trying to reach you about your warranty...
—Universal telemarketer pitch

The rest of the day had Lee explaining to Gunderson what had just happened. He helped unpack their "trade goods"—more fruit juice, some vegetables, jerky made from beef as well as wild goats and the occasional wild hogs from the windward valleys. Special items included two barrels of beer from the home brewers in Waimea, and one of the two jugs of mead given to them by Ben Peachtree in Waikoloa.

Lee also conferred with Copley on a list of items to send up to the garrison for future trade. Rechargeable batteries, socks, and more juice topped the list, and Lee knew they'd be good for it. They would also need to see if they could bring fresh beef as well.

Lee and Gunderson spent the night in one of the Quonset huts. It wasn't luxury quarters, but it beat camping on the trail, or the tent city Lee and Allie lived in back in Waimea. If they could arrange a regular supply run, it might be a good idea to move some of the people with prior service up to the garrison to relieve crowding and marginal living conditions in the refugee camps.

In the morning, the two men prepared to head back to Waimea, and they wouldn't be going empty-handed. They'd be taking back additional weapons, notably M4s and select-fire M16s, and plenty of the 5.56mm ammo used by those rifles. Lee was sure that van Tuyl would appreciate a squad automatic weapon or two, but Copley just laughed and suggested they revisit the idea on the next trip. He smirked and claimed to have "something better for zombie hunting."

They would also be taking several handheld military radios, and an encrypted radio for direct communication with both Pohakuloa and the Hole. Copley had Lee accompany him to the radio room to have the frequencies and encryption set, then surprised him one more time before Lee and Gunderson left.

"There's one more thing to do. I've been thinking about what you asked me yesterday. I talked to Lieutenant Cortez, and one of our own refugees. He was up at the housing for the astronomers, Hale Pohaku. He thinks you're right about survivors, so you and I are going to call HI-SLOPE."

Copley switched on the console labeled HI-SLOPE. When all lights were green, he pressed TRANSMIT and spoke into the microphone. "HI-SLOPE Logistics to HI-SLOPE Command."

There was an absence of the usual crackling noises that Lee associated with the radios he'd seen and heard at the ranch.

There was no response, so Copley called again. "HI-SLOPE Logistics to HI-SLOPE Command."

This time there was a click and a young male voice answered.

"Hello?"

Copley looked over at Lee and raised his eyebrows. Lee just shrugged.

"This is First Sergeant Robert Copley at Pohakuloa Training Area. I handle logistics for HI-SLOPE. To whom am I speaking?"

"Um, wow. We . . . never get messages over this line." The first words were tentative, but the rest came out in a rush. "Anyway, I'm Lugnut . . . er . . . Zach Lugnut . . . no wait, actually, it's Zachariah Ludwig, but the last person who called me that was my mom. Anyway, are you really calling us there's someone out there that wants to talk to us oh wow I should get the professor— Hey, Professor! There's someone calling on the closed-circuit fiber line I think you need to . . ." The voice faded away and they heard footsteps on metal.

Lee and Copley just looked at each other. It was clear that the NCO was trying not to laugh.

After a few minutes, they could hear footsteps again and the voice returned.

"...and the signals came in on the fiber line from downslope there's people out there calling us and I figured they needed to talk to you Professor Hummer sir."

"Easy, Lugnut. Take a breath." A deeper, but no less excited sounding voice could be heard approaching. "It also seems you left the line open, so they've heard your excitement."

"Professor?" asked Copley.

"Yes, that's what Lugnut calls me. Hamilton V. Forsyth, MD, PhD. Acting site director. We already have a doctor, so he decided to call me Professor."

"Good to speak with you Dr. Forsyth. This is First Sergeant Robert Copley at Pohakuloa Training Area. We're the Army logistics unit for HI-SLOPE."

"Really? So, you're just downslope. Good to know. We've been listening to the radio and thought the closest group was the ranchers."

Copley cleared his throat. "Well...I have one of their people here as well. It was his suggestion to call you. We couldn't reach you when everything fell apart and thought you all left."

"Ah, yes, the damned simulated communications blackout raises its ugly head again. Sorry, Sergeant, we were locked out of all communication for almost three months. Once we had communications restored, there was no one to talk to."

"Well, we are here, Doctor. When things got bad, NASA and the Mars-and-Beyond Consortium transferred your logistics to us. We're the ones who actually delivered your resupply, as it was. VennSystems wasn't happy with that, but after a day or so, we didn't hear from them, either."

"You and us both, it seems."

"Oh? Hmm, you said 'acting director.' Where is Mr. van Der Venn?"

"Missing, presumed coward."

"Um, what?" Lee couldn't restrain himself. He had meant to remain silent and let Copley do all of the talking.

"He left. Took off in the middle of the night, and good riddance. He did more damage to the morale of this crew before we even heard about H7D3."

"Ah, so you are aware of the Haole Flu," Copley asked.

"Haole...ah, yes, I suppose that would fit. It would have been brought in by tourists. So, yes. We have all the data dumps from the

CDC before they went offline, and we eventually managed to get a shortwave radio set up to listen for survivors."

"You've had no other communication? We understood that there was an override emergency channel. We even tried to contact you on it to tell you to lock yourselves up. We had supplies for you here, but you shouldn't have been exposed up there."

"Yeah, well, that ship has sailed. When the simulated blackout ended, it took us a while to go through the backlog, then we discovered that someone had tried to message us via the override channel but locked it out instead. We think they went zombie right in the middle of the process."

"Yeah, that happens. We had something similar happen with a C-130 on approach." Copley looked over at Lee, who was listening with rapt attention. "Anyway, I apologize for not having contacted you. We assumed that you had all evacuated."

"We lost a few to the disease after sending some folks down to Hale Pohaku. We then lost a few more at the summit, and we had some folks leave us in a helicopter that was up there."

"How long ago was this?" Lee broke in.

"At least five months ago. We made the summit expedition about, oh, seven months ago. We lost two, had a few badly hurt, but one of our people was rotary wing certified, and our communications engineer led a group that wanted to leave."

Lee nodded. "Folks at the Paniolo Ranch saw a helicopter leave the summit that long ago. It looked like they headed toward Kawaihae."

"The rest of us stayed because we're immunocompromised. We have no resistance to the disease, and no vaccine. Our doctor is working on one with information from the CDC briefings, but he was never able to ask questions before they went off the air."

Copley nodded even though he knew the man on the other end wouldn't see it. "Well, we need to see what we can do about that. There's at least one vaccine expert in the Hole at Offutt. We don't have any vaccine down here, either, but we've also all been exposed. There's probably not much reservoir of infection here at sixty-five hundred feet."

Lee tapped Copley on the shoulder. Then waved his hands back and forth, then tapped his right forefinger against his chest.

"Oh, that's right," the NCO continued. "We just reestablished contact with Waimea, so it might not be *that* safe. We can still try bringing you out. We don't have a doctor, but we do have a dentist, and Waimea has a senior medic."

"I think we'll stay for now. We *do* have a doc, and he's still working on his vaccine."

"Good. That's for the best, then. So, what's your personnel status? How many of you are there?"

"Twelve of us. We started with twenty-five; sent two to Hale Pohaku, one got killed, the other bitten, and made it most of the way back. Two of ours broke containment to check on them and got infected. Brought it back to their wives, but that section of the habitat was already sealed. Van Der Venn deserted. We lost two at the summit, including the XO, then the four who took the helicopter and left."

"Well, your supplies should stretch further. We have the next shipment that was supposed to go to you down here, still in isolation packaging. Is there anything else you need?"

"We get some fruit and vegetables from the greenhouse, but we have no meat that isn't dehydrated. Water is recycled, we have plenty of power, and we have computer access to worldwide networks, but no one's talking. Maybe some juices or concentrates and some fresh meat? Some eggs? Hell, we'd even take *Spam*."

"Funny you should mention that," said Copley.

Lee's eyebrows shot up. Spam was considered valuable down in Waimea. If the garrison had Spam, then that was something else they could trade for.

"Oh, that would certainly be different."

Lee cut in again. "Dr. Forsyth, this is Lee Eller. I've come up from Waimea and the Paniolo Ranch to set up trade with PTA. I think we might be able to include you in that. Beef, hog, goat, eggs. We can do this."

"Mmmm. Fried eggs and Spam. We've got rice, I am *so* making spam musubi," said another voice over the comm.

"Hush, Duke. We have to make sure we can get it safely," Forsyth said off-mic. "Forgive my associate, he's incorrigible. It sounds like we need to get busy."

"We do, but leave the worry about contamination to us. We have a sterilizer to handle your supplies. NASA docs predicted you'd be a bit immunocompromised," Copley told him. "Anyway, I've got to get this bewildered lieutenant on the road back to Waimea. And *he* needs to get his superiors briefed on many things. For that matter, I need to call the Hole and tell them about *you*. Welcome back to the world!"

There was the sound of a deep sigh on the other. When Forsyth spoke, his voice was heavy with emotion. "It's good to be back."

CHAPTER TEN

RALLYING CRY

Mauka—toward the mountain (or summit).
Makai—toward the ocean.

With a thirteen-thousand-foot volcano dominating the landscape, mauka and makai make a lot more sense than left, right, north, south, east, or west.

—I. Makano, senior ranch hand, Paniolo Ranch

The trip back down the mountain went much faster than the way up, although neither Lee nor Gunderson rode the wagon. For the steepest part of the slope, Gunderson walked the mules pulling the wagon and Lee walked 'Mua. Once they got back to the relatively level road of Route 190, Lee rode while Gunderson drove the wagon. It had been a fruitful mission, although perhaps not quite in the manner that Jules had intended; Lee knew it would come as a shock that he was now a military officer. On the other hand, if it bought them assistance from the Army, that wouldn't be a bad thing, would it?

General Brice had assured Lee and the garrison leaders that the Army would provide assistance, as long as it didn't overly deplete their own supplies. That meant arms and ammunition, clothing, hot and cold weather gear, and rations. What Waimea and the Paniolo Ranch wanted had been vehicles and fuel. The garrison had vehicles, but unless the ranchers could find their own source of fuel, those vehicles wouldn't do them any good.

Fuel was a problem that people of much higher authority than him would have to work out.

Pohakuloa was getting an unexpected benefit out of Lee's visit,

277

however. Contact with HI-SLOPE could lead to more access to electrical power and the possibility of repair for electrical and electronic equipment. More power could also mean the ability to recharge batteries for the transport of power downslope to Waimea and Waikoloa.

Access to computer networks also potentially meant access to satellite data. Lee had only rarely listened to the radio messages from Wolf Squadron, but Copley had brought him up to date on several items of interest as they'd worked out lists of trade goods. Apparently, Commodore Wolf's people had retrieved the International Space Station astronauts who'd returned to Earth after the Fall and landed on an island in the Caribbean. They'd brought back images detailing civilization's rapid decline, and slow rebirth.

There were still satellites up there—many with cameras pointed toward Earth. It was possible to pull readings and images from weather satellites, even if there were no meteorologists to interpret them. The Global Positioning System satellites were also still functioning. There'd been reports over marine radio bands of growing errors in coordinates, but that changed a few weeks ago. Lee had learned from Copley that someone had managed to upload a patch to the GPS system to recalibrate the systems and keep them functioning for several more years. The spy satellites of various nations still covered the globe with cameras if one had the codes to access them and control the paths.

All of these systems were now potentially accessible thanks to the young man they'd first spoken with at HI-SLOPE. Lugnut was apparently a genius with computer networks as well as electronic devices. He was the sort of person Lee would've hired back at his old company—what the industry called a "white-hat hacker": someone who could break into secured systems, but who worked through official government channels to fix the unfixable. Lugnut had subsequently told General Brice and Mr. Galloway that he could access weather satellite information. He didn't have the training or the knowledge to interpret it, but surely the military or the handful of scientists who'd been holed up in the Keck Telescope analysis lab in Waimea had someone who could assist with that.

In fact, the more Lee thought about possibilities, the more he realized how pivotal was the outcome of his mission. He'd made connections, and the community of survivors in Hawaii had grown accordingly.

☙❧

It took about four hours to return to Waimea compared to the eleven hours for the trip upslope. He was coming to understand why Hawaiians had adopted a system of directions referring either toward the mountains, *mauka*, or toward the sea, *makai*. On the slopes of the volcanoes, whether active, extinct, or merely dormant, those were the only truly meaningful directions. Even the trip to Waimea—at just short of three thousand feet elevation—wasn't exactly "toward the sea," but from the perspective of mauka, it was makai indeed.

Van Tuyl and Jules greeted them on their return. The former took charge of the munitions and other supplies that had come down from Pohakuloa, while the latter sat Lee down for his report. Upon hearing of the conversations with the Hole, he took Lee immediately to see Maleko and Maile.

Lee repeated his report, and then again as they were joined by van Tuyl, Cody, a couple of the other senior people from the community, and José, who'd just returned from Waikoloa. As the conversation among those individuals turned to plans of what to do next, both regarding the need for fuels and to defend or fight back against Ku and his followers, Lee stood to excuse himself.

"No, Lee, stay," Maleko told him.

"Sir, it's clear this is a leadership meeting. I should go attend to my horse."

Cody laughed. "I'm glad you're thinking of your horse, but don't worry. Darkhorse is taking care of him."

"In case it hasn't occurred to you yet, *Lieutenant*, you now are part of the leadership in this community." Maleko had given him a rather pointed look as he'd mentioned Lee's new rank, but he'd smiled as he'd done so, indicating that he approved. "You may even be more important than most of us in this room, Lee."

"I doubt that, sir, but thank you."

"I don't doubt it at all."

The first topic of conversation for the meeting of the Paniolo Ranch leadership was how to take advantage of the new working relationship with the Army and the stranded scientists near the summit of Mauna Kea.

"So, that's where that helicopter came from all those months ago. Do we have any idea where they went?" asked Paul Clithero, who'd been summoned from his workshop at the airport, along with Michael Horgan. As mechanic and blacksmith, respectively, their expertise was sought regarding how to create offensive and defensive capabilities from their limited supplies.

"Dr. Forsyth didn't say, and First Sergeant Copley really didn't know," Lee told them. "They had a few reports of them headed down slope in the direction of the harbor. There's supposedly a helicopter base down near there."

"Two, actually. Waikoloa and Hapuna. Those are strictly for tourist helicopters, but if your people were having any trouble, they might have tried to set down at either place there for fuel or repairs."

"I don't think so, Paul. Waikoloa was overrun and the Hapuna place burned fairly early on," van Tuyl corrected him.

"They wouldn't necessarily know that, would they? Or did they have access to satellite imagery then?"

"No, I don't think so," Lee told him. "According to their tech person, that was a fairly recent development. Apparently, someone accessed a GPS satellite ground station and uploaded a patch. That unlocked several communication channels, which is how they have satellite access at HI-SLOPE now. It's something to do with the GPS synchronizing the clocks used to track and map the other satellites."

"Okay, I suppose all of that is just sitting there with no maintenance. Huh. Man, it must have sucked to be the poor astronauts sitting in the ISS, watching civilization fall and waiting for the air to run out."

"Ah, actually, there's some good news on that front. By the way, sir? Do you have a charged laptop? If not, the garrison assigned me a notepad and I can have someone fetch it."

Nalani motioned to the desktop computer on Maleko's desk. She flipped a switch, and the people in the room could hear a generator kick on somewhere in the house. "We can run this one on battery power most of the time. The generator keeps it topped off."

"Oh, good. Thank you, ma'am." Lee pulled a thumb drive out of his pocket and handed it to her. "There's a video file on there. You should all watch this, I've seen it, and it explains a lot of what's going on in the world right now."

The room sat in silence as they watched a video of Earth turning beneath them. At first it was full of light and activity, but slowly, the lights on the night side went out. When the globe was completely dark, a match flared and a single candle was lit. Words on the screen referenced lyrics about lighting a candle rather than cursing the darkness, as music with a rock/electronic beat started up. The video went on to show people at sea pulling survivors onto boats, a young lady loaded down with knives, guns and ammo fighting off a horde of Infected as if she were performing some sort of danse macabre... but coming out triumphant in the end. There was a scene of an island with a streak of light descending from the sky. Rockets fired and parachutes opened above a space capsule. The next scene showed space-suited individuals being pulled from the capsule and rushed into isolation in a truck sealed with plastic.

Later scenes showed soldiers and civilians advancing on islands, and even a military base somewhere on the U.S. East Coast. There were boats, helicopters, and a few aircraft. The final scene showed an M1 Abrams tank, painted pink, leading a column of military vehicles, plowing through Infected as they traveled down a street somewhere on the U.S. mainland.

The video ended, and Lee could see that every person in the room was wiping at their eyes.

A rallying cry had been sounded.

CHAPTER ELEVEN
LIGHTING A CANDLE

A pink tank. Oh my. Someone has a sense of humor.
—J. Thompson, Foreman, Paniolo Ranch

"Apparently they use the tank as a test of state of mind," Lee told them. "Anyone who protests on the basis of military regulations gets told the story of *Trixie*—that's the tank—and Lieutenant Shewolf. If they can accept that, they're reactivated and rejoin the active military forces. Anyone too inflexible to accept that things are different in a zombie apocalypse, is quietly shuffled to a rear area job."

"Flexible . . . like a courier being elevated to a leadership role in his community?" asked Maleko with a smile.

Lee just nodded.

"What is the music? I admit that's not what I usually listen to, but there was something in there about 'the dawn of humanity' which seemed appropriate." Nalani looked at Lee curiously.

"The band is Nightwish, and the song is 'Last Ride of the Day.' I've heard them a few times. Copley told me that it's very popular with the marines these days. Probably because they see Shewolf as their mascot, even if she is Commodore Wolf's daughter."

"Hmm. I like it. I may have to ask in town if anyone has more of their music."

"Ah, I may have some on my music player, ma'am. It was good running and training music."

Lee was stunned by the brilliant smile she gave him. "We'll talk later. I'm sure my husband would like to get back on topic."

"Certainly, ma'am. Anyway, the astronauts got down safe, but the instruments are still there, and the Hole and HI-SLOPE can access them. It may not be the latest and greatest, but we have possibilities."

"Exactly. So how do we use this capability?" Maleko asked.

"Well, sir, even though the video shows all the lights going out, if you zoom in, there were still scattered light sources: the Caribbean, Tower of London, scattered locations in the Carolinas, Indiana, Nebraska, Utah, and several right here on the Islands. Obviously, we know of many of those now. Here and the garrison, of course. HI-SLOPE shows up on infrared even though they don't put out any visible light. Perhaps if we take a close look, we can figure out what some of those places are, and then ask if there is a way to get satellite images."

"That's not a bad idea, and frankly, it gives me another one. Jered, you said that the heliport burned, right?"

"Yes, sir," van Tuyl said. "We saw smoke from that area."

"Where else could a helicopter go? Would they go to Kawaihae? Paul?"

"There's no helipad there, but there's a wide-open cargo yard, and a beach where the LSVs unload," Clithero told them.

"LSVs?"

"Landing ships," Clithero clarified. "The great big Navy variety, not the little ones that island hop. There's one, the USAV *Robert T. Kuroda*, LSV-7, which makes regular stops. It's actually owned by the U.S. Army and can carry a battalion's worth of tanks, vehicles, and equipment from Pearl or Kaneohe. They pull into the south side of Kawaihae Harbor, drop the bow ramp, and the equipment rolls on or rolls off."

"Kawaihae's got fuel storage, too," van Tuyl mused. "Probably more than at the airports in Kona and Hilo."

"Ah, I see where you're going," spoke Jules for the first time in a while. "I wouldn't want to try salvage and clearance operations in Kona or Hilo without at least five times the number of hunters and fighters we have right now. But Kawaihae?"

"How many people do you need?" Maleko asked.

"At least a hundred."

"The payoff, though, could be worth it. Gasoline and diesel for sure. Probably had some bunker fuel for the cargo ships. Avgas for the Abrams and helicopters at PTA."

"Without dipping into essential ranching and farming personnel, plus those incapable of fighting... but how many can we raise? According to my census, not a hundred. We might get a few more from Waikoloa if we ask Peachtree."

"Lee..." Maleko started to ask a question, stopped, then restarted. "Lieutenant, can we ask the Army?"

"Marines, more likely, they make up more than half of the garrison right now. I will have to ask, and it will probably have to go to the top, General Brice and Mr. Galloway," Lee told him. "Sir? Are those your orders? Your official request to your military liaison?"

Maleko thought for a few moments. He looked around the room at the faces of his people. Lee's report had given them hope; the video had given them even more. If all of the survivors banded together, they could do more than just survive... they could thrive.

They could rebuild.

"Yes, Lieutenant, this is an official request."

"In that case, sir, I was instructed to pass on a specific suggestion from Mr. Galloway. We— Nope. You. Speaking for the country here," Lee muttered. "You need a government. A quorum of community leaders can appoint an acting civil authority pending a scheduled open election. With that in place, I can accept a request from the local head of civilian government."

"I move that Makaio Maleko be appointed governor *pro tem* of the territory of Hawaii," Jules said immediately. "Second?"

"Seconded," spoke several voices at once.

Maleko's face turned slightly pink as he ducked his head. "No, not governor. We don't represent enough people. Also, I won't run unopposed."

"Mayor of Waimea," corrected Jules. "Second for the change?"

Again, several people spoke in unison.

"Mayor of Kamuela," Nalani spoke quietly, using the name assigned the town by the U.S. Post Office.

"Yes, agreed. Let the Kauaians have Waimea. This is bigger than the ranch, bigger than the town, bigger even than the outlying areas of Kohala and Waikoloa," Maleko said.

Jules called the vote, and it was unanimous.

"Lieutenant Eller? The mayor of... Kamuela, in the territory of Hawaii... would like to request the assistance of the U.S. military. Let's light another candle."

"Very well, sir. I'll head back upslope in the morning."

Lee was a little slow to wake up the next morning. Conversation had gone quite late the night before, and today would see him heading back upslope to the garrison. If he were still in his role as a runner, he'd have been heading to Waikoloa and the outlying camps and settlements to spread word of the upcoming election. True to his word, Maleko would not run unopposed, and suggested that Ben Peachtree run against him for the seat. Peachtree had been contacted by radio, and first refused, until Maleko further suggested that they handle the election much as the original 1789 presidential election in which the runner-up took the next highest position.

It was also necessary to gather information and volunteers for the upcoming trip to Kawaihae. Some of the people at the meeting were hesitant to call it a "mission," but it hadn't taken Lee long to recover the mindset of his days as a cadet and brief service. This was a mission, and like it or not, he would be leading it. It wasn't that different from finding himself at the head of a commercial business when his activity watch and software designs turned a hobby into a thriving company. He just needed to consider it a similar challenge to deciding to run an extreme endurance race.

The large hotels and resorts along the coastline were still considered to be too much trouble for them to attempt clearance and salvage. He'd learned that, globally, most people who had the flu-like version of H7D3 survived. The problem was that they spread it like crazy, and there was hardly anyone alive who hadn't been exposed. Normally, a five percent mortality rate was serious for influenza, but not earth-shattering. With H7D3, though, a large proportion—over twenty percent—did not survive. Of the survivors, about half developed a constant, low-grade fever, which after several days manifested as a blood-borne virus termed D4T3. The latter was the one that killed another twenty to thirty percent of people, and turned the rest into Infected, or ferals, or zombies, depending on local preference in names. With double-digit percentages of the population dying outright, and a large portion of the remainder turning into mindless biting machines, any large population area, particularly if that population was largely transient tourists, was an extreme hazard.

Lee and Allie had witnessed the Infected attacks firsthand in Kailua-Kona, and then again in Waimea as the ranchers gradually rescued survivors and cleared the Infected from the town. Now the area was relatively safe as long as one stayed aware of where the Infected could hide or hibernate. There were too many of those places in Kona, Hilo, or the beachside resorts. For an isolated port like Kawaihae, however, it might be doable.

Working as a runner exposed him to all of that, but at a low level. From many points along Route 190 he could see all the way to the coast and witness the destruction left by the Infected. Being a military leader would put him right on the front line. It was *that* conversation with Allie that had kept him awake for so much later than the meetings. Eventually they'd drifted off to sleep, not in their tent, but outside where they could watch the stars.

Today he was headed back upslope, and he'd be taking fresh fruit, vegetables, and both fresh and preserved beef for the garrison and HI-SLOPE. It would also be a longer trip, since he'd have to consult with Captain Silver and General Brice, and coordinate with First Sergeant Copley if they agreed.

There would also be a need to talk more with HI-SLOPE. While the amateur band radios at the ranch could receive signals from many different sources around the world, and even talk to some sites such as Kauai and the group at the Pacific Missile Range Facility, they didn't have the wide-band encrypted digital communications systems that the garrison used for their links to the Hole and HI-SLOPE. Lee wanted Copley's assistance in talking with Lugnut to see what satellite data he could access. They would probably need General Brice to supply some of the access codes, so this would be a lengthy conference call, but it might also result in some contacts much farther away than the Islands.

Lee had to admit that the group he *really* wanted to talk to was Wolf Squadron, but that would likely have to wait for another time.

This trip would also let Lee do something he hadn't been able to do on his courier missions: take Allie with him. For much of the last year, she'd supported the clinic originally set up for ranch personnel, but now expanded to all of Kamuela. She'd leveraged her time in nursing school, particularly her training in emergency medicine, to volunteer at the clinic and pay back those who'd helped her. José Clavell had found study books and coached her through the EMT course while Lee was on the road—literally. While there was no way to certify her, José had assured her that having the skill was much more important than having the certificate. This was actually the justification given for her accompanying Lee to the garrison. Clavell called it her "final exam and internship." While Lee spent most of his time with Copley or in the communications room, Allie would work with Dr. Rickabaugh, the garrison's dentist, learning about emergency dental procedures. She'd also work with the two Navy corpsmen to assist with routine procedures to keep the soldiers healthy.

Gunderson would also be going with them and would drive the wagon. Allie would ride with him while Lee rode 'Mua. Copley had promised they'd have better facilities for the horse and mules upon their return, but they weren't expecting much. Once the supplies were packed, it would be time to go back up the slope to the saddle between two volcanos.

Lee couldn't think of a better place to light a candle.

CHAPTER TWELVE
THE WIZARD OF HI-SLOPE

It's nothing like a video game. It's better.
—Z. Ludwig, HI-SLOPE

First Sergeant Copley was at the gate again, and led them inside immediately, not bothering to peace-bond the weapons this time. The wagon was taken to an oversized Quonset hut next to a large lot filled with military vehicles. The wagon could be wheeled directly inside, and half of the cargo was loaded onto a conveyor belt leading into a large machine.

"HI-SLOPE has to be kept under strict quarantine. They did even before the Haole Flu, so we take packaged or unpackaged food, irradiate it, then double-pack it in a cargo container as if it was a space station delivery," Copley told them. "They used to be on a reversed day-night cycle. We'd drive the cargo up every few months during the day and load it into a conveyor so that they could simulate receiving mid-flight supplies the next morning."

As each item moved along the conveyor belt, two workers removed all plastic packaging and replaced it with a heavy brown paper. The food then entered a larger enclosure, where it remained for about ten minutes. The conveyor belt exited the machine directly into an area closed off with plastic sheeting, where workers wore full isolation suits. There the food was repackaged into plastic, then placed into metal containers and stacked inside a hexagonal crate about a meter tall. Multiple crates were then placed on a pallet and wrapped in plastic, then loaded into a larger shipping container that could be placed on the back of a truck.

"We'll send that up to them tonight. They're no longer on the reversed cycle, but we'll still do this when they're sleeping so that we don't risk contaminating them. There's a tunnel under the complex leading to a processing area where the shipping pod will be decontaminated and unloaded by a robot into their storage hold."

"Wow, that's quite a process," Allie told Copley.

"We sterilize the best we can. We have presterilized supplies for them as well, but we've always had this way of ensuring we could send them fresh stuff. They really liked pineapple, but we can't get that right now."

"Another few months," Lee told him. "We have a shipment coming up from Waipio in two months. We're also waiting on news from a group plying the channels between islands. If we can secure Kawaihae, we'll have a good way to bring food in from other islands."

"When, not if."

"Yes, First Sergeant."

"You're *my* lieutenant now, Lee. Call me 'Top.'"

"Yes, Top."

"Good, you can be trained. Now, let's do something with that."

Even with authorization codes from General Brice, Lugnut was unable to access live satellite footage of Hawaii. "Gentlemen, I'm not surprised. Those satellites had set courses and were usually tasked to look at areas of concern," she told them. "Hawaii just wasn't that much of a concern prior to the Fall. Getting a satellite to change its orbital track and look at different locations requires additional authorizations, time, and maneuvering fuel. Even before, it could take several days before a re-tasked satellite could give us pictures of an area we needed to look at. Frankly, without the National Reconnaissance Office, we don't know all of the precise orbits, nor how much orbital adjustment fuel is left. Without an orbit specialist, we don't even have a way to calculate a new path. I can have someone look into it, but I'm afraid it would not be a fast process, and that's if we can even find someone."

"That's okay, General. I think I've got something that might be of help," Lugnut told them. "The PhotoEarth project had their own satellite taking pictures around the world, and automatically uploading them. They were photographing Hawaii when everything fell apart, and those images are probably just sitting on their server. It's unclassified, so should be accessible."

"That will have to do. Let's see what you have."

"Okay." There was a pause, with a faint clicking of keys in the background. "And...I'm in. The images seem to be indexed by location. The base coordinate is the Kona airport, and I should be able to work northward from there."

Lee and Copley were in the communication room at PTA, working at one of the secured military computers linked to a larger monitor on the wall of the room. The console was normally used for communication with military command, but they'd linked in Lugnut's console at HI-SLOPE for the video conference and to view the overhead imagery. The current conference call included Brice and Galloway in the Hole, Lugnut and Forsyth at HI-SLOPE, and Lee and Copley at PTA. Captain Silver had been in and out, particularly when they'd first started the video conference, but he was also keeping an eye on the preparation of supplies for HI-SLOPE and meeting with the Marine company NCOs to select marines to assist at Kawaihae. He'd instructed the two of them to call him or Lieutenant Cortez when they had images of the harbor.

The screen switched from the faces of the teleconference participants to an overhead view of mottled browns and blacks. Two-hundred-year-old lava flows from Hualalai and Mauna Loa looked like dark river deltas flowing into a brilliant blue sea. The view zoomed in to show a single runway airport right near the edge of the water.

"Okay, that's Keahole." Lugnut pronounced it "KEY-hole" which was a common mispronunciation.

"That's 'KAY-uh-hull-uh' Lugnut," corrected Ham. "We just call it the Kona airport."

"Named for astronaut Ellison Onizuka, just like your astronomy center," interjected Galloway. There were murmurs in the background, and he responded, "What? I visited Hawaii many times as an under deputy to Sec-Def. The listening stations on Oahu, Kauai, and Hawaii were essential to nuke monitoring. I *love* Hawaii. That's why I'm so glad we can help them out."

"Okay, so...Kona. Let's scan north to find the harbor." The image zoomed out jerkily, and they could see that from Kona, the coastline actually extended northeast, and not due north. The old lava flows were darker and narrower, now looking like a black riverbed, until they finally gave way to brown dirt and scrub grasses as the passed the resort areas of Waikoloa. Just as the coastline turned north, and then northwest, he zoomed back in to show a roughly polygonal stretch of sand next to concrete piers, enclosed by a breakwater. The water showed the green of reefs and shallows but was a darker color at the northern tip of the breakwater indicating the harbor entrance.

Zooming in, they could see a vessel parallel to the large, paved area onshore.

"That should be the civilian cargo terminal," Galloway told them. It looked like lots of containers, but they were irregular in placement. Not lined up the way you'd see them at a normal cargo port.

"There's none of those big cranes...you know, the ones that look like walking tanks from that movie?"

"Those are only in the big ports that have to unload quickly and efficiently, Lugnut," Ham told him. "Hawaii operates on 'Island time.' No worries, no hurries."

There were a couple plumes of smoke, one from the cargo area, the other from a tall, cylindrical structure at the north end of the complex.

"Fires, that's not good. Is that a fuel storage tank?" asked Lee.

"Maybe," said Copley. "I've been down there a few times. There's two clusters of fuel storage tanks, plus silos for the cement company. We don't have the resolution to see for certain."

"Oh, look. I've don't remember if I've seen that before. What ship is that?" Lee pointed to a ship that appeared to have run aground on the sandy area at the southern end of the harbor.

"That is your target, Lieutenant," said Silver, as he and Cortez entered the room. "The USAV *SSGT Robert T. Kuroda*, LSV-7, is a roll-on, roll-off landing ship for transporting battalion equipment from Pearl and Kaneohe. It can hold fifteen M1 Abrams tanks, two dozen trucks and technical, eighty CONEX cargo containers, or a combination. It also has surplus tankage for fuel, plus room for food and troops."

"Has it been there all this time? I mean, lots of times I'm on Route 190 just outside of town and look downslope toward the harbor. The land slopes down in a straight line and you can see Kawaihae, the beach resorts, and most of the way back toward Kona. I didn't realize it was a ship."

"It was supposed to bring equipment for the battalion exercise, and we hadn't unloaded when we lost contact. Do we have a way of knowing the date of these pictures?"

"No, sir. Not the date it was taken, only the date it was uploaded. It's an automatic process and didn't require anyone to approve. Only national security restricted sites required approval—the White House, Pentagon, Area Fifty-one..."

"Which doesn't exist," said three voices in unison.

"Okay, so when was it uploaded?" Silver continued.

"About the time we came out of blackout, which was..." Lugnut paused.

"Sixty-two days after the explosion at Pearl," Ham finished for him.

"Okay, then," said Silver. "We have a few fixed points in time. We can pan to Oahu and look for evidence of the explosion, or up to the garrison for Penguin Four-two, it crashed the next day."

"I remember..." mused Lee. "I remember the day before we left Kona, there was a fire at the county park just past the bay-side tourist area. It's the old Kona airport. Nice beach walk: the runway is now a road, and the terminal building is the county events center. It's kind of strange riding down there, and all of a sudden, you're on an old runway, but it's a great training area. Someone set fire to the pavilion and it burned, so they closed the park. I wanted to do some sprints there, but with the fire and park closure, Allie and I cycled instead. Good thing, since I'm not sure we would have had enough advanced warning to get out of there."

"Okay, so that's three points of reference. Can we pan to Pearl?"

"I'm not sure that's a good idea, Captain, sir," Lugnut replied. "Oahu photos wouldn't be the same day, week, or month. Best we stick to this island."

"Do it, then. Let's look at Kona first."

Lugnut began to scroll the images back down toward Kona, passing the airport and zooming in on Kailua Bay and the Kona waterfront. As he started to zoom in, they could see a cruise ship in the bay. Several light-yellow blotches were in the dark blue water next to the ship— one directly at the debarkation port in the side of the cruise liner, one just in front of the platform, and another awaiting its turn to load or unload passengers.

"The park is west of Ali'i Drive," Silver said.

"No, wait," said Lee. "Zoom in on the bay."

Lugnut zoomed in as far as he could, but it wasn't much more than they already saw. Large vessels and buildings had clear edges, but not much detail. Smaller objects like the transfer tenders were fuzzy, but it was what Lee saw in the water around the tenders that made his blood run cold.

Various colored dots could be seen along the deck of the cruise ship, and there were white dots and streaks in the blue water.

"Pan over to the beach," he instructed Lugnut. The image lurched to the side, and they could see the seawall lining Ali'i Drive, as well as the two sandy areas at each end of the seawall. Dark dots, with no sign of the bright colors of standard Aloha-wear could be seen in the water, on the beaches, and starting onto the streets.

"Fuck. It's the day."

"What? Lee, what's wrong?" General Brice asked.

"It's the day Kona fell. That's the cruise ship that brought the Infected to Kona." Lee's voice was tight with emotion. The next part came out in a whisper. "The day Allie and I barely escaped."

"Oh my God, Mr. Eller, I'm so sorry," Lugnut told them.

"Don't be," Lee said gruffly, then cleared his throat. "No, I should be glad Allie and I survived." He turned to Captain Silver. "But please don't let her see this."

Silver nodded in acknowledgment.

"My apologies, Lieutenant, but that's our date stamp," Galloway said after a few moments.

"Right. We know that the *Kuroda* was in port on that day. The Kona cruise ship was two days before the Pearl explosion, and three before the evacuation of K-Bay. It's possible that the *Kuroda* could get underway in those three days, but where would they go? Pearl and Kaneohe were already closed and turning away ships," Brice assured them.

"I can confirm that I've seen it at the port. I didn't know what it was, because I only saw it from ten miles away and three thousand feet of elevation, but I've seen a structure in that location. It has to be the ship."

"Very well, Lieutenant. And thank you, Lugnut, this is very important information. And now that we know the date for these images, Mr. Galloway and I are going be very interested in looking at other satellite imagery, especially around Pearl Harbor and our other Pacific bases, but we'll save that for later."

Brice paused and consulted someone off-screen. After a moment, she continued. "Lieutenant Eller, are you okay to proceed? Captain Silver, I suggest you give him a platoon of marines."

Lee swallowed. He didn't know if he was prepared to continue, but he knew he needed to. "Yes, ma'am, I'm ready."

"Frank and I hate to put all of this on you, but you are the person on the scene, and your history suggests that you can get it done. You have good help. Rely on your NCOs. Use your best judgment."

"Yes, ma'am, I will do my best."

"That's all we ask, Lieutenant."

CHAPTER THIRTEEN

CRUSADE

Who was Carl Gustaf? I have no idea, but his name has gone
down in history with Browning, Colt, and Smith & Wesson.
—J. van Tuyl, armorer, Paniolo Ranch

The trip back down the mountain, five days after their ascent, was
once again uneventful. This time, rather than guns and ammunition,
they carried prepackaged meals—the infamous "meals-ready-to-eat"
or MREs that Lee remembered from active duty. They seemed to
have a better selection than he recalled, though. First Sergeant
Copley had suggested the MREs, given that they would be sending a
force out to clear their way to Kawaihae, and portable rations would
be much more convenient and enable the force to keep a lower
profile. The meals didn't have to be cooked over a fire, but had
thermochemical heaters that only required water, one of the most
abundant resources on the island.

They did bring additional firearms. Captain Silver had sent several
M3 recoilless rifles. Commonly misidentified as a "bazooka," the M3
was the U.S. Army designation for the well-known "Carl Gustaf"
recoilless rifle introduced by Sweden in 1946, and in extensive use
around the world. The M3 updated the original design and allowed
compatibility with modern battlefield optics and targeting. However,
its main advantage for the upcoming battle was that the standard anti-
tank/anti-structure rounds could be supplemented with ADM401
area-defense rounds that released over one thousand flechettes in a

cone, dispersing to cover one hundred square meters at a distance of a hundred meters. It was hoped that the antipersonnel properties of the rounds would assist in dealing with mobs of Infected, and the other munition types could assist in taking down fortifications by enemies of the intelligent kind.

When Lee sent word of the munitions back to van Tuyl, he'd begged for additional 84mm high-explosive rounds. The man was not just a certified gunsmith and the ranch's armorer, he'd worked for a major ammunition manufacturer in Mississippi many years back. He told Lee that he'd worked on a round for the M3 that dispersed steel ball bearings instead of fletchettes. He argued that Infected might not be incapacitated by the small needles of the ADM401 rounds, since they didn't feel pain, and that, much like a Claymore mine, a "rain of steel" would be needed to drive off the zombies. Using the 84mm HE rounds, he planned to produce some heavier rounds for the M3.

Lee was also taking Claymores and C4 explosive to be able to improvise traps and defenses against incursions or pursuit by the Infected. Everything was planned to provide the maximum firepower against mindless hordes.

Allie had had an interesting few days working with Dr. Rickabaugh and the corpsmen. They planned several more exchanges, including bringing Rickabaugh down to the ranch clinic to treat several severe dental cases. As a follow-up, there would be an effort to recover and resupply a dental office in Kamuela to provide an alternative to simply pulling affected teeth.

Most importantly, they were equipped with information, including topographical maps of the island, terrain maps around Kawaihae, satellite images, and more.

The garrison was sending thirty marines, set to arrive in Kamuela in three days and assist in training the civilian force raised by the ranch and outlying communities. Lieutenant Eller was starting to feel less daunted by his new role, but that just meant he needed to listen even more closely to his superiors, Top, and his squad NCOs.

This was now a military operation, and he would be in charge. He wasn't too worried about how Maleko and Jules would take the news; they'd already made it obvious that they accepted his role when they'd included him in the strategy session following his previous trip. He did worry about how Allie would perceive his new role, but the way she snuggled up behind him while riding 'Mua was a pretty good indication that she approved.

Approaching town, they were surprised to see the sign welcoming visitors to Waimea had been replaced with one welcoming them to Kamuela. He'd been told by Nalani that the town had been considering the name change for many years, and the signs had been in storage in anticipation. There were also announcements about the upcoming mayoral election and town council. In addition to Maleko and Peachtree, handmade signs announced that both Scotty and Jules Thompson, and José Clavell were on the ballot for town council.

Gunderson muttered something about needing to see Lee's name on the ballot, but Lee dismissed it as friendly banter. He'd need to speak with Jules about that, though. His military duty should preclude elected office. On the other hand, he was a reservist, and this was a zombie apocalypse. Did he *want* a role in the new government?

He set the thought aside. The days to come would be busy, and they would be dangerous. Lee was at ease. He knew they could do this. He was pretty sure *he* could do this. It was an important step toward bringing back civilization to the Hawaiian Islands.

As Lee had predicted, his return was the start of a round of meetings to determine the best way to approach the harbor at Kawaihae. While the others worried about approaching by road or across the fields, Lee had to concern himself with disposition of the military that would accompany them. He would have what amounted to a short platoon of marines. As a cadet he'd learned that a Marine platoon consisted of three squads of thirteen riflemen, capable of dividing up into three fire-teams of four men each, and a sergeant (E-5) leading the squad. However, a platoon that size would have taken half of the marines away from the garrison. While Command had determined that this was an important mission, not all of the marines at PTA were combat-effective, so a reduced platoon structure was offered. Lee would have four squads of six men led by a corporal or sergeant; each capable of being divided into two fireteams led by a lance corporal or corporal. In place of a marine platoon sergeant, Lee had Top. He also had a marine gunnery sergeant (E-7) as assistant platoon sergeant. There was no headquarters squad *per se*, but he'd been assigned a private first class as a combination runner, messenger, and radioman.

A few garrison soldiers would be attached to the civilian support elements. Dr. Rickabaugh and a Navy corpsman would follow well back from the platoon, and additional radio operators were being provided to the civilian combatants and ranch headquarters. An Army E-6 would also be working with the civilians as a trainer to assist with organization and movement. It was quite the investment on the part of the garrison. Then again, Kawaihae represented a military objective as well as civilian since it held military supplies in the form of the LSV-7 and its cargo. The force represented a third of their marines, and about half of the Marine effective combat strength. The garrison would keep their oversized Army platoon in reserve. Those individuals comprised the "OpFor" or "Opposition Force" permanently stationed at the garrison, and before the Fall had generally deployed as a counterforce to the battalions training. There were also trained as mountain troops, and it was thought that amphibious assault-trained marines would be best for this operation.

Copley volunteered to fill in as platoon sergeant—rightfully the gunny's job—so that he could act as guide and assistant to Lee. Gunny Kalama would still be the de facto platoon sergeant given that General Brice had accepted Copley's offer and tasked him with "keeping the lieutenant's head down."

Lee was honored and terrified.

The troops would arrive in three more days and be housed in their own tents on the other side of Route 190 from the tent city at the state forestry facility. Lee and Allie were being moved to indoor housing converted from the state tree nursery buildings so that he'd be near the troops and the training area for the civilian volunteers. The ranch stables and rodeo arena formed one side of a triangle bounded by the airstrip and Route 190, and it was the perfect location to house and train the fighters. Almost fifty civilians had volunteered and would form a unit of irregulars to complement the marines. Many were former military, but they would need time to get used to working as a unit before battle.

None of these preparations meant anything when dealing with Infected. However, the message given to Waikoloa by the supposed servant of Ku suggested that at least some of the Infected could follow directions or be driven toward particular targets.

The caused a discussion of a different sort. The idea of intelligence behind the mindless zombies was abhorrent. On the other hand, if they could be driven to attack people, what else could they do? What else was *Ku* driving them to do? And if he could get them to do his bidding, why didn't he use the ability to *help* people instead of attacking them?

In the end, the questions didn't matter. If there was someone controlling the Infected, the marines would push through and neutralize that party while the irregulars dealt with the zombies.

Maleko had called for strategy sessions each evening, with a large portion of the time on the radio they'd set up to talk with the Hole. The rest of the time they spent examining satellite photos and maps and talking strategy. The leaders pledged support for Lee and gave him absolute autonomy to command the civilian troops in addition to his marines. Jules reminded him that any unit was going to have assholes who wouldn't listen to orders but suggested just sending troublemakers back home. Volunteers were being offered shares in supplies recovered from Kawaihae, and anyone sent home would lose their share. The irregulars would gather a day before the marines arrived, and Lee was scheduled to speak with them and interview each person to place them in an appropriate role for the crusade.

Kawaihae Harbor represented a Holy Grail in the form of fuel. A clear road between waterfront and highlands would allow access to water-borne trade. The beachhead would be the starting point for retaking the Kohala and North Kona Coast, and even if they bypassed the population center of Kailua-Kona Coast, it was still a gateway to the rest of the island. Lee felt that the enthusiasm exhibited by the people of Kamuela was starting to feel like the eleventh-century campaigns to retake the Holy Land.

CHAPTER FOURTEEN
SECURING THE FUTURE

How do I make blades? I start with a piece of carbon steel, heat it until the metal is bright orange, then beat it with a hammer. When the metal cools to red, it goes back in the fire until it's orange again. Heat, beat, and repeat. Quench it in oil, then grind it to sharpness. You can do it with power tools or by hand, it's still just heat, beat, and repeat.

—M. Horgan, blacksmith, Paniolo Ranch

The crusade analogy seemed to have occurred others as well. Jules proposed a unit of mounted fighters who could be quickly deployed anywhere that Infected might break through and threaten the flank or the rear of the main forces. He cited the effectiveness of cavalry and knights to protect the flanks on a battlefield. Cody argued against the idea. The horses would have no defense, and the Infected would simply see the horses as more food. Zombies, Infected, victims, or whatever you wanted to call them, they didn't have any conscious thoughts, couldn't be intimidated, nor their spirit broken. The only solution was to slaughter them all. Ultimately, a compromise was agreed: six riders on horseback, with their horses protected by makeshift leather armor, would accompany the support element in the rear to act as messengers, or to rapidly extract key personnel who got mobbed.

Logistics was a minor problem. The marines would carry their own gear, food, and ammunition, but the civilians would not be as well equipped. Rear area supply caches would be placed at the old honeybee farm three miles upslope from the intersection of Route 19 and Route 270. For the irregulars, a second cache would be placed near the Hapuna Heliport just upslope from the golf course at the Mauna Kea resort. Those two points also marked the locations where the marines would switch from following Route 19 to an old stream bed, and the irregulars would head off the coast road to Mau'umae Beach so that the two forces could approach the harbor from different angles. Visibility was such that the harbor would be visible to both forces. The reverse was also true, so they all hoped there was no intelligence directing the Infected there.

The preparations would take a week once troops arrived, and it would be a week that Lee spent nervously, considering how he had gone from runner to commander in an equally short period of time. He also received one more piece of information that greatly disturbed him: Allie would be accompanying the support element. Clavell had approached Lee to explain that she had volunteered to be part of the medical support element.

It left him unsettled; it wasn't like being at the ranch was perfectly safe all the time. Lee placed himself in danger every time he ran a courier mission. They'd faced danger together the day they'd left Kona. Allie risked infection and more in the clinic since they were still seeing new cases a year after the initial outbreak. Going out and seeking trouble in the form of taking Kawaihae, though, was a major risk. The thought of Allie joining that risk kept him up many nights.

"I'm . . . conflicted about you going on the mission, Allie," Lee told her late that night. It was their last night in the tent, so they'd taken the bedding out into the tree nursery next to the housing area and found a secluded spot. They were moving into one of the nursery buildings the next day in time for the arrival of the marines. He just wanted a private moment before they got too busy.

"You're going," Allie said.

"I have an obligation."

"So do I, love. I am as obligated to caring for the people going on this mission as you are to leading them."

"I'm just a lieutenant."

"What? Of course, but you're the one entrusted to do this."

"No, I mean you're being the Captain's Lady, and I'm here all worried that you'll be hurt."

"You're not a captain—yet."

"Not much of a chain of command, and I essentially just got called up. It's okay, I'll be the best damn lieutenant I can be."

"That you will. I have faith in you."

"Hmm."

"And I know *you* have faith in you, too."

"Do I?"

"Look up there!" Allie pointed to the sky. They were among low trees, with a good view of stars while still secluded from other eyes. "You gave me a book back when you first found out I read science fiction. In it, a man and woman sat watching the stars and talking about far-flung civilizations and spacefaring heroes. Look up there and tell me you aren't in awe of it all."

"Barsoom, Trantor, and the Ringworld."

"Exactly. And just like the people in that book, we've survived the end of the world and lived to tell about it. And do you know why we survived—thrived even?"

"Because you won't let me quit?"

"Because *you* won't let *you* quit, Lee. You built your company. You ran, biked, and swam your way to success. You challenged yourself every step of the way and never let *yourself* quit."

"Yeah, I guess that's true, but this mission? It's become all too real."

"And you will go out there every day. Make the plans. Train your troops. Solve the problems. Just like you pushed yourself to always go one more mile."

"Huh. One mile more."

"And someday, that one mile more will be our future. Our gift to ourselves, and our children."

"Children?"

"Children, Lee. It's time."

"Oh . . . Oh!" Lee stood up, then got down on one knee.

Allie laughed and drew him back down to her before he could even ask. "Yes, yes, a thousand times, yes."

The mission may have become too real to Lee, but for this night, talk of galactic empires and the future led to a promise for the following day . . . and the future. It would be dangerous, but it was time to have faith that they would *have* a future together. Lee would speak to General Brice and Mr. Maleko about performing the ceremony, but they would proceed with the expectation and the will to survive and get through this.

They would be there for each other and rebuild the world for their children.

The marines arrived at midday, having left the garrison soon after sunup. Knowing the type of rations the marines lived on, Lee made sure the community cooks had prepared a meal of steak, eggs, and fresh fruit. The servings were small, and would be supplemented with preserved goods, such as beans and jerky, but it was a great way to welcome the troops prior to the hard work.

Lee took Copley aside and requested his assistance at the ranch headquarters. He took the first sergeant in to meet Mr. Maleko and the community leaders, but then sprung the request to act as his best man. They set up the conference call with the Hole, asking General Brice to do the honors, but she demurred, saying that Mr. Galloway might be more appropriate. When the man acting as provisional leader of the United States of America agreed, Maleko offered to act as the civil leader's "hands" on the ceremony. Nalani entered the room, dressed in an elegant business suit, then Allie entered behind her, dressed in a beautiful Hawaiian dress. Copley had brought the appropriate military wear for Lee, so he stood in his Army uniform, knees locked, feeling like he was going to faint at how beautiful Allie looked.

He was barely aware of Galloway's words over the conference call. He remembered hearing "Do you, Captain Leslie Eugene Eller, take Malia Noelani to be your lawfully wedded wife?" and answering, "I do." Somewhere in there, Allie answered the same question in reverse, and he was told to kiss the bride.

He was still in a daze when the ceremony ended, but there was something tugging at his subconscious. "Wait—Captain?"

Allie laughed at him. "You just now noticed?"

"Noticed what?" Nalani asked. She'd stepped up to hug Allie, while Maleko held out his hand to congratulate Lee.

"That Mr. Galloway called him a captain," Maleko laughed. "General Brice told me earlier. Lee has enough time in grade with his prior service, so they promoted him."

"But what about Captain Silver? Lieutenant Cortez?" Lee asked.

"Silver's being bumped to Major, that way he's only one step below what the garrison commander should be ranked. Cortez was promoted a month before the Fall, so you have seniority on her, Lee. It's okay, we all want this for you." Maleko held his hand out to his side, spread his fingers wide, and gestured at the room. "All of this. Kamuela is proud of you."

"Well then, I need to be worthy of it. Time for me to get to work."

He had a future to save.

As it turned out, Copley had the training situation well in hand. The marines needed to set up their camp. In turn, they would assist the civilian volunteers in setting up their own facilities, and it was necessary to prepare the training field and issue materials for the next week. Gunny Kalama took over the platoon, and Copley managed the irregulars, so there was nothing for Lee to do for the remainder of the day.

Maleko offered the use of a room in the ranch house. He'd offered the room to Lee and Allie on a permanent basis, but neither of them felt that they deserved such comfort when so much of the community made do with temporary housing.

Still, for a one-night honeymoon, it was greatly appreciated.

In the morning, they would join their respective training groups. Lee had to be a leader, and Allie was going to be a medic. It scared them but was necessary. Allie also needed to be trained in firearms, just in case. She'd had little opportunity to learn, and was somewhat reluctant, having seen gunshot injuries up close, but she'd studied martial arts in the past, including Kali, a discipline well suited to bladed weapons. José promised to take charge of her weapons training. It seemed contradictory that a nurse should be so familiar with taking lives, but Lee realized that the man's twenty-five-year career as a combat medic and nurse meant that he had seen it all—and likely done it all—during his time in uniform.

José reassured him that he would watch over Allie and make sure she learned what she needed to know. Meanwhile, for one day, Lee and Allie could relax and just be together until it was time for Lee to take charge of his military and civilian task force.

CHAPTER FIFTEEN

PARA BELLUM

"Si Vis Pacem, Para Bellum"
If You Want Peace, Prepare For War
—motto of the 96th Communication Squadron,
U.S. Air Force

Training involving both marines and volunteers was interesting. Horgan, the ranch blacksmith, routinely made tools that were easily converted to bladed weapons. Many had been forged the normal way, heating the metal, hammering it into shape, quenching, and sharpening. The result was strong, sharp blades that could chop wood, flesh, or bone without breaking. Unfortunately, the mission required many more weapons than he had prepared, so he'd switched to cutting and grinding spring steel and tools. The blades would be prone to breakage, and not stay sharp as long, but it would suffice for what was hoped would be a short battle, especially if they could reduce the numbers with the flechette or ball-bearing rounds for the M3s.

Horgan and Clithero had gone up to PTA the previous day, Michael to use the machine shop to speed up production of blades, and Paul to assist in increasing the electrical power available to the machine tools. He would also take a look at the damaged valve heads and pumping gear to see if it was possible to recover any of the remaining fuel in the underground tanks. If they could get access to fuel storage, there was a truck with a small transfer tank at the garrison that could be used to distribute fuel from the harbor.

All of the effort was centered around getting a fighting force ready to clear their way down to the harbor and push back the Infected. The military cargo on the LSV-7 was known, but they had no way of knowing what they might find in the civilian cargo at the pier. It might make a difference for long-term survival.

Lee and Copley watched the latest training exercise. The marines were currently acting as opposition force—an unarmed, undisciplined, unthinking mob. They rushed the civilians and attempted to overpower them. The irregulars were armed with imitation bladed weapons made of wood, foam, plastic—anything available in the right size and length. Each weapon was liberally coated in the reddish-brown volcanic soil, so that it would be obvious when they'd scored a "touch" on an Infected. Of course, that lasted only for the first half hour, after which everyone on the field was covered in dirt anyway. After that point, Gunny Kalama called his men in, spoke to them briefly, then sent them back to reform on the field and run the next iteration. He announced that since it was no longer possible to *see* evidence of touches, all participants were on an honor system for reporting when they were "cut" by a weapon.

Lee noticed that the marines were now ignoring most touches, and only reporting neck or head contact. "They're cheating."

"Yes. They are. Gunny told them to. Just watch."

At the next break, several of the civilians voiced accusations that the marines were cheating. Gunny Kalama stepped into the middle of the field, blew a whistle, then barked out a command.

"*Listen up!* You think my men are cheating, but how many of you *boys* have fought Zeds?"

Every Marine hand went up, and most of the civilians.

"How many of you have fought more than five at a time?"

All of the Marine hands stayed up, although about half of the civilians put theirs down. Lee and Copley had their hands up.

"Okay, how many of you have seen a mob of more than twenty?"

Most of the civilians lowered their hands. Copley lowered his, Lee kept his up.

"Over one hundred?"

All civilian hands went down. One of the marines lowered his hand. Lee still kept his raised.

"Look at the hands. My marines held the fences at Kaneohe as the base was evacuated. When we got the call to board the C-130, we left behind brothers and sisters facing thousands of Zeds, and not a few civilians trapped in the mob. You need to understand right now: Zeds, or Infected as you call them, are mindless. They are a mob. They don't feel pain. They don't get scared. They don't run off if they hear you rack the slide of your shotgun. They. Just. Keep. Coming.

"Only a headshot or decapitation will stop them for sure. Skewering them through the heart will work, but the damned zombies will keep moving until they bleed out, so don't make a strike and turn your back.

"One last thing. Your *captain* kept his hand up. You may not want to listen to me, but Captain Eller is one of you. Until last week, he was a civilian, like you. But he has seen the elephant. He and his wife escaped Kona even as it was being overrun with thousands of Zeds. He did not panic. He did not curl into a ball. He *escaped* when it was the *smart* thing to do, but he is going *back* into danger because *that* is the *right* thing to do.

"Remember that when the Zeds are coming at you and you are in the thick of it."

"I didn't realize it was Saint Crispin's Day, Top," Lee whispered to Copley.

"That speech from *Henry V* has worked for centuries. Shakespeare's pretty inspiring."

"So it would seem. They look a bit more serious now. I'm curious, though: you haven't faced the mob?"

"I've been at the garrison the whole time. We had almost five hundred in anticipation of the battalion exercise. Half of those had just arrived, and most turned. I've faced between fifty and a hundred, but Gunny was making a point."

"I should have lowered my hand. I saw that many but didn't really face them like you did."

"No, you shouldn't have. *You* were the point he was making. They'll respect you that much more now, and you're going to need that."

Training also involved daily conferences with General Brice and Major Silver. The gift of radios for Kamuela had included two—one for the community as a whole, and one for Lee. While Maleko's was at the ranch HQ, Lee was set up at the airport where he'd be close to the training grounds.

Many days, the discussion turned to how to handle the unknowns of the mission. They wouldn't know the answer to many of the questions until they were in contact with the Infected, and any enemy actors at the harbor. Lee was the sort of person who preferred to address unknowns, resolve them as much as possible, and create contingency plans.

One of those had just reared its ugly head in the latest joint conference with HI-SLOPE.

"I don't have all the tools to analyze and predict weather patterns, but I can look at the pictures," Lugnut was telling them. "I can send images to you, and if you have anyone who can analyze it, please do. Otherwise, here's the picture. There's a rotating storm to your east, and it looks like it might have an eye. Looking back at the cache of previous pictures, it seems to be heading mostly west, with a slight bend to the north. Maybe five degrees or so. If I draw a straight line, it'll pass north of the island of Hawaii, south of Oahu, but right over Maui. That should keep it well clear of Kauai. There's no way for me to predict wind speed to know how strong a hurricane, but it seems small, and the eye is small, too."

"Unfortunately, we don't have ocean temperature, wind speed, or direction to give you a better track, Lee," General Brice told them. "Lieutenant Stagg's a meteorologist here in the Hole, but without those other indicators, he can't do much more than look at the pictures, either."

"When is it supposed to be here?" Lee asked. "Best guess."

"Best guess? If it keeps on course, about three days," Lugnut said.

"Stagg is sitting right here looking at the images, and he says the same thing," Brice confirmed.

"We have noticed an increase in clouds, Lee, and it's a bit breezier," Copley added.

"Joy. So, just as we're about to take the harbor, we could be fighting a hurricane *and zombies*?" Lee started to run his hands through the stubble on his head. Allie had cut it for him the previous night and had made it as close to a military regulation as she could manage.

"One more thing," General Brice said. "Stagg was flipping through images in sequence to judge the rotation and I noticed something. This must be an unusual point in the orbit, or it's just a different angle, but I can clearly see your island, Lee."

"Okay, well, good to know. We might want to update our plans."

"You'll need to. I can see your port, and there's movement."

"What?" Lee stood up in shock.

Copley had stepped to the door to look out at the weather and turned back in alarm.

"It looks like a mass of bodies, and they're moving."

"How many?"

"I'll need to have an analyst check it . . ." Someone was speaking off-mic. "Oh, thanks. Stagg showed me a scale bar. I can't give you numbers, but I can give you area. The mass seems to start about a kilometer from the *Kuroda*, and it looks to be about a third to half a kilometer across, filling the area just southeast of the harbor."

"Pu'ukohola Heiau," said Copley. "Sacred site."

"Shit."

"Ku, I'd be willing to bet," Maleko said. "The bastard was a showman when he was caught before the Fall."

"Half a klick across, what would that translate to in bodies, Top?"

"Conservatively? Figure a round area, pi-arr-squared, fifty thousand square meters. How tightly packed?" Copley asked the general.

"Not enough resolution, but it doesn't look densely packed, and they're moving a lot. We wouldn't see that if they were packed tight."

"Okay, so, top end, fifty kay, Lee. Most likely in the ten thousands."

"Shit. Shit, fuck. Fucking Ku." Lee brought his left hand up to his face and rubbed his eyes. He finished the motion by tugging at his nose and looked up at Copley. "Have I told you I fucking hate zombies, Top?"

"Temper, Captain. We play the hand we're dealt. Better to know now."

The sound of a throat clearing brought their attention back to the radio. "We do have something else that we can offer and it should be getting there soon," Major Silver told them.

The sound of people shouting outside became audible in the meeting room. There was also the rumble and clanking of heavy machinery growing in volume. Lee looked around at faces showing surprise and concern. General Brice told them to go see their surprise, then ended the call.

Maleko, Lee, and Copley stepped out of the airport communications room to see a crowd gathered to gawk at a large, armored vehicle as it pulled into the field just behind a row of bushes from the airstrip buildings.

It was a large, tan box with a wedged front, sitting on tank treads, with a turret and several guns sticking out the top. The barrel of the biggest gun looked a bit small to fire tank rounds.

"A tank? You've sent us a tank?"

"No, it's a Brad . . . an M2 Bradley Infantry Fighting Vehicle. An IFV."

"It has treads, armor, a turret, and a cannon on top. It's a tank!"

"No, that's a twenty-five-millimeter M242 Bushmaster. There's an M240 machine gun firing seven six two rounds right next to it." Gunny had walked up to the pair as they stood in awe of the fighting machine. "I see they left the anti-tank missiles, but you won't need them. You want armor and crowd control."

A hatch opened in the back. Horgan, Clithero, and four more soldiers exited the vehicle.

"Congratulations, Captain," Paul told him. "You now have an armor squad."

"Someone must have decided the fuel expenditure was worth it," Copley said.

"Paul was busy fixing valves and pumps," Horgan told them. "PTA has access to fuel again. It looks like you lost about two thirds of a full load, but you've got fuel again. Still not worth running generators at full power all the time, but the garrison has lights, fans, and stoves."

Several of the marines pumped their fists and were grinning at the prospect of not eating MREs on their return. Two more vehicles came down the road, both the size of large pickup trucks, and they were loaded with crates and boxes.

"That's the bladed weapons, more guns, and more ammo, plus some combat medic packs."

"A tank. You got me a tank!" Lee mused. "Can I paint it pink?"

"NO!" shouted Top and Gunny simultaneously.

CHAPTER SIXTEEN

STORM FRONT

Do you have a backup plan?   —Commodore Wolf

No, but I've got lots of guns and knives and a machete. I'm still looking for a chain saw.   —Shewolf

Lee and Copley stood watching the marines and civilians train the next day. The Kamuela volunteers had now gotten good enough that they could play OpFor against the marines, and even pair up by squads in mixed teams. They'd incorporated the IFV and mixed squads just in case everything went to shit.

"It's a good plan," Top told him. "Now, test time, Captain. In the heat of conflict, you don't want to screw up comms. Quick—team names."

"We're Taskforce Runner. Peachtree has Team Golf. Darkhorse's mounted force is Team Knight, and the marines are Team Anchor, for the globe and anchor."

Copley laughed. "Okay, so Runner Actual?"

"I prefer Runner Six."

"And I'm Runner Seven."

"Nope, you're my XO, not my senior NCO. Gunny is Seven, but he's also Anchor Six, so we're not using Seven. You're Runner Five. The big Five-O."

"Oh, hell no, I'm no Steve McGarrett."

"*Duh-duh-duh-duuuuh-daaaa-daaaa, duh-duh-duh-duh-daaaaaa.* Nope, you're right, not even Jack Lord."

"I'll make sure you regret that, Captain. And by the way, you're wrong. I'm Runner Six. *You're* Runner Actual. I may have to answer comms in your stead. KISS: Keep it simple, stupid."

"I'm *sure* you *will* make me regret it, Top. And in keeping with KISS, we're not using the terms 'Infected' or 'zombies' on comm. They're Zeds. Succinct and clear."

"You pass, Cap. Now, final point; no plan survives contact with the enemy. What's your backup plan?"

Lee looked down at himself and his equipment. He'd been provided with desert camouflage gear similar to what the marines were wearing. The clothing was lightweight but resisted tears and punctures. He had long pants legs tucked into the tops of desert-tan military boots, and long sleeves with the cuffs tucked into thin leather gloves. Around his neck was a shemagh, a lightly patterned cloth wrap for neck and head that was common in desert environments. It functioned as neck protection, head cover, and mask, all in one, and while it wouldn't completely stop an Infected bite, it would prevent blood splatter from reaching his skin when the combat devolved to hand-to-hand fighting. For armament, Lee carried an M4 carbine, several of Horgan's knives, a machete, and an Army M9 handgun.

"Backup plan? If anyone has a chain saw, I think I'll have it covered." He looked down at the eighteen-inch length of steel reinforcement bar of the type normally embedded in concrete. One end was bent into a crook; both ends had been flattened and sharped. "Oh, and I've got a crowbar. If I'm down to the crowbar, this will count as a very bad day."

Copley laughed. He recognized the spirit, if not the exact words, from the video released by Wolf Squadron and pushed out to all the military forces by the Hole. It came from the time Shewolf first reported back from the deck of the cruise ship *Voyage Under the Stars*. That time, she'd nearly single-handedly cleared the deck of almost one hundred Infected. The act, and her spirit, endeared her to the submarine crews who could only watch and not break quarantine. Shewolf was considered something of a mascot by the East Coast and Atlantic forces . . . but from the looks of the marines who'd overheard the exchange, Lee had just had a similar effect on his troops.

∾∾∾

The leader meeting that evening was greatly expanded. In addition to Maleko, Thompson, Cody, and Lee, they were joined by Ben Peachtree, First Sergeant Copley, Gunny Kalama, and Darkhorse. There were also quite a few individuals joining over the radio—General Brice and Mr. Galloway in the Hole, Major Silver at the garrison, and Ham, Cro, and Lugnut from HI-SLOPE. An unfamiliar voice introduced himself as Jackson Toivo of the Kauai community. He apologized that his Kalaupapa counterpart couldn't join, but that group was still en route from Kauai to Molokai. In addition to national leadership, the meeting represented the leaders of the largest concentrations of survivors so far in the Hawaiian Islands.

Maleko started the meeting with a report from Darkhorse.

"Cody and I rode down Route 19 before dawn. I know we've never tried to contact the luxury vacation homes down there because they're too close to the beach and Infected, but with the offshore breeze, we were upwind and decided to risk it. We came across a family hiding out in one of the houses and convinced them to evac uphill. I got word they'd checked in at the community center around midday. Met an old coot who wouldn't budge, and he said there were others, but we didn't see them."

"Saw plenty of Zeds, though," Cody added.

"Right. I left the horses with Cody. I wanted to get close enough to estimate numbers, and the Infected seem awfully fond of horseflesh."

"Why is that?" Galloway asked. "We don't have contact with anyone using horses for transport."

"There's Texas," Brice corrected him.

"True, but they haven't said anything about Infected pursuing their horses."

"I don't actually know why. My mount is trained to be as quiet as possible. Infected have good hearing, but it's not that good. It might be smell. Zombies don't like the heights that much, very few infiltrate up from the lowlands, but Pu'u Wa'awa'a Ranch is about a thousand feet lower than us. They had a mob infiltrate up from Kona or someplace downslope about six months ago. It was strange how they ignored people and pursued the horses. We rescued survivors from the ranch but lost all of the horses."

"Good to know. Thank you," said Galloway.

"Anyway, I got all the way past the junction of Routes 19 and 270, almost to Spencer Beach Park Road before I got a good enough view. I'm going to call it three thousand, give or take a couple hundred."

"That's low," said Lee.

"Yeah, well, there's trees along the edge of the port. Take a mass of sun-darkened bodies, mix them in with the trees, and it'll look like more, or at least a large area."

"The weather satellite resolution wasn't high enough to be precise. I'd be happy to be wrong," General Brice said.

Lee looked over at Copley, who just gave a small shrug and said, "Okay, that's not great, but better. Any sign of Ku?"

"I don't know if it was him, but there was an old surfer-dude with a ratty aloha shirt," Darkhorse told them.

"Ku," said Maleko and Copley, simultaneously.

Surprisingly, Toivo said the same over the radio. "That's him. The guy we met called himself 'Larry Vale.'"

"Our guy called himself Ed Serra," Peachtree added.

"Hmm, so he's been to Kauai, too," Jules mused. "Laurentino Edgar Vale Serra is the name of the pre-Fall psycho who called himself Ku."

"Okay," said Lee with a sigh. "We have a few thousand zombies, endangered civilians, and Ku. Can this get any better?"

"Don't forget the storm," said Copley, quietly.

"Right. The storm. Alright. Let's get back to this."

"Wow, it's just like a raid!" said Lugnut.

"Raiding what?" asked Maleko.

"Like an RPG—a role-playing game. When you have an event in the game with an objective, lots of mobs and a mega-boss, you need more than just a group for the dungeon, so we assemble a bunch of teams into a raid, just like you did here. The ranchers are druids—or DPS, not sure which. Marines are the tanks. Zombies are the mobs. Ku is the Boss."

"I got some of that," Lee said. "I was never a gamer, but I've heard some of the terms. RPGs required groups of five to six people with a balance of abilities. I know that tanks usually lead and soak up damage. The Boss is the big bad monster you have to defeat to win. Mobs? DPS? Don't know those terms."

"Monsters are mobs—mobile damage dealers—they're the enemy.

DPS stands for damage per second—anyone firing a weapon or fighting hand-to-hand is DPS."

"Sorry about that, folks," Ham cut in. "Please forgive our youngest teammate. He's missing his online gaming."

"That's okay, Ham," said Maleko. "I think I get it. This . . . raid . . . is something that requires all of us—ranchers, military, and everyone willing to participate. One question, though, Mr. Ludwig: What do you see yourself as?"

"We're the wizards, Mr. Mayor. Surveillance, analysis, communication . . ."

"And healing." Dr. d'Almeida spoke for the first time. "It's been hard doing this the *right* way instead of the *easy* way, but my vaccine is ready and, hopefully, a treatment for acute bites by Infected. I'll also be available to consult on any medical cases."

"Oh, that's good," said General Brice. "Are you going to be able to be onsite for triage?"

"Alas, no, General. My good friend the headshrinker forbade me from testing the vaccine on myself, so I'm actually the *last* to be fully vaccinated. My assistant is a med-tech; we might be able to send her down."

"You're sure about the vaccine?"

"We had another breach, General," Ham said. "An atmosphere pump failed in Hex Six, our surface-access garage, and it got contaminated. We lost two more people, but Cro's vaccine saved three. It's good. He and I are the last to be vaccinated. We need a booster, but in about two weeks we should be fine to finally rejoin the outside world."

"Well, then," said Maleko, rubbing his hands together. "Druids, warriors, and wizards. I like that. But we need to make sure this part of the world is still here in two weeks. We have a raid to finish planning. The Kawaihae Raid."

For once, the meeting did not go late into the night, since the various groups would be moving into position in the morning. It did split up into primary and secondary leadership, though. The gunny took Darkhorse and van Tuyl off to meet with the NCOs and civilian leaders to review squad-level plans for the mission. He also included the medical staff, José, Allie, Dr. Rickabaugh, and the IFV crew to ensure that the support elements were squared away.

The final disposition of leadership was also formalized. Lee was in overall command, with Copley in charge of the military element. The Marine platoon would be led by Gunny Kalama, and the support elements would self-organize into medical, logistic, and armor squads as needed. Ben Peachtree would lead the civilian volunteers, with Cody as his second. Darkhorse would lead the six-person mounted quick-reaction force, which would split off from the marine support element to act as forward observers and from the slopes of Kohala Mountain overlooking the harbor.

Lee decided that Lugnut was right. They had an almost literal tank, damage-dealers, healers, and a quick reaction force of knights. The hard part—for both Lee and Copley—would be coming up with plans of attack and adapting the battle as needed. Wizards, indeed.

The next morning dawned gray and windy. Rain came in spurts of very fine droplets driven by the wind. This was the morning that the forces would all move to their staging areas for what everyone was now calling the Kawaihae Raid. In order to get all forces to reach the harbor at the same time, the volunteers would leave for Waikoloa this morning. From there they would work their way down to the Queen Ka'ahumanu Highway and follow it to the golf course, just short of the large Mauna Kea resort complex. There they would spend the night, preferably inside some maintenance buildings, or in well-secured tents away from the main complex if not. With the worst of the hurricane still two days away, the risk of camping outside was considered worth it to get the group in position to approach the harbor from the south. Besides, if the weather was too bad, they could always attempt to clear a few of the villas at the edge of the resort.

The marines would be moving to the edge of the original town of Waimea. The community stretched for five miles in each direction east and west from the ranch along Route 19. They would set up their base camp at an elevation of twelve hundred feet above sea level, at the site of a landscaping supply business and several large homes off Waiemi Place road. Clearance crews from the ranch had secured and locked up the homes and buildings—many were badly damaged and unusable—but there was sufficient space and cover to set up the field hospital and logistic supply. The location was also two and a half miles from the junction of Routes 19 and 270, and just over three miles from the harbor, with a good view of both.

The medical support team, including Allie, José, Dr. Rickabaugh, and a corpsman, would set up their facility in one of the houses in better condition than the others. It would also act as a supply point for food and ammunition brought by truck down from Waimea in the morning.

After walking through increasingly stormy weather, all groups reported in that they had reached their objectives for the day. They called an early night so that the marines could be up and ready to secure the junction before bringing in the IFV and the irregulars. That evening, Lee and Copley had one last meeting with the troops, including the support element.

After reiterating all of the plans, movement orders, waypoints, signals, and tasks, Lee stood in front of the assembled task force to close out the briefing.

"Alright. We've talked about alternatives if things go sideways. Now, everyone knows to disengage and retreat to the support element if it all goes south." Lee caught Allie's eye and spoke the next words as if directly to her. "Support element, you've got our docs and medics. If you are threatened *at all*, return to Kamuela. We can't afford to lose you."

Allie ducked her head. She knew he meant everybody, but she also knew he especially meant that *he* couldn't afford to lose *her*.

"Finally, if it all turns into a shit-show, we form a fighting retreat back up Route 19 until we're within range of Kamuela and every mother-lovin' son-of-the-earth that can hold a gun, spear, sword, or garden rake will be waiting to back us up."

"Daughters, too," said Allie.

"Right. Daughters, too. Now, sideways? Pivot. South? Retreat. Pear-shaped? Return. Shit-show? Fighting retreat. Got that?" Lee asked with a grin.

The group laughed as the tension was broken.

Slightly.

"Okay, everyone to positions. In the morning, we go to battle."

Morning came with the sound of gunshots. The winds had picked up, and the rain was steady. Lee and his seniors had hoped that the storm would limit the activity of the Infected, but a cluster of five had come out of a building at the end of Waiemi Place and were quickly joined by another ten coming around the large, expensive homes at the end of the drive.

"They were not there last night, sir," Gunny Kalama reported as Lee exited the building housing the field hospital. "My men cleared those homes, and there's no other structures for several miles. It's possible they were attracted to our lights and noise last evening, but we stuck to condition orange. There were no immediate threats, but we acted as if there were."

"Understood, Gunny. It may be that the rumors are right and Ku can control the Infected. We dare not be surprised. Maintain condition orange and be prepared for condition red the moment we move out."

The Infected were quickly dispatched, and the marines immediately broke camp and prepared to move out. They continued to encounter Infected in small groups of two to five as they left the last of the housing developments on Route 19 behind them. The force was now below five-hundred-foot elevation above sea level and could see the intersection ahead of them, with the harbor off to their north. The LSV-7 was still there, as well as a half-loaded cargo barge, not to mention a lot full of cargo containers. The bow ramp of the landing ship was closed, which was fortunate, since it might mean that there were no Infected aboard, or at least minimal numbers. Several cargo containers had been moved out of strict rows and formed a perimeter with additional containers. The fences and gates had been knocked down at one point, although there were locations that appeared to be repaired.

It could be that someone had survived, at least for a time. The ship was intact, the near and far fuel tanks were not burned, and there was cargo to be salvaged.

The problem was they would have to fight through a mob of Zeds both inside and outside the fence to get to it. Lee considered the situation for a few moments, then reached for his radio.

"Runner to Golf. Report."

"This is Golf Five. We're approaching the service buildings for Spencer Beach Park. We can see Zeds ahead, mostly just milling around. They haven't heard or smelled us yet, so I've got a squad working their way through the trees at the waterline to get a better look. We'll let you know when we engage."

"Roger, Golf. Team Knight?"

"Knight is in position at Pahihi Gulch. Most of us are in the gulch staying out of line of sight, but Knight Actual is up on the rise looking down at the harbor. He reports about a hundred Zeds inside the fence, mostly milling around that cluster of shipping containers. Just a few Zeds between there and the fuel tanks. The *Kuroda* is clear, they seem to be ignoring it, but you've got a shit-ton of Zeds between there and the road."

"Metric or imperial?"

"Imperial. Knight Actual confirms the scouting estimate at well over two thousand, but likely less than five. They're packed in on the sand and pressing up against the fence. There's breaks in the fence line up north, but they're just pressing out on the intact sections instead of going around."

"Got it, Knight. Anything else?"

"Do you want normal or weird?"

"Well, since weird means something's not going to go according to plan, give me weird."

"Right. Well, you know the old sacred ruin just outside the sandy side of the harbor?"

"Yes, Top is looking at it through the binocs."

"There's a guy up top of one of the platforms in robes and a fancy feathered hat. It makes him look like a dragon. There's more Zeds at the base of the ruin, and they're all looking up at him."

Copley nodded and handed the binoculars to Lee. There were at least three individuals on the elevated temple ruins. One of them was dressed the way Knight had described, with a feathered headdress, tattoos over his body, and paint exaggerating his mouth into a grimace clearly visible at a grimace.

"Ku."

"That's what Knight Actual says."

"Okay, Knight, hold fast. We'll let you know when we advance."

"Runner to Golf. Are you seeing the Zeds at the heiau?"

"This is Golf Actual. It's worse, Runner. There's a sacrifice tower on the makai side of the temple, There's a body on it, and it's one of ours."

"What the fuck? *Who*?"

"Golf Five says it's El Coquí. Clavell."

"What? How? They took him from base?" A cold chill ran down Lee's spine. If they somehow got José, where was Allie?

Copley was on his own radio calling the support element. "Runner Five to Starbase. I need a report on section Mike." The support facility—Team Starbase—consisted of Lima, logistics, Mike, medical, and November, the armor team. The radioman would have been with the armor and would need to go from the IFV, in position to start down the road, to the field hospital. Not giving the medics a radio was an obvious oversight but considering that Lee would have entrusted that to Clavell, it was a moot point.

After several minutes, the radioman reported back. "Starbase Mike is short one. Medic Clavell is missing. All others accounted for."

Lee breathed a sigh of relief. Allie was safe, for now, but he still didn't know how Ku or his people—zombies?—had gotten to José. Still, he had to compartmentalize.

"Roger, Starbase. Acknowledged. Missing person is accounted for, but in danger. Tell November to roll now." Lee clicked off the radio and turned to Copley "No plan survives...right?"

"The enemy gets a vote, Captain."

"Yeah. I hear that." He lifted the radio to his mouth once more and spoke one word, and it wasn't the one everyone was waiting to hear: "Hold."

CHAPTER SEVENTEEN
THE TEETH OF THE STORM

War is the realm of uncertainty; three quarters of the factors on which action in war is based are wrapped in a fog of greater or lesser uncertainty. —Carl von Clausewitz

"Do we try to negotiate, Top?"

"We can try, Captain. Doesn't mean it's a good idea, but we can try."

"Okay, someone get me a white flag."

"No, sir. You know that part where a good NCO keeps his young officer from doing something stupid? This is that part. You. Do. Not. Go."

"Understood, Top. How do we do this, First Sergeant?"

Copley motioned for the PFC serving as messenger and radioman to hand him the commander's radio. He clicked the send button twice to get attention, then spoke, "Runner Six to Anchor Six. Send me a private."

The radio clicked once, followed by the voice of Gunny Kalama's subordinate. "Anchor Six acknowledges."

Lee raised an eyebrow at Copley, who just shrugged. "Gunny knows it's me, but he also knows to treat it as if you gave the order. That's why I used Runner Six."

"Got it. Thank you, Top."

"My job, Captain."

Private Robert Vancel, attached to Anchor's first squad, arrived carrying one of Horgan's spears and a square of folded white cloth. It was proof that Gunny understood the situation perfectly, including the dilemma placed upon his commander. Lee handed him a roll of paper with a parlay request and sent him off with instructions to stop just short of the ruin and call out for Ku.

Copley handed his binoculars to Lee while the private double-timed down the road and stopped just short of the mass of Zeds. There was no way to hear anything, but the marine's body posture indicated that he was calling out.

Much to Lee's surprise—and Top's, given that he heard a sharp intake of breath—a single Zed separated from the pack and approach the private with a hand out as if to take the scroll.

"He's trained them." Lee looked over to see that Top had procured his own binocs, and was watching the scene, too.

"Yes, he has, the bastard." Lee went back to watching.

Just when it seemed that the Zed might act in a strangely civilized manner, it lurched toward the marine and swiped sharp fingernails across his face. When Vancel grabbed at the scratches and bent over, the Zed advanced and bit him on the neck.

"Well, there's our answer."

Lee said nothing, just motioned to the PFC for his radio, put it to his lips, clicked the button, and spoke.

"Attack."

As if the words were prophetic, a bolt of lightning crossed the sky and the rain began to pour down. Lee was glad he'd dressed in his poncho this morning. The ripstop nylon was plain, and somewhat heavy, not to mention rather humid inside, but with the hood up, he had additional neck protection and he could strap on all his gear over the waterproof garment. Gunny had shown him the best way to apply oil and wax to his knives and magazine pouches to keep them relatively dry as well.

The rain was a nuisance, but anyone who lived in Hawaii knew that daily rain was a fact of life. This near-blinding, soaking rain, though, reminded him of the time he'd run a marathon as the remnants of a hurricane passed through Washington, D.C., on a Labor Day many years back. At least then he'd been able to wear moisture-wicking race gear that got wet, but not heavy. The current situation was much more like ROTC Basic Camp at Fort Knox.

Well, he was an Army captain now, not a cadet. He needed to suck it up and get the job done. The advantage of the heavy rain was that it would mask their scent and sound. Suckage was good when it served a purpose.

The marines spread to each side of the road as the IFV came down from the base and turned right onto Route 270. As soon as the vehicle made the turn, the Zeds inside the harbor fence broke down that barrier and started running toward it. The Bushmaster started to fire on the crowd immediately but did not have much effect in reducing their number.

"Anchor and Golf, Romeo Charlie Romeo teams, load and fire two rounds of ADM." Lee had received twelve of the recoilless rifles—RCRs spelled out in military phonetic alphabet—from the garrison, and distributed four each to teams Anchor and Golf, keeping two in reserve and sending one each with the IFV and Team Knight. The flechette rounds wouldn't necessarily kill Zeds in one shot, but they should disrupt a charge, allowing the rifle teams to take more time to identify targets.

Lee wanted to advance with his men, but Copley held out a hand to hold him back. "Let them do their jobs. Stay where you can see the battle."

"I could see it a hell of a lot better from where that bastard's standing." Lee gestured in the direction of the heiau.

"True, but we have to get through the Zeds to earn that vantage point. The plan's a good one. Stick with it for now."

"And José?"

"It's combat, Captain. Deal with the problem in front of you."

"What happened to 'never leave a man behind'?"

"Leave this one to your NCOs. Concentrate on the big picture."

"Right, Top. Thank you." The rain suppressed the flash and smoke of the RCRs, but they could see the front rows of Zeds stagger as sixteen thousand flechette rounds hit the mobs.

Copley took the radio and spoke quietly to someone Lee couldn't hear over the rain. Even though he couldn't make out the conversation, he suspected this was about El Coquí. As Top said, he needed to trust his subordinates. When Copley was done, he handed the radio back.

Big picture, Lee thought.

"Numbers are greater in front of Team Anchor. There's no chance of flanking them," he said to Top, then spoke into the radio. "RCR gunners, give us another two rounds of ADM, then load with Hotel Echo and aim for center of the mobs. We're going to have to just stick it in and grind." Lee was hoping that alternating flechette rounds with high explosive would disrupt the mobs enough to allow the fighters to isolate and eliminate smaller clusters of Zeds. Once the ADM rounds were launched, the Bushmaster chain gun on the IFV fired up again, to give the M3 teams time to get their munitions changed out. There was then a much more visible effect on the Zeds as the high-explosive rounds began to go off in the midst of the mobs.

"I wonder..." Lee began.

"...if we can put a round on top of Ku?" Copley finished for him.

"Yeah, that's what I was wondering."

"We can. It's about five hundred meters from Golf, but only about three hundred from Anchor. The problem is Anchor is facing the wrong way, and Golf is about at the end of the range for an HE round."

"Where's Clavell?"

"Golf said it was makai side of the temple ruin."

Lee clicked the radio. "Runner Actual to Golf. What's the position of our missing tree frog?"

"Golf Five to Runner. I make it one hundred yards southwest of the ruin. The temples on a slight rise, about thirty, fifty feet difference from the sacrificial tower."

"Acknowledged, Golf. Runner out."

"The angle from the IFV to Ku is about three hundred degrees, Clavell's at about two-eighty, and thirty or fifty feet lower. Gunny mentioned that the TOW pack was still on the Brad. Those are guided anti-tank missiles, and the IFV can guide the missile in right on top of Ku. The armor penetration is overkill, but it's much more precise. We can blow the shit out of Ku while barely touching the top of the that temple."

"Huh, limiting collateral damage. The natives will still hate me for it."

"Just offer to rebuild it. That's worked wonders for the U.S. in the past."

"Heh. Yeah. Sounds like Manifest Destiny."

"The best kind. Want me to instruct them?"

"Yes, Top, I do."

"Roger." Copley keyed the radio and spoke, "Runner Five to November. We need one Tango-Oscar-Whiskey special delivery to that feathered fucker on top of the temple. Time immediate. You are cleared to disengage the Mike two-four-two while you make this happen."

The radio clicked twice in acknowledgment and the Bushmaster fell silent. The rectangular box at the side of the turret began to rotate up to a horizontal position. It no sooner oriented on the temple than a flare of rocket exhaust erupted from the rear of the box and the projectile came out the front. The launch force caused the rocket to rise slightly, but then it dipped toward the temple, and the ruin seconds later.

"Boom."

"Let's hope that worked."

"Maybe, but I didn't see Ku right there at the end," cautioned Copley. He keyed the radio again. "Thank you, November, you may resume perforating Zeds."

Since there were Zeds in an arc pushing out from the front of the now-ruined temple, the Bushmaster started up immediately, and simply swept the field back to its original targets. The smoke of the explosion persisted even in the heavy rain, and stones were falling all over the mob. The numbers were starting to thin out for the heiau mob, but they still had a thousand or more left to clear before Taskforce Runner could approach the harbor.

Area denial courtesy of the IFV and recoilless rifles had reduced the number of Zeds but there were still too many. Taskforce Runner was fixed in place, as the Zeds continued to advance and spread out between the harbor and heiau. They'd started at over two thousand, and there was still around half that number left.

On the one hand, that meant someone could potentially get in there to check on José, but on the other hand, the front line of the Zeds was now spread out over half to three quarters of a mile. Lee's people were positioned along two fronts, which was inefficient to address this mob. There was a real danger of breakthrough between Teams Anchor and Golf, which would allow the enemy to get behind them.

Team Anchor was supposed to be pushing down Route 19 toward the harbor, but that put them side-on to the Zeds from the heiau. They'd had to rotate in place to avoid being flanked, but now they were not in position to advance toward the harbor. Team Golf was intended to harass the flank of a force in the harbor but were now facing a mob in front of them.

The failure of Plan A lay in there being not a single mob, or random drifters, but two mobs that seemed to have a bit of intelligent direction. Hopefully Plan B had taken out that intelligence. Lee needed Plan C, and he needed it *fast*.

"Knight, this is Runner Actual. I need a report on the harbor. Is there any sign of movement in the cargo yard or from the LSV that *isn't* Zeds?" At this rate, it would take them all day just to reduce the mob to reasonable numbers that would allow an advance on the harbor.

Even worse, there had been leakers and individual Zeds that closed with Lee's forces, particularly in the region between Golf and Anchor. He now had quite a few casualties of his own men. He could ill afford to continue losses at that rate if they were going to achieve their objective.

Lee's thoughts briefly went back to Allie as he heard a truck come down Route 19. That should be the medevac team coming to pick up the seriously wounded members of Team Golf. He found himself hoping Allie wasn't in the truck. He didn't want her in the middle of danger but knew she wouldn't shy away from it either.

"Runner, this is Knight. Visibility is deteriorating. We can't see the deck of the *Kuroda* in this rain, but there have been a few flashes of light. Cooper says he saw a head over top the CONEX barricade, but that hasn't been confirmed."

"And the Zeds?"

"Aside from a few random walkers, all the activity is focused on you."

Lee turned to Copley. "We need a way to get some forces in behind them. What if I move two squads from Golf out to the highway and send two Anchor squads up to join the Knights?"

"If you're going to pull your DPS away from the tanks, you'll need to do maximum damage while they move. The Carl Gustavs are your best damage-dealers, so send all four of the reserve guns with Anchor Charlie and Delta squads, leaving their own with Alpha and Bravo with instructions to unload the remaining four ADM rounds into the Zeds as the movement starts."

"Right. I'm planning on bringing Golf, Alpha, and Bravo in from the shoreline—the Zeds aren't really that close to them, and are mostly focused on us. But hugging the shore doesn't buy us anything."

"Good. Have Golf Alpha and Bravo hand off their M3s to Charlie and Delta to cover the movement."

"Thanks, Top. I've become worried that the mob from the heiau will work its way around between the two forces. I want to flank them and get a force into the harbor. You said there's tanks and other vehicles on the *Kuroda*. Major Silver sent us ten canister rounds just in case we could get an M1 operational. If we could get a small force in, or even find someone inside to help, we could end this."

"Even if it costs you the entire task force?"

"Would it?"

"Perhaps. It's sound thinking, and you have to be prepared to do exactly that if you deem it necessary. It's a very 'Special Forces' approach. You ever meet a frogman?"

"You mean a SEAL?"

"Yup, had a friend, built like a fireplug but with perfect hair. He told me some of the SpecOps philosophy over beer and bourbon one night. Every one of them knew that their job was to get in, and hopefully out again. In a dynamic conflict, regular troops were to tie up the enemy so that he could do his job. Every frogman knew that men would die so that SEALs could achieve the objective. It's a very different thing from being willing to sacrifice your own life. It was very sobering, and we'd had a *lot* of whiskey that night."

"You're telling me I have to decide if the value of taking the harbor is worth sixty lives."

"Exactly. But you also have to keep in mind that marines don't fight for objectives, they fight for the brother to the left and to the right. It can't be a suicide march. They have to believe that their own sacrifice will allow a brother to live."

"Then there will be no undue sacrifices. We reinforce our front while making it possible for a small force to get in behind. At the very least, we harass them from the rear with more ADMs."

"Good. I'll call it in and have them square up the line."

Once the troops began to move, Lee watched carefully to see how the Zeds responded. They didn't seem to recognize that the makai flank was now open and concentrated on the reinforced line pressing in from Route 270.

"I don't know if he was controlling them, but if there was an intelligence behind them now, they'd rush for the seaward gap," he told Copley. "I think we got him."

"It's hard to argue with a TOW, but don't make assumptions, Lee. I don't know how the fuckers managed it in Afghanistan, but the worst of the warlords always seemed to get away. As I said, I didn't see him right there at the end. Don't count Ku out just yet."

With plans A and B busted, and C in play, it was time to come up with plans D, E, and F. Lee hoped it didn't come down to the "guns, knives, and chain saw" backup plan, but the mob still outnumbered them twenty-to-one. They needed an advantage. An M1 off the *Kuroda* would do, but even that pipe dream might not be enough.

Lee snapped his fingers. "Mines. I'm going in."

CHAPTER EIGHTEEN
DERECHO

Derecho: A line of intense wind, and sometimes thunder-storms, which moves *fast* across a great distance and is characterized by the damage it causes.

—Dictionary definition

"No, Captain. I know you want to lead by example..."

"That's not it, Top. I have something very specific in mind and it requires someone in the backfield with the big picture. I'm going to take Knight and the detached Anchor squads and punch though into the harbor. Mike Cooper is with the Knights, and he's a demo expert—former EOD with the Air Force and worked for Hawaii Concrete as a quarry tech. We've got all those Claymores and C-4. We're going to set up mines and then draw the Zeds onto them."

It was dangerous, but Lee was right. They needed to reduce the Zed numbers, and they just didn't have the area denial weapons they needed. "Alright, but how are you going to draw the mob your way?"

"The rest of the ADM rounds and use the horses as bait."

Copley sucked in a breath. "That's pretty bold. It won't endear you to the ranchers... but it might work." Worst of all, his captain was right—Lee was the only one who could get the Knights to sacrifice their mounts. He'd have to do that in person just in case they resisted.

"Alright, go, but there's someone you need to take with you." Copley got on the radio and requested a marine from Anchor Bravo to join them at the observation post. In a few minutes, an absolutely *huge* sergeant reported for duty.

Julius Borja San Nicholas Salinas was Samoan. He was nearly as broad as he was tall... and he was certainly tall. Lee was reminded of a certain native Hawaiian singer who stood six foot two inches tall and wore a size 10XL Hawaiian shirt. This man, however, didn't appear to be obese, just... big.

"Boorj is your guard. You aren't going to be popular with the ranchers or the Zeds. Boorj, protect the captain," Copley told the big man.

"Yes, First Sergeant."

"Also, Boorj is a tank mechanic. He's been known to crack tread all by himself. *If* you get to the *Kuroda*, and *if* you can get to the M1s, Boorj will make sure they're running, even if he can't get inside."

Boorj smiled. "I'll ride on top."

"Alright. Now go, Captain, before I think better of the idea."

Copley was right. The six mounted ranchers were not at all happy with Lee's plan. They had no issue with trying to punch through the flank of the mob and enter the harbor proper—after all, they'd been itching to do so ever since they saw the bulk of the Zeds moving in the direction of Teams Anchor and Golf. However, the idea of deliberately dangling the horses in front of a gang of zombies was utterly offensive.

Darkhorse led the protest and was even about to draw his gun on Lee before Boorj stepped between the two and put one of his large hands on Darkhorse's shoulder and squeezed. The wince on the man's face showed that although Boorj had used a little bit of force, it was just enough to get the message across. The big man said nothing, just stared at the other five members of Team Knight.

Mike Cooper broke the silence. "I can lay mines. I've got a full load of Claymores and I can set them up with timers or radio detonations so we don't have to run wire. Where do you want the C-4?"

"I want a line of Claymores in the sand in an arc between the gates and the *Kuroda*, Coop. Behind that, give me pockets of C-4 covered with rocks, plates, and the kind of shrapnel that can take down a Zed in one go."

"I can do that. It'll take an hour, maybe ninety minutes. You'll have to keep the stragglers off me. I don't want to get in a fight and set off the mines prematurely."

"You're okay with the plan?"

"Not the part of using horses as bait, but I'm all for blowing up Zeds."

"Good. I will do my best not to lose any horses, but they are the most attractive meal for the Zeds out here—more than we are. Anchor Charlie will go with you and be your guard."

Cooper nodded and reached around in his saddle to pull up his satchel of mines. "Oh, and you should know that I saw what looked like someone jumping down off that circle of shipping containers and running over to the Navy ship."

"Army, not Navy," Boorj said quietly.

Lee decided not to correct Cooper. "You're sure?"

"No. Rain's messing with us, and I can't be sure. Looked like it, though."

"Okay, Darkhorse, you and the rest of the Knights go to the shipping containers and see if anyone is home. If someone is there, make contact. If not, it'll keep the horses nearby, but out of the way for now. While you're doing that, Squad Delta, Boorj, and I will head over to the *Kuroda* and see what we can find." Lee stared at James Stephens, then dropped his hand to the holster at his waist and unsnapped the flap. "Darkhorse. This is my operation and I gave you an order. I'd rather not shoot you, but I will."

Darkhorse glowered back, but he eventually nodded to acknowledge the order.

"Okay, move out. Knights, stay to our right flank. Charlie, you lead. Delta has the left flank." Lee tried to keep the relief out of his voice.

The augmented Team Knight moved out and Lee started toward the port. He knew it wouldn't be that easy. They still had upward of a hundred Zeds in this part of the harbor. To avoid drawing attention with gunshots, the marines had pulled their machetes, and were dispatching any Zeds they encountered with their blades. Lee was at the center of the formation and had yet to draw his own weapons.

The gate was still intact, but two sections of fence had been knocked down by Zeds. The opening to the left of the gate would have them moving into the rear of the mob, but the opening to the right was relatively clear. The right was closer to the civilian cargo yard and the rows of shipping containers, but the left was close to a line of trees circling the military cargo area in front of the *Kuroda*. Farther to the left in that enclosure was an area where sand gave way to the rocky substrate that had been used as fill to build up the harbor. Coop would set his line of Claymores in front of the patch, and the C-4 mines in the rocks. He just needed to get through about twenty Zeds to get there.

Lee and Boorj needed to go straight ahead to a sand and asphalt road toward the *Kuroda*, but they had their own force of Zeds to contend with. Lee knew that from the gate, it was twenty-three hundred feet to where the *Kuroda* was pulled up to the shore. The LSV could maneuver in twelve feet of water, and drop the ramp in unload in four feet, but there was a small channel cut at the end of the sandy beach allowing the ship to pull onshore and drop its bow ramp completely on land. The problem was that once they fought through their two dozen Zeds, they risked Coop's batch at their backs.

They needed to clear all of the southern harbor at once. Shooting them risked friendly fire, so Lee pulled his machete and held it in his right hand, with the crowbar in his left. "Okay, this day officially sucks."

Two squads should have consisted of twenty-four men in a realistic platoon, but Lee's reducing manning halved that number. In addition, Charlie had lost one of their marines to a Zed that managed to close to within hand-to-hand distance. This was back when Ku was still directing the mob, and a few of the "brighter" Zeds seemed to be able to avoid getting shot. Delta had one serious injury who'd been medevaced, leaving the escort force at ten, plus Lee, Boorj, and Coop. Thirteen against nearly forty remaining Zeds, armed only with bladed weapons, was indeed a bad day.

The marines formed a perimeter around Lee and Coop as they advanced into the loose grouping of Zeds. Lee noticed that the demo expert held a strange, basket-hilted sword in his right hand, and a large-bore revolver in his left.

Seeing his glance, Coop grunted. "Always preferred wheel guns. A forty-four Magnum can take specialty loads, so I went with low-velocity fragmenting rounds. They'll penetrate a body but won't travel any distance. Perfect for the scrimmage."

Lee would have replied, but at that moment a Zed got through the perimeter of marines and came straight at him, and he had to go to work.

෴

The next twenty minutes was a blur of screeching Zeds, biting teeth, spraying blood, and nearby gunshots. Lee had stabbed, sliced, swung, and clubbed his way free of the scrimmage. They'd lost two more marines, and Coop was nursing his left arm, where he'd been injured as a Zed stepped right into his revolver and the shot had ricocheted off bone. Fortunately, he'd had been wearing a firefighter's turnout coat, and the bloody shrapnel couldn't penetrate to his skin. Some of the fragments had hit Lee as well, as the two men had been back-to-back at the time. Again, the ripstop nylon poncho had held.

It hurt like a son of a bitch, though.

The tide had finally turned, and the Zeds in the immediate area were down. The last one fell with the crooked end of Lee's crowbar through its skull.

He patted Coop on the shoulder—the good one—and sent him off to place his mines. Charlie Squad hadn't lost any members, so they deployed to keep the area safe while the demo expert got to work.

The three remaining men from Delta accompanied Lee and Boorj toward the *Kuroda* and their final objective.

"Okay, so now we're here. How do we get in?" Lee looked up at the side of the support vessel. "It's not like there's a big door or a ladder."

"This way, Captain. There's a ladder, just not the kind you're used to," Boorj told him as he pointed to a series of rungs painted the same color as the hull and mounted to the side of the vessel's bow. The Samoan headed in that direction but stopped at the screeching sound of metal rubbing against metal.

"Or we could just wait for them to open the door," Lee quipped as the large bow ramp began to move. A new sound began to rise in volume, sounding a lot like a jet engine winding up.

"That's an Abrams. The engine is a gas turbine, a jet engine for tanks. There's people in there and they've got one working!" shouted Boorj over the noise.

Lee allowed shock to overtake him for just a moment as he watched the huge ramp drop, then shook his head as the implication sunk in. He reached for his radio.

"Darkhorse. New orders. Disengage and get someone back to Starbase. There's one or more survivors on the *Kuroda*, and it sounds like they're trotting out a welcome mat. Go get me the canister rounds for the M1."

Lee saw one of the mounted men over in the cargo yard straighten up from where he'd been slashing at a Zed with his machete. He spurred his horse, which reared up and struck down the creature with its hooves, then wheeled and dashed off toward the gate.

Although blowing rain obscured their vision and the wind muffled sounds, Lee could hear more distant engine sounds. Boorj nudged him and pointed to the north end of the harbor where a truck was running over a section of fallen fence. There were two more trucks behind it, likely from the garrison, seeing as they looked just like ones Lee had seen during his visits. The beds were covered with canvas, except where portions were raised to provide gunports along the sides. As they got closer, he could see marines in the backs of the trucks, confirming their origin.

"Huh. They're coming south down Route 270. That means they took the long way around. I'd put money on them having your canister rounds, Captain," Boorj told him He took out a flare gun and fired a round into the air to mark their position. It didn't last long in the blowing rain, but it was enough to get the attention of the lead driver. The trucks turned and started their way as the *Kuroda*'s ramp continued to descend.

CHAPTER NINETEEN

WE GO ON

There is nothing more terrible than war . . . except the aftermath.
—M. Cooper, USAF Explosive Ordnance Disposal (ret.),
Demolitions Specialist, Hawaii Concrete Co.

Military trucks with reinforcements and tank munitions made their way through the harbor. The bow of the *Kuroda* continued to lower until was in contact with the sand. The wide bow ramp could accommodate two of the M1A1 Abrams tanks, or three trucks at a time. Only one of the fighting vehicles came out, though. It made its way about twenty yards, then a loud squeal—even louder than the metal-on-metal sound of the bow ramp—sounded, the tank abruptly pivoted toward the side, and one of the treads stopped moving.

"Road wheel froze up," said Boorj. "Not surprising. I doubt they've been doing periodic maintenance. Even in depot, you have to do PM every few months. I'll get on it, though. As long as they can move that cannon, we should be good."

As if his words were prophetic, the long tube at the front of the turret elevated slightly, and turned to bear on the mob of Zeds beyond where Coop was setting his mines. A hatch opened up on top of the turret, and a man stuck his upper body out and waved to Lee. At the same time, another man walked out of the bow of the *Kuroda* holding a rectangular box at the end of a long thick cable.

"Well, that's at least two survivors: one in the Abrams, one controlling the ramp," Boorj said as he followed Lee over to the tank.

The man standing in the hatch stopped waving and called out as Lee approached.

"Are you a tanker?"

"He is," Lee said, pointing his thumb back over his shoulder at Boorj, "not me."

"Well, that's good to know because frankly we don't know the first thing about these things other than how to drive them on and off the LSV." The man wasn't dressed for combat or for the rain and was already soaked through to the skin. His name tape said ZELINSKI, and his rank insignia was for a private first class.

"Well, Private, I'm certainly happy to see you, and we'll be happy to take that tank off your hands." Lee turned to Boorj and lowered his voice. "Um, Sarge, can we?"

Boorj laughed and shrugged. "Ask these guys."

The first of the military trucks pulled up and disgorged a mixed dozen Soldiers and Marines. They formed a perimeter, while a staff sergeant in a dark green uniform stepped up to Lee.

"Staff Sergeant Aaron Haskins, Captain. Major Silver sent me down here with the M1028 canister rounds and a tank crew, just in case. When we heard your call, we figured we should come in. We've been waiting in Kawaihae town."

"How the hell did you get there without us seeing you, Staff Sergeant?" Lee asked.

Haskins laughed. "The long way over the Kohala Mountain Road to Hawi and around. There's survivors over that way. We met them when we got a bit stuck in after missing the turnoff for Hawi Road. It was an absolute bitch to clear. We were supposed to be here last night but arrived in the area an hour ago."

"We're very glad to have you, although you're cutting it close. We're not doing as well as we could."

"Well, I'm not much use to you unless you have a tank, but this M1A1 looks like it will do. Needs maintenance, though, Boorj, you're slacking off."

"It just got here, A-Ron—I mean, Staff Sergeant Haskins."

Haskins laughed. "I know, I'm just looking forward to seeing you crack tread all by yourself. Again."

"Fuck you, too, Staff Sergeant. Let's see what they have for us, first."

꧁꧂

"We're glad to see you all," Zelinski said. "There's only three of us, two from *Kuroda* and one from the Madison Line tug assigned to the civvy side. We've been holed up in a cargo container—used the propane forklifts to move them into a defensive shelter until the fuel ran out. When we saw you make contact with the zombies, Rodriguez and I figured we should break out *Bessie*. Figured we could just run them over if we had to."

Haskins laughed. "Yeah, that's been done. Remind me to show you video of a tank drifting."

"Can't be done, A-Ron. That is, unless you smear about a hundred and fifty Zeds into paste to lubricate the pavement, first," Boorj said as he used a long-handled wrench to loosen a lug on the frozen wheel.

"Exactly, Boorj. Exactly."

"So, 'Bessie'? Why did you name the tank?" Lee asked, thinking of a certain sixteen-year-old Marine lieutenant and her pink tank.

"Well, it was that or 'Vanessa.' This one's got some new electronics inside with the VSE label on them. Venn-something. Well, Rodriguez started calling her 'Vessie,' which became Bessie because Roddy's allergic to something that keeps making his lip swell."

"Much better than painting it pink and calling it *Trixie*," said Haskins with a wink.

"I don't understand," Zelinski said, looking confused.

"Never mind. I will show you everything later," Boorj told him. He motioned the other man from the Kuroda over and pointed to a section of track. "Congrats, Privates, you're now tankers. Hold this out of the way while I get these wheel lugs."

By this time, six marines had come out of the back of the second truck carrying two cases—each requiring two men to lift it and a third to help steady it.

"What are those?" Zelinski asked, looking up from his work, causing Boorj to grumble.

"Canister rounds," Haskins told him. "M1028 one twenty millimeter antipersonnel canister. Think of it as a shotgun shell, except instead of bird- or buckshot, it's got over a thousand nine-mil bullets. Works wonders on Zeds."

"Come to Papa," Lee said. "Just what we need. Let's use a round or two to get their attention, soften them up with Coop's mines, then suck then in and mow them down."

"That's the idea. Sir, you've still got a battle to manage. We've got this," Haskins told Lee and saluted.

Lee returned the salute. In the back of his mind, he reflected on how odd it was to be saluted in the field. On the other hand, this was the first time he felt like he might have earned it.

It took another twenty minutes for the tank to be ready to move out. By that time, Coop had finished laying his mines and Lee was ready to spring the trap. The backside of the Zed mob had started to notice the action behind them, and the sound of gunfire from the Anchor and Golf front line was starting to slow down as the mob changed its focus. Lee began to think it wouldn't be necessary to dangle the horses as bait to draw the Zeds into the killing zone.

He keyed his radio. "Knight, you are relieved. Back to the observation overlook." He also sent the remnants of Charlie squad north with the two men from the Kuroda, and an additional civilian the Knights had found at the container fort. The Marine reinforcements broadened the perimeter behind the tank, while the soldiers got the tank ready for action.

"Golf, Anchor, shift your line to the east side of the highway. That's mauka of the highway. Retreat under fire to keep the attention on you for the moment, but don't let any of them cross the road. Makai is a hot range. Repeat, the ocean side of Route 270 is in the range of fire. Report when in position."

The calls began to come in almost immediately—the men had already been using Route 19 as their skirmish line. It still took another ten minutes of sporadic gunfire before all Golf and Anchor teams reported they were in position. Some of the mob had attempted to follow, but by concentrating his forces, they were able to pick off the stragglers with ease. All of which meant that the Zeds were now turning back to the harbor.

When Boorj had finished with the tank team, he'd come back and pushed Lee and Coop well clear of the tank and mines. He'd also handed them heavy earmuffs and showed them how to plug into their radios.

Lee clicked his radio three times and was almost knocked off his feet by the roar and pressure of the M256 120mm main gun firing.

That got their attention. Most of the mob was now turned to the rear and starting back into the harbor.

Right into the minefield.

As the explosive went off, Lee was glad for the hearing protection. He would be deaf by now from the sheer power of the explosions.

The Abrams fired again, and parts of the front line of the mob, staggered by the Claymores and other mines, simply . . . disappeared.

The Abrams didn't even have to move. In ten minutes, all that were left were scattered Zeds. Lee sent a cease-fire order to the Abrams, followed by ordering Anchor and Golf to start mop-up operations.

The contents of ship and harbor were everything they were hoping for. The *Kuroda* held three more tanks, four IFVs, ten armed transports, and assorted armaments, munitions, guns, ammo, uniforms, and food. There was even a limited supply of the highly filtered kerosene fuel favored by the Abrams.

The harbor was a treasure trove of household goods. Some of it was spoiled, such as the grocery stocks, but there was packaged food, clothing, sundries, and the ever-popular hygiene supplies. Some of the cargo containers were earmarked for the garrison, and included stocks for *after* the battalion training, to replenish those used by the exercise. There was furniture, building supplies, and even plumbing and electrical supplies.

Copley came up to him while Lee stood staring at a container filled with pet food and supplies. "Pets were a luxury of civilization, Lee."

"It's odd, Top. Of all the things we've lost . . . we've lost our most faithful companions. There's cats and dogs at the ranch, but those are working animals—herding dogs and mousers—not pets."

"Yeah, loss hits you at the oddest times. Doesn't matter that they were animals. They and their owners typically didn't survive the Haole Flu and the hungry Zed aftermath. It's only a small piece of a greater loss."

"Then why does it hurt so much?"

"Because you're trying *not* to think of the other losses of the day."

"José?"

Copley shook his head. "Didn't make it. Probably dead before the sun even came up."

"Damn."

The fuel storage at the harbor yielded mixed results. One cluster of four tanks was nearly full, with gasoline, diesel, and bunker fuel for the tugs and cargo ships. The second cluster of tanks was nearly empty. The ground around the tanks was scorched with remnants of an old fire. The valves to those tanks were open, and Copley surmised that defenders at the harbor had attempted to keep Zeds out using fire and drained the tanks to fuel it.

What they didn't have was avgas, the light, purified kerosene used for aircraft engines . . . and the Abrams. While the gas-turbine engine of the M1A1 could burn a wide variety of fuels, using avgas cut down on maintenance, and got the most out of the power plant. The other thing missing was tanker trucks to transport the fuel.

On the good side, there were several of the "low-boy" transporters used to move tracked vehicles over the road, sparing the asphalt and concrete from the damaging treads. As Lee was reporting the findings back to Kamuela, the garrison, and the Hole, Lugnut broke in to say that he'd located what appeared to be three intact fuel tankers around the island. One was at the Kona airport, with another out in Hawi, where Haskin's crew probably just missed it as they passed Hawi Road on Route 270. The third was technically in the town of Kona, but along Route 190, where it sat at nearly two-thousand-feet elevation mauka of the town, proper.

It would have to do. For now.

Lee ordered his troops to spread out and inspect the rest of the harbor. They needed to look into any of the places where Zeds might hide, or even where refugees might hole up. He finally took the time to assess the overall status of his troops and tally the losses. Of thirty marines, he'd lost six directly to conflicts with the Zeds. The civilians lost ten people.

Three marines were severely injured with likely contamination. Zed blood had splashed on, or close to, their own wounds. They would be treated with the new vaccine from HI-SLOPE, and watched to ensure that they didn't turn. Team Anchor had eight more wounded of varying severity. Team Golf had two potential Zeds, and nine wounded. All wounded would be receiving the vaccine as a precaution, although Doc d'Almeida had told them it would be a lower dose than those with blood exposure.

In all, he'd potentially lost nine of thirty marines, and twelve of thirty-five volunteers. Plus José. Copley reassured him that a thirty percent loss on a battlefield as dynamic as this was acceptable for the marines. Limiting the loss to forty percent on the civilian side was amazing.

Lee didn't feel that way. He'd led men, and they died. That was something he would have to live with. On the other hand, he knew that those were the risks they signed up for when they took their oath.

Lee nodded to himself. He swallowed and looked up at his first sergeant. "I don't like it, but I'll accept it."

Copley looked at his captain with understanding. "That's all anyone can ask."

The medical section came down from Starbase and set up in the harbormaster's offices just inside the gate from where Lee and Team Knight first entered the area. He was happy to find that Allie was safe and uninjured. It dismayed him to learn that she had been in a truck extracting seriously wounded from the battlefield. She'd made several trips, and only had one incident. She'd been trying to stabilize a member of Team Golf for transport, when a Zed broke through the line and got to within twenty feet before a marine had taken it out with a headshot. It was sobering, but just stiffened her resolve to do everything she could for the combatants.

Lee loved her all the more for it.

The next part of the wrap-up was something Lee personally felt distasteful but knew he had to do. He could—and would—order his troops to go through the battlefield and ensure that each Zed was either decapitated or head-shot, but he would also participate in the action himself. He felt he owed it to his men. After that was a trip to the sacrifice tower to recover José's body. The tower had collapsed, with one leg chewed up by the TOW rocket explosion on the temple ruin. Clavell's body was nearby, chest torn open and heart removed. It had probably been done with the man's own saber, now lying atop the body, like a tribute.

Top said he didn't see Ku on the temple mound right before the TOW hit, Lee mused. *Could the fucker have escaped?*

Lee gathered the few items next to Jose's body. He was torn whether to return them to the ranch or see that they were buried with his friend. Marines were coming to retrieve the body. It would be handled the same as all the others they'd lost today.

He was still standing on the battlefield, staring at the ruins, when Darkhorse stepped up.

"So, you won."

"Did I? José died. Sacrificed on the altar of Ku's madness."

"Ku's dead."

"Is he?"

"Doesn't matter. Still, I owe you something."

Lee turned toward the man, expecting something like an apology for his actions earlier. He wasn't expecting the right cross.

"What the hell?" Lee staggered back, his right hand coming up to his face while he held the other out defensively and backed away.

"You sacrificed the horses." Darkhorse started to circle around to Lee's weak side.

"Hell, no. They were safe all along." Lee continued backing away as he furiously tried to think of how to react.

"You used them as bait."

"Did you lose any? No." Lee swung his right hand out and down to counter the punch he anticipated, but that only served to further expose his middle.

Darkhorse closed and grappled, putting his arms around Lee's torso, and squeezed.

Lee beat at the man's back, struggling to break free, seemingly forgetting what was actually *in* his left hand. Once he remembered, though, he twisted his left wrist enough so that his right hand could grasp the hilt of José's saber. He let go of the scabbard and flicked his wrist to free the blade, then brought it down in a glancing blow across the back of his opponent's left leg.

The saber cut the man's pants and left a line of blood in the exposed skin. Darkhorse yelled and released his hold. He stepped back with his right foot and grabbed the crowbar off Lee's belt as he moved. When he attempted to move his left leg and take another step back, his leg buckled, causing him to stumble.

Lee's eyes were still teared up from the punch, and he was gasping for breath, so he didn't see the Darkhorse swing his right arm—and crowbar—toward his leg.

Lee crumpled to the ground and screamed in agony as excruciating pain struck his left knee. The pain was so intense, he had to struggle not to black out, as that would leave him at the mercy of the other man.

He was barely cognizant of the sound of a gunshot and the appearance of a red bloom on the horseman's chest.

Lee came awake to a sharp pain as he felt hands moving his injured leg. He turned his head enough to see someone tying a splint, with Gunny Kalama standing watch—rifle at the ready.

"Darkhorse?" he gasped as the corpsman tightened the straps.

"He'll live. It was only five five six," Gunny said. "He'll live to stand trial, then likely be executed for mutiny."

"No. No, we don't want that. We can't turn on each other. That's what Ku did. What he wanted." Lee's radio crackled, and he heard what sounded like laughter. After a moment, the radio went silent.

"We are *better* than that," Lee said.

INTERLUDE
NO LONGER ALONE

Hold your loved ones, keep them close, pray for them when they are away. Welcome them home. Love them unconditionally.
—M. Noelani Eller, Nurse/Medic, Kamuela, Hawaii

Dear Abi,

As always, I send these messages out into the void, not knowing if you're receiving them. You told me to have faith, though, so I write and send. I hope against hope that you're out there, and eventually will receive these messages.

Things have gotten, shall we say, "interesting."

Once we started talking to the folks downslope, we found ourselves drawn into a big battle. The military and ranchers combined to raid a port and clear out the Infected, and we helped!

A person calling themselves "Ku" seems to be able to train the Infected to do what he wants them to do. And what he's taught them to do is attack healthy people. Well, they do that anyway, but the Infected are brainless. Ku's mob acted with some intelligence behind it. Hungry, angry, violent zombies are bad enough. *Intelligent*, hungry, angry, violent zombies are too much.

The very idea has Cro incensed. The idea that someone who could control the Infected wouldn't try to cure them, or at least treat them well, is abhorrent to him. He worked for months to develop a vaccine the *hard way*—growing cultures, isolating the active proteins, and synthesizing antibodies. He says using the spines of live Infected is barbaric and swore he would not only make his vaccine without doing that, but also work on finding a cure.

His vaccine works, we know that. He treated people who'd been bitten or splashed with Infected blood, and they never showed a sign of the blood-borne phase of H7D3. It saved the lives of five people from the ranch and Army base who'd been exposed during battle.

They won the battle at the port. The truth is, *we* won it, all of us. It took the ranchers, equipment from the military, and tech and overwatch from HI-SLOPE. We've learned a lot more about our neighbors in the process. We've all started to exchange visits. It's good to get out of the Hab and talk to other people. I'm headed down to meet with Mayor Maleko in Kamuela tomorrow, then spend some time talking with Captain Eller, who led the battle. He wants my opinion as a psych professional about Ku. It's possible the person using that name is someone I interviewed in Halawa prison when I was deciding who *not* to recruit for HI-SLOPE.

Whatever Ku did with the Infected, numbers are down all along the coast down to Kailua-Kona. The town still has too many for the limited fighters we have, but teams have now successfully cleared isolated areas near Kona, such as the airport and industrial areas. Route 19 is still impassable at Kona, but we can get around that to Route 11 southeast of town. That opens up the South Kona district . . . and coffee.

Funny, it's been almost a year and they're still finding survivors. Anyone who survived this long is either in a deep hole, or has already formed a community. Captain Eller says that it's fine for folks to stay in small communities as long as they can defend themselves, and has been working to build up defenses in the outlying areas.

Mayor Maleko is starting to talk about the "Hawaii Territory" and about pushing to renew statehood. I think he wants to be governor if we can ever build up enough population. "Five Thousand Free Men" is the requirement. We need a governor, secretary, and three judges, and a plan to hold an election for one senator and congressman. With the entire Kona and Kohala districts, plus Kauai, and Molokai, we're now pushing a thousand.

It's so good to not feel like HI-SLOPE is just standing still. We're no longer hiding out in our cinder cone high on Mauna Kea. It's even possible to leave the island. The Kauai and Molokai folks have a lot of boats and are starting up trade routes between the islands.

Ham paused the recording for moment as he heard a knock on the door to his quarters. He answered it to find Lugnut holding a tablet with readings from one of the communication links.

"Hey, Professor, sorry to interrupt, but Doc needs you. Something about a vaccine. Also, Mr. Bigfoot and I will be in the Hex Six garage working on drones. We're going to service them all, and I'm teaching Littleshawn how to fly them. Crossbow's going to watch."

"Okay, probably a good idea to have a backup drone pilot or two."

"Right, Sean said he's embarrassed that the mission pilot isn't piloting the drones. Crossbow's just bored."

"Alright. Go play with your drones. Anything else?"

"No? Uh, maybe. Legs is complaining about a wonky sensor suite reporting seal degradation in one of the Hexes, but she can't tell which one. I've checked the logs and can't figure it out either. The report's logged, but there's no location. She's going to go hex-to-hex, so wants me to alert everyone so she doesn't interrupt."

"Yes, that could be awkward. Thanks, Lugnut."

"No problem, Professor."

When the outside world had immunity and we didn't, we had to stay isolated. No more. Now we're part of a community. Maleko's Hawaii Territory for now, the State of Hawaii again before too long. Unless he decides to rename it "Kamuela"!

It's been a year. Abi, but we're still here. We're stopped simply existing. More than just survive—it's time to thrive. *I believe it with all my heart.*

Just like I believe that you're out there. Surviving. Thriving. Living.

Be well, Abi, I miss you.

Love, Dad

Part Four

KAHUNA

CHAPTER ONE

HUNTERS

It's Kona. "For Coffee" is a perfectly appropriate rallying cry!
—T. Pearson, hunter

The hunt was going well despite the rain. A light afternoon rain wasn't uncommon in Hawaii, but this sort of all-day rain was typically confined to the windward shore, where moisture carried on the easterly trade winds piled clouds up against the central peaks. Kona District was on the *leeward* side, though, and only the rare Kona Storm would bring this amount of rain to the normally drier side of the island. The tech wizards at HI-SLOPE were predicting another day of unusual weather before conditions returned to normal for the tropical paradise.

The hunter team set out while the storm was relatively light. It was now possible to travel the Queen Ka'ahumanu Highway—formed by Hawaii State Road 19—through the North Kona District with only personal firearms. Tom Pearson's team and others based out of the reclaimed Kona airport were working to do the same for the South Kona district along the Hawaii Belt Road—Route 11.

Pearson drove the lead truck. It was equipped with extra lighting on the roll bar behind the cab to draw the Infected out of the tree-lined slopes along the road. Large speakers mounted to either side were currently blaring something about "ghost divisions" by a Swedish heavy-metal group. Pearson had found that heavy metal was often the best lure for Zeds.

Tom was driving back toward Kona rather slowly, not much faster than a walk, but he was headed straight into an ambush—not for him, but for the dozen Zeds following him. The theory had been that Tom would drive his darkened truck slowly and quietly down toward the town of Captain Cook, about ten miles south of Kailua Bay, turn on the lights and music, wait for Zeds to show, then lead them back to the roadblock set up just past the junction of 11 and 180. North of the junction, Route 11 led into what was still a no-go area in the town of Kailua-Kona, while Route 180, the Mamalahoa Highway, was the higher, safer road back north to Kamuela.

Tom had been instructed to turn around as soon as his saw the first signs of Zeds. The battle at Kahaiwae had drawn many of them north along the coast, so nightly patrols reduced the numbers of Infected along the highway even further. While not yet to the level of relative safety to be found in North Kona, not to mention the mostly secure Hamakua and Kohala Districts comprising most of Kamuela, armed and armored convoys were able to traverse Route 11 to reach the prime coffee, citrus, and macadamia nut growing region of South Kona. Over the last week, the numbers of savages attracted per trip had dropped from hundreds to just thirteen on this particular trip. Coffee that didn't need to be obtained from the assholes over in Kauai was a pretty decent incentive for the hunter teams.

Tom jumped as his passenger shot at a Zed attempting to get in front of the truck. It had come from the side of the road, and Moose Dennison, one of the engineers from HI-SLOPE, literally "riding shotgun" on this trip, had fulfilled his role of making sure that the live Infected stayed behind them and not in front.

Tom was happy for his ear protection. He didn't have to worry too much about the report from the shotgun, and it saved him from going deaf due to the excessively loud music. He spoke into the radio: "Fireteam, this is Pearson. Coming your way with about a dozen. Light haul tonight, we're almost clear here."

The response came back rather quickly. "Froggy Bear, this is Fireteam. Tell your buddy Moose to safe that firearm and not frag my shooters."

"I thought we agreed never to mention that name again...Dick."

"I didn't agree, Frog."

"You're a dick, Curran."

"Cut the chatter, Pearson, Curran. Pay attention."

"Yessir, Mr. Beck," said Curran quickly.

"Acknowledged, sir. On task," replied Pearson.

Dennison pulled his shotgun back in the window and held it facing up, muzzle just outside the window frame. "They know I wouldn't frag the guys on foot, Tom, for they are crunchy..."

"...and good with ketchup. Yes, I know, Moose. Hang on, I need to get a bit of a lead before I have to thread the needle." The truck sped up, opening the gap between them and the trailing mob of hooting and howling savages. As he cleared the first barricade, shooters standing above the concrete highway dividers opened fire on the Zeds. In less than five minutes, there was no one moving on the road past the roadblock.

"Not much of a haul tonight, Thomas," said Linaka Wicklund as Tom turned off the music and extra lights. The local girl was holding a clipboard and recording the numbers of Infected dispatched as a result of the runs tonight. "If we stay under ten for the next few trips, we can declare this section of highway open."

"True, Lin, but then we'll have to start clearing the houses and through the brush. I've listened to enough of Dr. d'Almeida's lectures to want to avoid the house-to-house thing. He doesn't dispute clearing the mobs, but he wants us to be 'compassionate with the isolated victims.' It's why I transferred to Pied Piper duty."

"He thinks we'll find people who haven't turned all the way. Something about their starting IQ, or whether the 'neuroendocrine milieu' can support the constant aggression."

"They aren't constantly aggressive as it is, Lin. They go dormant inside buildings and wait for their next meal to deliver itself." Tom shuddered at the memory of clearing the resorts, where Infected seemed to be in every condo, apartment, and hotel room.

"Well, get some rest, you're not due back out until the dawn run. After that, Beck wants you to check out reports of some kind of nest down by the State Park." The distant crack of gunfire and a hint of death-metal indicated another lure truck returning.

"I think I'll bed down in the truck. Not heading all the way back to the airport only to be back at dawn."

"It's your aching back and neck, Tom. Although, see me when you do get back to the airport tomorrow and I'll give you a neck rub."

"Thanks, Lin. I'll need it."

Seamus Curran was bitching. It was his usual lot in life to be stuck with all the shit jobs and garbage that rolled downhill to the lowest person in any organization. At least, that's what he kept telling anyone who would listen. He was often paired with Pearson, after all. Dennison's primary job was renovating the solar power array at the industrial park adjacent to the Kona airport. He'd spent years cooped up in HI-SLOPE and went out with the hunters for a change of pace.

"I came to Hawaii to hunt *hogs, goddammit!* I didn't *ask* to be stuck in a fuckin' zombie apocalypse! Why in hell couldn't Travis send a different team for this? I'm a *hunter*, not a fuckin' jungle guide!" He swiped at a low-hanging branch with his machete and went back to his tirade. When the going got tough, Curran got bitching. "And where did this damned *rain* come from?"

"Hey, it always rains in Hawaii. Every day for ten minutes," Pearson told him.

"Bullshit! There was *hail* in this shit last night and it hasn't stopped raining in two days!"

Despite the litany of complaints, Curran was surprisingly good at cutting brush, clearing trails, and all of the other aspects of ground clearance. He had a good eye for tracks and trails—animal and human—and today they were hunting humans.

As the numbers of Infected in the district dropped, the convoys passing through became ironically more prone to other attacks. Sailors called them pirates. Travis Beck, director of the Kona District Clearance Operation called it by the more accurate term: brigandry. The former U of H anthropologist had predicted that some form of highway robbery and thievery would arise once attacks by Zeds became less common. Pearson and Curran were tasked with figuring out where the latest suspected group of brigands was holed up. The town of Captain Cook and Kealakekua Bay were likely candidates, given access by both land and sea.

The hunters had been supplemented by a pair of locals from one of the farms cleared over the last six months. What made Curran's complaints amusing to Tom was that Kilika Woods and Akamu Gaffen were doing most of the clearance, while Pearson and Curran followed slowly in the pickup truck. The team had come down the dirt road most of the way to the coast when Curran pointed to a scrap of clothing hanging from a nearby bush, a wet dirt track leading from it, back into the scrub. Pearson parked the truck and he and Curran got out to follow the track. They left Rick Hailey with the pickup and a radio in case the truck was needed elsewhere.

It was hot, it was humid, it was raining, and there were flies, the latter giving Curran a new direction in his bitching. "Flies, man. Who ever heard of fuckin' flies on a tropical island? Are there flies in Waikiki? No, there are not. No flies in Hilo. No flies in Maui, but here in fuckin' Kona we have fuckin'... Wait... wait here." The constant complaining stopped for a moment as Curran held up a hand to keep Kilika and Akamu back from the clearing in the brush. Pearson moved up and tried to look past them. It wasn't easy, particularly while squeezed between the two large Hawaiians.

In the clearing was a... nest, for lack of a better term. The team had been looking for a 'nest of brigands,' in the more metaphorical sense, but this was a literal nest. Scraps of clothing had been arranged in a small pile, just about the size for a human to lie on. There were branches piled up to one side, with the bedding tucked partially under it as a form of shelter. There was a bit of trash, an old food wrapper, bones of a small animal, scraps of paper and cardboard, a discarded plastic cup and the leg off a small doll.

"What is this? A child's fort?" Pearson asked. "Get your shit, together, Dick, you've had us tracking some kid's secret play area."

"No, wait," said Curran, surprisingly calm despite his earlier mood and Pearson's anger. "This is recent. There's not enough rain collected in that cup and the bones can't be more than a day or two old. There's something strange going on here."

"Could it be someone who escaped the pirates?" Akamu asked. Kilika only grunted. "If we find them, maybe they could show us where the others are hiding." Kilika grunted again—that was probably agreement, given that Pearson had never known the islander to utter any word he didn't have to.

"There's another trail out the other side." Curran was moving forward again, carefully stepping over the nest. Akamu and Kilika followed, leaving only Pearson to continue staring at the clearing. "C'mon, there's some fresh tracks in the mud here." The team leader decided there was no point in not following. The former big-game hunter was in his element, so who was Pearson to argue?

The wider trail meant less hacking and cutting of the brush, and the hunting party moved more quickly down the trail. After about twenty minutes, there was a flash of skin ahead, and they caught a glimpse of a Zed, naked, holding something in its hands.

"Go. Now," Pearson ordered, as Woods and Gaffen raised their machetes and gave chase. Surprisingly, the naked . . . boy? . . . turned and ran. That was unusual behavior for a Zed. Unless seriously overwhelmed, they never ran, only attacked. This one ran, though, farther down the track, headed toward the sea. Pearson could now see that the boy—no, a young girl, probably early teens—was holding a doll clutched to her chest. None of the Infected he'd ever encountered, even going house to house in Kona, had so much as picked up a bone unless to eat, let alone carried any object or gave evidence of using tools.

"You might want to capture this one!" Tom called ahead. "Doc d'Almeida will probably want to examine it!"

The trail suddenly ended as the brush gave way to black sand, rocks, and dirt. The Zed ran out in the open, and visibly cringed at the sight of the open sky. Akamu and Kilika began to circle around to entrap the Zed when a voice cried out, "Stop!"

A young woman in a sarong stepped out into the rain, right between the hunters and the Zed. She was thin, as most were these days, but rather shapely in her flower-print dress. Her hair was long and dark, pulled back off her shoulders, and on her head was a circlet woven from leaves. She held no weapons, but her voice commanded them, nonetheless.

"This is the Pu'uhonua O Hōnaunau, the Place of Refuge. You may not hunt nor kill here."

CHAPTER TWO

ELDERS

Poker requires luck, bluff, and daring. Pinochle requires strategy, calculation, timing... and telepathy. You need to know what your partner is thinking. This is why husbands should never play against their wives.

—W. Bear, Shaman

Captain Bubba Gnad stepped off the wildly rocking boat onto the short, narrow pier. The Kona Storm had been lashing the Kalaupapa peninsula for several days already. He helped the last of the refugees regain their footing as they stepped off the RHIB, then turned to the tall, graying man at the helm.

"Okay, Tully, take her back out to the *Gifts* and set anchor. We won't be doing any more salvage or rescue until the storm blows over. You and Mamabear close everything down. Tell her I'll be over at the padre's after I check these folks in with Gran."

The big ships, such as Tully's *Simple Gifts*, and Steph Stephanidis's *Sails Proposition*, spent more time in-port than at sea. They were pretty much only used for ferrying VIPs, or for long-duration trips into the open ocean, away from the island. The various sailing vessels, family catamarans, and a few recovered tourist vessels were much more economical for routine trips between islands. Kiwi's two-masted ketch, *Eye of the Storm*, carried the bulk of trade around the islands from Hawaii Island to Kauai.

They'd been out for two weeks on this last run, and gone as far as Kiribati, over one thousand miles to the south. There were many inhabited atolls and islands in Micronesia, in an arc extending from Kiribati northwest to Johnston Atoll. Bubba's fleet was gradually working its way those islands, figuring that they were the most likely to adopt to an "island hopping" way of life after H7D3. Along the way, they found twenty-five drifting boats, but only five survivors. On the other hand, they'd encountered over a hundred islanders, including several sailing rafts in a clear rebirth of the Polynesian tradition.

Two local women took charge of the refugees and led them to the Community Hall, where they'd have an opportunity to get clean, eat some food that wasn't from a package or can, and stay out of the storm. Gnad slung a duffel bag over his shoulder and headed for a small house next to the hall. He deposited his bag in the dark house without bothering to light a lamp, then stepped over to the Hall to check in with Vanessa Landrum, the refugee coordinator.

The new arrivals were pretty obvious—thin, some very weak and sitting in rolling chairs—but clean and dressed in new muumuus. The large shirt/dress was the easiest garment to provide modesty and comfort for women and men alike. Refugees each received a basic clothing and food allowance—muumuus and stew in the community hall. Once they committed to farming, construction, or rescue operations, they were moved to temporary tent cities until better accommodations were built or arranged. There were a few who never left the tent cities and were recognizable by the fact that they never "graduated" out of muumuus and still sheltered in the receiving facility on stormy nights like tonight.

"What's the take, Gran?"

"Bubba, you probably know this group better than I do. You brought the latest ones in," she replied. "When are you going to stop bringing me refugees and start bringing me the supplies I asked for?" She tapped a handwritten list on the table, picked it up and handed it to him.

As he read the list, he stopped on one item. "Notions? What are 'notions'?"

"Sewing supplies." She indicated the refugees new and old, sitting eating their stew. "While we all appreciate the clothing we got in trade from Kawaihae, most of it was designed for big mainlander tourists." She gestured at her own thin figure. "Few of us qualify as 'big' anymore."

"Yes, I know of Jon's proposal to attempt salvage around Honolulu. I'm surprised you'd let him do that."

"He's been talking with Nardo about taking *Doc's Side* over to Hawaii Kai. There's a lot of shops right on the water, so they can minimize their onshore presence. It's his decision, and I trust him to stay safe. Besides, Wizardbear said the spirits have quieted."

"Not surprised he'd say that, and he might be right, but do you believe him?"

"Father Bart says he's been right before, and you know how those two snipe at each other."

Bubba mused and stroked his beard. "Well, I believe in Jon. He's the best clearance person this side of Kauai. Tell him to put a plan together and present it to the council. I'll endorse it."

He turned to leave, then turned back. "Oh! I nearly forgot! Here, this is for you." He reached into a small bag he'd been carrying over his shoulder and produced a large bottle of scented shampoo. "We found some well-aged Macallan and cigars for the padre, too."

Vanessa squealed with delight and got up to hug the captain. "Ooh, thank you. Now off with and go see Father Bart. If Bear is there, give him my shopping list for Honolulu. See if he can predict where Jon should go."

Bubba just shook his head at her words and headed back into the rainy night. He could take his truck, but there was no point in wasting the propane. The next boat from Barbers Point wouldn't be for another month . . . maybe two.

No, he'd walk. It was only a couple of miles to the rectory and the rain wasn't *that* bad . . . not like the hurricane at Ko Olina.

Father Bart Koa looked over his cards at his partner, David Wells. He considered himself a good judge of character, but somehow that didn't carry over to figuring out why Kiwi had run the bid up so high. Unsure of the logic behind it, he sighed, pulled four cards out of his hand, and passed them over to Wells. The New Zealander picked them up and placed them in his hands, grunted, then selected four of his own cards to pass back.

Bart looked at the cards handed him. *Hmm, king, two jacks and a nine. I guess he needed those face cards I passed.*

Wells cleared his throat. "Diamonds trump." He laid down four cards out of the twelve in his hand—four aces. "Aces around," he announced. Then he laid down the king and queen of diamonds, "Trump marriage," then the jack of diamonds and queen of spades. "Pinochle." Finally, he laid down the nine of diamonds. "And dix."

Bubba looked up at that last comment. "Y'know, I've never understood why you insist on this game with such arcane rules when we could be playing something sensible, like Spades!" Gnad's partner, William Bear, nodded agreement, but said nothing, just sorted his own cards and laid them on the table. The four men proceeded to play, talk, and socialize. Unlike some of their games in the past, there wasn't much drinking or eating. Bubba had arrived late, and wet. He'd walked the two miles across the peninsula from Kalaupapa Town to the rectory in Kalawao but brought gifts from the salvage. Crackers and cheese went to Micki Witt, Koa's housekeeper. The Macallan had been shared around. Bubba was nursing his glass, but Father Bart had finished his, and was now sipping from his second dram. Kiwi Wells passed on the alcohol, but was chewing on one of Bubba's cigars, unlit. Micki had already given him holy hell about smoking in the kitchen. Wizardbear was drinking guava juice, and also had a cigar, but was mostly ignoring it.

The frugality of Kalaupapa residents was already established before Bubba came to the peninsula. The twenty-two survivors had a warehouse filled with a year's supplies for a hundred people, from the barge wrecked in the surf a few hundred meters off the pier at Kalaupapa Town. The influx of survivors from Kauai, and even the additional folks rescued from the Ka'iwi Channel between Molokai to Oahu, actually benefitted the locals. The population had fallen below the minimum required to gather food by fishing or farming. Even with the new interisland trade, luxuries such as the gifts Bubba had shared were relished and nurtured.

Father Bart had been in favor of taking in refugees, and so far, it seemed to have worked. The Hawaiian-born Catholic priest cared for the parish built by Father Damien de Veuster, a Belgian priest who ministered to the leper colony in the mid-nineteenth century. His counterpart, friend, and all-around religious thorn in the side, William Bear, had been more cautious. The Hawaiian priest and animist shaman had responded positively to overtures by the Kauaians, and welcomed Bubba's flotilla, but he'd urged caution lest the colony grow too quickly and overwhelm the food supply. When interisland trade started up, Wizardbear admitted he was wrong, and even traveled to some of the outlying locations to serve their religious needs.

The two ministers were polar opposites in so many ways, but Father Bart had to admit that they served the same roles, ministering, comforting, and serving the residents and refugees alike. Neither was a stranger to working the fields, and if not for the (admittedly substantial) liturgical differences, Bart would be tempted to accept Wizardbear as an equal in ministry. As it was, he daily asked himself WWSDD—What Would Saint Damien Do? The answer to the question was a rather unsettling "accept him as I accepted the lepers." So, Bart swallowed his pride and shared his flock, his table, and his luck at Pinochle with the admittedly affable shaman. Just so long as they didn't have to compete for parishioners.

Bart was down to his last trump card, and it was a nine. He hadn't been very smart at counting the points during play and was still a bit worried about making the bid. Kiwi didn't seem too nervous, though, perhaps he had been counting. On the other hand, Bubba was acting as if he *knew* that his opponents were going to lose the game and was grinning from ear to ear as he played the last card. Before the hand was finished, however, Micki came back into the room and interrupted the game.

"Father Bart? Captain Bubba? There's a radio message for the two of you!"

"Radio?" asked Bubba. "Shortwave, ham, or marine? Ship or shore?" Bubba had brought multiple radio sets with him to Molokai.

Micki gulped a breath. "Captain Tully says it is the government ham station in Kamuela."

Wizardbear snorted. "I have little use for those who declare themselves the rightful 'leaders' of Hawaii." It was an old argument, and one Bart and Wizardbear rehashed many times, particularly in relation to the burgeoning government in Kamuela, and the idiocy of the madman claiming to be the incarnation of Ku.

"Well, then? What's the message?" Bubba was still figuring his points on the last hand. It looked like he might not have beaten Kiwi and Bart after all.

"It said..." Micki took one last deep breath, then let it all out in a rush. "He said the message was 'Captain Bubba, please bring priest to Hōnaunau, need *kahuna*.' It's from Noelani Sara Hiatt."

"Hōnaunau? Hawaii Island?" Father Bart grew up in Hawaii, but for seventeen years he'd barely traveled away from Kalaupapa even before the Fall.

"Yes, there's a bay, not bad anchorage, okay beach. Not much there," replied Bubba.

"Pu'uhonua O Hōnaunau," growled Wizardbear in his deep voice, "is the Place of Refuge. The Pu'uhonua is a sacred site where those who had broken Kapu, who were defeated in battle, or needed protection, could claim sanctuary, be sanctified by the high priest, and forgiven." He stood and looked down at the Roman Catholic priest. "She asked for *kahuna*, Bartholomeus. You may be island born, with the name of Koa, but you are not a priest of Wākea-Skyfather." He turned and strode for the door.

"Just a moment, there, William." The shaman bristled at the use of his Christian name, but he had started it when he called the priest by his own first name. "I know Sara Hiatt. She was christened in this very church and I performed the ceremony. She sent the message as Noelani *Sara*, not Noelani *Kala*, her Hawaiian name. She asked for me, not you, O wizard-who-is-a-bear."

"Sounds to me like you should *both* go. The young lady seems to want a priest rather badly. Can't imagine why the Biggies need either one of you, but why not both go?" Wells told them as he checked the cards, wrote down the score, then started putting the Pinochle deck away.

The two ministers looked at each stubbornly, then Micki put a hand on Father Bart's shoulder while Bubba reached way up to put one on Bear's. "Come, gentlemen," the captain ordered. "We have a boat to catch at first light. Pack light, but plan on getting wet. The Kona is not over, and it's going to be a rough crossing."

Kiwi left, with Bubba and Wizardbear following close behind. Micki started to fuss over the priest, planning what to pack for his trip. Bart watched the shaman's retreating back.

Mary, Mother of God, give me strength. That man can be a tribulation, he thought. Somehow, he knew the matter was far from settled, and yet he had a feeling that something very important had just happened. *Ah well, I'd better get ready. I wonder if Bubba has any scopolamine left? A boat is bad enough, but stormy seas will be... an ordeal.*

CHAPTER THREE

REFUGE

Those who do not remember the past, are condemned to repeat it.   —G. Santayana, philosopher and essayist

It was a *very* rough crossing from Molokai to Hawaii—the island. By direct measure, it was one hundred and forty miles. By air, it would have taken an hour, but by sea it was considerably longer. The most direct routes, either threading between the islands of Maui County—Molokai, Lanai, Maui, Kaho'olawe—or swinging west to avoid the narrow channels, rocks, and shoals, added a minimum of twenty-five miles. However, while the shallow waters of Maui County were generally protected from storms carried by the prevailing easterly trade winds, Bubba decided it was worth adding even more distance to take the eastern route around Maui to gain some protection from the westerlies of the Kona Storm.

They still had to contend with the wind whipping waves into ten-foot swells, deepening to twenty feet as they crossed the Maui Channel to the Big Island. On calm seas, *Simple Gifts* could make the direct crossing in just under five hours. With the storm, and out of consideration for his passengers, Bubba limited his speed, turning the transit into a twelve-hour, all-day trip.

Father Bart prided himself in only getting sick three times during the crossing. Bear, that miserable bast—ah, blessed soul, hadn't been sick at all, nor had any of Captain Bubba's crew. The priest's discomfort had only been alleviated by the fact that their additional passenger,

Abraham Krebs, had brought along of a bag of crystalized ginger he'd hoarded and rationed since the Fall.

Krebs was a short man, and like most, thin from his life since the Fall. He was a plastic surgeon from New York, whose divorce and consequent midlife crisis had brought him to the islands with a brand-new wife and fifty-foot Valiant sailing yacht. When Honolulu fell, Bram and wife hired two men to assist in sailing back to San Diego. He was in a hurry and desperate and didn't consider that the men he hired might want to keep the boat and its generous supplies—or his attractive wife—for themselves. One of them had turned, right in the middle of the attempt at piracy. The resulting scuffle had left both of the hired crew dead, and Krebs with a hard decision upon discovering his wife had been bitten. The surgeon had restrained her, cared for her, and ended her life himself when she turned. He then headed the yacht back toward Maui, figuring the less populated islands were better than Oahu. He ran aground on Kanaha Rock Islet, just a mile off the windward coast of Molokai, and remained there living off his supplies and the occasional fish, until rescued by a pair of young Kalaupapa boatmen in a hand-built outrigger canoe.

Bart was grateful to Bram and had asked him to accompany them. It was not just to improve the odds against Wizardbear—Krebs had been *gabbai* in his synagogue in New York in recognition of his knowledge of the Torah—but also because he was one of only three full-fledged doctors identified so far in all the Hawaiian Islands. Sure, the Big Island had the dentist and the HI-SLOPE doctor, but the simulation "astronaut" was more researcher than physician, and Bart preferred to bring his own just in case.

After all, Sara had asked for a *kahuna*, and the word could be taken to mean healer as well as priest.

Hōnaunau had a boat ramp and a small pier, but it also had a reef blocking access to the small cove. Bubba had radioed Kamuela to inquire about using the more accessible harbor at Kealakekua, the town nearest the point where British captain James Cook had visited what he named the "Sandwich Islands" in 1778. The response to the request had been negative. While Hōnaunau was deemed secure by nature of clearance activities and the Pu'uhonua, most of the coast north to Kailua was still unsecured. While preparing to board the

RHIB for the trip to shore, they were all quite surprised to be met by Hawaiians paddling outrigger canoes that easily navigated the reef and quickly transported the party to shore.

Awaiting them on shore were a man and a woman in native attire, the woman short, with dark hair, dark skin, and a full figure. She was wearing a sarong made of a bright, colorful floral print fabric. The man was tall and burly, in shorts and a loose-fitting shirt of the same printed fabric. While the woman smiled in welcome at the newcomers, the man just scowled. Father Bart recognized the young woman—after all, her parents had been part of his parish until a few years ago.

"Sara!" he greeted her. "So good to see you looking well. Your parents? Are they ... well?" He stumbled over the last few words, realizing the blunder only after the words were already out.

She ran up and embraced him, gently, considering that he was still a bit wobbly. "Father Koa. Thank you, and I am happy to see you as well." Her expression fell. "No, I am sorry Mother and Father succumbed to the plague. Mercifully, they died from the fever and never turned. They are now with God." In response to this statement, her male companion made a sound of disgust. "Iona. Mind your manners!" she rebuked him, sharply.

Again, he snorted in disgust. "We need a *kahuna*," he stated bluntly, "not the pope." He spat the last word.

Father Bart actually smiled at that. He and Bear had discussed this at length during the crossing—at least during the intervals when his stomach was not heaving. "Then perhaps I should introduce my companions ... Iona, is it?"

Sara nodded. "Iona Glenn. He refuses to use the name of his birth, John, but then many here wish to follow the old ways." She shuddered slightly. "Within reason, of course." Glenn did not offer to shake hands, but he did nod his head ever so slightly at the introduction.

Bart turned to his companions and introduced the captain first: "Brian Gnad, known to all as Captain Bubba."

Bubba leaned forward and kissed Sara's hand. She giggled and embraced him much as she had the priest.

"The shrimp beside me is Bram Krebs, our doctor."

Krebs emulated Bubba and kissed Sara's hand. He nodded to Iona, who inclined his head very slightly in response.

"This big bear beside me is Wizardbear or just Bear." Bear also bent and kissed Sara's hand. He crossed his right fist across his chest, then opened it to reach out and take Iona's hand in a forearm-to-forearm grip. The two nodded at each other. There was no need to explain that Bear was likely the *kahuna* that Glenn had desired.

"The sun is going down, and I'd like to see this refugee without relying on flickering lamp or candlelight," Bart told her. He hadn't realized that the trip would take nearly all of the precious daylight.

"Not one, but two refugees," another voice interrupted them. The newcomer was a big man. Well fed, which meant that he was one of the Kamuela ranchers. He had a wandering eye that gave the appearance of watching you even when his attention was elsewhere.

"Travis Beck, Director of Clearance for South Kona District." He held out his hand to Father Bart. "One of them is a problem, but we can deal with that. But the other will be a *problem*, if you catch my drift!"

"I'm not sure I understand," said the priest, returning the handshake. "Director of Clearance?"

"My boys have been cutting down the number of Zeds roaming free in this area. We're clearing Routes 180 and 11 from the population centers to the farms and orchards. We help provide security and teach folks to fend for themselves. The High Road to Waimea is passable with only small arms during the day." He seemed pretty self-satisfied with the description.

Sara also motioned for another individual to come over and a woman a few years older than Sara stepped up. She was quite lovely and had a simple beauty that many women sought through cosmetics but was generally only gained through good genes and years of attention to personal fitness.

Beck introduced her, "Malia Eller, our nurse and head of clinic in Kamuela."

"Miz Eller. Wife of Captain Lee Eller?" Koa asked.

"I am, indeed, Father. Call me Lia, please." She turned and looked in the direction of a small hut with evidence of lantern light through the window. "Mayor Maleko is interested in this development and wanted a representative present."

Sara took him aside to say that she'd summoned him due to a claim for asylum and sanctification according to the old traditions of the sacred refuge. Bart knew he'd need to get much more information about this proposed ceremony before commenting on it. Fortunately, he was saved by Bubba's approach with Bram in tow.

Bubba clearly knew Lia and introduced Bram in a near repeat of the prior introductions. His next words confused Bart. "Allie, I'm so sorry for your loss."

"Ah?" was all Bart could manage.

"Thank you, Bubba. If Lee were here, he'd say we just have to move on. We have a world to rebuild."

Bart was confused, not just by the name Bubba used, but because while he'd understood that the Hero of Kawaihae had been seriously injured, he'd survived the battle, or so he thought.

Lia saw the confused look on his face and laughed. It was a gentle, delicate laugh, accompanied by a smile. She also placed a hand on her lower stomach. "He means my miscarriage, not my husband. Bubba knows very well that Lee's on Kauai, conferring with the soldiers from the Pacific Missile Range Facility."

"Oh, my condolences, too," Bart said. "But . . . Allie? You said to call you 'Lia.'"

She laughed again. "Bubba's spent too much time ferrying Lee around the islands. My husband calls me Allie, but Lia's the more traditional shortening of Malia. At least he doesn't call me 'Mal.'"

All five laughed at the thought.

"He's integrating them into the Hawaii Territorial Guard? Jackson's not going to like that," Bubba said.

"I guess we'll find out. Lee and Mr. Toivo are on their way, too. This event is bigger than any of you might know. It's become a serious political issue. To top it off, I'm here because Dr. d'Almeida came down from HI-SLOPE. He has definite opinions as to what we should do with the Infected."

"Oh, so that's why Kōkee took *With the Wind* out into the teeth of the storm." At Lia's questioning look, Bubba clarified. "It's a racing trimaran. The only choice for fast transit from Kauai all the way down here."

"Oh joy," Koa said. "'Political' doesn't even begin to describe this."

"We should go in and see the refugees," Krebs prompted.

"Yes, let me take you there," Lia said.

As they walked over to the building, Krebs introduced himself to

Beck and struck up a conversation. "May I ask how you perform this 'clearance'?"

"Send out a team at night, armed and armored," Beck answered. "Show a lot of light, make a lot of noise, and the Zeds come out to play. My boys are protected, and the savages can't really get to them, but they sure will follow! We lead them right into the kill box and BLAM! No more savages!"

Bram shuddered. "That's barbaric!"

"These *are* barbarians, old man. That's why my people call them savages; the term 'Infected' is too . . . well, it's too kind to them." Beck spat on the ground. "Have you ever seen them take down an armed man and chow down on his face? Or women? Or children? I fought at Kawaihae and it was bad, but it was even worse clearing the resorts down the coast. We'd find survivors and lose half of them to the Zeds. Then we get down here to South Kona and have to deal with pirates."

"Not all of the Infected are savages," interjected Sara with some passion. There was a fire in her eyes as she faced the burly uplander. "Some of them are like children. Come, Father, let me show you Ewa."

She led them past the building—apparently the former park headquarters—to a small corral of some sort. It smelled of pigs, although there were none present. At the farthest end was a bit of roofing and what could only be called a *nest* of foliage, cloth, and wooden boxes. In the nest was a very young, very naked teenage girl. An older female, dressed much like Sara, was also present, as well as two people in "moon suit" isolation garments. The girl was visibly shaking in fear and clutching a teddy bear in the manner of a scared child. The adult was brushing the child's hair and comforting her as one of the people in a moon suit examined her.

"We call her Ewa. The name means 'she who brings life to everything.' In the Hawaiian language, though, the word also means 'ill-fitting.' She doesn't fit our understanding of the Haole Flu. She shows every sign of having had it, but she's not aggressive, not angry, not dangerous. She ran here to the Refuge and we have given her sanctuary. We require a *kahuna* to perform a ceremony of sanctification so that she may rejoin humanity."

CHAPTER FOUR

POLITICS

Politics is a game to some, a way of life to others. I, for one, enjoy the give and take, but I'm sure that for most people, having a situation become political is to be devoutly avoided.
—R. Staba, President of the United States

An Infected that was not dangerous? That just didn't make sense to Father Bart.

"Yes, we've seen reports of this." That was one of the men who'd been in the isolation suits. Bart had never met the HI-SLOPE people personally, but he recognized the voice of Hamilton Forsyth, leader of the surviving "astronauts." Forsyth had apologized for the moon suits, explaining that while all his people were vaccinated, their doctor had insisted he wear the suit given that the girl may have a variant of H7D3 against which their vaccine would offer no protection.

With nightfall, the group had moved indoors to a large hall that had once been a visitor information center and museum. The exhibits had been moved aside, although many of the more useful artifacts had been put into daily use by the residents. Both men from HI-SLOPE had now removed the isolation garments. In addition to Forsyth, the second man had been introduced as Dr. Anson d'Almeida. Krebs and d'Almeida had stepped aside for a few private comments, mostly figuring out common mentors and acquaintances, but rejoined the group for this discussion.

"Seen one or two myself," said Beck.

"What do you do to them?" d'Almeida asked with a cold tone to his voice.

"They mostly ran off. The rest got caught in the meat grinder."

"Hmph. Ran off. I bet they did," said d'Almeida. "I may not have seen it firsthand, but I've talked to the CDC folks from the Hole and gone over all the reports from the early stages of the Haole Flu. H7D3 virus works a little bit like rabies and invades the nervous system with a vengeance. It's unique, though, in that it suppresses the frontal lobes, amps up the limbic system, and juices the adrenal glands, turning infected individuals into rage zombies. It stands to reason, for those who actually engage in reason"—he glared at Beck—"that there would be a few victims whose amygdala and adrenals can't maintain that high activity. The girl won't sit still for much of an examination, and I haven't been able to draw blood yet, but Bram and I concur that she's *probably* a Nea—what the CDC docs call a 'beta.'"

"Neas? Betas?" asked Bear. He'd taken out an ornately carved pipe and was filling it with tobacco—and it *was* just tobacco. He might play up appearances to suit his role as an animist, but Bart knew that Bear was an educated man, and the medical lecture clearly triggered his own professorial habits.

"Beta, as in a second form of Infected. Aggressive Infected are alphas, nonaggressive are betas. Personally, I like 'Nea' for *Neanderthalensis*. Neanderthals were very likely a gentle and simple people. Of course, my HI-SLOPE colleagues call me 'Cro' for 'Cro-Magnon,' so, I might be biased."

D'Almeida reached for the cup of tea Sara had provided. Bear puffed his pipe, and Bart found himself wishing for the bottle of Macallan they'd left in Kalaupapa.

Beck waved his cigar back in the direction of the corral outside. "I was an anthropology professor. You're telling me that this girl has no sense of self? If she has no aggression, how can she have a sense of self-preservation? After all, she ran."

"No, that's not what I said. I didn't say anything about sense of self."

"But you compared her to a Neanderthal."

"Who *did* have the sense of self."

Beck snorted but said nothing.

D'Almeida took that as permission to continue. "She has few or no higher cognitive functions, only survival and feeding. Those are instinctual. However, she is a mimic. You noticed the toy? She has been treating the teddy bear exactly the same way others have been treating her. That indicates she can be taught some very basic skills."

Father Bart thought for a moment. "And do what? Once she's taught a skill, that is?"

"I suppose she could pull weeds on a farm, wash clothing, pound grain for meal." Beck sighed. "We could take her up to Lalamilo Farm and put her to work, but Noelani and Iona insist that she needs the sanctification ceremony, first."

"That would be slavery," rumbled Bear. Father Bart knew the signs, the big man was about to lose his temper, so he put a restraining hand on his companion's arm. Surprisingly enough, he was seeing the same look on Dr. d'Almeida's face.

"Only if they toil for others with no reward," Father Bart said quickly. "If she works on behalf of herself, or a guardian, she would be protected. She is still just a child. She could be a ward of the Church!" Bear snorted. "Okay, either church, Bear. Yours or mine." At a look from Krebs, he added, "Ward of the State?"

Lia Eller laughed, but it was without humor. She knew that the territorial government—a long way from being a state, yet—would likely not want to spare the resources for a "ward" unless there was a substantial gain in labor.

"Indenture, vassalage, peasantry, sharecropping—doesn't matter what fancy name you give it, without cognitive consent, it's still slavery," d'Almeida said.

"No, Bartholomeus has a point," Bear grumbled, but the imminent explosion of his temper seemed to have been deferred.

"Well, that's not why *I'm* here." Beck changed the subject, punctuating his comment with a puff of his cigar. "*My* problem is that we found a nest of pirates and one of them escaped. He'd heard my men talking about the beta, or Nea or whatever, and ran right here to claim Sanctuary for himself." He glared at Iona Glenn.

"He reached the Pu'uhonua before his pursuers. Sanctuary is his right. But then he tried to leave. I explained that if he left before the sanctification ceremony, he was still a criminal and the Ali'i could hunt him. He came running back within five minutes." Iona grimaced. "If we truly followed the old ways, we would have cast him out for violating the sanctuary, but he insisted on speaking to the *Kahuna* first."

"And that would be why I'm here and my husband is on his way," Lia Eller said. "We can talk, plan, or whatever you want to argue, but until he gets here, the final decision is deferred by order of Mayor Maleko."

"He doesn't speak for us," Iona said.

Beck began to protest, but Lia held up her hand.

"Mayor Maleko is the senior-most elected official in Hawaii Territory, and the *only* elected official on Hawaii Island. In case you haven't heard, we actually have a functioning U.S. government and president who was elected, not appointed. I spoke with President Staba this morning. By tomorrow we will have representatives of Kauai and Kameula here. Do our *kahunas* speak for Molokai?" At their nod, she continued. "My husband was ordered here by the Commander in Chief, Joint Forces. If we have to, we can fetch someone from Hana or the LDS enclave in Liae, but with our friends from HI-SLOPE, we will have representation from every polity—secular, religious, and military—in the islands."

She paused and looked at each of them in challenge. "The eyes of Hawaii and the world are on us. We need to act like it."

No one spoke for several moments as they pondered her words.

Father Bart had a thoughtful look on his face. "Hmm, I'm beginning to get an idea. Bear, my old friend and rival, I believe that the sanctification ceremony is more in your line of work than mine. However, it may be that we need to talk to this man, this bandit... What is his name?"

"Duncan, Johnny Duncan, and yeah, he definitely said he needs to talk to a priest if we had one," Iona said.

"Okay, then, it sounds like I need to hear this Mr. Duncan's confession."

The weather began to clear the next morning. Captain Bubba sent the *Gifts* back to Kalaupapa at first light with a list to fulfill Wizardbear's need for ceremonial supplies. Beck did the same, sending a truck up to Kamuela for several items on Bart's and Bram's lists as well. Tully radioed ahead for Mamabear and Gran to gather the items, with the storm abating, *Simple Gifts* should be back shortly after nightfall.

It would still be tomorrow at the earliest before they could hold the service since they were still awaiting Toivo and Eller to make the three-hundred-mile sail from Kauai. *With the Wind* might be the fastest sailing ship they had, but it would still be a minimum of ten hours, even without sailing into the diminishing headwinds of the Kona Storm.

Father Bart settled in to listen to Bubba and Lia discuss the trade goods on offer now that reasonably clear passage had been established between Kamuela and the South Kona communities. The first harvest of coffee beans in over a year was sitting on the bushes upslope from Hōnaunau, not to mention citrus from the groves farther south.

Bubba countered that he could get coffee from the former Kauai Coffee Company plantation outside the settlement at Hanapepe. Lia insisted that the Kona Mountain Coffee farms had the superior product. She also raised her ante with macadamia nuts.

"Well just need to arrange a taste test, then," Bubba said. "I'm sure Jackson will be bringing coffee with him. He likes to flaunt it."

"I think upland Maui might want in on that. They'll call your macadamia nuts and raise with chocolate." Ham Forsyth turned from where he'd been sitting, enjoying a breakfast of guava juice and fish. "Any chance of adding some chicken to the trade, Bubba?"

"How did you hear from upland Maui?" Bubba asked. "We've only been in touch with Hana."

"Lugnut received a bounce off an OSCAR satellite. It originated from a ham station in Kula. According to him, they're broadcasting to the satellite, but not directly. A good thing, too, Haleakala is in the way."

"Oh. The amateur radio satellites. We don't have any satellite dishes, though. I guess we'll have to salvage one."

"We can get you one from Mauna Kea, Captain. Not a—" Whatever Ham was going to say was lost in a noise that most of them hadn't heard since before the Fall.

"Helicopter?" Father Bart asked.

"Helicopter!" someone shouted from outside.

CHAPTER FIVE

CONVERGENCE

Million-to-one chances crop up nine times out of ten.
—C. Ironfoundersson, Ankh-Morpork guard

Everyone rushed out of the former museum to see a very large helicopter circling overhead. It made a low pass of the buildings, then moved out over the water of Keone'ele Cove, then to Hōnaunau Bay. After hovering for several moments, it moved over a rectangular rock platform at Pu'uhonua Point. It descended, hovered over the platform, then the pilot must have decided that the landing area was too small.

The helicopter rose up, drifted over the empty parking lot, and then off to the rocky soil and scrub that made up most of the park. After a few minutes of searching, it rose up and flew off to the north.

"It seemed like they were looking for a place to land," said Bubba.

"Best place for that might be up near Kealekekua Bay. That sucker's big." Beck came up holding a handheld radio. "My boys say it's been spotted at several points along the coast headed down from Kawaihae."

"Do you think they went to the port first? If so, why come down here?"

"Don't know, but no one from Kamuela has seen it land anywhere."

"Where are they from?"

"That was a CH-53E Super Stallion. It's either from a ship or a base, but they've only got a six-hundred-mile range. Under most conditions, that is," Iona told them. In response to the quizzical looks he got from

Bubba and Beck he shrugged. "I was Navy—a mechanic. I *fixed* those birds."

"If they come back..." Ham started.

"When, not if. That was a scouting pass. We only have a few places with sufficient area for eighty-foot rotor span. They were trying to judge width and substrate stability. They might try to set down on the reef. The surf's low enough, but they'd have to drop a frogman, first."

"Eighty feet, you say?" Bubba asked, looking across the elliptical drive and parking lot, with its low, mostly clear island between loops. A single, rusted GMC Yukon sat at one end. He knew from a ferry job years ago that the big SUVs were fifteen to twenty feet long. The parking area was easily four times that at its widest, which would make it barely eighty feet, but if the helo landed on the grass between the loops, it would easily clear all the features. He pointed to the lone obstructions in an approximately one-fifty-by-two-hundred-foot space. "Iona? How quickly can we remove those three small palm trees in the island, there?"

The big Hawaiian grinned. "Want me to do a FOD-walk? Lots of potential for flying object damage, but we can do this." He turned and ran into the old museum, returning five minutes later with an axe and two more islanders, plus Wizardbear. They made short work of the four- to six-foot trees, and then started picking up any large objects on the ground in the parking area far from most of the museum and park buildings. Within thirty minutes, Iona declared the area as clear as it was going to be, just in time to hear the returning beat of helicopter blades. Beck had called for one of his men to bring a road flare, and the pickup arrived in time, the passenger handing off the flare just as the helo came into view.

Iona shooed everyone back into the museum, away from the improvised landing area. He took the flare from Beck, crouched low and ran out to the center of the cleared area, lit the flare, then stood up and waved it in the air. He then went to the farthest point from the buildings, which just happened to be upwind, and placed the flare on the ground. He then crouched down and ran back to join the few onlookers, brave enough—or foolhardy enough—to stay out on the porch of the museum.

The helicopter came in high, hovered over the clear area, then rotated to align its nose with the flare. It slowly settled to the ground and they heard the engines reduce power, but not shut off, although the rotors began to slow.

Iona kept everyone away from the helo. "Even though the rotors are twenty feet up, we're not going to risk it. Those seven blades can do a number on you."

"Considering the dirt and gravel flying around, I'd agree," Bart said.

On being told it would be several more minutes before the rotors stopped, a brief discussion ensued as to who would greet the newcomers. Despite competing claims by Beck and Wizardbear, Lia ended the discussion with her recommendation.

"They came to the Place of Refuge. It should be Noelani."

Once the rotors finally slowed, the rear ramp opened. Sara stepped up to welcome them, but never got to. Lia Eller rushed past her to grab the man carefully walking down the ramp, leaning on a cane.

Everyone present, even those who hadn't met him personally, knew of Captain Lee Eller, the Hero of Kawaihae. It looked as if Lia tried to drag him out of the aircraft, but he held up a hand, seemed to speak into a microphone attached to heavy headphones, then took them off and allowed her to help him step down.

The engine sound began to wind down. Bart had covered his ears against the noise; as it decreased, he took them down, and realized that his ears actually felt numb, as if anesthetized. He stuck a finger in each and wiggled them around to relieve the uncomfortable feeling.

"It'll go away," Iona told him. "But that's why we wear earpro on the flight line."

Lia appeared to be speaking to her husband as she led him away from the helo, but he just shook his head and tapped his ears. She grabbed his right arm and linked it with hers. He still used the cane, but appeared to lean a bit more on his wife as he walked toward the group. An older man wearing a weathered polo with "Cap'n Jack's Tours" embroidered on the breast pocket, followed them.

As they approached, Bart was finally able to hear the conversation, and apparently, so was Captain Eller. "I *said*, 'What are you doing in a helicopter?' Are you expanding the Army again?"

Eller just laughed. "Navy, Allie, my dear. We found some new friends."

"Of course you did." She led him up to Sara, who began the greeting she'd prepared, and the group agreed on, even though it seemed a moot point at this time. "Welcome to Pu'uhonua O Hōnaunau, the Place of Refuge. Are you seeking sanctuary?"

To Bart's surprise, Lee bowed low. "With respect to the holy refuge, I am but a humble messenger. My *Alaka'i*, General Montana, has sent me as an emissary."

With a smile on her face, Sara bowed slightly, and stepped to repeat the greeting to the man behind him, who just seemed to scowl and wave her off.

"As sociable as ever, Jackson," Bubba said.

The man gave Bubba a slight smile, but then returned to a neutral expression with just the hint of a sneer. His body language showed that he was deferential to Eller, but no one else in the group.

Bart noticed another figure appear on the ramp of the Sikorsky. A woman in a flight suit stood there, took her helmet off and handed it to someone inside, then stepped out of the craft and moved to join them.

"Abi?" he heard someone say, turned and saw that it was Forsyth. "Abi!" The man ran as fast as he could to greet the helo pilot, but stopped short, uncertain.

"Dad?" she said, eyes widening in shock. "Daddy!" She leapt forward and threw herself in his arms.

The helo pilot, introduced as Abigail Forsyth, daughter of Hamilton Forsyth of HI-SLOPE, was sitting drinking her first cup of good coffee since the Fall. As Bubba had said, Jackson Toivo liked to show off, and had brought a fifty-pound bag of roasted coffee beans along with various coffee-making tools from the coffee plantation gift shop. The group was all sitting in the museum listening to the latest tale of survival.

"I was flying out of K-Bay transporting marines needing medevac. I'd just come back from Tripler when the alarms went off because of a mob at the gate. At first it was people, then Infected." Abi shuddered at the memory. "There were ships about fifty miles offshore from a big FleetEx. We were told to evacuate the base by taking folks out to the ships. It was Bill Jung's shift, and he was already taking people to the destroyer, *Port Royal*. I was assigned to take folks to the *Yukon*. It's an oiler, fleet replenishment."

"Gas, grub, and gear," Bubba said. He, too, had been glad to see the young lady who'd worked for his fishing charter company one summer.

"You know of it?"

"One of my boat captains is a former Coastie—one our Captain Eller has *not* succeeded in enticing back to his Hawaii Territorial Guard. Flip told us about the evacuation and the *Yukon*."

"Ah, so you know the story."

"I've heard it," said Bubba. "But do go on."

"Not much more to it. Mine was the last flight. Bill got off first, then a C-130 headed for Pohakuloa. Mike Fowler took a big risk. I heard he didn't make it."

"His men did, though. And I wouldn't be here today if not for them," Lee said.

"Bill was overloaded because we got word the fence had fallen. He had a sling load filled with people just to rescue as many as he could. I started our lift as soon as the C-130 cleared our airspace, but had to put us back down in a hurry because we saw Bill wobbling and the load swinging our way. The radio signal was chaotic. Best we could figure, someone went zombie and attacked Bill. They buzzed us, and it was close. If Jimmy hadn't spotted him, we'd have collided. It was bad, though. I watched his loadmaster fall . . ."

Abi teared up for a moment, and Ham reached over to hug her. Lee reached out and placed his hand over hers, using his other hand to hold Lia. He nodded to the pilot. "Never good to lose a friend."

Abi swallowed several times. Lia offered her some guava juice from Kamuela. Sara laughed and countered with fresh-squeezed orange juice from the farms upslope. Jackson offered noni fruit, but pretty much everyone at the table had been warned off of the notoriously foul-tasting "health food."

"We made it to the *Yukon* but landed hard. Tom's sudden maneuver had cracked the left landing gear and it gave out. We canted and the rotor hit the aft railing. We threw pieces of railing all over, killed one of the ship's crew, and injured several others. A fragment took out the *Yukon*'s radio mast, too. If it hadn't been the last possible flight from K-Bay, that would have done it for sure."

"Flip told us about *Port Royal* and the collision, too. But we always wondered why *Yukon* never refueled you and sent you back out," Bubba said.

"Couldn't. We had a machine shop on *Yukon*, but no one to do the work. Once the boomer *Louisiana* joined us, the machinist mates got to work and fixed the *Yukon*'s steering gear, disconnected her bent shaft, and fixed my bird."

"Lieutenant Forsyth, once the current business is done, I'd like to get you up to the garrison and on the horn with Higher," Lee told here. "The president's in Jacksonville, Florida, along with CINC Navy. CINC Joint Forces is off in California somewhere, but we can get him on a secured line, too. We have a working chain of command and they'd love to hear about you, *Yukon*, and the *Louisiana*. You've all been thought lost."

"We've been sitting at French Frigate Shoals. The captain wanted to get to Midway, but we couldn't make it. Only about halfway. It's a protected anchorage, probably why the *Louie* and Japanese sub surfaced there."

"Japanese sub?"

"*Zuiryū*. It means 'Auspicious Dragon.' It's a diesel, only two years in service, pulled out of Yokosuka the day Tokyo fell. Joined us about five days after we got there, running on fumes. We could refuel them, but frankly none of us knew where to go. It took me two months to convince Captain Knox to let me fly to PMRF on Kauai. It's actually too far for a Stallion's normal round-trip range, but I have extra fuel tanks. I met Captain Eller there yesterday. We came right here, and I have to tell you, if you can't refuel me, I can't go back."

"We have avgas at the Kona airport. It's cleared and ready for business," Beck said.

"Well then, I guess it's 'Welcome back to the world' for all of us."

"Indeed, Lieutenant." Lee turned to Lia, then looked at the men clustered around the table. "Well then, gentlemen and ladies, I believe we have a mess to sort out!"

CHAPTER SIX

RITUAL

It's just a jump to the left and then a step to the right...
—Dr. F.N. Furter, famous ritualist

Despite their religious differences, Father Bart realized that the sanctification ceremony planned by Wizardbear was not unlike an old Hebrew temple sacrifice for forgiveness. He discussed it with Dr. Krebs, who offered to assist at creating a multi-denominational service that could stand as an example of the unity of the Hawaiian spirit. He suggested they ask Kamuela for a young goat. Jewish tradition mandated a lamb or kid, but the few remaining Hawaiian sheep were rare and protected by tradition and law. Goats, on the other hand, roamed the island and had been considered a nuisance when they infiltrated tourist areas and munched on the cultivated floral displays.

Father Bart was not entirely comfortable with the concept of animal sacrifice, certainly not as a component of pagan practice, but he was enough of a realist to understand that the traditional Hawaiian luau had its origins in exactly that sort of ritual. Wizardbear had promised that there would be no overt sacrifice, just symbolic use of the blood— arguing that Catholic communion and ceremonial incense were simply the most recent implementations of the ages-old prayers of atonement and sanctification. The goat itself would be for a feast following the ceremony that would also form the basis for mutual support and trade agreements between Kamuela, Molokai, Kauai, and the South Kona coast.

When preparations were made, Bart had an informal meeting with the captured brigand, Duncan. He'd made it clear that the meeting was not a confession, but rather a time to discuss what information the priest would keep confidential under the seal of the confessional. The ranchers considered Duncan a criminal but they agreed that if he went through with the sanctification ceremony, they would issue him a conditional parole—not a pardon, but a parole provided he perform services to the community. The implication was that work in the cleaning and clearance crews was better than being shot outright, or hanging from a gallows on the beach in Kealakekua.

The alternative was to leave the island with Father Bart and work the fields in Kalaupapa for his own sustenance. The Church might consider him forgiven, but he would still be responsible for atonement. The priest encouraged the young man to search his soul regarding what information he might wish to provide to Kamuela as part of that atonement as well as to ease his own burden of conscience. When they were done speaking, Travis Beck came into the room while Bart left to retrieve his vestments.

An hour later, Beck exited the office looking rather satisfied. Father Bart reentered the room and observed that Duncan appeared to be much more at ease. He said that he wished to leave the Big Island for good. The now-former brigand looked forward to a positive change in his life and felt he could do that best helping the colony grow. As he listened to Duncan's confession, Bart thought back to many he'd heard over the years since seminary. He wondered how many lives might have been changed with the opportunity to truly earn a clean slate and literally take their lives in their own hands. H7D3 might have been the worst thing to happen to humanity, but in this small way, in this Place of Refuge, it might have been the best thing as well.

The sanctification ceremony was held two days later, which happened to coincide with the full moon. HI-SLOPE's youthful tech wizard, Lugnut, came down from the mountain to set up video and audio broadcast and recording. The signal was sent live to Jacksonville for President Staba, and recorded for rebroadcast, in much the same spirit as the "Light a Candle" video. Although General Brice and Under Secretary Galloway no longer held the reins of government, they were invited to join the live teleconference because of their role in bringing the various Hawaiian communities together. Vice President Stacy Smith and her husband, Commodore Wolf, would also be watching. Father Bart, Bear, and Krebs would perform the ceremony. Sara Hiatt and Kukana Nainoa, the woman who had been caring for Ewa, would assist. Ewa was very nervous around other people, so only those individuals would be involved with her ceremony. Duncan's sanctification would be separate, and by his own choice include a pledge of atonement to the Hawaiian Territory. Beck, Toivo, and Bubba, along with Lee and Lia Eller, would be present at that ceremony to receive the pledge.

The animal sacrifice was purely symbolic—the ranchers had trapped several goats and sent the youngest kid down to Hōnaunau. It was slaughtered in a manner prescribed by both Bear and Krebs, then prepared for roasting with only a bit of the blood saved for the ceremony. Wizardbear was in full ceremonial robes and offered up a prayer to Wākea-Skyfather, then smeared a dab of blood on the girl's forehead and dashed droplets of blood from his fingers onto hot coals. The thick smell of cooking meat filled the air.

Krebs elbowed Bart and whispered, "Not unlike ceremonial incense, no?"

Bram was next and read from Genesis 22 about God testing Abraham's willingness to sacrifice his own son to the will of God. Father Bart read from Hebrews 10, regarding Christ's sacrifice for sin. Bear offered ceremonial wine. Bart had argued for a full communion service but had been talked out of it by Krebs and Bear. Still, the feast to follow would certainly suffice as a sacrament. Ewa would not drink, so Kukana dipped a finger in the wine and placed it on Ewa's lips.

Again, Krebs whispered, "As we do with infants. There are not so many differences between us, I think."

Father Bart nodded. This was less a pagan ceremony than one that paid homage to many religions. Soon this ceremony came to a close. A strangely calm Ewa was led back to her nest by Sara and Kukana, and the larger group gathered for the second sanctification ceremony.

Duncan was dressed in rough cotton shorts and a floral print shirt similar to those worn by the Hōnaunau residents. He sat perfectly still for the ceremony, until the final part, where he had requested to be able to make his pledge and read the final passage from Hebrews in place of the priest. At the appropriate time, he stood, made a simple statement of apology and atonement, then preempted Father Bart to read the final passage from Hebrews, chapter ten, verses sixteen through eighteen:

> This is the covenant I make with them
> after that time, says the Lord.
> I will put my laws in their hearts,
> and I will write them on their minds.
> [...] Their sins and lawless acts
> I will remember no more.
> And where these have been forgiven,
> sacrifice for sin is no longer necessary.

It was a grand feast, with much talk of politics and trade. Abi Forsyth sat quietly throughout most of it, although Father Bart noticed that she had caught young Mr. Ludwig's eye. After a while, and the visible urging of Lia Eller, Lugnut went up to talk with her. After several minutes, she gestured to a chair and motioned for him to sit. Bart only caught a few words, but the two seemed to be talking about video games and something called "Twitch."

A commotion on the other side of the museum caught his attention. He heard raised voices between Jackson and Dr. d'Almeida. He knew he'd missed the start of it, but ...

"They are people, Mr. Toivo. The Infected are victims. I've tried— God knows I've tried. *Any* of the gods invoked here today have to know how hard I've worked to develop not just a vaccine, but to try to figure out if there's a cure. We can't save the alphas, but maybe we can do something for the betas. The Neas—betas—are our first sign of hope."

"They're beasts, not humans," said Toivo. "We put beasts in the field and hitch them to the plow."

"That's slavery. You're no better than Ku. I don't know how he managed to train Infected, but he did. The fact that he manipulated them to attack was just plain evil, and you want to do the same thing!"

"Whoa, whoa, whoa, there, Doc. He said no such thing." Beck was standing next to Toivo, apparently on his side of the argument. "He just said that if the betas can be trained to do basic tasks, then put them to work and free up intelligent people who can do other work."

"And the doctor said that if Neas can't consent, any other use is slavery, and I agree." Wizardbear's booming voice now had everyone's attention.

It appeared as if the men would come to blows. The argument between Beck and d'Almeida four days ago was bad enough but the addition of Toivo fanned the flames. Mediation came from a surprising place. Johnny Duncan stepped between the men and spoke quietly.

"When I leave this place tomorrow, my sins are forgiven and I am free to make my own way. I pledged atonement, and that I will do. Why do you think Ewa will be any different? Kukana says she responds to kindness and will emulate those who are kind to her."

"It's different. You're sentient," Toivo sneered.

"Am I? What makes me different from an animal?" He addressed this last to Wizardbear.

"Your immortal spirit," the *Kahuna* said, followed by nods and murmurs of agreement from Bart and Bram.

"And can any of us say that Ewa has no spirit? No soul?"

Wizardbear smiled and shook his head. "No."

Toivo turned bright red and looked to argue, but Captain Eller stepped up and tapped the floor with his cane. He stood next to Duncan but looked straight at Bart.

"Father Koa, does Kalaupapa still minister to the downtrodden, the forgotten, the outcasts?"

"As long as the church at Saint Philomena's stands," Bart responded.

"Good. Let Ewa go there. She needs a caretaker, though."

"Kukana will go." Sara added to the now calmer atmosphere.

"Very well. Mr. Duncan, will you be Ewa's guardian? You'll still have to work the fields and serve the colony. Be her guardian. Let no harm befall her, nor shall you allow her to be exploited. If she chooses to emulate you and work beside you, so be it. This can be the terms of your atonement. You will work for yourself and for her, and both of your shares of the community welfare. Will you agree to this as a condition of your parole?"

"I will."

"This decision is now backed by the U.S. Army and the Hawaiian Territorial Guard. The matter is closed."

Jackson Toivo stomped off angrily. Beck followed, trying to talk to him.

The young man with the surprisingly inspiring presence beckoned to Bart and Wizardbear. "Thank you, Father, Kahuna. You were correct. He will be a problem. He was *very* unhappy about me swearing the PMRF people back to military service. I'm glad you suggested this, Brother Bear."

"Wait, you came up with this?" Koa looked incredulously at his counterpart.

Wizardbear just grinned.

"Huh. Good thing we're friends. I won't let you forget this, though."

Wizardbear's expression fell, and he grumbled, then brightened and laughed.

CHAPTER SEVEN

THE RETURN

You have earned a curse to your line, but I will live on. Through the blood sacrifice and by consuming the heart of a warrior, Ku lives on. —Anonymous radio message

The next morning Father Bart bid a fond farewell to Sara Hiatt, and even had an affable parting with Iona Glenn. He spoke a few parting words with the HI-SLOPE and Kamuela representatives. Abi Forsyth's helicopter—and crew—would be remaining for a few days while she took a trip up the mountain to visit Pohakuloa, HI-SLOPE, tell her story to the national leadership, and spend a bit more time on her reunion with her father.

Jackson Toivo had already left. A small catamaran had pulled into the cove before sundown the day before and departed, presumably with Toivo, at first light.

Krebs and d'Almeida had given everyone cursory checkups, including Ewa. D'Almeida provided an inhaled tranquilizer to ease the voyage back to Kalaupapa. The two doctors pledged to keep in touch, with Krebs sending d'Almeida periodic updates on the girl.

It was time to go.

But the sound of moaning, and a small watercraft engine offshore interrupted the leave-taking...

"That bastard. Jackson *would* leave before it gets spicy!" Bubba said.

"What?" Father Bart asked.

"Out there." Bubba pointed to where the reef off Two Step Beach opened into Hōnaunau Bay. A mass of Infected was wading in the surf toward them. Beyond was a single figure on a Jet Ski.

Lee Eller stepped up beside Bart, placed a hand over his eyes to shade them from reflection off the water, then turned and motioned to Beck.

"Do you have binocs?"

"No, but Pearson's on his way to pick me up. I'll call to find out how far out he is."

"Okay." Eller turned back to peer out at the oncoming attack. It was slow. The Infected weren't moving quickly through the less-than-knee-high water. "Strange, they weren't that slow when they came out of the surf on Ali'i Drive."

He reached down to his belt and grabbed the military radio, clicked it twice and held it to his lips. "Top. Walker Actual. Mob of Zeds. I need marines to Pu'uhonua O Hōnaunau. Now!"

"That's two hours, Cap," Bart could hear the voice on the other end of the radio say.

"Shit. One working helicopter and it's *here*, while my marines are *there*." Eller put the radio back on his belt and turned to Abi, who was just tightening a cuff on her flight suit. "Lieutenant. How long to get your bird in the air?"

"Jimmy did the daily run-up this morning, so everything's pre-pressurized. If it starts on first try, I can have it in hover inside four minutes. If I have to do a second attempt, we've got to hand-pump it back up to three-kay pounds of pressure in the APU hydraulic lines. That'll take time. If I have to do a third...I won't be apologizing for my language. This bird was fully broken for most of a year. As it is, it's only been getting regular PM for a month."

"Go. Do. I'll ignore any salty language." She turned and headed for her helicopter. As she did so, she put her right hand in the air, index finger pointed up, and made a circular motion above her head, signaling her copilot to begin startup procedures.

Eller turned to Bart. "Forgive us, Father, soldiers don't hold back when the shit hits the fan. You should have heard my men trying to fix a frozen road wheel on an M1A1 while Zeds advanced on us through a minefield."

"Fuck yeah," the padre said with a grin. "By the way, the stories I've heard of you call you 'Runner,' but you identified yourself as 'Walker.'"

Lee grinned back, but then turned serious. "I don't run anymore, Padre." He tapped his left leg with his cane.

"Kawaihae?"

"After. Civilian volunteer attacked me for endangering his horses. Gunny shot the guy in the shoulder to stop the attack. Top—my first sergeant—called it mutiny and wanted him tried and executed. The guy's worse off than I am, though, so it was left at that."

"You attract danger, young man. I will pray for you."

"I appreciate it, Padre." Eller turned at the sound of vehicle engines. "Well, it looks like we have reinforcements from Kamuela."

He rotated slightly so that he wasn't shouting in Bart's ear. "Beck! Binocs?"

"Pearson's here. Ten seconds."

A man hustled up with a semiauto rifle in one hand and a pair of binoculars in the other. "Give the captain the binos, Tom. I'll take the M4."

"No!" shouted Sara Hiatt, jumping in front of the men and turning to face them. "No violence. No killing. This is the Place of Refuge!"

"But we're unarmed," Beck protested. "They'll run right over us."

"It's Ku," Eller said, lowering the binoculars. "Same ratty old blue shirt with the pink flowers. He's got a wilted, old flower lei around his neck now. He's also looking a hell of a lot like his Zeds, except for the clothes."

"Is he a Zed?" Bubba asked.

Someone tapped on Bart on the shoulder. He turned and saw Wizardbear in the outfit he'd worn for the sanctification ceremony. His other hand was holding Bart's vestments. "Abraham is getting ready. You should, too."

"What are we doing?"

"Praying."

A whine began to sound behind them. It got louder, and higher pitched, then began to cycle in both pitch and volume. Once, twice, then on the third time a faint rumbling started. The whine faded out, replaced by the growing roar of a jet engine.

"Oh, good. We won't have to listen to Abi bitching later."

Tom Pearson had brought several trucks full of men. Iona stood at the entrance to the parking area and would not allow them to enter with their weapons, so they backed up a hundred feet and turned down a public access road to the waterfront. It wasn't a beach per se, but it did have access to the water. It had a short pier, boat ramp, and smooth-topped lava rock instead of sand.

It also had Zeds.

Strangely, the Infected weren't headed toward the side of the cove leading into the Pu'uhonua, but rather to the public beach side. The men arrayed themselves in and out of their trucks and faced the Zeds. Seamus Curran had brought his compact Toyota truck fitted with a mortar in the bed and an M240 mounted to the roll bar. One of the Pu'uhonua workers was standing on the opposite shore waving at them, trying to get them to stop.

Pearson didn't care, they weren't technically on Refuge land.

"Open up!" he commanded.

CHAPTER EIGHT

RESOLUTION

The soldier above all others prays for peace, for it is the soldier
who must suffer and bear the deepest wounds and scars of war.
—Gen. D. MacArthur, West Point, 1962

Sara Hiatt was crying. Lee could see that the girl was distraught. This
was a refuge, and it was clear to him that it was *her* refuge. When he
had a moment, he'd look for Forsyth and see if he'd talk to her. For
now . . . Oh. Allie was leading her away.

Lee was torn. He wanted to be respectful. He'd learned a lot from
the people who'd lived here all their lives. He knew he was a haole, and
it was only by virtue of working for mutual survival that outsiders got
accepted here. But respect for tradition was another part. He wouldn't
take lava rock from its rightful place, wouldn't deface natural beauty,
and wouldn't desecrate a burial ground—of his own volition. Ku
desecrated the Pu'ukohola Heiau at Kawaihae. Lee put an end to it.

It looked like the same thing was about to happen here, but he
would do his damnedest to not kill Zeds—people, according to Doc
d'Almeida—within the Refuge. Hawaii needed its traditions and
beliefs. They wouldn't restore a worthwhile Hawaiian way of life
without them.

It was up to him to keep the desecration *out* of this place.

His radio vibrated; it was getting hard to hear. He reached into the
breast pocket of his uniform shirt and pulled out his earpro. It had a
Bluetooth link to his radio—not perfect in light of three jet engines
starting up at his back, but it would do.

"Walker Actual."

"Walker, this is Five-O. What's the sitrep?"

"We have upward of three hundred Zeds, Top. That's three-zero-zero Zulus wading onshore at Hōnaunau Bay."

"Shit. What manpower?"

"Eleven ranchers, a technical, three priests, BubbaFleet Actual, and a Super Stallion."

"A what? I can't hear you over the background noise."

"I said, a Charlie-Hotel-five-three-Echo Super Stallion helicopter originally from K-Bay and now the USNS *Yukon*."

"Oh God, the ghost ship! You found them?"

"They found me. At PMRF. You were supposed to be our next stop. I'd planned to take the pilot upslope today to talk to Jacksonville."

"They armed?"

"Well, duh. They'd be foolish to go unarmed in a zombie apocalypse. *Yukon*'s got gas, grub . . ."

". . . and gear, right, and enough ammo for a Marine Expeditionary Unit—or three. Gunny's going to be thrilled. What's their ETA?"

"By Lieutenant Forsyth's estimate, they should be wheels up in one more minute."

"Forsyth? As in . . . ?"

"One and the same. She's the professor's daughter."

"Damn, son, how do you keep landing in the shit and coming up smelling like hibiscus?"

"No hibiscus, orchids, or roses here yet, Top. Just Zeds."

"Well, I'll call up and see if Lugnut can get visual."

"He's down here. Professor has him and the noncombatants tucked away."

"Shit. Okay, well, Gunny's barreling your way downslope in an MRAP. There's two trucks on their way, but you know how he drives, he'll probably be there in another forty-five minutes, half an hour ahead of the second squad."

"If we're still here in forty-five minutes, he can have what's left."

"If I tell him that, he'll make it thirty. 'It's only fifty-five miles,' he said, 'all downhill.'"

"Hah. Sounds like Gunny. Don't tell him what I said, though. I want live marines."

"Acknowledged, Walker. I can send two squads more if needed. Oh, and ask your lieutenant if *Yukon* has any more pilots. We've got two UH-60s sitting here idle with no one to fly them."

"I'll ask later. Right now, it's time to get in the scrimmage, Five-O. Walker out."

The helicopter was lifting. Lee checked his watch. Running and cycling had kept the self-winding mechanism operating for so many years. Now he had to actually wind it.

Three minutes, fifty seconds.

Abi had given him a frequency for the helo, so Lee set the channel on his handheld and called his new air-support element.

"We have approximately three-zero-zero Zeds on the beach. That's your target."

"Do we engage the lone tango on the Jet Ski?"

"Negative. Suppress the Zeds first, then prosecute the tango."

"Aye aye," came the response. It hadn't been Abi, so the voice on the radio was likely Medlock, her copilot. He'd been introduced last night at the feast but they hadn't really talked. Yet another thing that was supposed to be rectified today—if they survived.

The helo lifted higher, then tilted forward and moved northward over land before turning west, over the water. Lee switched back to the frequency shared with the ranchers and heard them setting up positions along a low rock wall that separated the Hōnaunau Beach Road from a small parking and picnic area. It provided neither cover nor concealment but was a decent line of demarcation between the rocky beach and the land.

A short pier separated Keone'ele Cove from the beach, and the gun truck had set up right at the foot of the pier, with a good view of the beach, cove, and even the sandy shore of Pu'uhonua.

Lee had moved to the sandy walk that followed the shoreline of the Refuge. To his right, across the water, were Two Step Beach and the ranchers. To his left was Pu'uhonua Point, with its thatch hut and tiki statues. He wasn't happy with the idea that the ranchers had a mortar. If they aimed anywhere south of their position, it would hit Refuge land... and him.

He keyed his radio. "Beck forces, be advised, do not fire heavy ordnance left of the tiki statues. That's Refuge land. Stick to the public areas to the north and west."

"But they'll flank us!" came a voice over the radio.

"These savages aren't *over* there," said another voice, likely Beck's.

It was true. Lee stepped out on to the beach and saw that there were no Zeds moving his way. It was curious, but there was no time to think about that now.

He felt a strong rush of wind, and the helo passed by overhead, angling to target the Zeds without hitting the ranchers. The gust almost knocked him over but gave him an idea—one that might achieve both objectives: stopping the Zeds and honoring the Refuge.

"Walker Actual to *Yukon* helo. How low can you hover over that beach?"

There was a moment while the helo lined up and fired some shots into the crowd of Zeds, but it was likely the pilot wasn't happy with the angle. Abi's voice came over radio. "What do you have in mind, Walker? We can put down on the rocks or even get our feet wet, but there's an awful lot of debris. It'll be worse than a sandstorm and hailstorm combined."

"That's the idea, *Yukon*. If you hover over the beach, it'll knock the Zeds down, and FOD will likely take some of them out. It'll be easier for the ranchers to deal with them immediately after. You can then lift and move offshore to drive them into the guns."

"That's . . . not bad, Walker. I wasn't happy with the angles, too much chance for ricochet and overshoot. Oh, and while I understood you, the call sign's actually '*Ghostbird*.'"

"Got it, *Ghostbird*. Give me a half a minute to warn the ranchers to take cover."

"Acknowledged, Walker. *Ghostbird* out."

Lee switched radio frequencies again. "Beck forces, you have two-zero seconds to get to cover. The helo's going to drive the Zeds to ground, but it's going to get rocky for a few minutes."

He would need to take cover himself, and walked between the park buildings to a private residence marking the shoreside edge of the park. Sitting down beside another rock wall, he watched the helo get into position. He was easily three hundred feet away, but still felt the strong winds and gravel thrown by the rotor downdraft. He ducked his head, and waited until he heard the helicopter move away.

Most of the Zeds were down, struggling to get back to their feet. Quite a few were down and not moving. The Super Stallion moved about a quarter mile north of the beach, and then did the low hover a few more times to drive some stragglers along the Hōnaunau Beach Road toward the ranchers.

The stunned Zeds were no longer a relentless mob, and the ranchers began to have success in reducing the numbers. The Toyota truck was on its side, a victim of rotor wash. That relieved Lee's fear of the ranchers overshooting their target, given that the mortar was no longer in play. The M240 was still able to bear on the mass of Zeds, though, and added to the success in suppressing the attack.

Lee noted that there were small groups of Zeds that quickly stood back up after the helo passed and were making their way off the beach and into the trees that would lead behind the ranchers.

Intelligent Zeds, just what we need, thought Lee. They still weren't moving into the Refuge, though. *There might be something to this holy place.*

He switched back to the helo's radio channel. "Walker Actual to *Ghostbird*. One more time on suppression in the cove, Lieutenant, then we can deal with the leader. Take out the tango in the blue shirt any way you can."

"Acknowledged, Walker. Jimmy's out of practice with his Barrett, but a Golf-Alpha-Uniform-two-one's hard to argue with. Proceeding to splash the tango."

Lee warned the ranchers, then the helo made one more close pass over the mass of Zeds before rotating toward the figure on the Jet ski, who'd turned and was headed out to sea. He could hear the fifty-cal machine gun begin firing and saw sprays of water from where the bullets hit the surface. A puff, and then plume of black smoke suggested a round had hit the Jet Ski, and the device seemed to turn in the water, headed back to shore. A moment later, and the figure on the watercraft was down, and floating in the water.

With Ku down, the Zeds began to mill about, directionless. Even this was unusual for Infected, since they were driven by basic instinct, and once attracted to a target, they wouldn't stop until they or the target were dead. Lee radioed Beck to warn about the ones he'd seen headed into the trees, but those were easily rounded up, no longer acting with intelligent direction.

Bubba called on *Simple Gifts* to send a RHIB to check out the body in the surf. It hadn't moved, and was still visible, so Lee began to think that the battle might be over. He kept watch until he saw the body being pulled from the surf, then turned to go back to the museum to check on everyone who'd been sent to cover during the conflict.

Stepping back onto Refuge grounds, he noticed the three holy men, standing tall, praying. Lee stopped and bowed. Allie and Sara came running out to them, and he straightened and addressed them all.

"No shots were fired on the Pu'uhonua O Hōnaunau. The Infected never came in this direction. This is truly a holy refuge, and may it always be so.

"One more candle in the darkness."

EPILOGUE

RIVER OF FIRE

Go, tell it on the mountain, over the hills and everywhere!
—African American spiritual

My Dearest Abi,

I know it's only been a week since your last visit, but I miss you already. I lost you once, but now that I've found you again, any time between visits seems an eternity.

It's been quiet here. Captain Eller says there's been no sign that Ku repeated his miraculous escapes. Thanks to you. Eller, Bubba, First Sergeant Copley, and even Ben Peachtree viewed the body and confirmed that it was the guy who'd threatened them. I can't tell if it's the guy I interviewed all those years ago, but it could be.

He certainly *looked* like an Infected, just with clothes on. Lee said he'd deteriorated with each attack, so maybe he really *was* just a different sort of Zed.

I'd rather not think on the ramifications.

HI-SLOPE is done. Today is the day the grand experiment was due to end. Three years of our lives, and way too many sacrifices. Many of the crew are talking about moving out. Red Kirby has been aimless ever since we lost Medusa. Duke and Legs are heading to Hana, Maui; they're outdoors types, and HI-SLOPE is too confining. Bigfoot and Moose are already at Kawaihae getting it ready for the *Yukon*.

Cro will stay; his lab is here, and Eggnog will help him part-time. She and Mrs. Eller are setting up a clinic at Hōnaunau, so she'll be splitting her time. Lugnut will stay and

401

even be joined by some civilian and military tech folks. He and his new team are turning one whole hab into a communications and technical center for the island.

I'm leaving, but it's more of a convenience move. Major Silver requested my assistance with reintegrating the recovered and rescued military members. It's been a challenge, many are well past their ETS dates, but have nowhere to go. I'm going to have a house at the garrison, with a guest room.

In other news, Father Bart, Wizardbear, and Dr. Krebs have been called upon to perform the sanctification ceremony many times now. Twice more at the Pu'uhonua, once for a beta recovered on Molokai topside, plus twice again for betas brought in by Bubba's fleet. Mayor Maleko is talking about making *Kahuna* an official position with the government. Those three will be the first.

Johnny Duncan has been a surprise. He built a large open-sided shelter and lives there with his "children." He's enclosing a bedroom and bath in the middle of the structure for Kukana Nainoa, but he stays with the betas, cares for them, and works the fields with them by his side. Father Bart visits them every day, praying and blessing them. Wizardbear says the old priest considers them his flock and his mission, much like Father Damien did with the lepers over a hundred years ago. Bear also says they made the right decision— whether they call Him Wākea-Skyfather or Yahweh, these are truly children of God.

No betas have ever been sent over from Kauai. I think we knew that would happen. Toivo will be a problem. We're up to thirty-two hundred in the census, only eighteen hundred from a statehood vote, but Maleko is no longer sure he'll run for governor. It will need to be someone who can deal with Toivo. He suggested Lee Eller, but I'm not sure the captain would accept; General Montana is going to be pushing promotion on him, even jumping him up a couple of grades. Perhaps his wife will do it. Either of their wives, actually; Nalani and Malia are both formidable women.

⊚◎⊚

"Hey, Professor, sorry to interrupt, but the servers over at HVNP are going nuts."

"HVNP? You mean the volcano observatory? The servers are still working?"

"It's all automated, but yeah. They were all set for remote monitoring. Pretty obvious why, I guess."

"Okay, so seismic activity isn't unexpected. Mauna Loa is almost always rumbling."

"Not Mauna Loa, per se. Not Kilauea, either. This is east of the active vent. In fact, the sensors say the Pu'u O'o vent has finally stopped erupting. This activity is in the East Rift Zone near the coast. It looks an awful lot like an eruption. I found some air sensor data showing pyrrolics—that's combustion by-products—and silicates."

"Hah! Bet it's a new vent. Just what we need, things start to go right and we get a volcanic eruption."

"Not much we can do about it, Professor, but I thought you should know. I'll package this up and send it to all parties. I can head down to the garrison tomorrow and ask Sarge Copley if they have a drone with the range to go take a look-see."

"Not a bad idea. Good call, Lugnut."

"Thanks, Professor. I'm actually kind of excited. I never spent time in Hawaii before the mission. I'd love to see a river of fire."

"From a distance, I hope."

"Yeah, that's true. Okay, sorry to have interrupted. I'll get the OSCAR uplink ready for your letter as soon as it's done."

"Thanks, Lugnut."

Well, it seems that every time things get settled, something new happens. I suppose we all should have been expecting Pele to wake up.

Take care, my brave and beautiful daughter, and drop your old man a line when you can.

All my love, always,
Dad

THE END

PLAYLIST

John Ringo includes playlists of the music he listened to while writing his novels. The playlists associated with *Under a Graveyard Sky* and the rest of the Black Tide Rising novels introduced me to many new, favorite songs. I also have a few of my own.

My playlist is organized by the parts of the novel due to the different theme and tone of each section. My overall source of listening pleasure for writing is the music of Two Steps from Hell and, in particular, cofounder Thomas Bergersen. There are so many good compositions, that I often just put the whole collection on shuffle and play them all while writing, driving, and relaxing.

Part 1: Explorer

"Mountain Call"—Thomas Bergersen—*Humanity: Chapter I*
"Wings"—Thomas Bergersen—*Humanity: Chapter I*
"Humanity"—Thomas Bergersen—*Humanity: Chapter I*
"Illusions"—Thomas Bergersen—*Illusions*
"Flight of the Silverbird"—Two Steps From Hell—*Battlecry*
"Goodnight Moon"—John Tesh—*Monterey Nights*
"Home"—Michael Bublé—*Caught in the Act*
"Fight Song"—The Piano Guys—*Uncharted*

Part 2: Seafarer

"Never Forget (Midnight Version)"—Kazuma Jinnouchi—
        HALO 4: Original Soundtrack
"Arrival"—Neil Davidge—*HALO 4: Original Soundtrack*
"Winter Wind"—The Piano Guys—*A Family Christmas*
"We Know the Way"—Opetaia Foa'i and Lin-Manuel
        Miranda—*Moana (Original Movie Soundtrack)*
"The Islander"—Nightwish—*Dark Passion Play*
"Turn Loose the Mermaids"—Nightwish—*Imaginaerum*
"Enchantress"—Two Steps From Hell—*Vanquish*
"High C's"—Two Steps From Hell—*Vanquish*

"Drink (We Are Here to Drink Your Beer)"—Alestorm—
Sunset on the Golden Age
"He's a Pirate"—Klaus Badelt—*Pirates of the Caribbean:
Curse of the Black Pearl (Official Soundtrack)*
"Miracles"—The Piano Guys—*Limitless*
"Eye of the Storm"—Crüxshadows—*DreamCypher*

Part 3: Iron Man
"The Endless Road"—John Tesh—*Monterey Nights*
"Sogno di Volare (The Dream of Flight)"—Christopher Tin—
Civilization VI Soundtrack
"Last Ride of the Day"—Nightwish—*Imaginaerum*
"Winter Born (This Sacrifice)"—Crüxshadows—*Ethernaut*
"82nd All the Way"—Sabaton—*The Great War*
"The Price of a Mile"—Sabaton—*The Art of War (Re-Armed)*
"The Last Stand"—Sabaton—*The Last Stand*
"The Attack of the Dead Men"—Sabaton—*The Great War*
"Birth of A Hero"—Two Steps From Hell—*Nero*
"We Are Legends"—Thomas Bergersen—*Humanity:
Chapter II*

Part 4: Kahuna (plus rewrites and editing of all parts)
"Ghost Division"—Sabaton—*The Art of War (Re-Armed)*
"The Lost Battalion"—Sabaton—*The Last Stand*
"Love Suite"—Thomas Bergersen—*Humanity: Chapter III*
"Iron Will"—Thomas Bergersen—*Humanity: Chapter V*
"One Last Day"—Thomas Bergersen—*Humanity: Chapter V*
"Aventura Suite"—Thomas Bergersen—*Humanity: Chapter V*
"My Last Love: In Paradisum"—Ailee—*Sisyphus: The Myth
(Original Television Soundtrack)*